FACE OFF

"You're not a veterinarian. Veterinarians give dogs rabies vaccines. They don't throw elementals around."

Kiyo regarded me levelly. "And Web designers don't banish elementals to the Otherworld."

"Yeah, well, sometimes I moonlight."

The faintest ghost of a smile flickered across his face. "We need to talk about this—"

"No. Don't get any closer." If I could have cocked the wand like a gun, I would have.

"What are you going to do? You can't cast me out. It won't work."

I hesitated, wondering about that. He seemed so human. He had felt human. I hadn't sensed anything from him like I would one of the gentry, yet his speed and strength had been superhuman.

"What do you want from me? Why did you bring me back here?"

"Look, Eugenie, just put the wand down. We'll talk. We'll figure this out."

"I thought you couldn't be cast out," I reminded him. "Why are you afraid of the wand? Maybe the Otherworld couldn't hurt you . . . but what about the Underworld?"

He didn't answer. I sent my will into the wand and felt the air crackle with power. Fear crossed Kiyo's face. So. He was afraid. That was all I needed to know. The words were on my lips to send him to the crossroads, but suddenly he moved with that rapid speed I'd seen earlier. He backed up toward the sliding glass door, opened it up, and then ran out and over the edge of the balcony . . .

Books by Richelle Mead

SUCCUBUS BLUES

SUCCUBUS ON TOP

SUCCUBUS DREAMS

STORM BORN

Published by Kensington Publishing Corporation

STORM BORN

Richelle Mead

ZEBRA BOOKS
Kensington Publishing Corp.
www.kensingtonbooks.com

ZEBRA BOOKS are published by

Kensington Publishing Corp.
850 Third Avenue
New York, NY 10022

All Kensington titles, imprints, and distributed lines are available at special quantity discounts for bulk purchases for sales promotion, premiums, fund-raising, educational, or institutional use.

Special book excerpts or customized printings can also be created to fit specific needs. For details, write or phone the office of the Kensington Special Sales Manager: Attn. Special Sales Department. Kensington Publishing Corp., 850 Third Avenue, New York, NY 10022. Phone: 1-800-221-2647.

ISBN-13: 978-1-4201-0096-9
ISBN-10: 1-4201-0096-3

First Printing: August 2008
10 9 8 7 6 5 4 3

Printed in the United States of America

For Michael, who always liked this one best.

Chapter One

I'd seen weirder things than a haunted shoe, but not many.

The Nike Pegasus sat on the office's desk, inoffensive, colored in shades of gray, white, and orange. Some of the laces were loosened, and a bit of dirt clung around the soles. It was the left shoe.

As for me, well . . . underneath my knee-length coat, I had a Glock .22 loaded with bullets carrying a higher-than-legal steel content. A cartridge of silver ones rested in the coat's pocket. Two athames lay sheathed on my other hip, one silver-bladed and one iron. Stuck into my belt near them was a wand, hand-carved oak and loaded with enough charmed gems to probably blow up the desk in the corner if I wanted to.

To say I felt overdressed was something of an understatement.

"So," I said, keeping my voice as neutral as possible, "what makes you think your shoe is . . . uh, possessed?"

Brian Montgomery, late thirties with a receding hairline in serious denial, eyed the shoe nervously and moistened his lips. "It always trips me up when I'm out running. Every time. And it's always moving around. I mean, I never actually see it, but . . . like, I'll take them off near the door, then

I come back and find this one under the bed or something. And sometimes . . . sometimes I touch it, and it feels cold . . . really cold . . . like . . ." He groped for similes and finally picked the tritest one. "Like ice."

I nodded and glanced back at the shoe, not saying anything.

"Look, Miss . . . Odile . . . or whatever. I'm not crazy. That shoe is haunted. It's evil. You've gotta do something, okay? I've got a marathon coming up, and until this started happening, these were my lucky shoes. And they're not cheap, you know. They're an investment."

It sounded crazy to me—which was saying something—but there was no harm in checking, seeing as I was already out here. I reached into my coat pocket, the one without ammunition, and pulled out my pendulum. It was a simple one, a thin silver chain with a small quartz crystal hanging from it.

I laced the chain's end through my fingers and held my flattened hand over the shoe, clearing my mind and letting the crystal hang freely. A moment later, it began to slowly rotate of its own accord.

"Well, I'll be damned," I muttered, stuffing the pendulum back in my pocket. There was something there. I turned to Montgomery, attempting some sort of badass face, because that was what customers always expected. "It might be best if you stepped out of the room, sir. For your own safety."

That was only half-true. Mostly I just found lingering clients annoying. They asked stupid questions and could do stupider things, which actually put me at more risk than them.

He had no qualms about getting out of there. As soon as the door closed, I found a jar of salt in my satchel and poured a large ring on the office's floor. I tossed the shoe into the middle of it and invoked the four cardinal directions with the silver athame. Ostensibly the circle didn't change, but I felt a slight flaring of power, indicating it had sealed us in.

Trying not to yawn, I pulled out my wand and kept holding the silver athame. It had taken four hours to drive to Las Cruces, and doing that on so little sleep had made the distance seem twice as long. Sending some of my will into the wand, I tapped it against the shoe and spoke in a sing-song voice.

"Come out, come out, whoever you are."

There was a moment's silence, then a high-pitched male voice snapped, "Go away, bitch."

Great. A shoe with attitude. "Why? You got something better to do?"

"Better things to do than waste my time with a mortal."

I smiled. "Better things to do in a shoe? Come on. I mean, I've heard of slumming it, but don't you think you're kind of pushing the envelope here? This shoe isn't even new. You could have done so much better."

The voice kept its annoyed tone, not threatening but simply irritated at the interruption. "*I'm* slumming it? Do you think I don't know who you are, Eugenie Markham? Dark-Swan-Called-Odile. A blood traitor. A mongrel. An assassin. A murderer." He practically spit out the last word. "You are alone among your kind and mine. A bloodthirsty shadow. You do anything for anyone who can pay you enough for it. That makes you more than a mercenary. That makes you a whore."

I affected a bored stance. I'd been called most of those names before. Well, except for my own name. That was new—and a little disconcerting. Not that I'd let him know that.

"Are you done whining? Because I don't have time to listen while you stall."

"Aren't you being paid by the hour?" he asked nastily.

"I charge a flat fee."

"Oh."

I rolled my eyes and touched the wand to the shoe again. This time, I thrust the full force of my will into it, drawing upon my own body's physical stamina as well as some of the power of the world around me. "No more games. If you leave on your own, I won't have to hurt you. *Come out.*"

He couldn't stand against that command and the power within it. The shoe trembled, and smoke poured out of it. Oh, Jesus. I hoped the shoe didn't get incinerated during this. Montgomery wouldn't be able to handle that.

The smoke bellowed out, coalescing into a large, dark form about two feet taller than me. With all his wise-cracks, I'd sort of expected a saucy version of one of Santa's elves. Instead, the being before me had the upper body of a well-muscled man, while his lower portion resembled a small cyclone. The smoke solidified into leathery gray-black skin, and I had only a moment to act as I assessed this new development. I swapped the wand for the gun, ejecting the clip as I pulled it out. By then, he was lunging for me, and I had to roll out of his way, confined by the circle's boundaries.

A keres. A male keres—most unusual. I'd anticipated something fey, which required silver bullets; or a spectre, which required no bullets. Keres were ancient death spirits originally confined to canopic jars. When the jars wore down over time, keres tended to seek out new homes. There weren't too many of them left in this world, and soon there'd be one less.

He bore down on me, and I took a nice chunk out of him with the silver blade. I used my right hand, the one I wore an onyx and obsidian bracelet on. Those stones alone would take a toll on a death spirit like him without the blade's help. Sure enough, he hissed in pain and hesitated a moment. I used that delay, scrambling to load the silver cartridge.

I didn't quite make it, because soon he was on me

again. He hit me with one of those massive arms, slamming me against the walls of the circle. They might be transparent, but they felt as solid as bricks. One of the downsides of trapping a spirit in a circle was that I got trapped too. My head and left shoulder took the brunt of that impact, and pain shot through me in small starbursts. He seemed pretty pleased with himself over this, as overconfident villains so often are.

"You're as strong as they say, but you were a fool to try to cast me out. You should have left me in peace." His voice was deeper now, almost gravelly.

I shook my head, both to disagree and to get rid of the dizziness. "It isn't your shoe."

I still couldn't swap that goddamned cartridge. Not with him ready to attack again, not with both hands full. Yet I couldn't risk dropping either weapon.

He reached for me, and I cut him again. The wounds were small, but the athame was like poison. It would wear him down over time—if I could stay alive that long. I moved to strike at him once more, but he anticipated me and seized hold of my wrist. He squeezed it, bending it in an unnatural position and forcing me to drop the athame and cry out. I hoped he hadn't broken any bones. Smug, he grabbed me by the shoulders with both hands and lifted me up so that I hung face to face with him. His eyes were yellow with slits for pupils, much like some sort of snake's. His breath was hot and reeked of decay as he spoke.

"You are small, Eugenie Markham, but you are lovely and your flesh is warm. Perhaps I should beat the rush and take you myself. I'd enjoy hearing you scream beneath me."

Ew. Had that thing just propositioned me? And there was my name again. How in the world did he know that? None of them knew that. I was only Odile to them, named after the dark swan in *Swan Lake,* a name coined by my stepfather because of the form my spirit preferred to travel in while visiting the Otherworld. The name—though not particularly terrifying—had stuck, though I doubted any of the creatures I fought knew the reference. They didn't really get out to the ballet much.

The keres had my upper arms pinned—I would have bruises tomorrow—but my hands and forearms were free. He was so sure of himself, so overly arrogant and confident, that he paid no attention to my struggling hands. He probably just perceived the motion as a futile effort to free myself. In seconds, I had the clip out and in the gun. I managed one clumsy shot and he dropped me—not gently. I stumbled to regain my balance again. Bullets probably couldn't kill him, but a silver one in the center of his chest would certainly hurt.

He stumbled back, half-surprised, and I wondered if he'd ever even encountered a gun before. It fired again, then again and again and again. The reports were loud; hopefully Montgomery wouldn't do something foolish and come running in. The keres roared in outrage and pain, each shot making him stagger backward until he was all the way against the circle's boundary. I advanced on him, retrieved athame flashing in my hand. In a few quick motions, I carved the death symbol on the part of his chest that wasn't bloodied from bullets. An electric charge immediately ran through the air of the circle. Hairs stood up on the back of my neck, and I could smell ozone, like just before a storm.

He screamed and leapt forward, renewed by rage or adrenaline or whatever else these creatures ran on. But it was too late for him. He was marked and wounded. I was ready. In another mood, I might have simply banished him to the Otherworld; I tried not to kill if I didn't have to. But that sexual suggestion had just been out of line. I was pissed off now. He'd go to the world of death, straight to Persephone's gate.

I fired again to slow him, my aim a bit off with the left hand but still good enough to hit him. I had already traded the athame for the wand. This time, I didn't draw on the power from this plane. With well-practiced ease, I let part of my consciousness slip this world. In moments, I reached the crossroads to the Otherworld. That was an easy transition; I did it all the time. The next crossover was a little harder, especially with me being weakened from the fight, but still nothing I couldn't do automatically. I kept my own spirit well outside of the land of death, but I touched it and sent that connection through the wand. It sucked him in, and his face twisted with fear.

"This is not your world," I said in a low voice, feeling the power burn through me and around me. "This is not your world, and I cast you out. I send you to the black gate, to the lands of death where you can either be reborn or fade to oblivion or burn in the flames of hell. I really don't give a shit. *Go.*"

He screamed, but the magic caught him. There was a trembling in the air, a buildup of pressure, and then it ended abruptly, like a deflated balloon. The keres was gone too, leaving only a shower of gray sparkles that soon faded to nothing.

Silence. I sank to my knees, exhaling deeply. My eyes closed a moment, as my body relaxed and my consciousness returned to this world. I was exhausted but exultant too. Killing him had felt good. Heady, even. He'd gotten what he deserved, and I had been the one to deal it out.

Minutes later, some of my strength returned. I stood and opened the circle, suddenly feeling stifled by it. I put my tools and weapons away and went to find Montgomery.

"Your shoe's been exorcised," I told him flatly. "I killed the ghost." No point in explaining the difference between a keres and a true ghost; he wouldn't understand.

He entered the room with slow steps, picking up the shoe gingerly. "I heard gunshots. How do you use bullets on a ghost?"

I shrugged. It hurt from where the keres had slammed my shoulder to the wall. "It was a strong ghost."

He cradled the shoe like one might a child and then glanced down with disapproval. "There's blood on the carpet."

"Read the paperwork you signed. I assume no responsibility for damage incurred to personal property."

With a few grumbles, he paid up—in cash—and I left. Really, though, he was so stoked about the shoe, I probably could have decimated the office.

In my car, I dug out a Milky Way from the stash in my glove box. Battles like that required immediate sugar and calories. As I practically shoved the candy bar into my mouth, I turned on my cell phone. I had a missed call from Lara.

Once I'd consumed a second bar and was on I-10 back to Tucson, I dialed her.

"Yo," I said.

"Hey. Did you finish the Montgomery job?"

"Yup."

"Was the shoe really possessed?"

"Yup."

"Huh. Who knew? That's kind of funny too. Like, you know, lost souls and soles in shoes . . ."

"Bad, very bad," I chastised. Lara might be a good secretary, but there was only so much I could be expected to put up with. "So what's up? Or were you just checking in?"

"No. I just got a weird job offer. Some guy—well, honestly, I thought he sounded kind of schizo. But he claims his sister was abducted by fairies, er, gentry. He wants you to go get her."

I fell silent at that, staring at the highway and clear blue sky ahead without consciously seeing either one. Some objective part of me attempted to process what she had just said. I didn't get that kind of request very often. Okay, never. A retrieval like that required me to cross over physically into the Otherworld. "I don't really do that."

"That's what I told him." But there was uncertainty in Lara's voice.

"Okay. What aren't you telling me?"

"Nothing, I guess. I don't know. It's just . . . he said she's been gone almost a year and a half now. She was fourteen when she disappeared."

My stomach sank a little at that. God. What an awful fate for someone so young. It made the keres' lewd comments to me downright trivial.

"He sounded pretty frantic."

"Does he have proof she was actually taken?"

"I don't know. He wouldn't get into it. He was kind of paranoid. Seemed to think his phone was being tapped."

I laughed at that. "By who? The gentry?" "Gentry" was what I called the beings that most of Western culture referred to as fairies or sidhe. They looked just like humans but embraced magic instead of technology. They found "fairy" a derogatory term, so I respected that—sort of—by using the term old English peasants used to use. *Gentry*. Good folk. Good neighbors. A questionable designation, at best. The gentry actually preferred the term "shining ones," but that was just silly. I wouldn't give them that much credit.

"I don't know," Lara told me. "Like I said, he seemed a little schizo."

Silence fell as I held on to the phone and passed a car driving 45 in the left lane.

"Eugenie! You aren't really thinking of doing this."

"Fourteen, huh?"

"You always said that was dangerous."

"Adolescence?"

"Stop it. You know what I mean. Crossing over."

"Yeah. I know what you mean."

It was dangerous—super dangerous. Traveling in spirit form could still get you killed, but your odds of fleeing back to your earthbound body were better. Take your own body over, and all the rules changed.

"This is crazy."

"Set it up," I told her. "It can't hurt to talk to him."

I could practically see her biting her lip to hold back protests. But at the end of the day, I was the one who signed her paychecks, and she respected that. After a few moments, she filled the silence with info about a few other jobs and then drifted on to more casual topics: some sale at the mall, a mysterious scratch on her car . . .

Something about Lara's cheery gossip always made me smile, but it also disturbed me that most of my social contact came via someone I never actually saw. Lately the majority of my face-to-face interactions came from spirits and gentry.

It was after dinnertime when I arrived home, and my housemate, Tim, appeared to be out for the night, probably at a poetry reading. Despite a Polish background, genes had inexplicably given him a strong Native American appearance. In fact, he looked more Indian than some of the locals. Deciding this was his claim to fame, Tim had grown his hair out and taken on the name Timothy Red Horse. He made his living by reading faux-Native poetry at local dives and wooing naive tourist women by using expressions like "my people" and "the Great Spirit" a lot. It was despicable, to say the least, but it got him laid pretty often. What it did not do was bring in a lot of money, so I'd let him live with me in exchange for housework and cleaning. It was a pretty good deal as far as I was concerned. After battling the undead all day, scrubbing the bathtub just seemed like asking too much.

Scrubbing my athames, unfortunately, was a task I had to do myself. Keres blood could stain.

I ate dinner afterward, then stripped and sat in my sauna for a long time. I liked a lot of things about my little house out in the foothills, but the sauna was one of my favorites. It might seem kind of pointless in the desert, but Arizona had mostly dry heat, and I liked the feel of humidity and moisture on my skin. I leaned back against the wooden wall, enjoying the sensation of sweating out the stress. My body ached—some parts more fiercely than others—and the heat let some of the muscles loosen up.

The solitude also soothed me. Pathetic as it was, I probably had no one to blame for my lack of sociability except myself. I spent a lot of time alone and didn't mind. When my stepfather, Roland, had first trained me as a shaman, he'd told me that in a lot of cultures, shamans essentially lived outside of normal society. The idea had seemed crazy to me at the time, being in junior high, but it made more sense now that I was older.

I wasn't a complete socialphobe, but I found I often had a hard time interacting with other people. Talking in front of groups was murder. Even talking one-on-one had its issues. I had no pets or children to ramble on about, and I couldn't exactly talk about things like the incident in Las Cruces. *Yeah, I had kind of a long day. Drove four hours, fought an ancient minion of evil. After a few bullets and knife wounds, I obliterated him and sent him on to the world of death. God, I swear I'm not getting paid enough for this crap, you know?* Cue polite laughter.

When I left the sauna, I had another message from Lara telling me the appointment with the distraught brother had been arranged for tomorrow. I made a note in my day planner, took a shower, and retired to my room, where I threw on black silk pajamas. For whatever reason, nice pajamas were the one indulgence I allowed myself in an otherwise dirty and bloody lifestyle. Tonight's selection had a cami top that showed serious cleavage, had anyone been there to see it. I always wore a ratty robe around Tim.

Sitting at my desk, I emptied out a new jigsaw puzzle I'd just bought. It depicted a kitten on its back clutching a ball of yarn. My love of puzzles ranked up there with the pajama thing for weirdness, but they eased my mind. Maybe it was the fact that they were so tangible. You could hold the pieces in your hand and make them fit together, as opposed to the insubstantial stuff I usually worked with.

While my hands moved the pieces around, I kept trying to shake the knowledge that the keres had known my name. What did that mean? I'd made a lot of enemies in the Otherworld. I didn't like the thought of them being able to track me personally. I preferred to stay Odile. Anonymous. Safe. Probably not much point worrying about it, I supposed. The keres was dead. He wouldn't be telling any tales.

Two hours later, I finished the puzzle and admired it. The kitten had brown tabby fur, its eyes an almost azure blue. The yarn was red. I took out my digital camera, snapped a picture, and then broke up the puzzle, dumping it back into its box. Easy come, easy go.

Yawning, I slipped into bed. Tim had done laundry today; the sheets felt crisp and clean. Nothing like that fresh-sheets smell. Despite my exhaustion, however, I couldn't fall asleep. It was one of life's ironies. While awake, I could slide into a trance with the snap of a finger. My spirit could leave my body and travel to other worlds. Yet, for whatever reason, sleep was more elusive. Doctors had recommended a number of sedatives, but I hated to use them. Drugs and alcohol bound the spirit to this world, and while I did indulge occasionally, I generally liked being ready to slip over at a moment's notice.

Tonight I suspected my insomnia had something to do with a teenage girl. . . . But no. I couldn't think about that, not yet. Not until I spoke with the brother.

Sighing, needing something else to ponder, I rolled over and stared at my ceiling, at the plastic glow-in-the-dark stars. I started counting them, as I had so many other restless nights. There were exactly thirty-three of them, just like last time. Still, it never hurt to check.

Chapter Two

Wil Delaney was in his early twenties, with straw-yellow hair in need of a haircut. He had pasty white skin and wore wire-rimmed glasses. When I showed up at his house the next morning, he had to undo about twenty locks before he could open the door, and even then, he would only peek out with the security chain in place.

"Yes?" he asked suspiciously.

I put on my business face. "I'm Odile. Lara set up our appointment?"

He studied me. "You're younger than I thought you'd be." A moment later, he closed the door and undid the chain. The door opened again, and he ushered me inside.

I glanced around as I entered, taking in stacks and stacks of books and newspapers—and a definite lack of light. "Kind of dark in here."

"Can't open the blinds," he explained. "You never know who'll be watching."

"Oh. Well. What about the lights?"

He shook his head. "You'd be amazed how much radiation lights and other electrical devices emit. It's what's making cancer run rampant in our society."

"Oh."

We sat at his kitchen table, and he explained to me why he thought his sister had been abducted by the gentry. I had a hard time concealing my skepticism. It wasn't like this kind of thing was unheard of, but I was starting to pick up on Lara's "schizo" vibe. It was highly possible that the gentry could simply have been a figment of his imagination.

"This is her." He brought me a five-by-seven picture showing him and a pretty girl leaning into each other against a grassy backdrop. "Taken just before the abduction."

"She's cute. And young. Does she . . . did she . . . live with you?"

He nodded. "Our parents died about five years ago. I got custody of her. Not much different than how it used to be."

"What do you mean?"

Bitterness crossed that neurotic face, an odd juxtaposition. "Our dad was always off on some business trip, and our mom kept sleeping around on him. So it's always just sort of been Jasmine and me."

"And what makes you think she was taken by gen—fairies?"

"The timing," he explained. "It happened on Halloween. Samhain Eve. That's one of the biggest nights for abductions and hauntings, you know. Data supports it. The walls between the worlds open."

He sounded like he was reciting from a textbook. Or the Internet. Sometimes I thought Internet access was like putting guns in the hands of toddlers. I tried not to roll my eyes as he rambled. I didn't really need a layman explaining remedial information to me.

"Yeah, I know all that. But a lot of scary people—humans—roam around on Halloween too. And lots of other times. I don't suppose you reported it to the police?"

"I did. They weren't able to turn up anything, not that I really needed them. I knew what had happened because of the location. The place she disappeared. That was what made me know fairies did it."

"Where?"

"This one park. She was at a party with some kids from school. They had a bonfire in the woods, and they saw her wander off. The police traced her tracks to this clearing, and then they just stopped. And you know what was there?" He gave me a dramatic look, evidently ready to impress me. I didn't give him the satisfaction of asking the obvious question, so he answered it for me. "A fairy ring. A perfect circle of flowers growing in the grass."

"It happens. Flowers do that."

He shot up from the table, incredulity all over his face. "You don't believe me!"

I worked hard to keep my face as blank as a new canvas. You could have painted a picture on it.

"It's not that I don't believe what you're describing, but there are a lot more mundane explanations. A girl alone in the woods could have been abducted by any number of things—or people."

"They said you were the best," he told me, like it was some kind of argument. "They said you kick paranormal ass all the time. You're the real deal."

"What I can or can't do isn't relevant. I need to make sure we're on the right track. You're asking me to cross physically into the Otherworld. I almost never do that. It's dangerous."

Wil sat back down, face desperate. "Look, I'll do anything at all. I can't let her stay there with those—with those *things*. Name your price. I can pay anything you want."

I glanced around curiously, taking in the books on UFOs and Bigfoot. "Uh . . . what exactly do you do for a living?"

"I run a blog."

I waited for more, but apparently that was it. Somehow I suspected that generated less money than even Tim made. Hmphf. Bloggers. I didn't get why everyone and their brother thought the world wanted to read their thoughts on . . . well, nothing. If I wanted to be subjected to meaningless blather, I'd watch reality television.

He was still looking at me pleadingly, with big blue puppy dog eyes. I nearly groaned. When had I grown so soft? Didn't I want people to think of me as some cold and calculating shamanic mercenary? I'd vanquished a keres yesterday. Why was this sob story getting to me?

It was actually because of the keres, I realized. That stupid sexual suggestion had been so revolting to me that I just couldn't erase the image of little Jasmine Delaney being some gentry's plaything. Because that's what she would be, though I'd never tell Wil that. The gentry liked human women. A lot.

"Can you take me to the park she disappeared from?" I asked at last. "I'll get a better sense if fairies really were involved."

Of course, it actually turned out that I took him because I quickly decided I wasn't going to let him drive me anywhere. Having him as a passenger taxed me enough. He spent the first half of the ride slathering some really thick sunscreen all over him. I guess you had to take precautions when you lived in a cave and finally emerged into the light.

"Skin cancer's on the rise," he explained. "Especially with the depletion of the ozone layer. Tanning salons are killing people. No one should go outside without some kind of protection—especially here."

That I actually agreed with. "Yeah. I wear sunscreen too."

He eyed my light tan askance. "Are you sure?"

"Well, hey, it's Arizona. Hard not to get some sun. I mean, sometimes I walk to the mailbox without sunscreen, but most of the time I try to put it on."

"'Try,'" he scoffed. "Does it protect against UVB rays?"

"Um, I don't know. I mean, I guess. I never burn. It smells pretty good too."

"Not good enough. Most sunscreens will protect from UVA rays only. But even if you don't burn, the UVB rays will still get through. Those are the real killers. Without adequate protection, you can probably expect an early death from melanoma or some other form of skin cancer."

"Oh." I hoped we got to the park soon.

When we'd almost reached it, a traffic light stopped us under an overpass. I didn't think anything of it, but Wil shifted nervously.

"I always hate being stopped under these. You never know what could happen in an earthquake."

I again schooled myself to neutrality. "Well . . . it's been awhile since our last earthquake around here." Yeah. Like, never.

"You just never know," he warned ominously.

Our arrival couldn't have come a moment too soon. The park was green and woodsy, someone's idiotic attempt to defy the laws of southern Arizona's climate. It probably cost the city a fortune in water. He led me along the trail that went to Jasmine's abduction spot. As we approached it, I saw something that suddenly made me put more credence in his story. The trail intersected another one at a perfect cross. A crossroads, often a gate to the Otherworld. No circle of flowers grew here now, but as I approached that junction, I could feel a slight thinness between this world and the other one.

"Who knew?" I murmured, mentally testing the walls. It wasn't a very strong spot, truthfully. I doubted much could pass here from either world right now. But on a sabbat like Samhain . . . well, this place could very well be an open doorway. I'd have to let Roland know so we could check it when the next sabbat rolled around.

"Well?" Wil asked.

"This is a hot spot," I admitted, trying to figure out how to proceed. It appeared I was zero for two in gauging the credibility of these last two clients, but when

90 percent of my queries were false leads, I tended to keep a healthy dose of skepticism on hand.

"Will you help me then?"

"Like I said, this really isn't my thing. And even if we decide she was taken to the Otherworld, I have no idea where to look for her. It's as big as ours."

"She's being held by a king named Aeson."

I spun around from where I'd been staring at the crossroads. "How the hell do you know that?"

"A sprite told me."

"A sprite."

"Yeah. He used to work for this guy Aeson. He ran away and wanted revenge. So he sold the information to me."

"Sold it?"

"He needed money to put down a deposit on an apartment in Scottsdale."

It sounded ludicrous, but it wasn't the first time I'd heard of Otherworldly creatures trying to set up shop in the human world. Or of crazy people who wanted to live in Scottsdale.

"When did this happen?"

"Oh, a few days ago." He made it sound like a visit from the UPS guy.

"So. You were seriously approached by a sprite and only now thought to mention it?"

Wil shrugged. Some of the sunscreen he'd missed rubbing in showed on his chin. It kind of reminded me of kindergarten paste. "Well, I'd already known she was taken by fairies. This just sort of confirmed it. He was actually the one who mentioned you. Said you killed one of his cousins. Then I found some locals that backed up the story."

I studied Wil. If he hadn't seemed so hapless, I almost wouldn't have believed any of this. But it smacked too much of truth for him to be making it up. "What did he call me?"

"Huh?"

"When he told you about me. What name did he give you?"

"Well . . . your name. Odile. But there was something else too . . . Eunice?"

"Eugenie?"

"Yeah, that was it."

I paced irritably around the clearing. The second of two Otherworldly denizens to know my name in as many days. That was not good. Not good at all. And now one of them was trying to get Wil to lure me into the Otherworld. Or was it truly a lure? Sprites weren't really known for being criminal masterminds. If I'd killed his cousin, I suppose he might hope some other motivated creature would take me down.

"So what? Are you going to help me now?"

"I don't know. I've got to think on it, check up on some stuff."

"But—but I've shown you and told you everything! Don't you see how real this is? You have to help me! She's only fifteen, for God's sake."

"Wil," I said calmly, "I believe you. But it's not that simple."

I meant it. It wasn't so simple, no matter how much I wanted it to be. I hated Otherworldly inference more than I hated anything else. Taking a teenage girl was the ultimate violation. I wanted to make the guilty party pay for this. I wanted to make them suffer. But I couldn't cross over with guns blazing. Getting myself killed would do none of us any good. I needed more information before I could proceed.

"You have to—"

"No," I snapped, and this time my voice wasn't so neutral. "I do not have to do anything, do you understand? I make my own choices and take my own jobs. Now, I'm very sorry about your sister, but I'm not jumping into this just yet. As Lara told you, I don't generally do jobs that take me into the Otherworld. If I take this one, it'll be after careful deliberation and question-asking. And if I don't take it, then I don't take it: End of story. Got it?"

He swallowed and nodded, cowed by the fierce tone in my voice. It was not unlike the one I used on spirits, but I felt only a little bit bad about scaring Wil with it. He had to prepare himself for the highly likely possibility that I would not do this for him, no matter how much we both wanted it.

On the way home, I swung by my mom's place, wanting to talk to Roland. Sunset threw reddish-orange light onto their house, and the scent of her flower garden filled the air. It was the familiar smell of safety and childhood. When I walked into the kitchen, I didn't see her anywhere, which was probably just as well. She tended to get upset when Roland and I talked shop.

He sat at the table working on a model airplane. I'd laughed when he picked up this hobby after retiring from shamanism, but it had recently occurred to me it wasn't so different from working puzzles. God only knew what stuff I'd find to keep me busy when I retired. I had the uneasy feeling I'd make a good candidate for cross-stitching.

His face broke into a smile when he saw me, making laugh lines appear around the eyes of the weathered face I loved. His hair was a bright silver-white, and he'd managed to keep most of it. I was five-eight, and he was only a little taller than me. But despite that height, he was solidly built and hadn't lost muscle with age. He might be pushing sixty, but I had a feeling he could still do some serious damage.

Roland took one look at my face and gestured me to a chair. "You're not here to ask about Idaho." I hadn't really understood their recent vacation choice, but whatever.

Giving him a quick kiss, I held my arms around him for a moment. I didn't love many people in this world— or any other—but him I would have died for. "No. I'm not. But how was it anyway?"

"Fine. It's not important. What's wrong?"

I smiled. That was Roland. Always ready for business. If my mom would have let him, I suspected he'd still be out there fighting, right by my side.

"Just got a job offer. A weird one."

I proceeded to tell him all about Wil and Jasmine, about the evidence I'd found for her abduction. I also added in Wil's bit of information about this Aeson guy.

"I've heard of him," said Roland.

"What do you know?"

"Not a lot. Never met him, never fought him. But he's strong, I know that much."

"This gets better and better."

He eyed me carefully. "Are you thinking about doing it?"

I eyed him back. "Maybe."

"That's a bad idea, Eugenie. A very bad idea."

There was a dark tone in his voice that surprised me. I'd never known him to back down from any danger, especially one where an innocent was involved.

"She's just a kid, Roland."

"I know, and we both know that the gentry get away with taking women every year. Most don't ever get recovered. The danger's too high. That's the way it is."

I felt my ire rising. Funny how someone telling you not to do something can talk you into it. "Well, here's one we can get back. We know where she is."

He rubbed his eyes a little, flashing the tattoos that marked his arms. My tattoos depicted goddesses; his were of whirls, crosses, and fish. He had his own set of gods to appeal to—or in this case, God. We all invoked the divine differently.

"This isn't a drop-in and drop-out thing," he warned. "It'll take you right into the heart of their society. You've never been that deep. You don't know what it's like."

"And you do?" I asked sarcastically. When he didn't answer, I felt my eyes widen. "When?"

He waved a hand of dismissal. "That doesn't matter.

What matters is that if you go over in body, you'll get yourself killed or captured. I won't let you do that."

"You *won't let* me? Come on. You can't send me to my room anymore. Besides, I've gone over lots of times before."

"In spirit. Your total time over in body's probably been less than ten minutes." He shook his head in a wise, condescending way. That irked me. "The young never realize how foolish something is."

"And the old never realize when they need to step aside and let the younger and stronger do their jobs." The words came out before I could stop them, and I immediately felt mean. Roland merely regarded me with a level look.

"You think you're stronger than me now?"

I didn't even hesitate. "We both know I am."

"Yes," he agreed. "But that doesn't give you the right to go get yourself killed over a girl you don't even know."

I stared at him in surprise. We weren't exactly fighting, but this attitude was weird for him. He'd married my mom when I was three and adopted me shortly thereafter. The father-daughter bond burned in both of us, obliterating any longing I might have had for the birth father I'd never known. My mom almost never spoke about him. They'd had some sort of whirlwind romance, I knew, but in the end, he didn't want to stick it out—not for her, not for me.

Roland would have done anything for me, kept me away from any harm that he could—except when it came to my job. When he'd realized I could walk worlds and cast out spirits, he'd started training me, and my mother hated him for it. They were the most loving couple I'd ever met, but that choice had nearly broken them apart. They'd stayed together in the end, but she'd never been happy about what I did. Roland, however, saw it as a duty. Destiny, even. I wasn't like one of those silly people in the movies who could "see dead people" and go crazy from it. I easily could have ignored my abilities. But as far as Roland was concerned, that was a sin. To neglect one's calling was a waste, especially when it meant others would suffer. So he tried to treat me as objectively as he would any other apprentice, fighting his personal feelings.

Yet, for some reason now, he wanted to hold me back. Weird. I'd come here for strategy and ended up on the defensive.

I changed the subject abruptly, telling him about how the keres had known my name. He cut me a look, not wanting to drop the Jasmine topic. My mom's car pulled in just then, giving me a temporary victory. With a sigh and a look of warning, he told me not to worry about the name. It happened sometimes. His had eventually gotten out too, and little had come of it.

My mom came into the kitchen, and shamanic business disappeared. Her face—so like mine, down to the shape and high cheekbones—put on a smile as warm as Roland's. Only hers was tinged with something a little different. She always carried a perpetual concern for me. Sometimes I thought it simply had to do with what I did for a living. Yet, she'd had that worry ever since I was little, like I might disappear on her at any moment. Maybe it was just a mom thing.

She placed a paper bag on the counter and began putting away groceries. I knew she knew what I was doing there, but she chose to ignore it.

"You going to stay for dinner?" she asked. "I think you've lost weight."

"She has not," said Roland.

"She's too skinny," complained my mom. "Not that I'd mind a little of that."

I smiled. My mom looked amazing.

"You need to eat more," she continued.

"I eat, like, three candy bars a day. I'm not depriving myself of calories." I walked over and poked her in the arm. "Watch it, you're being all momlike. Smart, professional moms aren't supposed to be that way."

She cut me a look. "I'm a therapist. I have to be twice as momlike."

In the end, I stayed for dinner. Tim was a great cook, but nothing could ever really replace my mom's food. While we ate, we talked about their vacation in Idaho. Neither Jasmine nor the keres ever came up.

When I finally got back home, I found Tim getting ready to go out with a gaggle of giggling girls. He was in full pseudo-Indian regalia, complete with a beaded head wrap and buckskin vest.

"Greetings, Sister Eugenie," he said, holding up a palm like he was in some sort of Old West movie. "Join us. We're going to a concert over in Davidson Park, so that we may commune with the Great Spirit's gift of springtime whilst letting the sacred beat of the music course through our souls."

"No thanks," I said, brushing past him and going straight to my room.

A moment later, he followed sans girls.

"Oh, come on, Eug. It's gonna be a blast. We've got a cooler of beer and everything."

"Sorry, Tim. I don't really feel like being a squaw tonight."

"That's a derogatory term."

"I know it is. Very much so. But your bleach-blond posse out there doesn't deserve much better." I eyed him askance. "Don't even think about bringing any of them back here tonight."

"Yeah, yeah, I know the rules." He flounced into my wicker chair. "So what are you going to do instead? Shop on the Internet? Work puzzles?"

I'd actually been thinking of doing both those things, but I wasn't about to tell him that.

"Hey, I've got stuff to do."

"Fuck, Eugenie. You're becoming a hermit. I almost

miss Dean. He was an asshole, but at least he got you out of the house."

I made a face. Dean was my last boyfriend; we'd broken up six months ago. The split had been kind of unexpected for both of us. I hadn't expected to find him screwing his real estate agent, and he hadn't expected to get caught. I knew now I was better off without him, but some niggling part always wondered what about me had made him lose interest. Not exciting enough? Pretty enough? Good enough in bed?

"Some things are worse than staying home alone," I muttered. "Dean is one of them."

"Timothy?" one of the girls called from the living room. "Are you coming?"

"One moment, gentle flower," he hollered back. To me he said, "You sure you wanna hole up here all night? It isn't really healthy to be away from people so much."

"I'm fine. Go enjoy your flowers."

He shrugged and left. Once by myself, I fixed a sandwich and shopped on the Internet, exactly as he'd predicted. It was followed by a puzzle depicting an M. C. Escher drawing. A bit harder than the kitten.

Halfway through, I found myself staring at the puzzle pieces without seeing them. Roland's quiet, fierce words played over in my head. *Let Jasmine Delaney go.* Everything he'd told me had been true. Dropping this was the smart thing to do. The safe thing to do. I knew I should listen to him . . . yet some part of me kept thinking of the young, smiling face Wil had shown me. Angrily, I shoved some of the puzzle pieces aside. This job wasn't supposed to be about gray moral decisions. It was black and white. Find the bad guys. Kill or banish. Go home at the end of the day.

I stood up, suddenly no longer wanting to be alone. I didn't want to be left with my own thoughts. I wanted to be out with people. Clarification: I didn't want to talk to people, I just wanted to be around them. Lost in the crowd. I needed to see my own kind—warm, living and breathing humans, not undead spirits or magic-infused gentry. I wanted to remember which side of the fence I was on. More important, I wanted to forget Jasmine Delaney. At least for tonight

I threw on some jeans and the first bra and shirt I could find. My rings and bracelets always stayed on me, but I added a moonstone necklace that hung low in the shirt's V-neck. I brushed my long hair into a high ponytail, missing a few strands. A dab of lipstick, and I was ready to go. Ready to lose myself. Ready to forget.

Chapter Three

I'd been people-watching for almost an hour, so I saw
him as soon as he walked in. It was hard not to. The eyes
of a few other women in the bar showed that I wasn't the
only one who'd noticed.

He was tall and broad-shouldered, nicely muscled but
not over the top in some crazy Arnold Schwarzenegger
way. He wore khakis with a navy blue T-shirt tucked into
them. His black hair was not quite to his chin, and he had
it tucked behind his ears. His eyes were large and dark,
set in a smoothly chiseled face with perfect, golden-
tanned skin. There was some mix of ethnicities going on
there, I suspected, but none I could discern. Whatever
the combo, it worked. Extremely well.

"Hey, is anyone sitting here?" He nodded at the chair
beside me. It was the only empty one at the bar.

I shook my head, and he sat down. He didn't say anything else, and the only other time I heard him speak
was to order a margarita. After that, he seemed content
just to people-watch, like me. And honestly, it was a great
place to do it. Alejandro's was right next to a midlevel
hotel and drew in patrons and tourists from all sides of
the socioeconomic scale. TVs showed sporting events or
news or whatever the bartender felt like putting on. A

few trivia machines sat at the other end of the bar. Music—sometimes live, but not tonight—forced the TVs to have closed-captioning, and dancing people crowded the small space among the tables.

It was humanity at its best. Teeming with life, alcohol, mindless entertainment, and bad pick-up lines. I liked to come here when I wanted to be alone without being alone. I liked it better when drunk, stupid guys left me alone. I wasn't sure about articulate, good-looking ones. One nice thing I soon discovered was that with Tall, Dark, and Handsome sitting next to me, no losers dared approach.

But he wasn't talking to me either, and after a while, I realized I'd kind of like him to—not that I'd have any clue what to say back. With the glances he kept giving me, I think he felt the same way. I didn't know. A sort of tension built up between us as I nursed my Corona, each of us waiting for something.

When it finally came, he started it.

"You're edible."

Not the opening I'd been expecting.

"I beg your pardon?"

"Your perfume. It's like . . . like violets and sugar. And vanilla. I suppose it's weird to think violets are edible, huh?"

"Not so weird as a guy actually knowing what violets smell like." It was also weird that he could even smell it. I'd put it on about twelve hours ago. With all the smoke and sweat around here, it was a surprise anyone's olfactory senses could function.

He shot me a crooked grin, favoring me with a look that could only be described as smoky. I felt my pulse quicken a little. "It's good to know what flowers are what. Makes it easier to send them. And impress women."

I eyed him and then swirled the beer in my bottle. "Are you trying to impress me?"

He shrugged. "Mostly I'm just trying to make conversation."

I pondered that, deciding if I wanted to play this game or not. Wondering if I could. I smiled a little.

"What?" he asked.

"I don't know. Just thinking about flowers. And impressing people. I mean, how strange is that we bring plant sex organs to people we're attracted to? What's up with that? It's a weird sign of affection."

His dark eyes lit up, like he'd just discovered something surprising and delightful. "Is it any weirder than giving chocolate, which is supposed to be an aphrodisiac? Or what about wine? A 'romantic' drink that really just succeeds in lowering the other person's inhibitions."

"Hmm. It's like people are trying to be both subtle and blatant at the same time. Like, they won't actually go up and say, 'Hey, I like you, let's get together.' Instead, they're like, 'Here, have some plant genitalia and aphrodisiacs.'" I took a drink of the beer and propped my chin in my hand, surprised to hear myself going on. "I mean, I don't have a problem with men or relationships or sex, but sometimes I just get so frustrated with games of human attraction."

"How so?"

"It's all masked in posturing and ploys. There's no honesty. People can't just come up and express their attraction. It's got to be cleverly obscured with some stupid pick-up line or not-so-subtle gift, and I don't really know how to play those games so well. We're taught that it's wrong to be honest, like there's some kind of social stigma with it."

"Well," he considered, "it can come out pretty crass sometimes. And let's not forget about rejection too. I think that adds to it. There's a fear there."

"Yeah, I guess. But being turned down isn't the worst thing in the world. And wouldn't that be easier than wasting an evening or—God forbid—months of dating? We should state our feelings and intentions openly. If the other person says 'fuck off,' well, then, deal. Move on."

I suddenly eyed my beer bottle suspiciously.

"What's wrong?"

"Just wondering if I'm drunk. This is my first beer, but I think I'm sounding a little unhinged. I don't usually talk this much."

He laughed. "I don't think you're unhinged. I actually agree with you."

"Yeah?"

He nodded and looked remarkably wise as he contemplated his answer. It made him even sexier. "I agree, but I don't think most people take honesty well. They prefer the games. They want to believe the pretty lies."

I finished off the last of the Corona. "Not me. Give me honesty anytime."

"You mean that?"

"Yes." I set the bottle down and looked at him. He was watching me intently now, and his look was smoky again, all darkness and sex and heat. I fell into that gaze, feeling the response of nerves in my lower body that I'd thought were dormant.

He leaned slightly forward. "Well, then, here's honesty. I was really happy when I saw the empty seat by you. I think you're beautiful. I think seeing the bra underneath your shirt is dead sexy. I like the shape of your neck and the way those strands of hair lay against it. I think you're funny, and I think you're smart too. After just five minutes, I already know you don't let people screw around with you—which I also like. You're pretty fun to talk to, and I think you'd be just as much fun to have sex with." He sat back in his chair again.

"Wow," I said, now noticing I'd put on a white shirt over a black bra in my haste. Oops. "That's a lot of honesty."

"Should I fuck off now?"

I played with the rim of the bottle. I took a deep breath. "No. Not yet."

He smiled and ordered us another round.

Introductions seemed like the next logical step, and when his turn came, he told me his name was Kiyo.

"Kiyo," I repeated. "Neat."

He watched me, and after a moment, a smile danced over his mouth. A really nice mouth too. "You're trying to figure me out."

"Figure you out how?"

"What I am. Race. Ethnic group. Whatever."

"Of course not," I protested, even though I'd been trying to do exactly that.

"My mother is Japanese, and my father is Latino. Kiyo is short for Kiyotaka."

I scrutinized him, now understanding the large dark eyes and the tanned skin. Human genes were exquisite. I loved the way they blended.

How cool, I thought, to have such a solid grip on your ancestry. I knew my mother had a lot of Greek and Welsh, but there was a mix of all sorts of other things there too. And as for my deadbeat father . . . well, I knew no more about his heritage than I knew anything else about him. For all intents and purposes, I was very much the mongrel the keres had called me earlier.

I realized then I'd been staring at Kiyo too long. "I like the results," I finally said, which made him laugh again.

He asked about my job, and I told him I worked in Web design. It wasn't entirely a lie. I'd majored in it and in French. Both areas had turned out to be completely irrelevant to my job, though Lara swore having a Web site would drive up our business. We mostly relied on word of mouth now.

When he told me he was a veterinarian, I said, "No, you aren't."

Those smoldering eyes widened in surprise. "Why do you say that?"

"Because . . . because you can't be. I just can't see it." Nor could I imagine telling Lara tomorrow: *So I was in a bar last night and met this sexy veterinarian . . .* No, those concepts somehow didn't go together. Veterinarians looked like Wil Delaney.

"It's God's truth," Kiyo swore, stirring his margarita. "I even take my work home with me. I have five cats and two dogs."

"Oh, dear Lord."

"Hey, I like animals. It goes back to the honesty thing. Animals don't lie about how they feel. They want to eat, fight, and reproduce. If they like you, they show it. If they don't, they don't. They don't play games. Well, except maybe the cats. They're tricky sometimes."

"Yeah? What'd you name all those cats?"

"Death, Famine, Pestilence, War, and Mr. Whiskers."

"You named your cats after the riders of the apocal—wait. Mr. Whiskers?"

"Well, there are only four horsemen."

We talked for a while after that about whatever else came to mind. Some was serious, some humorous. He told me he was in town from Phoenix, which kind of disappointed me. Not local. We also talked about the people around us, our jobs, life, the universe, etc., etc. All the while I kept wondering how this had happened. Hadn't I just been noting how I lived outside of society? Yet, here I was, talking to a guy I'd just met like I'd known him for years. I barely recognized the words coming out of my own mouth. I didn't even recognize my body language: leaning into him as we talked, legs touching. He wore no cologne but smelled like he looked: darkness and sex and heat. And promises. Promises that said, *Oh, baby, I can give you everything you've ever wanted if you'll just give me the chance. . . .*

At one point, I leaned toward the bar to slide an empty bottle across it. As I did, I suddenly felt Kiyo's fingers brush my lower back where my shirt had ridden up. I flinched as electricity crackled through me at that slight, casual touch.

"Here's more honesty," he said in a low voice. "I like this tattoo. A lot. Violets again?"

I nodded and sat back in my chair, but he didn't remove his hand. That tattoo was a chain of violets and leaves that spread across my lower back. A larger cluster of the flowers sat on my tailbone, and then smaller tendrils extended outward on both sides, almost to my hips.

"Violets have sort have become my patron flower," I explained, "because of my eyes."

He leaned forward, and I almost stopped breathing at how close his mouth was to mine. "Wow. You're right. I've never seen eyes that color."

"I've got three more."

"Eyes?"

"Tattoos."

This got his interest. "Where?"

"They're covered by the shirt." I hesitated. "You know anything about Greek mythology?"

He nodded. A cultured man. Cue swooning.

I touched my upper right arm. My sleeve covered the skin. "This one's a snake wrapped all the way around my arm. It's for Hecate, the goddess of magic and the crescent moon." What I didn't add was that Hecate guarded the crossroads between worlds. It was she who governed transitions to the Otherworld and beyond. This tattoo was my link to her, to facilitate my own journeys and call on her for help when needed.

I moved to my upper left arm. "This one's a butterfly whose wings wrap around and touch behind my arm. It's half black and half white."

"Psyche?" he asked.

"Good guess." He really was cultured. The goddess Psyche was synonymous with the soul, which the butterfly represented in myth. "Persephone."

He nodded. "Half black, half white. She lives half her life in this world and half in the Underworld."

Not unlike my own life. Persephone guided transitions

to the world of death. I didn't travel there myself, but I invoked her to send others across.

"She governs the dark moon. And back here"— I tapped the spot behind me where my neck connected to my back—"is a moon with an abstract woman's face in it. Selene, the full moon."

Kiyo's dark eyes held intense interest. "Why not one of the more common moon goddesses, then? Like Diana?"

I hesitated with my answer. In many ways, Diana would have served the same purpose. She, like Selene, was bound to the human world and could keep me grounded here when I needed it. "The others are . . . solitary goddesses. Even Persephone, who's technically married. Diana's a virgin—she's alone too. But Selene . . . well, she doesn't get a lot of press anymore, but she was a more social goddess. A sexual goddess. She opens herself up to other people. And experiences. So I went with her. I just didn't think it'd be healthy to be marked with three goddesses who were all alone."

"What about you? Are you alone, Eugenie?" His voice was velvet against me, and I could have drowned in those eyes. They were like chocolate. *Chocolate is an aphrodisiac.*

"Aren't we all alone?" I asked with a rueful smile.

"Yes. I think in the end, we all are, no matter what the songs and happy stories say. I guess it's just a matter of who we choose to be alone with."

"That's why I come here, you know. To be alone with other people. There's isolation in a crowd. You're hidden. Safe."

He looked around at the buzzing, moving sea of people in the bar. They were like a wall surrounding us. There but not there. "Yes. Yes, I suppose that's true."

"Isn't that why you're here too?"

He glanced back down at me, his expression a little less sexual and a bit more pensive. "I don't know. I'm not sure. I guess maybe I'm here because of you."

I didn't have any quick retorts for that, so I started

playing with the bottle again. The bartender asked if I wanted another, and I shook my head.

Kiyo touched my shoulder. "You want to dance?"

I was pretty sure I hadn't danced since high school, but some force compelled me to agree. We stepped out into a crowd of very bad dancers. Most were just sort of floundering around to a fast song with a heavy beat that I'd never heard before. Kiyo and I weren't much better. But when a slower song came on, he wrapped me to him, pressing us together as close as two people could be. Well, almost as close.

I couldn't ever remember anything like this happening with a guy I'd just met, a desire for someone I actually wanted and not just someone who was available. His body felt hard and perfect against mine, and my flesh kept concocting ways to touch his. I was already picturing him naked, imagining what it would be like to have his body move against and inside of mine. What was going on with me here? The images were so vivid and real, it was a wonder my feelings weren't written across my face.

So I didn't really mind when he slid his hand up the back of my neck and brought his mouth down to kiss me. It wasn't a tentative kiss either. No first-date kisses here. It was the kind of kiss that meant business, the kind of kiss that said, *I want to consume every inch of you and hear you scream my name.* I'd never really made out in a public place, but it seemed kind of a trivial concern as that kiss burned between us, our tongues and lips exploring the contours of each other's mouths.

But when his other hand slid up and cupped my breast, even I was surprised. "Hey," I said, breaking off slightly. "There are people around." Amusing, I thought a moment later, that I was less concerned about him doing it than being seen doing it.

He kissed the side of my neck, just below my ear, and

when he spoke, his words heated my skin. "People only notice if you make a big deal about it."

I let him kiss me again and didn't say anything else about the hand that continued to stroke the curve of my breast and tease my nipple into hardness beneath the shirt. His other hand slid down to my ass and ground me closer to him, letting me feel exactly what was underneath his jeans. The fact that we were doing this in public suddenly made it a lot sexier.

I let out a small, trembling sigh and then broke away from the kiss again. Only this time, it wasn't because of any prudish feelings. It was from need. My body's suddenly urgent and excruciating need.

"Are you staying next door?" I asked, indicating the hotel adjacent to the bar.

"No. Out at the Monteblanca."

I let surprise show on my face. That was in the region near where I lived, in the Santa Catalina foothills. "That's not a hotel. That's a resort. A really nice one. Veterinarians must make a lot."

He smiled and brushed his lips against my cheek. "You want to see it?"

"Yes," I told him. "I certainly do."

Chapter Four

We were on each other before we even made it to his room. If our actions on the dance floor had been racy, our grappling in the elevator was downright X-rated. Fortunately no one else rode up with us, which was a good thing, considering the disheveled state of our clothing when we finally made it inside.

All the while, some reasonable voice in my mind kept whispering, *You don't do this kind of thing*. But I was. And I wanted to, very badly.

It was a nice room, not surprising in such a nice hotel. A king-size bed offered comfort in the moonlit room, and beyond it, a sliding glass door opened out to a balcony that overlooked the desert. I didn't have time to admire the view because Kiyo pushed me down onto the bed, pulling my shirt off at the same time. I'd already done a fair job at undoing his pants in the elevator, so I had an edge in the race.

When we were both naked, I saw him sit up and lean over the side of the bed, fumbling with the grocery store bag on the floor. We'd had to make an unromantic—but necessary—stop for condoms. I was on the pill, but even in the heat of passion, I wasn't so foolish as to trust going into unprotected sex with a stranger, no matter how charming. Kiyo's eager hands practically tore the box apart, causing the little packets to scatter on the floor. He picked one up and opened it, and I helped him put it on.

I smiled both at his reaction to my touch and the fact that the condom was a deep scarlet. When it was on, I admired him for a moment. Everything about him was perfect: the shape of his body, the sculpted muscles, the tanned skin. His eyes were dark and demanding in the dim lighting, black depths that wanted to wrap me up. There was an intense quality to him, something primal and feral. He regarded me in a similarly scrutinizing way just before pulling me down onto the bed with him, laying his body across mine.

All he did was kiss me at first. Everywhere. He tasted my lips again and then my neck, tracing its shape with his tongue. My breasts held his attention for a long time after that, but then, breasts occupied most guys' attention as a general rule. He held them and kissed them, biting the nipples, keeping his eyes locked on mine the entire time. For me, it was like traces of fire shooting under my skin, like his touch was some kind of drug my body needed to survive.

When his face moved between my legs, it was only to nuzzle against the sensitive skin down there, to run his tongue along the place where my thigh connected with the rest of my body. He inhaled deeply, burying himself against me as though he needed to take more of me in.

He moved back up so that we were face to face once more, his body again on top of mine. My own body was in agony, uncertain as to why we weren't expediting things. I don't know what look was on my face, but he smiled at me. It was a knowing smile, an animal smile.

"There is nothing in the world," he said in a soft, burning voice, "like the smell and look of a woman about to let you have her."

"'Have?'" I laughed. "Are you calling me a possession?"

"We're all possessions during sex, Eugenie."

And then I felt him slide into me, slowly at first as though he would inch his way in and catch me unaware, and then plunging all the way. I thought the earlier delay around the tour of my body might have made him less hard, but if anything, he felt harder and bigger than when I'd put the condom on. He moved at a rough, fast pace that in any other man would probably have ended things in thirty seconds. Somehow I suspected that wouldn't be the case here.

It wasn't.

I dug my nails into his back, arching myself up as though I could drive him farther and farther into me. Already I was almost painfully full, but it was a good pain, the kind that danced with pleasure, making the two inextricable. He moved with long, rapid strokes, watching my face carefully to see how I reacted to every movement and shift of position. When he hit a spot that made my lips part and cries grow louder, he thrust harder and more fiercely. My cries bordered along the edge of screaming, and he moved his hands to hold my wrists and keep my bucking body from moving. The wrist that had been hurt with the keres complained a little, but it was lost to the building sensation between my legs, that burning liquid heat waiting to explode through me. Besides, I wasn't being gentle either. I slipped my hands from his hold and clutched at his back, letting my nails dig in fierce and deep, almost hard enough to draw blood, I realized. That knowledge didn't make me stop. If anything, I dug deeper until he snatched my wrists back and held me down again. It was the roughest sex I'd ever had. And probably the best.

"Don't close your eyes," he told me.

I hadn't even realized I'd been doing it. Vision seemed a superfluous sense at the moment, compared to everything else I felt.

"Look at me," he whispered. "Look at me."

Our eyes locked as the pressure within me finally exploded, sending my body thrashing and shaking. My screams faded to one low moan, the only way I could give voice to the feelings coursing through me. One might have thought Kiyo would slow down after that, but he didn't. He kept up the same ardent pace, still holding me, and it was almost too much after that orgasm. I could see from his face that my reactions aroused him, drove him on further. I was his possession in that moment, just as he had said.

My combative, fighter nature flared up just then. I decided that I didn't want to be the possession anymore. Dominance and power ruled my days; it would with sex too. I moved my hands from his back to his upper arms and shoulders. Relying on the element of surprise, I rolled him over, using my legs to pin him down, wrapping them around his hips. Pleased surprise poured over his face. He hadn't expected me to be so strong. He shifted as though he might try to throw me, and I shoved him down. It turned into a rougher motion than I intended, but he didn't mind. If anything, it made the passion on his face grow.

"You submit now," I growled, pressing my palms down onto his chest.

A smile twisted at his lips. "Sure."

I guided him back into me, exultant that I was the one in control now. I moved my hips up and down, leaning over so I could watch him slide in and out of me. My hair, long since freed from its ponytail, hung over him, grazing his skin. I have hair the color of cinnamon, a tawny russet not dark enough to be auburn, nor light enough to be strawberry. In this lighting, however, it was only a dark veil between us. He brushed it aside and rested his hands gently under my breasts so he could feel their movement as I rode him. Looking up through my hair, I watched his face now that I was the one controlling him. It was exquisite. I moved faster and harder, bringing him all the way into me, watching and adjusting as I did. I

wanted to see him come so badly, see the look on his face
when he lost control.

I knew we were close when his hands dropped from my
breasts to grip my waist and hips. His fingers clenched
tightly into my skin, just as mine had earlier. He kept his
gaze on me, bold and unafraid of me seeing him in
climax. I moved more fiercely, urging him on, and then
I heard a soft, ecstatic sound issue forth. His eyes never
left mine, and his hands slid to the backs my shoulders,
suddenly raking down my flesh as his body released itself
into mine.

I yelled out in surprise at the pain from where he'd
scratched me. How sharp were his nails? Did he have
talons? I'd dug into him too but nothing like what he'd
just accomplished on me. When he'd recovered, and his
frantic gasps had returned to normal, he seemed to realize what he'd done.

"Oh my God, I'm sorry," he said, his breathing still
heavy. He pulled me to him, putting his arms around
me, careful to avoid the places he'd gouged. I laid my
cheek against the warm, sweaty skin of his chest. "Did I
hurt you?"

I didn't know which part of sex he referred to—
probably that last bit of scratching—but really, it didn't
matter. "No," I lied. "Of course not."

When we'd both sort of come back to ourselves, we
ransacked the shopping bag again and produced the
cheap wine we'd purchased along with the condoms. It
had seemed hilarious at the time, considering our earlier conversation on courtship gifts. We sat naked and
cross-legged in bed, drinking from the glasses that had
already been in the room. We talked a little, and though
the conversation was a bit less substantive than in the
bar, it still felt comfortable. It was hard to be eloquent
after the wild, animal experience we'd just had.

I went to the bathroom at one point and peered at my
back in the mirror. He'd missed my tattoos but definitely

drawn blood and torn skin. It was startling. I wet a washcloth and cleaned my stinging back as best I could, then pulled on one of the plush white robes hanging on the back of the door. Kiyo still sat on the bed, watching me, but I left him there and took my wine outside to the balcony.

It was a gorgeous night. The cacti and other desert plants stood painted in shadows and moonlight cast from a full silver moon. Selene was out tonight, and I guessed she'd come through for me just now. Crystalline stars adorned the blackness. I had a telescope at home and mused that it would have been a good night to study the heavens.

Except that it looked like the weather would turn on us soon. This surprised me, considering how clear it had been most of the day. Rain was rare this time of year. But dark clouds were tumbling quickly across the sky, blotting out the stars they passed. On the horizon the clouds came from, I saw a faint flicker of lightning. A wind picked up, the kind of wind that rises and falls like one's breath. The air was warm and alive, building up tension and power. It wouldn't be a dismal, glowering storm; it would be the kind of storm that left you awestruck about the power of life and nature.

I felt alive too in that moment, as restless and wild as the tempest about to come. I felt pretty confident I had never opened myself up to anyone as much as I had to Kiyo just now. I had let myself go. It was frightening and thrilling at the same time.

I heard him step out onto the balcony a few minutes later and then I felt his arms slide around my waist and his chest press against my back. He rested his chin on my shoulder. All was quiet around us. We were far from the highway, and no one else seemed to be awake. There was only the sound of the wind blowing around us and thunder growing louder.

Kiyo's hands slipped to my waist and loosened the ties. He then reached up and tugged at the robe so that it fell off, leaving me naked to the elements. I started to turn away, shy, but he held me where I was.

"No one's out," he murmured, running his hands over my body, grazing my breasts as he moved farther down. "And even if they were, you have nothing to be ashamed of. You're beautiful, Eugenie. You are so amazingly beautiful."

He buried his face against my neck, and I leaned into him as he kissed me. His hand slid down between my legs and stroked me as the wind caressed my skin. When I whimpered out of desire, he released me for a moment, and I heard a slight rustling. He'd brought a condom outside with him. Presumptuous bastard.

He had it on in seconds and then returned his hands to me, positioning me so that I bent over, my hands holding on to the railing. He pressed up behind me, and then that hard thickness was inside me again, once more claiming possession. I was almost rubbed raw from our last round, but as he kept moving into me, I eventually grew wet again, allowing the line between pleasure and pain to blur once more.

It seemed crazy, having sex out here in public like this, but it was the kind of crazy that felt pretty damned good. Apparently he had an exhibitionist streak. But no one was out here. It was just us and the desert and the storm.

I hadn't thought I could come any more tonight, but he proved me wrong just as the first warm drops of rain began to fall. Thunder and lightning occurred together around us now; the storm had reached us, screaming its own ecstasy to the earth. Still Kiyo moved into me, oblivious of the weather, intent only on me and him. At last, when we were in a full downpour, I felt him shudder and give a few last hard strokes before pulling out.

Then he turned me around and drew me to him again. I could hear his heart beating in his chest almost as loudly as the thunder around us. The desert flickered and flared to life in the lightning, and the pounding rain threatened to drown us.

But neither of us noticed.

I fell asleep pretty quickly after that, lying under the covers in his arms once we'd both toweled off. No insomnia tonight.

Yet, I woke up a couple hours later, not entirely certain why. Then I knew. Kiyo's hand was pressed against my mouth, making it hard to breathe. The storm had stopped; all was silent in the dark room.

I started to struggle, and then his mouth was by my ear, his voice barely audible.

"Shh. Something's in here."

I nodded my understanding, and a moment later, he released his hold. We both lay perfectly still, and I thought about his choice of words. *Something,* not *someone.*

Literal and figurative chills suddenly crept over me. Following Kiyo's gaze, I looked up at the wrought-iron headboard and saw ice crystals spreading along it like fine white lace. Our breath came out in small clouds, and my bare skin shivered with the cold.

A shape moved into my field of vision, shining in the returned moonlight. I had known what it was before seeing it. An ice elemental. A creature vaguely anthropomorphic and composed of sharp, glittering ice crystals.

Technically, however, it was just one of the gentry. Some of them could not pass physically into our world, just as some shamans could not cross physically into theirs. Gentry not wanting to come in spirit but lacking the strength to come over with bodies intact would sometimes cross in an altered, flawed form. An elemental form.

Of course, the thing was, any gentry not strong enough to come physically was not even close to being as strong as me. I could kick any elemental's ass easily. Well, if I had the right tools, of course.

At the moment, all I had—aside from my own physical

strength—was my jewelry, which was more defensive than offensive. All of my weapons had been left at home, save my wand, which was in my purse. Unfortunately, my purse still sat over by the door where it had been dropped immediately upon entering the room, lest it hinder Kiyo and me ripping each other's clothes off.

A dilemma, truly. But the ice elemental could see we were awake now, and a cold smile—seriously—crossed its face.

Screw this. I was going to have to make a move for the door and hope I was faster than it. I started to tell Kiyo just to stay still, but suddenly he leapt from his lounging position and nailed the elemental squarely with a kick straight to the solar plexus.

The elemental flew backward, hitting the wall, and for a moment, I could only stare. I'd barely seen Kiyo move. One minute he was with me, the next he was on the elemental. And was he on it! I mean, I was stronger than a lot of people, but I could not have landed that blow. I knew of few who could. It was my will or weapons that fought a creature like this in the end, not my body. How had Kiyo done that? I stared at him incredulously, then realized I was missing my window here.

I sprang from the bed, slipping out of Kiyo's reach. "No, Eugenie! Stay away!"

I made it to the door, but the elemental was getting up. Its eyes focused on me, and my stomach lurched, knowing I had attracted this creature here and possibly put Kiyo at risk. The elemental gave a tinny laugh as it watched me empty out the purse onto the floor.

"Yes, Eugenie Markham, stay away. Stay away, little swan." It took a step toward me.

Frantically, I searched for the wand. Where had all this shit in my purse come from?

"How do you know my name?" I asked, hoping to distract it. Gentry, no matter their form, loved to hear themselves talk.

"Everyone knows your name. And everyone wants you." I'd never thought a walking chunk of ice could look lascivious, but this one pulled it off. I shuddered and not from the cold. "But I see someone has already tasted you tonight. No matter. I don't mind following in another's wake, nor will I be the last to spread those soft legs—"

The creature was so fixated on me and what it wanted to do to me that it'd forgotten about Kiyo. Kiyo had surveyed the room during the exchange, and I'd seen his eyes rest on a tall, wrought-iron lamp. His eyes glittered with a dark heat, almost frightening in its ferocity. With the elemental distracted, Kiyo dashed for the lamp, again moving with incredible speed, and then in one motion, swung it at the elemental, hitting it with the force of a tank.

A large chunk of ice broke from the elemental's body, and it roared in agony. Iron or steel will always hurt the gentry, regardless of which world they walk. I wondered if Kiyo had known that. The elemental lunged at him, and the two of them wrestled on the floor, rolling over and over as they struggled to land a hit. Kiyo fought savagely, and each time he dug his fingers into the monster, it would hiss in pain.

I had my wand now and advanced toward the two of them. I thrust it out, making it an extension of my arm. With alcohol still metabolizing in my body, as well as me being physically exhausted, I knew I couldn't destroy the elemental, but I could sure as hell send it back to the Otherworld.

The air tingled around me, and again I smelled ozone. The elemental realized what I was doing and released Kiyo, trying to stop me. Kiyo did not let his prey go so easily, however, and moved forward, his foot again connecting with the creature—this time on the back. The weakened elemental stumbled to its knees.

I could usually do expulsions on my own, but tonight I needed a little divine help. "By Hecate's grace, I cast you from this world. In Hecate's name, I return you to your own realm." The elemental screamed its fury, but it was already dissolving. "Leave here, and return no more, you fucking bastard. *Go.*"

The elemental shattered in an explosion of ice. Some of the crystals grazed my skin, cutting it. An onlooker might have thought it had been destroyed, but I had only damaged its elemental manifestation. It had gone to the Otherworld in its own body.

I could hear the blood pounding in my ears, adrenaline surging through me. Another creature had known my name. And like the keres, it had seemed terribly interested in me in a . . . Biblical way. Bleh.

But I had more pressing problems. Slowly I turned to stare at Kiyo who was watching me with equal caution, taking in my posture and the charged wand in my hand.

Kiyo.

Dark, sexy Kiyo, who had wooed me in the bar and just given me the best sex of my life.

The same Kiyo who had just fought an elemental with more strength and speed than I ever could have mustered—more than any human could have mustered. He had also not turned into a blabbering, shocked idiot like most humans would have—*should have*—around an elemental. He had seen one before. He knew what it was, just as he knew what my wand and incantations were.

What had earlier seemed like a passionate encounter for me suddenly had a vile edge. Fear traced my spine as we stared at each other, neither of us certain what to do. The words were on my lips, but he asked them first.

"What are you?"

Chapter Five

The fact that we were having a standoff while completely naked might have been hilarious under ordinary circumstances. But these were not ordinary circumstances, and even my twisted sense of humor had its limitations.

"Me?" I demanded. "What about you? You're not a veterinarian. Veterinarians give dogs rabies vaccines. They don't throw elementals around."

Kiyo regarded me levelly. "And Web designers don't banish elementals to the Otherworld."

"Yeah, well, sometimes I moonlight."

The faintest ghost of a smile flickered across his face. He relaxed a little, found his pants, and pulled them on. Not me. I stayed rigid and ready to strike. I was also trying very hard to think of him only as a potential threat, not as the man I'd just slept with. Because if I thought about that, I might falter. Worse, I might have to face the fact that I had just let a creature of the Otherworld—

His pants now on, he approached me. "We need to talk about this—"

"No. Don't get any closer." If I could have cocked the wand like a gun, I would have.

"What are you going to do? You can't cast me out. It won't work."

I hesitated, wondering about that. He seemed so human. He had felt human. I hadn't sensed anything from him like I would one of the gentry, yet his speed and strength had been superhuman. And that wasn't even counting his unholy stamina. That should have been a dead giveaway right there.

"What do you want from me? Why did you bring me back here?"

His eyebrows rose. "I thought it was obvious. I wanted to have sex with you."

"No, damn it! There's more to it. What's going on? What are you trying to get from me?" My cool demeanor was plunging rapidly. "Did someone send you?"

"Look, Eugenie, just put the wand down. We'll talk. We'll figure this out."

"I thought you couldn't be cast out," I reminded him. "Why are you afraid of the wand? Maybe the Otherworld couldn't hurt you . . . but what about the Underworld?"

He didn't answer. I sent my will into the wand and felt the air crackle with power. Fear crossed Kiyo's face. So. He was afraid. That was all I needed to know. The words were on my lips to send him to the crossroads, but suddenly he moved with that rapid speed I'd seen earlier. He backed up toward the sliding glass door, opened it up, and then ran out and over the edge of the balcony.

A small scream escaped me in spite of myself. We were three floors up. I dropped the wand and dashed off to the balcony, peering around on the ground for him. No way could he have survived that uninjured.

Yet, there was no sign of him. A few bats flew up over the eaves of the building, and around the far side of it, I saw the flicker of headlights. A coyote howled from far out in the desert, and a cat slunk into the shadows. There was life out here but not the kind I sought. With a lot of maneuvering, I hung over the side of the balcony, making sure he wasn't hiding under it like escaping people often did in movies. Nope. Nothing.

I gazed back over the desert, wondering what had happened to him. It was possible he could have "jumped" figuratively to the Otherworld. He'd have to be a very powerful gentry to do that without a thin spot nearby, but similarly, a strong gentry would have also been able to hold a perfect physical shape in this world. I supposed it was also possible someone so powerful could pass themselves off as human. I hadn't encountered any who were that strong.

Walking back inside, I sat on the bed cross-legged, wrapping my arms around me. The residual ice from the elemental had melted into small puddles. The bed smelled like Kiyo and sex, and I swallowed down the nausea building within me. Oh God. What had I done? Had I had sex with a monster? Had I had sex with the very kind of thing I hunted and hated and killed? Kiyo had spoken to me about honesty, yet it seemed to have all been a lie. At least it had been safe sex.

Worst of all, I had liked him. Really liked him. When was the last time that had happened? Dean and I had seemed to date and sleep together simply because neither of us had anything better to do. With Kiyo, I had started to feel a real connection. Real chemistry. His betrayal hurt me deeper than I liked to admit.

I opened my eyes, thinking. Most gentry were too technologically inept to function seamlessly in the human world, yet he had navigated it well. He'd had a car back at the bar, one we'd passed over in favor of letting me drive. He'd also had a wallet and cash to pay for drinks and the condoms. And if he was checked into a hotel, he had to have a credit card. Credit cards were traceable. If he had a dual life in our world, I should be able to find out something.

I picked up the phone and hit the button for the front desk.

"Good morning, Mr. Marquez," a pleasant desk clerk answered.

Kiyo Marquez. It was a start.

"Um, actually this is Mrs. Marquez. I was wondering if you could tell me if my . . . husband already prepaid for the room?"

A pause while she looked it up. "Yes, he did upon check-in. He left the same card on file for incidentals."

"Can you tell me the number on the card he used?"

A longer pause. "I'm sorry, I can't give that out to anyone but the cardholder. If you can put him on the phone, I can tell him."

"Oh . . . I don't want to bother him. He's in the shower. I just wanted to make sure we weren't maxing out the wrong card."

"Well . . . I can tell you it's a Visa ending in 3011."

I sighed. That wouldn't do me much good, but I doubted I'd get more from this woman. "Okay. Thanks."

"Is there anything else I can help with you?"

"Yeah . . . can you connect me to room service?"

I ordered breakfast on Kiyo and then showered while I waited for it to show. I needed to wash away the sweat, to wash away the scent of his body on mine. When the food arrived, I munched on toast and ransacked the room for some kind of evidence. Kiyo's wallet had been in his pants, so that was gone. He had no other personal possessions in the room, save the other discarded clothing from last night. I explored every drawer and nook, just in case he'd hidden something away.

The sun was well up over the horizon when I finally left the hotel. When I arrived back home, I called Lara and told her his name. I asked her to see what connections she could find to it, Phoenix, and vets. She excelled at that kind of thing, but I knew it might take a few days. Fortunately, a career in banishing and destroying is a great way to relieve frustration while waiting.

My first job the day after the Kiyo incident involved frisking a marid out of someone's bathroom. Marids are one of the djinn—genies to most Americans—and are tied to the element of water. Like the keres and most other djinn, marids tend to occupy some sort of physical object. Only, rather than a bottle or lamp, they prefer someplace wet—say, like, a sink pipe.

Annoyed at being troubled with such an idiotic task, I cast my circle in the large, black-tiled bathroom and used the wand to yank the marid out of the pipe. She materialized before me, looking very much like a human female, save for her death-pale skin and rippling blue hair. A silk dress hung from her body.

I saw her tense up, instinctively ready to lash out at me with her power. Then she did a double take, sizing me up from head to toe. A funny look came over her face, and moments later, she lit up with a schmoozing smile. She swept me a low bow.

"My lady," she said grandly. "How may I serve you?"

"You can't," I told her, holding up the wand.

She kept the smile, but there was tension in it. "Of course I can. I have the ability to conjure up riches and other wonders. I can make your dreams—"

"Stop it. I'm not falling for this."

The myths about djinn granting wishes aren't entirely fabricated. She wasn't all-powerful, but she could definitely pull some tricks out of her hat. When faced with danger, a djinn's most common strategy is to try bargaining with the enemy. Unfortunately, the "wishes" they grant rarely turn out the way others expect.

Uneasily, she backed up toward the wall. She hit the edge of the circle first. Glancing around, she realized she was trapped. The smile slipped, replaced by true fear.

"Surely there's no need for violence," she said. Her eyes widened. "Please."

I stared. I rarely had Otherworldly creatures beg for mercy. I hesitated for a moment, then my Kiyo-induced bad mood took over. I poured my will into the wand, ready to push her through the gate.

She felt the power charge up in the air and kicked into true self-defense mode, now that she realized her wheeling and dealing wouldn't work. Her magic trickled into the circle. It reminded me of mist or fog, a soft dampness filling the air. I blinked in surprise. I didn't usually sense magic in this way. Most often, I felt Otherworldly power as a tingle or a pressure. This was tangible.

She saw my surprise. Her eyes widened with hope. "You see? You have no need to tear me apart. Like calls to like."

Like? I was puzzled but didn't hesitate to take advantage of her distraction. Her magic might be weaker in my world, but I still didn't want to fight it head-on. Far easier to deal with her this way.

A moment later, I had made my connection to the Underworld. She grew more pale when she realized I'd used my wand to ensnare her and begged me again for mercy. Gritting my teeth, I thought about the way Kiyo had used me and grew angrier. No. No quarter for Otherworldly creatures.

And yet . . . staring into her eyes, I recalled the brief feel of mist from her magic. *Like calls to like.* I didn't know what that meant, but it had struck me. At the last possible second, I decided to spare her after all—in a manner of speaking. There was no way I could allow her to stay in this world. Instead, I shifted my focus to the Otherworld and sent her over there in entirety, rather than giving her instant death via the Underworld.

When it was all over, I stared at the empty bathroom, wondering what had come over me. "Going soft," I muttered.

It took Lara awhile, but she found something about Kiyo a few days later, the same day I decided to go see Roland and break the news that I was going to go after Jasmine. Something about that encounter with Kiyo and the elemental in the room had made me decide I couldn't leave that poor girl to the mercy of the Otherworld. Roland might not like it, but he couldn't stop me, not anymore. My powers had surpassed his awhile ago. I also intended to ask him about my newfound status as bachelorette of the year in the Otherworld.

At least in the few days since being with Kiyo, there had been no other attacks specifically targeted at me. Wil had left a million messages with Lara, but we'd been putting him off. I'd had only a handful of small jobs: one banishing and a couple of exorcisms. I could almost have said it was a slow week. Not much was happening while I waited.

What also wasn't happening was any healing of the scratches on my back. The blood had dried up and scabbed a little, but the marks didn't fade at all. They stayed red and angry-looking, although they didn't hurt. Every morning I would look at them, hoping they had disappeared. They never did.

I harbored a secret thought that if the scratches went away, so would my feelings about Kiyo. I couldn't stop thinking about him. I'd spend my days venting and fuming over him, and at night, scandalous dreams would play through my head, making me wake up hot and restless. I didn't know what was wrong with me. I'd never behaved this way, especially with a guy who represented everything I stood against.

"I finally turned up a Kiyo Marquez at a vet hospital in Phoenix," Lara told me as I drove out to my mom's house. "I had to call around a lot. They say he doesn't work a full schedule there and is on vacation for the next two weeks. I couldn't get anything else. His address and phone number are unlisted."

I thanked her and pondered this. So Kiyo hadn't completely lied. He had a job, a very human one. It still didn't mesh with what I'd observed or knew.

I saw my mom bent over in her garden when I arrived, requiring me to sneak inside quietly so I could speak with Roland in private. I found him in the kitchen, almost exactly in the same place as last time.

We exchanged greetings, and then I dove in, deciding to save the Jasmine thing for last.

"More of them know my name. I've fought with two now who knew me as more than Odile. I also heard about a third who knew who I was."

"Were the attacks specifically targeted at you, then? Like revenge attacks?"

"One was. The other was part of a job. Why? Did they come looking for you when your name got out?"

"A little. Inconvenient, but not the end of the world."

"The weird thing here . . ."

"Yes?"

"Well . . . they've also sort of been, like, soliciting me . . ."

He arched an eyebrow. "Like for sex?"

"Yeah." Roland undoubtedly had done all sorts of sexual things in his life—most with my mother, God help me—but he was enough of a father figure that I didn't feel entirely comfortable discussing such things with him.

"Well, you know how they are with human women. If one were trying to get back at you . . . well, rape is a common enough act of retaliation."

"Great. I'd rather they just beat me to death."

"Don't make jokes like that," he warned. "If your name was just discovered, it's probably pretty hot right now. But I imagine the hype will die down eventually. Just wait it out. In the meantime, watch your back—not that you don't already. Do the usual things. Keep your head clear. Stay armed at all times. Don't drink." He cut me a look. "Stay away from the peyote."

I rolled my eyes. "Come on, I haven't done that in years."

He shrugged. "You've got something else to unload. I can see it in your eyes."

"Well . . . speaking of watching my back . . ."

I stood up from the chair and took off the loose button-up shirt I wore over a tank top. I swept my hair aside and turned around so he could view my back.

He gave a small grunt when he saw the scratches. "Those look nasty. You get in a fight today?"

"They're from four days ago. They won't heal."

"Do they hurt?"

"No."

"What gave them to you?"

"Not sure. He looked human, but . . . I don't know." I let my hair drop and turned around, putting the shirt back on.

"How'd he get you at that angle and position?" Roland looked puzzled. "Were you wrestling?"

"Uh, that's really not important," I said hastily. "Have you ever seen anything like it?"

"Not exactly, no, but I've seen enough to not think this is too out there. If there was enough magic or whatever used to inflict them, they may just take awhile to heal."

That didn't really make me feel better, but I was unwilling to elaborate on my encounter with Kiyo.

I took a deep breath. "There's one more thing."

"I know. You're going after the girl."

So much for my dramatic proclamation. "How'd you know?"

"Because I know you, Eugenie. You're foolish and headstrong with a naive sense of righteousness. You're like me." Not sure if that was a compliment or not.

"Then you understand."

He shook his head. "It's still dangerous. And stupid. You cross in your own body and—"

"And what?"

We both looked up like guilty children. My mother stood in the doorway in a wide-brimmed hat and dirt-covered gloves, further evidence of her gardening. I had a few planters out in the rock garden that passed for my backyard, but she maintained a veritable oasis. Her long, slightly graying hair streamed down her back as she regarded us. Her hair lacked my reddish hue, and her eyes were just blue, not violet-blue. Otherwise, everyone said we looked alike. I wondered if I'd age like her. I hoped so, although I would probably dye any gray away.

"What are you planning on doing, Eugenie?" she asked in a level tone.

"Nothing, Mom. Just hypothetical stuff."

"You're talking about going over *there*. I know what that means."

"Mom—" I began.

"Dee—" Roland began.

She held up a hand to stop us both. "Don't. I don't want to hear it. Do you know how much I already worry about you in *this* world, Eugenie? And now you want to walk right into their homes? And you." She turned on Roland, her eyes flashing. "I spent twenty years worrying about you. I'd lie awake, wondering which night would be the one you didn't come home. I thanked God the day you retired, and now you're encouraging her to—"

"Hey, whoa, he's not telling me anything here. Leave him out if this if you want to thrash somebody. This is just me. He's not involved."

Roland turned on me. "Eugenie, if you insist on going, I might as well go—"

"Mom's right. Your fight's done. This one's mine."

My mom turned on me. "It's not yours either! Why can't you just worry about keeping them away from here? Why go after them?"

I told her. She kept her face proud and stony the entire time I spoke, but I could see her eyes betray her. The severity of the situation wasn't lost on her, even as her words continued to deny that truth.

"You're just like him. Too noble for your own good." She suddenly looked older than her age. "You're compensating for some sort of lack of attention as a child, aren't you?" There she was, slipping into therapist mode again.

"Mom, she's fourteen, er, fifteen now. If this were someone kidnapped locally, you'd agree to any measures to get her back."

"I'd agree to measures that involved backup, not you alone."

"I have no backup."

"Except for me," piped in Roland.

"No," my mother and I told him together.

She turned to me and used that deadliest of weapons known to mankind: the Mom Card. "You're my only child. My baby. If something happens to you . . ."

I was ready for her. "Jasmine's someone's baby too, even if her mom is gone. That almost makes it worse, actually. She lost her parents. She has no one. And now she's trapped, being held hostage by some asshole who thinks it's okay to kidnap and rape unwilling girls."

My mom flinched as though I'd slapped her. She looked at Roland. They exchanged one of those long looks that couples who have been together for ages can do. I don't know what they communicated, but she finally looked away from both of us.

"When . . . you get her back, bring her to me. It doesn't matter if it's . . . gentry or humans. She'll need the same kind of therapy any other victim would." I knew she did that kind of counseling with patients all the time, but I'd never thought of her as helping gentry victims. It was very kind for someone who tried to pretend the Otherworld didn't exist.

"Mom—" I attempted.

She shook her head. "I don't want to know anything else about it until it's all over. I can't know."

She left us then, returning to the peace of her garden.

"She'll recover," Roland told me after a quiet moment. "She always does."

Forced to accept the fact that I would be going over now, he was only too willing to flood me with as much tactical information as possible. It grew dizzying.

At one point, after I'd refused his third request to go with me, he said, "I assume you'll be taking your *other* help."

The tone in his voice showed undeniable derision for my "other help." I knew he didn't approve, but he had to recognize the benefits. "You know they're an asset."

"So is a grenade—until it goes off in your hand."

"They're better than nothing."

He scowled but said no more, instead discussing more logistics with me: where and when to cross over and what weapons to bring. We decided it would be best for me to wait until the moon was in crescent phase, so I'd have a stronger connection to Hecate. She facilitated transitions, particularly to the Otherworld, which might be useful if I needed a hasty retreat. There'd be a nice crescent in about four more days.

I left their house without seeing my mother again. I hoped she wouldn't take her feelings out on Roland, and I wondered how much it must suck to love someone who always walked into danger. I decided if I ever got married, I'd choose someone with a normal job whom I could expect to be home at normal hours. Like an electrician. Or an architect.

Or a veterinarian.

Ack.

As I got into my car to depart, I saw the strangest thing. A red fox watched me from the tree line on the far side of my parents' house. More surprising than seeing it watch me so seriously was the fact that it was a red fox in the first place. They weren't common in southern Arizona. You were more likely to see a gray fox or one of the silly-looking little desert kit foxes. I stared into this one's yellow-brown eyes and shivered. Too many weird things were happening lately for me to feel comfortable with a studious fox, no matter how beautiful.

When I got back to my house, I knew it was time to solicit the "other help." This was one of the areas where my path had split from Roland's. He'd been my mentor and had years more experience, but we both knew I'd grown stronger. He could never have done what I was about to do. If he could, he might have understood why I relied on this sort of assistance.

I closed my bedroom door and then shut the curtains

and blinds. Darkness fell, and I lit a candle, letting it be my only light source. I was strong enough to do a summoning without the stage tricks, just as I could cast out a spirit without divine help, but I didn't want to waste the extra strength today.

I produced the wand and touched the smoky quartz crystal on it, strengthening my connection to the spirit world. Closing my eyes, I focused on the being I wanted and then recited the correct words. I often improvised words when I cast out creatures—hence my frequent use of expletives—but it didn't usually matter, so long as my intent and meaning proved clear. For a summoning like this, however, I had to have everything right. I was essentially invoking a contract, and as any good lawyer knew, technicalities were everything.

The room grew freezing cold when I finished the incantation, a different kind of cold than the elemental had caused. A pressure sort of swirled around me, and then I knew I was no longer alone. I looked around and found him in the corner he usually appeared in, a black shape hidden among the shadows. Red eyes gleamed out at me from the darkness.

"I am here, mistress."

Chapter Six

I turned the light back on.

"Hey, Volusian, how's it going?"

He stepped forward, blinking with annoyance at the light, just as I'd known he would. He was shorter than me, very solid and humanoid in shape, which indicated a fair amount of power. He had smooth, almost shiny black skin and those narrow red eyes that always unnerved me a little. His ears had a slight point to them.

"I am the same as always, mistress."

"You know, you never ask how I am. That hurts."

He answered my lazy smile with a long-suffering scowl. "That is because you are also always the same. You smell of life and blood and sex. And violets. You are a painful reminder of all the things I once was and all the things I will never be again." He paused thoughtfully. "Actually, the scent of sex is stronger than usual. My mistress has been . . . busy."

"Did you just make a joke?"

I said this partially to deflect the sex issue but also to keep teasing him. Volusian was about as damned as a soul could be. I didn't know what he'd done when alive, but it had been evil enough that someone had cursed him from ever entering the world of the dead. His soul would never find any peace. So he had haunted my world and the Otherworld until I'd discovered him tormenting a suburban family.

He was so powerful, as was his curse, that I had not been strong enough to destroy him and send him on. The best I could have done was cast him to the Otherworld, but I had no guarantees he wouldn't return. So I'd done the next best thing I could: I'd enslaved him. He was bound to me until I released him or lost control. This way, I dictated his actions. I usually kept him in the Otherworld until I needed him. Teasing him was a way to project confidence in my control, like I wasn't worried at all. I couldn't show any weakness with him. He had made it perfectly clear a number of times that he would kill me horrifically if he ever broke free.

He didn't respond to my last comment. He simply stared. He was only obligated to answer direct questions.

"I need some advice."

"I do as my mistress commands." There was an implied *until I can choke the breath from her body* at the end of that seemingly subservient statement.

"I'm going to be crossing over into the Otherworld soon. Physically."

That almost surprised him. Almost. "My mistress is foolish."

"Thanks. I have to find a human girl that some horny gentry abducted."

He reconsidered. "My mistress is brave and foolish."

"She was taken by a guy named Aeson. Do you know him?"

"He is king of the Alder Land. Powerful. Very powerful."

"Stronger than me?"

Volusian stayed silent, thinking. "Your powers do not diminish in the Otherworld, as some humans' do. Even so, he will still be at his full strength. It would be a close battle. Were you to fight him in this world, there would be no contest. He would be weaker by far."

"I don't think I can manage that. What about you guys? I'm going to bring you along. Will it help?"

"I feared my mistress would say that. Yes, of course it will help. You know my binds force me to protect you, no matter how much angst it causes me."

"Aw, don't sound so glum. Think of it as job security."

"Make no mistake, mistress. I may protect you now, but as soon as I have the chance, I will rip the flesh from your body and tear your bones apart. I will ensure you suffer so gravely that you will beg me for death. Yet, even then, your soul will not find relief. I will torture it for all eternity."

He spoke in a flat tone, not as a threat, but simply as a statement of fact. Honestly, after my week of propositions, statements about my impending death were kind of a refreshing return to normality.

"Looking forward to it, Volusian." I yawned and sat on the bed. "Anything else constructive you've got to offer? In rescuing the girl, I mean."

"I suspect my mistress is too . . . set in her ways for my advice, but you could solicit help."

"Solicit it from whom? I don't have anyone else to go to."

"Not in this world you don't."

It took me a moment to get what he was saying. "No. No way. I'm not going to some gentry or spirit for help. Not like they'd give it anyway."

"I would not be so certain of that, mistress."

Gentry were petty and dishonest. They had no regard for anyone but themselves. No way would I appeal to one. No way would I trust one.

Volusian watched me. When he saw I would not respond, he said: "It is as I thought. My mistress will not hear anything she doesn't want to. She is too stubborn."

"No, I'm not. I'm always open to things."

"As you say, mistress."

The look on his face somehow managed to be angelic

and scream *you fucking hypocrite* all at the same time. "All right," I said impatiently, "let's hear it."

"There is another king, Dorian, who rules the Oak Land. He and Aeson hate each other—in a polite-faced, political manner, of course."

"No surprise there. I'm surprised they aren't all turning on each other. That doesn't mean he'd help me."

"I believe Dorian would be very happy to see someone come and kill off Aeson. Especially if he did not have to actually do it himself. He might offer a great deal of assistance to see you do it."

"'Might' being the operative word. So you're suggesting I just show up at his door and ask for help?"

Volusian inclined his head in the affirmative.

"Have I ever killed or cast out any of his people?"

"Likely."

"Then I think it's 'likely' he'd kill me the moment I set foot on his land. I can't imagine any gentry's keen on letting their biggest assassin in the door."

I wasn't touting ego in that statement. Much like Volusian's death threats, I simply stated a fact. I knew my own worth and reputation as far as the Otherworld was concerned. I mean, it wasn't like I was reaching genocide levels or anything; I just had more notches on my belt than most.

"Dorian has . . . an odd sense of humor. It might amuse him to welcome an enemy like you. He would enjoy the sensation it would cause among others."

"So he uses me for entertainment and then kills me." I couldn't believe Volusian was even suggesting a plan like this. He hated me, but he also knew me. If he hadn't had such a stick up his ass, I would have sworn he was messing with me. Yet, his bindings forced him to sincerely give the best of his counsel if I asked it.

"If he gives you his word of hospitality, he is honor-bound to keep you safe."

"Since when do gentry keep their word? Or have honor?"

Volusian regarded me carefully. "May I speak bluntly, mistress?"

"As opposed to usual?"

"Your hatred of the gentry blinds you to their true nature. You are also blind to the only thing that might let you escape this mad scheme alive—not that I would mind if you were torn to bloody shreds by Aeson's people. But whatever else you believe, one of the gentry will stake his life on his word. They keep their oaths better than humans."

I honestly didn't believe that. No matter how much I might need help with this, it wasn't worth it. I would not make a deal with the devil.

"No. I won't do it."

Volusian gave a small shrug. "As my mistress wishes. It makes no difference if you speed your own death. I cannot die, after all."

I stared at him in exasperation. He stared back. Shaking my head, I stood up for another summoning.

"Okay, if that's all, I'm gonna call the rest of the gang."

He hesitated. "May I . . . ask my mistress a question first?"

I turned in surprise. Volusian was the epitome of don't-speak-until-spoken-to. He only answered what was asked of him. He did not seek out other information. This was new. Wow. What a week of earth-shattering events.

"Sure, go ahead."

"You do not trust me."

"That's not a question, but no, I don't."

"Yet . . . you came to me for advice first. Before you spoke to the others. Why?"

It was a good question. I was about to summon two other minions. I didn't trust them either, but they had more reason to show loyalty than Volusian. They did not describe my graphic death on a regular basis.

"Because no matter what else you may be, you're smarter than they are." I could have elaborated on that, but I didn't. That was really all there was to it.

He thought about this for a long time. "My mistress is less foolish than she normally appears." I think it was the closest he could come to thanking me for a compliment— or giving one.

I took out the wand and summoned my other two spirits. I didn't bother with candles or darkness because these ones were easier to call—especially since I was technically only "requesting" one to come, not ordering him.

The coldness and pressure came again, and then two other forms appeared. Volusian stepped back, arms crossed, not looking impressed. The two newcomers glanced around, taking note that I had gathered all of them. The three of them never interacted much in my viewing, but I always wondered if maybe they hung out for coffee or something in the Otherworld and made fun of me. Kind of like how people make fun of their boss after work during happy hour.

Still affecting unconcerned, lazy control, I unwrapped a Milky Way and sat back on my bed again. Leaning against the wall, I surveyed my team.

Nandi was less powerful than Volusian, so she had a less substantial form in this world. She appeared as a translucent, opalescent figure that seemed vaguely female in shape. Centuries ago, she had been a Zulu woman accused of witchcraft by her people. They had killed her and, like Volusian, cursed her from finding rest. Unlike Volusian's, I could break this curse and send her on to the land of death. I had encountered her haunting this world, more frightening than harmful, and bound her in service to me in exchange for eventual peace. I had demanded three years of loyalty, one of which she had fulfilled. When the other two were up, I would let her pass on. Whereas Volusian always seemed sullen and sarcastic, Nandi was always sad. She was the poster child for a lost soul. A real downer.

Finn, however, was a different story. Of the three, only he looked happy to be here. He too was not powerful enough to have a solid form. He translated to this plane as small and glittering, barely there, much like how humans perceived Disney-type pixies. I had no claims on Finn. He had started hanging around because he found me entertaining. So he popped up from time to time, followed me, and would generally come when called. I had the power to force his service, but—even as much as I disliked all things from the Otherworld—I was hard-pressed to do so without provocation. I didn't entirely trust anyone who offered help so freely, but he had never given me reason to doubt him either. Indeed, he'd always been very helpful. I had no idea what his story was, if he too was a cursed spirit. I'd never pressed for the details.

His shining body settled upon my dresser. "Hey, Odile, what's new? Why do you smell like sex? Did you get some? Why are we all here?" Too much exposure to my world and television had given him a better grasp of our slang than the others.

I ignored the questions. "Hey, Finn, hey, Nandi." The female spirit merely nodded in acknowledgment of the greeting. "So," I said in my best boardroom voice, "I'm sure you're all wondering why I called you here today." None of them found that funny, so I just kept going. "Well, brace yourselves: I'm going to be paying you guys a visit. In the flesh. The real deal."

Nandi showed no reaction whatsoever. Finn leapt up in excitement. "Really? Truly? When? Now?"

Nice to know someone appreciated me. I debriefed them, telling them the story. Volusian leaned against my wall, letting his body language convey to me what an utter waste of his time it was to have to hear this all again.

Finn's enthusiasm diminished a little. "Oh. Well. That's ballsy but also kind of . . ."

"Foolish," said Nandi in her typically gloomy monotone. "It will end in despair. Dark, bitter despair. You will die, and I will never know peace. My suffering will be without end."

"Never thought I'd hear you two agree with Volusian."

Finn shrugged. "It is a good cause, honest. But you can't really just walk into Aeson's castle and take the girl. Not that I'm saying you aren't tough enough or anything. You'll just need a plan. A really good one. Yeah. What's your plan?"

"Um, well . . . to walk into his castle and take the girl."

Volusian sighed loudly. It was hard to tell with those red slits, but I think he rolled his eyes.

I shot him an angry glance. "Hey, it's a hell of a lot better than your plan. Would you like to share it with the rest of the class?"

He did.

When he finished, Finn said, "Now, that's a good plan."

I threw my hands up. "No, it's not. It's a horrible plan. I'm not asking one of the gentry for help."

"King Dorian might help you," offered Nandi, "although his help would most likely only offer a brief flaring of hope, which would then make our ultimate defeat that much more tragic."

"Stop with the maudlin crap, Nandi." I wished they made ghost Prozac. "Anyway, it's a moot point. We're taking on Aeson directly. End of discussion."

I gave them the time and location of our meeting spot, binding them to silence about the plan. I had to take it on faith that Finn wouldn't let the cat out of the bag, but once he'd reconciled himself to my possible demise, he seemed pretty stoked about the whole idea.

"I have one more question for all of you before I release you. In the last week, three denizens from the

Otherworld knew my name. What's going on? How many of them know who I am?"

None of the spirits answered right away. Finally, in a voice that sounded like he couldn't believe I was asking, Finn said, "Why, everyone. Well, almost everyone. Everyone that counts. It's all they've been talking about for the last couple of weeks. Odile Dark Swan is Eugenie Markham. Eugenie is Odile."

I stared. "Everyone's been talking about this?"

The three spirits nodded.

"And none of you—*none of you!*—thought this was worth bringing to my attention?"

More silence. Finally Nandi, compelled to answer any direct question, merely said, "You did not ask, mistress."

"Yes," agreed Volusian dryly. "Had you summoned us and asked, 'Is my name known in the Otherworld?' then we would have readily answered."

"Smartass."

"Thank you, mistress."

"It wasn't a compliment." I ran a hand through my hair. "How did this happen?"

"Maybe someone guessed," said Finn.

Volusian cut him a glance. "Do not be an even bigger fool than you already are." The dark spirit turned back to me. "Not all creatures come to this world to fight you. Some may have spied. For someone quiet, discovering your identity would not have been so difficult."

"What are they saying, then? Are they all going to try to kill me?"

"Some are," said Finn. "But most of them are weak. You could probably take them in a fight."

"Unfortunately," added Volusian.

Great. This was not good news. Some part of me had been hoping only a few knew, but now it seemed my identity was the gossip du jour in the Otherworld. I wondered if it would be worthwhile to find a local witch and set wards around my house. I could also keep the spirits on permanent guard duty, but I didn't really know if my patience was up for large doses of their idiosyncrasies.

"All right, then. Get out of here. Come back at the time we set up. Oh, and if any of you hear anything that might be useful about Aeson and the girl, come tell me. Do not wait until I explicitly ask you." Those last words were a growl.

, Finn vanished instantly, but Nandi and Volusian watched me expectantly.

I sighed. "By flesh and spirit, I release you from service until next I call. Depart to the next world in peace and do not return until my summons."

The spirits faded into nothing, and I was left alone.

Chapter Seven

I couldn't believe it when Wil told me he wanted to go too. Why did everyone suddenly want in on what was probably the most dangerous trip of a lifetime? I sure as hell didn't want to go. Why did they? If only I could have given up my spot.

"No," I told him. "You'll get yourself killed." I sounded just like Roland now.

"Yeah, but you said I wouldn't actually go in body. Only my spirit would go."

"Doesn't matter. The spirit is still your essence, still tied to your being and body. Someone does enough damage to it, then your body's toast too."

He didn't seem to care, which I found ironic for a guy who seemed to be so afraid of everything else. His final argument was that Jasmine would be scared and traumatized; his presence would comfort her in the face of being carted off by more strangers. He had a point, I supposed, but I warned him he would only be a reflection in that world, bearing little resemblance to his human self. She might not know him. Accepting this, he remained undaunted, and I decided if he wanted to get himself killed, that was his problem. So long as he didn't drag me down in the process.

I also made sure he paid me beforehand. Best not to take chances.

When the appointed night came, I brought Tim with me. Since Wil would not be able to go physically, we'd need someone to watch his body. Tim treated it like going to summer camp, bringing a tent and a drum and everything. I told him he was an idiot, but he had grand plans for how he could later tell his groupies he went on a vision quest. The way he saw it, he would only be half-lying. I could have brought Roland and had a little less absurdity, but I didn't trust him not to sneak in after me. So Tim it was.

We drove outside of town, traveling winding roads that snaked through the desert. Wil waited for us in a secluded spot, away from some of the more public access areas. It was a beautiful night, with the stars and moon crisp in the sky and saguaros standing watch. There were a few other thin spots between the worlds I could have used, but I chose this one because I liked the privacy and because it was one of the strongest. I wanted to waste as little power as possible in the transition over, particularly since I'd have to work to bring Wil along.

As it was, we had enough trouble even getting him into a trance.

"Jesus," I said irritably, watching him in the dim lighting, "how much coffee did you drink today?" He probably didn't even drink coffee. Too many carcinogens or something.

"I'm sorry." He attempted to stay still. "I'm just so worried about her."

He lay on a blanket near our small campfire, the smell of burning sage hanging in the air. Tim sat back near the tent with his iPod, smart enough to leave me alone and do my job. With the way Wil kept twitching, I doubted anything short of Valium would calm him down. Not that that ultimately would have done us any good.

"Are there coyotes out here?" he demanded. "Some

have been known to attack humans. Even with a fire. They could have rabies. And snakes—"

"Wil! You're wasting our time here. If you can't calm down soon, I'm going without you."

Already the crescent moon had reached its zenith; I didn't want to transition too long after its descent. At my wits' end, I produced the pendulum and hung it before Wil's face. I didn't really go for hypnosis, but I'd had good results with it in the past for clients needing soul retrieval. Hoping it would work on him, I began walking him through the stages of unconsciousness.

It worked. Or maybe just my threat to leave him behind did. Finally, I saw him fall into a waking sleep, the perfect time for his soul to loosen from his body. Holding out my wand, I drew his spirit to me so it clung like static, felt but not seen. Then, relaxing my own consciousness, I let my mind expand and touch the walls of this world, pushing its limits into the Otherworld as far as I could go. As I expanded out, I held on to an awareness of my body, working hard to bring it over in its entirety. Unlike so many others, I was even strong enough to bring other material things—my clothes, my weapons.

At first nothing seemed to happen, then the landscape around me shimmered, almost like we were trapped in a heat mirage. My senses blurred, making me feel disoriented, and then my surroundings clarified. I found myself breathless, a wave of dizziness sweeping me. The effects passed quickly. I was pretty good at crossing worlds.

"Oh my God," breathed a voice that sounded vaguely like Wil's.

Looking to my side, I saw his Otherworldly representation. Not even powerful enough to come over in elemental form, he appeared beside me much like any spirit in my own world would have: vague shape, translucent, and smoky.

"You did it. You really brought us over."

"Hey, I live to serve."

"Actually, mistress, that is our job."

I turned around and tried to hide my surprise. My minions stood before me but not as I knew them in the human world. In this world, the Otherworld, they were more corporeal, appearing in their natural forms and not as a projected sending.

Nandi stood tall and rigid, a black woman in her mid-forties. Her face had hard lines and angles, beautiful in a regal and hawklike way. Iron-gray waves of hair framed a face as bleak and expressionless as her spirit version's.

As for Finn, I'd expected him to be small and spritelike. He, however, was almost as tall as me with shining, sun-bright hair that stuck up at odd angles. Freckles covered his face, and the grin he showed me mirrored the amusement I usually saw when we were together in my plane.

Volusian looked the same as always.

I didn't exactly know what to say, seeing them like this. It was kind of startling. They watched me silently, waiting for orders. I cleared my throat, trying to appear haughty.

"All right, let's get this moving. Who knows the way to this guy's place?"

They all did, as it turned out. We stood at a crossroads, mirroring the one we'd left in my world. The country around us was beautiful, warm and balmy in the evening twilight, pleasant in a different way from Tucson. Cherry trees in full bloom lined the roads, shedding pink-white petals to the ground as the breeze rustled their leaves.

"We stand in the Rowan Land, mistress," explained Nandi flatly. "If we follow this road, we will eventually reach the part of the Alder Land where King Aeson lives."

I glanced at the road. "What, no yellow bricks?"

Nandi didn't get the joke. "No. The path is dirt. The journey will be long and must be taken on foot. Likely you will find it tedious and wearying, plunging you into misery and making you wish you had never set out on this quest."

"Quite the endorsement."

She stared at me, puzzled. "It was not an endorsement, mistress."

We set out, and I discovered in about five minutes that conversation with this group was pointless. So instead I focused on studying my surroundings, like any good soldier would. I had crossed over in body a few times, but I had never stayed long. Most of my jaunts had been to chase down wayward spirits. I'd always jumped in, done my duty, and jumped out.

With such beauty, it seemed incredible the residents here would want to keep sneaking over to my world. Birds sang a farewell to the setting sun. The landscapes we passed were gorgeous and exquisitely colored, like a real-life Thomas Kinkade painting. It almost looked unreal, like Technicolor gone crazy.

There was also magic here. Strong magic. It permeated the air, every blossom, every blade of grass. It set my hairs on end. I didn't like magic, not this kind, not the magic that filled living things. That was a gentry thing. Humans had no magic within them. We took it from the world with tools and charms; it was not inborn with us. Feeling it so heavy in the air unnerved me, almost making it hard for me to breathe.

Suddenly we crossed an invisible line, and cold wind blasted against my skin. Snow lay in drifts along the side of the road—which stayed miraculously uncovered—and icicles hung daintily on the trees like Christmas ornaments.

"What the hell happened?" I exclaimed.

"The Willow Land," said Finn. "It's winter right now. Here, I mean."

I glanced behind us. A chilly, white landscape stretched back as far as the eye could see, no cherry trees in sight. I wrapped my arms around my body.

"Do we have to go this way? It's freezing."

"You are the only who is cold, mistress," noted Volusian.

"Yeah," said Wil brightly. "I can't feel anything. How

cool is that? I bet those boots of yours won't protect you from hypothermia."

I rolled my eyes. Stupid spirits. All of them. Alive or otherwise.

"How much farther through here?"

"Longer if we keep standing around," said Volusian.

Sighing, I trudged along, pulling my coat tighter. I wore my usual one, the olive-green moleskin that went to my knees. I had put it on mainly to cover the arsenal underneath, and it had seemed too warm back in Tucson. Now it felt ridiculously thin. Teeth chattering, I followed the spirits, focusing mainly on putting one foot in front of the other.

In only a short while, we crossed another unseen boundary, and thick humidity slammed down on me, much like my sauna. Heat boiled around us, and this time I took off my jacket. In the fading light, deep green leaves rustled together, and cicadas sang in the trees. The flowers here were different than the delicate ones in the Rowan Land. These had richer, deeper colors, and their perfume was cloying. The minions informed me we'd crossed into the Alder Land. I cheered up, happy to find it wasn't winter here and that we were so near our goal.

Until we crossed back into the pink-treed valleys of the Rowan Land.

"What's this? Are we going in circles?"

"No, mistress," said Nandi. "This is the way to King Aeson's."

"But we just came out of the Alder Land. We need to turn around."

"Not unless you want to take days to get there. Your friend's body wouldn't survive that long." Volusian inclined his head toward Wil's ethereal form.

"That doesn't make any sense."

"The Otherworld doesn't lie like yours," explained Finn. "It's hard to notice if you haven't been here a lot.

It's more obvious when physical. The land folds in on itself, and sometimes what seems longer is shorter. And what's shorter is longer. We've got to cut back through here to get to Aeson's. Weird, but there you have it."

"It sounds like a wormhole," I muttered as I walked again.

"Worms do not travel this way," said Nandi.

I tried explaining what a wormhole was, how some physicists theorized space could wrinkle and fold, making it possible to travel through those folds and end up on the other side more quickly. As soon as I reached the word "physicist," I gave up, realizing I fought a losing battle.

We soon crossed into the Oak Land, a breathtaking landscape of fiery orange trees and scattered leaves, enhanced by the burning orange sunset. Here, it apparently was autumn. I swore I could smell wood smoke and cider on the wind. Something else also caught my attention.

"Hey!" I stopped and stared off into the trees. I had just seen a sleek orange form dart by, its white-tipped tail flaring behind it. "It was that fox again. I swear it was."

"What fox?" asked Finn. "I don't see anything."

"Neither did I," added Wil.

"My mistress has gone mad at last," Nandi said on a sigh.

"Long before this," muttered Volusian.

"There was a fox watching me back in my world . . . and now I just saw another one."

"The Otherworld has animals just like yours does," said Finn. "It's probably coincidence."

"But what if it's not?"

"Well, it could be a spirit fox. Was it really big? Sometimes they're—"

Volusian cried a warning just before the horses came crashing through the trees. I had my gun and athame out in a flash, firing without hesitation at the first assailant I saw. There were twelve of them, men and women, some armored and some not. Their clothing looked like something you might get if the cast from

Lord of the Rings went to a rave. All of them rode horses. Charmingly archaic.

The man I shot screamed. Steel bullets and gentry flesh don't mix so well. Unfortunately, he had shifted position at the last minute, so I only took him in the arm. In my periphery, I saw Volusian flare with blue light; I hoped he was fighting on my side. One of the riders bore down on me with a copper sword alight with magic. My iron athame caught it, and we stood locked there for a moment. Iron, the emblem of technology, fought back against the metal it had supplanted, but in the end his magic was stronger. There was simply more of it, and the wielder had more brute force.

He pushed me backward, and I stumbled into someone one of my minions must have unseated. In one fluid motion, I regained my balance and slashed at the man with my athame. Blood gleamed through his shirt, and then I clocked him in the head. He staggered, and then another hit took him down.

Another rider came at me. I fired, and she jerked backward as the bullet hit her in the chest. Underneath her shirt, I saw leather armor and wondered how much that would have softened the blow. I took aim at another rider, and then a sharp female voice called out to me.

"Stop, human. Unless you want your friend to die."

Glancing over, I saw a tall woman with long black hair worn in two braids. She inclined her head toward a young man whose arm extended gracefully outward. Above the palm of that hand, Wil's spirit floated. A golden, viscous glow encased him, giving him the appearance of an insect stuck in amber. I had no clue what kind of magic it was, but I knew he was trapped. And at risk.

Damn it. This was exactly the reason I hadn't wanted him along. He had indeed succeeded in getting both of us killed.

I glanced around. Seven of the riders were injured, unconscious, or possibly dead. Not bad for the four of us, I thought, as I assessed our odds of taking out the last five. My gun was still trained on my target.

The woman gave me a thin smile as though reading my mind. "You could kill him, but your friend would be dead before your next eye blink. As would you."

"What's it matter? You'll just kill us both anyway. At least this way I'll take company to the next world."

A new voice spoke: "No one's sending you to the next world. Not yet anyway."

One of the unhorsed riders clambered to his feet. Presumably one of my spirits had fought him, because I didn't recognize him. Yet . . . something about him struck me as vaguely familiar. White-blond hair hung to his shoulders, and ice blue eyes studied me carefully.

He approached slowly, a sly smile spreading over his face the closer he got. I didn't know who he was and wondered what tactical advantage I'd gain or lose by turning the gun on him instead. Was he the bigger threat? When he was only a couple feet away, his face lit up, and he lost himself to great, booming laughs.

"I don't believe this. I don't believe this! The mouse has walked right up to the cat. Unbelievable."

The black-haired woman fixed him with an irritated glare. "What are you rambling on about now, Rurik?"

He could barely contain himself. "Do you know who this is? This is the Dark Swan herself. Eugenie Markham, right at our doorstep." I flinched at the use of my given name, though I knew it shouldn't surprise me anymore. "By the gods, I never expected this. I fought her only a week ago, and now here she comes, offering herself to me."

"If you consider me shoving my gun down your throat offering, then yeah, I suppose I am." I eyed him curiously, and then I knew. "It was you. You're the ice elemental from the hotel."

He sketched me a bow. "And now I'll finish what I started. Happily, even. The sight of your naked body has haunted my dreams for many a night."

"Yeah? The only thing I remember about you is how easy it was to kick your ass."

Rurik grinned. "You'll remember a lot more before I'm done." Behind him, a few of the other men regarded me with renewed interest. I felt myself go rigid, despite my bold words.

The black-haired woman eyed Rurik distastefully. "If you think I'll let you give in to your . . . perversions here, you're wrong. You're as bad as them."

"Stop being so prim, Shaya. You know who she is."

"It doesn't matter. You can have her later if the king says so, but you're not doing anything while we're on patrol. *My* patrol."

I didn't quite take that as female solidarity, but it was better than nothing. I'd come expecting a grisly death, not a gentry gang bang. Wil might be a lost cause, but if I fired on one of the guys, my minions could probably do serious damage to the others. I tensed, ready to fire.

"Stop," Volusian suddenly said, moving forward. "Don't touch her."

"We don't take orders from you," replied Shaya.

Volusian was unfazed. "No, but you do take orders from your king, and my mistress has business with him."

I saw the men freeze. So did I. Business with their king? Ah, right. We were in the Oak Land where Dorian ruled, the king Volusian had originally wanted me to see. Suddenly I wondered if this winding way we'd taken had been a ploy of his to get us to Dorian after all. If so, I wondered if he'd imagined capture as part of the plan.

Shaya regarded me coolly. "King Dorian has no business with her."

A few of the men looked like they doubted this, and I jumped on it, as well as what Volusian had said about Dorian earlier.

"Are you so sure?" I smiled, portraying the same smug confidence I used with the minions, even as my heart pounded in my chest. Too many eyes on me. It was like public speaking. "I've come a long way to talk to him. How do you think he'll react if he finds out you've killed me before I've delivered my message?"

"Tell me your message," she said impatiently.

"I talk only to him. Alone. I don't really think he'd like you getting the gossip before he did. Or not getting it at all if you kill me."

"We won't kill you," said Rurik cheerfully. "We have plenty of other things we can do. You'll still get to the king . . . eventually."

Volusian fixed his red eyes on Rurik. "And how do you think Dorian will feel when he learns you've been at her before him? The king's tastes are quite . . . particular."

In another situation, I would have decked Volusian. Whose side was he on anyway? Stupid question, I realized a moment later. He was on his own side. As always.

The gentry all appeared put out. They looked like they really wanted to kill someone. The woman verified as much.

"They've killed our people. We cannot let that go unpunished."

One of the other female riders strode forward. "No, actually. Everyone's still alive. Some just barely . . . but if we can get a healer out here fast enough, they'll live."

All alive? So much for Team Eugenie. I'd known gentry were stronger in their own world, but this . . . It didn't bode well for our gallant attack on Aeson and his people. Next time I'd aim for the face. I doubted they'd come back from that.

"Let's kill the weak human anyway," suggested one of the others, "just for fun. We can still bring *her* to the king."

"The king's going to offer me hospitality," I informed them, still talking out of my ass, "for my whole group. He'll be pissed if you kill one of them. It'll make him look bad."

I was lying, and Shaya looked like she knew it. "You seem very sure of yourself, Odile, but I'm less convinced."

The other woman crossed her arms. "We have to get a healer. We need to go back for help now."

Shaya thought about this and then gave a sharp nod. She delegated people to stay with the wounded and others to escort my party back. Before she did, she ordered me disarmed. Rurik made a great show of this, touching me a lot more than was really necessary as he took away the athames—handle first, of course—and wand. When he wrapped his fingers around the butt of the gun, a look of shock crossed his face and he recoiled.

"Damn it!" he swore, cradling his hand. "It's . . . I don't know what it is. But it doesn't feel . . . right."

I smiled sweetly. Thank God for polymers. Almost as effective as iron.

The commanding woman's eyes flashed. "Someone take it from her."

No one moved.

"All right, then, one of you spirits. You take it."

My minions didn't move.

"They don't take orders from you," I said, parodying her earlier words.

"They do from you. Order one of them to do it now, or I will have the life squeezed out of your friend, regardless of King Dorian's anger."

I studied her, trying to decide if she bluffed. Wil suddenly made a piteous sound as the golden aura around him tightened. God, I hoped Volusian was right about this Dorian ridiculousness.

"Nandi," I said simply.

She strode forward and removed the gun from me. One of the riders offered up a cape so she could bundle it up. When it looked like a smothered baby, he reluctantly took it.

As for me, I was hoisted onto Rurik's horse for the trip back to Dorian's. The spirits needed no such transportation.

He wrapped his arms around me, ostensibly to reach

the reins, but I was pretty sure he didn't need to touch my breasts to do it. His hold tightened.

"I wouldn't want you to fall off," he explained.

"I'm going to cut your balls off the first chance I get," I informed him.

"Ah," he laughed, urging the horse into motion. "I can't wait for you to meet the king. He's going to love you."

Chapter Eight

The keep was like a cross between Sleeping Beauty's castle and a gothic church. Towers jauntily sprang up to impossible heights, creating black patches across the evening sky. We'd lost our light now, but I could still see that a lot of the windows looked as though they contained stained glass. I imagined they'd be beautiful in full sunlight. And framing everything, of course, were those brilliant, yellow-orange trees. Volusian had told me that the kingdoms' seasons were dependent on their rulers' whims and could last for extremely long times. This was beautiful, but I couldn't imagine living in a place that was perpetually autumn. I knew some claimed Arizona was perpetually summer, but, then, the people who said that didn't actually live there. The seasons were subtle, but they were there.

I had to keep reminding myself I wasn't in some kind of wacky movie as Rurik and his gang led us through twisted hallways lit with torches. People passed, giving us curious looks as they went about whatever one did in a medieval castle. Churning butter. Flogging peasants. I really didn't know, and I didn't care. I just wanted to get out of there.

"Wait here," Rurik told us when we reached a large set

of double oak doors. "I will speak to the king before you're shown into the throne room."

Wow. An honest-to-goodness throne room. He disappeared behind the doors, and a couple guards watched us but kept their distance.

"Volusian," I said softly, "did you purposely lead us here?"

"My only purpose, mistress, is to keep you alive. Being here will increase your chances."

"You didn't answer the question."

"You will also increase your chances," he continued, "if you are nice to King Dorian."

"Nice? They just assaulted me and threatened to rape me."

He gave me an exasperated look.

"The king will see you now," said Rurik dramatically, returning from inside the room. He held the door open for us. Trumpets wouldn't have surprised me.

The throne room was not what I expected. Sure, there was a dais with a chair on it, just like in the movies, but the rest of the room was in a state of disarray. A large space ran through the middle, for dancing or processions, perhaps, but the rest had an almost lounge sort of look. Small couches, chaises, and chairs were arranged around low tables set with goblets and platters of fruit. Men and women, again dressed in sort of a goth-Renaissance style, draped themselves on the furniture and on each other, picking idly at the fruit as they watched me. I was put in mind of the way Romans used to dine.

More than gentry lounged around, however. Spirits and sprites and trowes and wraiths were also in attendance, along with an assortment of Otherworld creatures. The monsters of human imagining, side by side with magical refugees who had immigrated to this world.

I wondered then if any other shaman had been this far into gentry society. I remembered Roland's warning, that I could be taken right into the heart of their world.

If only our kind had some sort of scholarly journal. *The Journal of Shamanic Assassination and Otherworldly Encounters*. I could have used this "research" to write a compelling article to share with my fellow professionals.

Conversation dropped to a low hum as the gentry leaned over and whispered to each other, eyes on me. Smirks and scowls alike lit their faces, and I put on the blank expression I would wear going to meet a new client. Meanwhile, my pulse raced into overdrive and breathing became a bit difficult.

Volusian trailed near me on one side while Rurik walked on the other. Wil and the others moved behind us.

"Why all these people?" I murmured to Volusian. "Is he having a party?"

"Dorian is a social king. He likes keeping people around, most likely so he can mock them. He keeps a full court and regularly invites his nobles to dine here."

We came to a stop. On the throne sat a man, Dorian, I presumed. He looked bored. He leaned into the arm of his chair, one elbow propped on it so he could rest his chin in his hand. It sort of made him view us at an angle. Long auburn hair, reminiscent of the trees outside, hung around him, highlighted with every shade of red and gold conceivable. He could have been autumn incarnate. He had the most perfect skin I'd ever seen in such a vivid redhead: smooth and ivory, with no freckles or rosy color. A cloak of forest-green velvet covered unremarkable dark pants and a loose, white button-up shirt. He had well-shaped cheekbones and delicate features.

"Kneel before the king," ordered Rurik, "and get used to being on your knees."

I gave him a withering glance. He smiled.

"I'll be happy to make you," he warned.

"Bah, enough. Leave her in peace," intoned Dorian laconically. He didn't change posture. Only his eyes portrayed any sort of interest in these goings-on. "If she's been with you for the last hour, she deserves a break. Go sit down."

Rurik's smugness flashed to embarrassment, but he bowed before the throne and backed off. That left Dorian and me staring at each other. He grinned.

"Well, come here. If you won't kneel, I at least want to get a good look at the 'terrible monster' they've brought to me. They all seem quite afraid of you. I confess, I didn't really believe it was you when they told me. I thought Rurik had been into the mushrooms again."

"Do you know how many of our people she has killed and forcibly banished, sire?" exclaimed Shaya from somewhere behind me. "She took out three in under a minute just now."

"Yes, yes. She's quite terrifying. I can see that." Dorian looked at me expectantly.

I shook my head. "I'm not moving until you offer us hospitality."

This made him sit up. He kept smiling. "She's clever too, though, admittedly, asking for hospitality before you crossed our humble threshold would have been more clever still since any of my subjects could have attacked you just now." He shrugged. "But we've made it this far. So, tell me, Eugenie, why—er, wait. Do you prefer Eugenie or Miss Markham?"

I considered. "I prefer Odile."

That smile twitched. "Ah. We're still clinging to that, are we? Very well, then, *Odile,* tell me what brings the shining ones' most feared enemy to my door, asking for hospitality. As you might imagine, this is without precedence."

I glanced around at all the watching, listening people. *Ignore them, ignore them,* an inner voice whispered. *Focus on Dorian for now.* "I don't really want to talk about it in front of the peanut gallery. I'd rather meet with you in private."

"Oh." He pitched his voice for the crowd. "Well, well. Odile wants to meet with me *in private.*"

I blushed, hating myself for doing it. Nervous laughter ran around the room, soon growing stronger and more confident as the king's did. Interesting, I thought. I remembered Volusian's comments about Dorian, and his soldiers' hesitation about his wrath. These gathered people were sheep, obviously, ready to dance or laugh at Dorian's command, but suddenly I wondered if they were sheep who also feared the whims of their capricious shepherd. I wondered if I should be afraid too.

I kept my silence, not acknowledging his joke. He leaned forward, putting both elbows on his knees, letting his chin rest in both hands now. "If I offer you hospitality, you must reciprocate in kind. I'll see that no one harms you in my household, but in return, you can harm no one under my roof."

I glanced back at Volusian. "You didn't mention that."

"Oh, for God's sake," he hissed, displaying a rare loss of patience. "What did you expect? Take it before your imminent death becomes more imminent and robs me of my chance to kill you myself."

I turned back to Dorian. I didn't like this turn of events. I didn't like being in a nest of gentry, nor did I want to be at one's mercy. Why was I here again? In my head, I summoned an image of little Jasmine Delaney, imagining her being tormented in a similar way over at Aeson's court. Only she would be subject to more than just mockery.

"I accept," I said.

Dorian regarded me in silence and then nodded. "As do I." He looked up at the crowd. "Odile Dark Swan is now under the protection of my hospitality. Anyone who so much as lays a finger on her will get his own fingers chopped off and fed back to him." He issued the threat with as much cheer as Volusian might have.

A buzz spread through the crowd, not entirely pleased. "What's to keep her from breaking her oath?" I heard someone mutter. Another said loudly, "She could slay us all!"

Dorian's eyes flicked back to me. "Did you have any idea what a creature of nightmare you are around here? Mothers tell their children Odile Dark Swan will come for them if they're bad."

"Hey, I don't seek them out. I only come for them if they come for me first."

"Interesting," he said, arching an eyebrow. "But if that's how you like it, so be it. I always admire women who know what they want in the bedroom."

"Hey, that's not what I—" I hadn't realized the extent to which our slang had permeated the gentry world. Theirs was a reflection of my own; things seeped through.

He cut me off with a gesture. "I gave you hospitality, now come up here. I want to see the terror that haunts the darkness."

I hesitated, both from distrust and defiance to his taunting. Volusian's voice whispered in my ear. "He will not harm you now that he's given his word."

"I don't know if I can really believe that."

"I do." My minion's voice was calmly serious. "You know I can't lie to you."

Turning back to Dorian, I took the steps until I stood at the same level as his chair. I met his gaze evenly. "Look at those eyes," he sighed happily. "Like violets in the snow. You smell like them too."

Beyond us, I heard another rise of murmurs in the crowd.

"What's got them all worked up now?" They couldn't hear our discourse.

His own eyes danced. They were golden-brown, the color of autumn leaves falling from the trees. "You've broken protocol. They expected you to stop one step lower. Instead, you've put yourself at the same level as me. The fact that I'm not chastising you means I'm treating you as an equal, like royalty. You should be flattered."

I crossed my arms. "I'll be more flattered when we have the private talk."

He *tsked* me. "So impatient. So human. You've asked for my hospitality. You can't expect me to not give it now." He made a gesture with his hands, and spirit servants appeared, bearing serving platters of food. For some reason, I suddenly started thinking of the song "Hotel California." "We were about to eat when you so kindly dropped in. Dine with us, and then we'll have as many 'private encounters' as you like."

"I'm not stupid. I won't eat anything in the Otherworld. You have to know that."

He shrugged, still sprawled out on his throne like a comfortable cat. "Your loss. You can sit and watch, then." He rose gracefully and offered me his hand. I stared at it blankly. Shaking his head with mirth, he simply walked with me down the steps, not touching.

"Where's the rest of my group?"

"Your servants and human friend are safe, I assure you. We've given them their own accommodations since they don't have a guest-of-honor seat at my table, that's all."

He beckoned toward a low, polished table, a bit larger than the others in the room. Like the rest, it was surrounded by sumptuous-looking chairs and sofas, patterned in bright brocades and velvets. Dorian settled down onto a small loveseat and patted the spot beside him.

"Keep me company?"

I didn't dignify that with an answer, instead sitting down in the chair next to his sofa. It was a single seat. No one could sit with me. We were soon joined by about a dozen others, including Rurik and Shaya. She reported to Dorian that the people I'd injured had been healed and were recovering.

True to my word, I didn't eat any of the food set out before us, but I confess, it looked pretty good. Stuffed Cornish game hens. Fresh bread with steam still rising from it. Desserts I would have committed murder for.

But I didn't give in. One of the first rules of the game was to never eat outside your own world. Stories and myths abounded about those foolish enough to ignore that precaution.

The other diners tried hard to pretend I didn't exist, but Dorian was fascinated by me. Worse, he flirted with me. At least he wasn't as crass as every other gentry I seemed to encounter, but I didn't rise to any of it—even if it was charming at times. I took it all in with a stoic face, which seemed to delight him that much more. The other women at the table were less resistant. Any look, any word, and they practically melted with lust.

In fact, many other people in the room also seemed to melt with lust. Very explicitly so. During and after dinner, I watched as people—couples usually, but sometimes more—touched each other brazenly. It was like being in junior high again. Some of it was just kissing. Some of it was heavy groping—a hand fondling the breast or sliding up the thigh. And some of it was . . . more. Across the room, I saw one woman climb on top of a man and strad-dle him, moving up and down. I was pretty sure they had nothing on beneath the voluminous folds of her skirt. At a table nearby, one woman was on her knees in front of a man, and she was—

I hastily averted my eyes, turning back to my own table. I found Dorian's gaze on me and knew he scruti-nized my every reaction. Through some unspoken com-mand, a blond slip of a woman slid into the empty seat beside him, the one I had refused. She draped a leg over his lap and wrapped her arms around him, kissing his neck. He moved one hand up her leg, pushing up the skirt to reveal smooth flesh, but he otherwise seemed oblivious to her as he regarded me and the other guests.

Aside from the free love and utterly medieval setting, there was almost something, well, normal about this place. The gentry I'd run into were always causing trou-ble in my world. Luring humans. Using magic indiscrim-inately. But this was like any other social occasion or party. People knew each other and regarded their friends with warmth. They discussed love and children and politics. True, they were still foreign and *other* to me, but I could also almost see them as human. Almost.

Needing to do more than sit there and stare, I reached into my coat and pulled out one of the two Milky Way bars I'd brought along. It was also a utilitarian move, seeing as how I was so hungry from watching all the feasting around me. Dorian immediately became intrigued.

"What is that?"

I held it up. "It's a Milky Way. It's . . . candy." I didn't really know what else to say about it. I wasn't even sure what was in it. Nougat? I had no idea what the hell that foamy stuff was, save that it was delicious.

He eyed it curiously, and I broke off a piece, tossing it over to him. He caught it deftly.

"Your majesty," exclaimed one of the men, "don't eat it. It's not safe."

"It won't hurt me here," rebuked Dorian in annoyance. "And don't even start in about poison or I'll let Bertha the cook have her way with you again."

The man promptly shut up.

Dorian popped the piece into his mouth, chewing thoughtfully. Watching the expressions his face went through was almost hilarious. It took him awhile to work through all that gooey scrumptiousness, and I fostered a compelling image of him with saltwater taffy.

"Entertaining," he declared when he'd finished. "What's in it?"

"I don't know. Some chocolate and caramel. A bunch of stuff sort of fused into other stuff."

One woman, her hair curly and brown, fixed me with a combative look. "That's so typical of them. They twist nature and the elements for the sake of their perverted creations until they no longer know what it is they do. They are an offense to the divine, bringing forth monstrosities and abominations they cannot control."

A snappy retort rose to my lips, but I bit it off. Volusian

had warned me to be nice. In light of their relatively civ-
ilized behavior at dinner, I could do no less, so my voice
stayed calm. "Our monstrosities do great things. We can
fix injuries you can't. We have plumbing and electricity.
We have transportation that makes your horses look like
dinosaurs."

"Like what?" asked one of the men.

"Bad analogy," I replied.

Shaya shook her head. "We can achieve many of the
same results with magic."

"Magic couldn't do much against my gun earlier."

"Our people survived. Only a human would brag about
her ability to wield death."

"And you in particular would have good reason to,"
pointed out Rurik. "No other human in memory has
killed as many of our kind—spirits or shining ones—as
you. You would have killed me last week if you'd had the
strength. You would have killed our people in the woods
today if you could have."

"I don't always kill. I even avoid it if I can. But sometimes I have to, and when I do . . . well, then, that's the
way it goes."

Glowers regarded me all around the table. Only
Dorian's face stayed politely curious.

"Rumor has it you've killed your own kind too," he
noted. "Doesn't it keep you up at night to have so much
blood on your hands?"

I leaned back in my chair, as always trying to keep my
emotions off my face. It did bother me sometimes, but I
didn't want them to know. I hadn't killed many humans—
only a handful, really—and most of it had been self-
defense. They'd been humans working with gentry or
other creatures to do harm in my world. That had justi-
fied the kills in some ways, but I could never ignore that I
was taking a life. A human life. A life like my own. The first
time I'd seen the light fade out of someone's eyes—
wrought by my hand—I'd had nightmares for weeks. I'd

never told Roland about that, and I certainly wasn't going to tell this group.

"Actually, Dorian, I sleep very well, thank you."

"It's *King Dorian*," hissed a plump man across from me. "Show respect."

Dorian smiled. The others glared further.

"The gods will punish a murderer like you," warned one of the women.

"I doubt it. I don't murder anyone. I defend. Everyone I've killed was doing damage to my world or—in the case of those humans—helping your kind cause harm. Those who merely trespass, I don't kill. I just send them back. It's not your world, so I protect my own. That's not a crime."

Dorian sent the blonde away with a quick motion of his hand and leaned over the couch so he could speak closer to me. "But you know it was once our world too."

"Yes. And your ancestors left it."

Shaya eyed me, cheeks flushing. "We were driven out."

Dorian ignored the outburst. "You gave us no choice. Once we were all one people. Then your ancestors turned away from the power within and sought it without. They built. They subdued nature. They created things with their hands and the elements that we had only thought magic capable of. Some even surpassed what magic could do."

"So what's wrong with that?"

"You tell me, Odile. Has it been worth it? You can't have it both ways. The ability to force 'magic' from the world killed the magic within. Your lives shortened as a result compared to ours. Your sense of wonder disappeared, short of anything that can be proven by numbers and facts. Your people will soon have no gods but their machines."

"And despite all this," observed Shaya bitterly, "humans continue to flourish. Why haven't they been cursed? Why do they spawn like cats and dogs while our numbers suffer? They are the abominations, not us."

"Their short lives, their burning need to create before they die, drive that. Their bodies can't help but produce life so readily. We do not feel that urgency." Dorian grinned. "Well, physically we do, but subconsciously . . . our souls know we have time."

"That's another wonder of modern medicine. We can help the infertile."

Dorian frowned, again more curious than angry. "Enlighten us."

I hesitated, suddenly regretting my comment. In as brief a way as I could, I explained artificial insemination and in vitro fertilization.

Even Dorian had trouble stomaching that one.

"This is how your numbers grow?" asked a woman near Shaya. Her voice was an awed whisper.

"Only for some," I told her. "Most don't need it. If anything, I think we have too many babies."

Seeing their shocked faces, I felt a little bad about upsetting them with all this. After all, I was a big advocate of respecting cultural diversity. Yet that core belief of mine wavered around these people. Maybe that was unfair, but I had spent my life being taught that they were not human. They might seem so now, but I didn't think one dinner could truly alter my ingrained views.

Shaya shook her head, face pale. "This, then, is what has displaced us from our homeland. These are the *things* that forced us from the place we came from and into the world of spirits and lost souls. We lost to twisted creatures who breed easily, who rape and pillage the earth in homage to their metal gods."

"Look, I'm sorry it upsets you all so much, but that's how it is. You guys lost. You have to deal. You did an okay job fighting, I guess. You still show up in a lot of fairy tales and myths. *But you still lost.* History's like that. There are wars, and unfortunately, in the end, who wins and who loses is more important than who's right or wrong."

"Are you saying your people were wrong, then?" asked Dorian quietly.

"No," I said with certainty. "Absolutely not."

"You're very loyal to your own kind."

"Of course I am. I'm human. There's no choice there—especially when your people do nothing but cause trouble for mine when they cross over."

"Look around this room. Of those gathered . . . I would say only less than twenty have ever visited your world. And of those, only a small amount 'caused trouble.' You have degenerates in your world too. Yet, you wouldn't use them to define your entire race as bad."

"No," I agreed. "But I'd still punish them. Look, maybe I'm overly jaded toward your kind, but then, the only ones I've ever met have been the deviants. It's hard not to judge."

Dorian stared at me for a long time, and I couldn't read him. Everyone else looked like they would have killed me on the spot, if not for the hospitality prohibition. I wondered if I'd made Dorian mad enough to regret giving his oath.

His thoughtful face changed to its typical expression, the perpetually amused and lazy one. He rose from his couch, sweeping the cloak behind him. Everyone else hastily followed suit. I took my time getting up.

"I thank you all for a lovely evening, but I must take my leave now." He spoke loudly, so that his words carried to more than just our table. Conversation in the room dropped. "I daresay my guest is growing restless and eager for some privacy, and I do so hate to disappoint."

The toadies laughed appreciatively, and I steeled myself not to blush again. Dorian glanced at me as we slowly walked out of the hall.

"If I offered my hand again, I don't suppose you'd take it?"

"Not a chance. I don't want to give them any ideas."

"Oh. Well. I'm afraid it's too late for that, once they see where we're going."

I cut him a warning look. "Where are we going?"

"Why, to the most private of places. My bedroom, of course."

Chapter Nine

"What's the point of a bedroom? I mean, you guys seem to be more into public sex anyway."

Dorian gestured me around a corner to his suite or wing or whatever. "What we do is natural. We don't hide it. Besides, it's actually quite titillating to know others are watching. Haven't you ever done it?"

"Sorry. I'm not an exhibitionist."

And yet, as soon as I said the words, I thought about Kiyo. We'd been all over each other at the bar, and then we'd had sex out on the balcony. We hadn't drawn that much attention, but we could have. Just thinking about it made me shudder—in a good way.

We passed through another set of double doors with two guards standing outside. They had weapons, but I knew their magic posed the true threat.

Once Dorian had closed the doors behind us, I turned and took in the room. "My God. Why would you have sex in the dining room when you could do it in here?"

"I do do it in here. I do it in there. Honestly, it doesn't matter. I like variety."

The room spread out for what seemed like miles, the far wall composed almost entirely of windows. It probably had a stellar view in the daytime. Everything from the paint to the enormous satin-covered bed was painted in shades of gold and wine. The torches on the wall added a charming, almost kinky touch. To one side I saw a room that must have served as a bathroom, judging from the giant marble tub. Opposite that, a parlor of sorts extended off on the other side of the room. He beckoned me there to an ornate chair with velvet cushions.

"Wine?" he asked, picking up a crystal decanter from a little table.

"You know the answer to that."

"I'm sure a small taste won't hurt."

"Yeah, and Persephone thought a few pomegranate seeds wouldn't hurt either. Now she rules the Underworld."

He poured himself a glass and sat down in a chair facing mine at an angle. "Would it be so bad to rule here?"

"I'm going to ignore that question. Now look, I need to talk to you about a guy named Aeson. He kidnapped a human girl—"

Dorian waved a hand to stop me. "No business yet."

"But I need to get her back soon—"

"And I will help you, I swear it. Now. One more hour won't matter. Sit with me, and I'll tell you a story."

"A story? You're serious?"

"My dear Odile, I assure you I am always serious—well, no, actually that's a lie. Most of the time I'm not. But this time I happen to be. So make yourself comfortable."

I sighed, slouched back in the chair, and took out the other Milky Way. Seeing his eyes on it, I broke it in half and handed him a piece. Nodding his thanks, he ate it with the wine, something that looked ridiculous and nearly made me smile.

"Now. Tell me something. Have you ever heard the story of Storm King?"

"No. Is or was he a real guy?"

"Very real."

"So what, is there, like, a Storm Land or something?"

"Not exactly. He did rule a vast area, but the title was more honorary due to his ability to control storms and the weather."

"Sounds reasonable."

He quirked me a half-smile. "I'm guessing you don't realize just how important that is."

"Not really. I mean, all of you have some kind of magic, right? Why not storms?"

"Ah, but to control storms and the weather is to literally control the elements. Water. Air. The fire of lightning. To see him in his fury was a terrible and amazing thing. He could call down the very heavens to smite his enemies. Few of us have such strength. I've never seen his equal, and I've lived almost two centuries. Even when crossing into your world, his powers didn't dim."

"What do your own powers do?" That was probably something I should have known before being alone with him.

"I can summon and control materials that come from within the earth. Dirt. Rocks. Magma on occasion."

"The magma sounds cool, but the rest . . . well, sorry. Not so impressive."

Those golden eyes sparkled. "I could call down the stones that have built this keep and reduce the entire building to a pile of rubble within minutes."

I glanced around us. "Yeah. Okay. That's impressive."

"Thank you. Anyway. With power like that, he inevitably drew followers. In those days, we were more fractured . . . split into smaller kingdoms. Our political and geographic divisions are always changing. Storm King sought to remedy this. He conquered and united a number of the smaller rulers, attempting to unite all of the shining ones under his rule. He made astounding progress."

"Was he a good king?" I was getting sucked in despite my best resistance.

"Depends on how you define 'good.' He was a good war leader, certainly. And he was ruthless—which is an ugly but sometimes necessary part of ruling. But, with such power, he had no qualms about taking what he wanted—no matter the inconvenience to others. Those who angered him died without question. If he wanted land, he took it. If he wanted a woman, he took her. Some of those women thought it was an honor, some were taken forcibly." Dorian paused, giving me a look both studious and sympathetic. "Some were human."

I stiffened. "Like Aeson."

"Unfortunately, yes."

"'Unfortunately'? You're one of them. You must have a thing for humans."

"Of course I do. We all do—men and women alike. You all smell like musk and sex. It screams fertility. It calls to our most basic, primal instincts to reproduce. For a people whose children are dwindling, that means something. So, yes, I understand men like Storm King and Aeson, but"—he shrugged—"I've never been with a woman who didn't want me, never taken one by force. Not even a human."

"You seem to be in the minority."

"No, as I told you earlier, it's only a small number of us who infringe on humans. You have your own rapists. They too are only a small number."

I shifted and leaned my head against the chair's back. "Fair enough. Get on with the story."

He paused a moment, looking surprised, like he couldn't believe I'd conceded a point to him. I could hardly believe it myself.

"Very well. Storm King's ambitions extended beyond conquering this world. He wanted to conquer yours as well."

"That's impossible."

"Not so. The desire to return to our homeland burns in all of us; it would push many to extreme actions. He drew a lot of support, armies willing to cross over for this dream. He had the power to make it happen. He planned a massive Samhain invasion, consisting of shining ones and spirits alike."

"What happened? Obviously it didn't work."

Dorian had propped up his elbow again, resting his hand in his chin as he had on his throne. That gorgeous hair hung off to one side, a stream of molten copper. "I'll tell you in a moment. First I'd like your opinion on all of this. What do you think about this plan of his in light of your earlier noble words about conquerors and how the conquered must simply accept their fate? If our forces took yours in fair warfare, would you accept that so easily?"

"I hate hypothetical questions."

He simply smiled.

"Okay, then. 'Accept' is a funny thing. I mean, I guess if our armies and infrastructure were destroyed, I'd have to accept that on a certain level. Would I like it? Would I just let it go? Probably not. I'd probably always keep fighting. Looking for some way to change things."

"Then perhaps you understand our attitudes toward you and the world you live in."

"Yeah, but . . . why not let it go? You have a perfectly nice world here."

"You're contradicting yourself."

"Well, in the scenario you described, we don't have a new world. We're subjugated in your new one."

"Would it make a difference?"

I stared off at one of the flickering torches. "No. Probably not. I don't know." He was making me empathize with the gentry, and I didn't like it. I turned back to him. "What happened, then? Is this Storm King someone I should go hunt down?"

"No, alas. He's already dead." Dorian watched me for a moment, weighing me for some purpose I couldn't understand. "Roland Markham killed him."

I straightened up. "What?"

"You didn't know that."

"No. Of course not. I've never even heard of this Storm King guy until tonight."

This answer turned Dorian pensive, momentarily halting his normal jocosity. "That rather astonishes me. Storm King must have been the greatest conquest of Roland Markham's career. How can you not know? Isn't he your father?"

"My stepfather. But he trained me." I turned the information over in my mind. "I don't know why he never told me. When did it happen?"

"Oh, about . . . thirteen years ago. Maybe fourteen."

That was around the time Roland had started training me. Coincidence? Had the threat of Otherworldly invasion frightened him into defying my mother's wishes?

When I didn't say anything, Dorian continued: "Not surprisingly, Roland Markham has his own reputation around here. But some say with your kills, you have surpassed him."

"I wish you guys wouldn't paint me like some bloodthirsty avenger."

"Prejudice works both ways."

"Yeah, but come on. Half the time, I just send them back here."

"You kill enough to scare most of the people out in the main hall."

"But that's not why you're telling me this story."

"True enough." He poured another glass of wine. "You are brave, Eugenie Markham. You are brave and strong and beautiful. But your perspective and view of the world—worlds—are flawed. You don't understand us. We don't behave as we do out of an evil nature. We have reasons for our actions."

"Just as I do for mine. I don't kill because I enjoy it."

"Well, I wonder about that, but yes, I get your point. You do what you do out of loyalty to your own kind. You want to protect them and see that they have the best lives they can."

"This is where you say you're doing exactly the same thing."

He laughed out loud, the sound rich and melodious. "Why, Eugenie, did we just have a moment of rapport?"

"You've stopped calling me Odile," I noted, deflecting the question.

"We aren't in public. It doesn't matter."

"Whatever. So . . . when Storm King was gathering his armies and followers . . . were you one of them?"

Dorian's levity faded. "Yes. I was. One of his biggest supporters, actually."

"Would you do it again? If you got the chance?"

"In a heartbeat. I would give anything to see his vision realized. Since his death, prophecies and omens have abounded, whispering of other opportunities that might come in the future. I pay attention to them all."

I didn't respond.

"What are you thinking about?"

"I'm trying to decide if I should break my hospitality vow and kill you."

His good humor returned. "Do you know how glad I am that you stopped by tonight? I haven't had this much fun in years. But you won't kill me. Not tonight, at least, and not even because of the promise."

I looked up at him again, a smile suddenly playing on my own lips. "Oh? And why are you so sure of that?"

"Because I told you exactly how I feel. If I'd lied and said I had no interest in the human world or following Storm King's vision, you wouldn't have believed me. In telling you the truth, I shall live another night. You may not like me, but I think honesty might have bought me your respect."

"It might have." Again, I lapsed into silence. Dorian seemed incapable of handling that.

"Now what are you thinking?"

"That you almost seem human."

He leaned toward me, a bit closer than I felt comfortable with. "Should I be flattered or insulted?"

I gave a small, rueful laugh. "I don't know."

"You have a lovely smile."

"Hey, don't start with that. I don't care how honest you are or how musky I smell."

He leaned back in his chair. "As you say."

I still couldn't get over the idea of a massive invasion. "So, is your attitude toward Storm King pretty common? Do others feel the same way?"

"Some do, some don't. Maiwenn, queen of the Willow Land, believes he was evil incarnate. She wouldn't join up with him and thought his plan would lead us to ruin. Others gave up after Storm King's defeat. If he couldn't do it, no one could. But others . . . well, many others still carry the dream. Including your King Aeson."

I sighed. "At last we get down to business."

"If we must. So. I gather you want to remove this girl from him."

"Yes."

"And how are you doing this? With your servants and that human?"

"Yes."

Now Dorian didn't say anything.

"Hey, I know it's crazy, but I don't have any choice."

"Which is why you come to me."

I nodded, and at long last, I saw the wisdom of Volusian's plan. If Dorian really could destroy this castle, he'd be a pretty good asset on a rescue mission.

"Despite my compelling story about protecting my own kind, you actually think I would go against Aeson."

"Volusian—my servant—told me you two don't get along."

"He's right. Aeson is one of our strongest leaders, but I don't like the way he rules or deals with his so-called allies. Yet, that doesn't mean I can walk over there with you and openly oppose him."

"But you said earlier—"

"That I would help. I still will. I'm just not going to do so in person."

Whatever kindly feelings I'd been building toward him disappeared. My voice turned icy. "Okay, so what are you going to do?"

"I have a servant here who used to be one of Aeson's men. I'll send him with you as a guide."

"What good is that? My spirits already know the way."

"They don't know the back ways. My servant knows the place intimately. He is far more likely to get you in unseen. I don't know much about human tactics, but I imagine even in your world, subtle and stealthy is safer than marching in openly. Especially when you're outnumbered."

I slouched back in the chair. "I suppose."

"Now you're pouting," he teased.

"No, I'm not."

"I don't mind. It's charming."

"No, it's not."

He touched my chin to turn my face toward his. "It is. But it's still unwarranted. Would you have helped me even a little if I'd come to you in a similar way?"

"No." I didn't even try to make a pretense otherwise.

He withdrew his hand, still smiling. "We are all honest tonight. Well, then. I suppose I should introduce you to Gawyn."

"Wait," I said. I stood up uncertainly. All of this honesty talk had put me in mind of Kiyo. So had the sex talk. Okay, everything made me think about Kiyo lately.

"You have another question?"

I studied Dorian carefully. He was one of the gentry, but something about this brief encounter made him . . . well, if not exactly trustworthy, then less untrustworthy. And really, he was the closest thing I might have to a true gentry resource.

"Yes. I do."

I took off my jacket and then turned around, facing

away from him. I wore no backless tank top today and had to completely pull off the long-sleeved shirt I had on. After a moment's consideration, I took off my bra too.

"Oh," said Dorian. "I think I'm going to like this question."

I wrapped my arms around my breasts, still keeping my back to him. "Do you see the scratches?"

"Of course."

"Do you know what they are? I think something Otherworldly made them."

I heard him stand up and approach me. Moments later, his fingertips lightly grazed the marks, following their tracks. His touch was slow and considering, one that truly sought to feel me. It shouldn't have been erotic—for a lot of reasons—but it was anyway. His fingers trailed all the way down the scratches and then back up.

"I can't tell you what made them," he said at last, "but I can tell you they were magically inflicted. If I had to guess . . . I'd say you've been marked."

"Marked how?"

"I think whoever—or whatever—made these did so to track you. As long as these are on you, the maker can find you."

I shivered, and it had nothing to do with being topless or the fact that his fingers were still on me. "Can you get rid of them?"

"No. They might eventually go away on their own, but I can't tell you when. Who made them?"

I hesitated. "A man."

Dorian spread his fingers out so that his palms were facedown on my back. "I'd be hard-pressed to scratch you like that standing here. I'd need to have my arms around you."

I didn't answer.

I could feel his soft laughter against my skin, and somehow, he now stood closer. "Why, Eugenie Markham, slayer of gentry, what have you done?"

"I don't know."

He ran his hands down my back until they rested on my hips. "And that's killing you, isn't it? That you might have let something you despise touch you like that. Did you enjoy it?"

"None of your business. And you're standing too close." I turned around, still wrapping my arms around me as I stepped away. "The inspection's over."

"If you wish. I'm not sure you really want it to be over."

"I don't do . . ." I stopped.

"Gentry?" He stepped forward again, resting his hands on my arms, holding more tightly than he needed to—not that he needed to be touching me at all anymore. I should have decked him, but I didn't. He had considerable height on me but had to lean down to close the distance between our faces. He smelled like cinnamon. "You know, in spite of your deadly reputation, any man in this keep would bring you the world to be your lover. Come to my bed tonight, and I'll take you to Aeson myself. I'll fight by your side."

I stared up at him, half tempted. I needed the help. And he wasn't too hard on the eyes. But I couldn't do it, no matter how reasonable he'd seemed tonight. I had gone to Kiyo unwittingly. I couldn't have sex with another of the gentry, knowing exactly what he was. That instinct wouldn't budge.

"No. You have plenty of women out there," I said lightly. "You don't need me."

"None of them will conceive like you. Your body promises many children."

"Not likely. I'm on the pill."

"The what?"

I explained it to him, and while he didn't back away from me, his eyes looked like he wanted to. He sighed. "I don't understand humans. You're gifted with fecundity, yet you stifle it."

"The world's overpopulated. And I'm not ready for a baby."

"I don't understand humans," he repeated.

"And here I thought we'd made such progress. I guess you can let go of me now."

"My offer still stands."

I felt my eyebrows rise. "Even with no chance of pregnancy?"

"Don't discount your many charms. I'd still sleep with you for other reasons."

"Like what? I mean, aside from the fact you'd probably sleep with anything female."

He looked down at me and then back up to my face, giving me the feeling I wasn't covering my breasts very well. "I won't bother with the obvious things," he said. "Honestly the main reason . . . well, in one night, I think I *might* have convinced you that not all gentry are monsters. *Might*. You still have a long way to go. But you've already been intimate with one—or something else from this world—and you can't stop thinking about it. And not because you hated it. You'll mix that with what you've seen tonight, and then you really won't know what to think.

"I want to make love to you while that indecision still torments you, while you're still not sure if I'm a god or a monster or simply a human like you. I want to be with you in that ultimate moment of vulnerability, when your desire wars with your instincts and every touch of my body triggers both fear and pleasure in you."

"Fear? Are you threatening to rape me like every other gentry lately?"

"No. I told you, I don't take women by force. But it doesn't matter. You'll come to me by choice."

"Not likely."

"Oh, very likely. Your own nature is conflicted, Eugenie. You're attracted to things you know you shouldn't be, even if you don't realize it consciously. You like playing with danger—it arouses you. That's why you fight the creatures of this world so aggressively. That's why you've come for this girl—despite how foolhardy you know it is. And that's why you'll return to me. You won't be able to help yourself. You want to walk that line, put yourself at risk, see how far you can let yourself go. You protect yourself so fiercely from the things you fear that the thought of letting down your defenses and submitting excites you. Now, you won't let someone you hate—like Rurik—touch you, but me? You don't hate me. Not quite. I'm the perfect mix. The perfect way—the safe way—to give in to what you want."

"You're crazy." I broke away, pushing with my hands, not caring if he saw my chest or not. "And you get off on some pretty crazy shit."

"No crazier than your own desires."

"You're wrong. Besides, if I were going to fuck one of you, it wouldn't be one who harbors plans to take over my world."

He shrugged, watching me put my clothes back on. "If you say so. Do you still want my earlier offer of help?"

I hesitated. His little sexual tirade had unnerved me— only I couldn't exactly articulate why. I still needed his help, regardless of my mixed feelings about him. That was becoming increasingly clear.

"Yeah, I'll still take your servant."

"Then let's introduce you."

Chapter Ten

By my count, we'd spent a little over two hours at Dorian's and almost an hour getting there. That did not please me. At this rate, we might not get home until dawn in our world. If we made it home.

Dorian's servant, Gawyn, looked like he was about a hundred years old. No, wait. Actually, that'd be pretty young for one of the gentry. Okay. He looked about a millennium old. I don't know. He was just old, plain and simple. His gray hair fell almost to his ankles, and as soon as I saw him hobble forward, I suddenly envisioned us taking another three hours to get to Aeson's, despite how close Dorian and the spirits claimed it was.

"He's ancient," I whispered to Dorian. "And he seems kind of . . . out of it."

Gawyn was currently telling Wil what lovely legs he had, despite the fact that Wil had none in spirit form. I wasn't entirely sure if Gawyn even realized Wil was male.

"His mind will be razor sharp when it comes to Aeson's castle. As for speed, I'll give you horses. You look like you could ride a number of things exceptionally well."

I ignored the innuendo, mostly thinking how it'd been years since I'd been on a horse—not counting my earlier capture. Horses had never done much for me. I didn't get why little girls wanted ponies. If I did more riding tonight, I'd likely be sore as hell tomorrow.

Once my weapons were returned, we set out. Dorian waved us off, telling me he'd be looking forward to my next visit. I stayed professional, simply thanking him for his help. I think this delighted him more than any other reaction could have.

The horses did give us more speed than walking and were the best I could have hoped for in a world without mechanical transportation. The horse I rode was midnight black with a small white star on its nose. Gawyn's appeared to be a palomino. The spirits and Wil merely drifted in our wakes.

In the darkness, I could just barely see Gawyn glancing over at me. "So you're Eugenie Markham. The Dark Swan."

"So they say."

"I met your father once."

"Oh?" I didn't bother making the father-stepfather clarification.

"Great man."

"You think so?"

"Absolutely. I know some don't think so . . . but, well, you should be proud."

"Thank you. I am."

Gawyn said no more, and I pondered his words, feeling kind of surprised. Considering what Dorian had told me, I hadn't expected Roland to have fans in the Otherworld. Then again, Dorian had also said that some—what was her name? Maiwenn?—had opposed Storm King. They might very well view Roland as a hero.

We traveled in relative silence after that, broken occasionally when Finn would happily spout about what a great party Dorian had had. Like before, we crossed in and out of the various kingdoms and their climatic changes. I still felt like we traveled in circles. More than once, Gawyn called us to a halt, scratched his head, and mumbled to himself. I didn't find that reassuring. At one point, he led us off the trail and into a forest, and I hoped one of my minions would speak up if we'd gotten completely lost. Everything was tropically warm and flourishing here, so presumably we rode in the Alder Land again. Gawyn came to a stop.

"Here," he said.

I looked around. Night insects sang in the trees around us, and the smell of dirt, fresh growth, and decaying plants permeated the air. It had been dark before, but now the canopy of leaves blocked out even starlight. Gawyn climbed off his horse, nearly falling into a heap on the ground. I started to get down and help him, but he soon righted himself. He walked a few paces forward and then slammed his foot against the ground. A hard, solid sound answered back.

I dismounted as well. "What is that?"

Volusian, back in a legged form, walked over. "A door of sorts. Built into the ground."

"Yes," said Gawyn triumphantly. "Built for sieges. But never used anymore."

"Does it lead into Aeson's fortress thing?" I asked.

"To the cellar. Stairs from the cellar lead up to the kitchen. From the kitchen, you take the servants' stairs—"

"Whoa, hang on."

I wanted to make sure I had it all. Volusian created blue flame to cast light, and we drew a map in a clear spot of dirt based on Gawyn's recollections. I might have doubted his memories, but he spoke with certainty, and he had managed to lead us to this obscure place. Maybe Dorian had been right in the "razor sharp" assessment. When Gawyn felt we had the directions to the residential wing memorized, he told us he wouldn't join us. He would wait here to tell Dorian what became of us. That was fine by me. I didn't really regard Gawyn as a battle asset—or Wil, for that matter. Unlike the old man, however, the ghostly conspiracy theorist didn't take being left behind so well.

"But I told you, I need to reassure her—"

"No," I said firmly. "I let you come this far, and you almost ruined things with those riders. Now you wait. If Jasmine's scared, she'll hold on a few more minutes until we bring her out to you."

I worried I'd have to bind him—I could actually do it since he was here in spirit, not in body—but it didn't come to that. He conceded, so I entered the trapdoor with just my minions in tow.

"Truly," remarked Nandi as we entered a darkened tunnel, "it is amazing that you have not died yet, mistress."

"Well, hang in there. The night is young."

Volusian provided light again, and we let it guide us along a stone-encased tunnel that smelled damp. Rats ran by at one point. Finn had been right. Apparently the Otherworld did have its share of animals and vermin.

When the tunnel sloped upward, I knew we had reached the end. A wooden door in the ceiling marked our next gateway. I asked the spirits to go into an insubstantial form. Hitherto, they'd walked along looking very human. I needed them obscured now. Compliant, all three shifted to what looked like a fine mist surrounding me.

I pushed open the door and climbed out, finding myself in a small enclosed space. The mist that was Volusian glowed once more, and I made out the shapes of bags and boxes. If Gawyn was right about this attaching to the kitchen, then those containers probably contained food or other supplies. Twenty feet in front of me, a doorway was outlined in light shining through from the other side. I walked up about ten steps and gingerly opened the door.

I now stood in a kitchen, a very rustic one compared to my own, but completely on par with what I'd seen at Dorian's place. All was quiet.

"Where is everyone?" I murmured.

"It's late now," Finn whispered back. "No one's

hungry. And Aeson's not into the party scene as much as Dorian."

We found the servants' stairwell exactly where Gawyn had said it would be. Unfortunately, when I opened the door, I found a servant there, just coming down. We stared at each other stupidly, and I had only a heartbeat to decide how to handle him. I wielded both gun and athame. In another state of mind, I probably would have just killed him. But something held me back. Maybe it was Dorian. Maybe it was seeing his people and having to acknowledge they were more than just a faceless mob. Whatever it was, I chose not to kill this time. I reached out, grabbed the guy, and gave him a hard jolt to the head with my fist and the butt of my gun. His eyes rolled back, and he collapsed to the floor.

Once he had been safely deposited in the cellar, we continued on our way. We encountered no one else on the stairs, nor in the magnificent hallway it led us to. Enormous stone pillars supported the high ceiling, and rich oil paintings of various landscapes turned the walls into seas of living color. We had reached the residential wing, just as Gawyn had said. If my other intelligence was correct, we'd find Jasmine Delaney behind one of the many doors lining the hall.

Fortunately, housekeeping had decided to leave open all of the unoccupied rooms. Sticking my head inside a few, I could see no one had occupied them in awhile. The beds were stripped of covers, and dust coated everything. Only two doors were actually closed. In some ways, that made my job easier. Yet, I might have enjoyed the build-up of opening a few false doors before the big payoff.

Weapons readied, I opened the first one. It led to a bedroom almost bigger than Dorian's, but no one was inside. All was dark and still. A smoldering fire provided the only source of movement. Pausing a moment, I admired the wall tapestries and canopied bed. It had a nice layout, almost circular, complete with adjacent rooms and high ceilings. It made my bedroom at home look like a closet.

"One left," I muttered, slipping back out.

We turned down the hall and approached the only other closed doorway. Unless Jasmine was locked in a dungeon, we should find her here, according to what we'd heard. I reached for the handle, then hesitated.

"You open it, Volusian."

Some of the mist coalesced into physical form. Once solid, Volusian slowly opened the door and peered in. It looked dark. I started to move forward, but he held up a warning hand.

"No, there's something—"

Light flared on, and suddenly we were under attack. I tried to back out of the room, but someone grabbed me, pulling me inside. With me at risk, the other minions poured into the room. They had no choice, their pre-emptive orders always demanding they look to my safety.

This was a bedroom, like the other one, but seven men stood here, armed with weapons and magic. I fired at the one who had grabbed me, aiming for the face and neck now that I knew what little effect I'd had on Dorian's people. It was bloody and messy, but I felt pretty sure even the best healing magic would have a tough time fixing that guy up.

Once free of him, I turned on the next one who came at me. He was smart enough to strike out at my gun hand, attempting to neutralize that threat. I slashed at him with the other hand, the one holding the athame. He flinched at the feel of iron, and I used that momentary weakness to grab him and shove him into the wall with my elbow. He collapsed to the floor, and a sharp kick to the gut made sure he stayed down.

I saw the spirits engaged in battle nearby, shoving and fighting with a strength that was literally inhuman. Two other men had been subdued or killed by them, and they now fought a third. That left two. One lunged at me, and I shot him, the gun's report loud in the small room. He fell backward, and I fired again, still not trusting gentry healing on their own turf.

I started to look for the last guy when I heard a small whimper on the far side of the room. I turned, pausing. It was her. Jasmine Delaney.

She was smaller and slighter than I'd thought she'd be. A long white gown covered her body, and she wrapped its voluminous folds around herself as she huddled in the corner. Lank, reddish blond hair nearly covered her face, but it couldn't hide her eyes. They were enormous and gray, filled with fear. They stood out sharply against her pale, gaunt face. Seeing my gaze upon her, she cringed further.

Anger boiled within me. And pity. I knew she was fifteen, but in that moment, she looked about ten. She was a child. And she was trapped here, taken against her will. Hotter and fiercer my rage grew. I needed to make her captor pay, to let him know he couldn't just—

My moment of emotion cost me. In those seconds I'd spent staring at her, I'd lost the last man. I felt a blade at my throat and realized I'd let him sneak up behind me.

"If you want to live," he said, "drop your weapons and call off your servants."

I didn't really think I'd live if I did that, but I was pretty sure I wouldn't if I didn't. So I did as he asked.

Yet, it wasn't entirely clear to me what this one guy could really do alone. A moment later, I had my answer as another man entered. Immediately, I knew he was Aeson. For one thing, the others had been dressed in a sort of uniform. He was not. He wore deep burgundy pants tucked into thigh-high boots made of black leather. A shirt of black silk clothed his upper body, billowing and gleaming. His gray-streaked brown hair was pulled back in a short ponytail, and a circlet of gold sat on his head. His face was long and narrow, with a mouth destined for good sneers. Arrogant or not, Dorian had never worn a crown in his own keep, I realized. There had been no need. His kingship was obvious to all.

Two guards followed Aeson, and upon seeing the situation, he sent one for backup. And here we'd been doing so well in evening the odds.

"If I'd realized you would decimate my men in minutes, I would have had the whole garrison up here," Aeson remarked. He leaned toward me, touching my cheek. "It really is you. Eugenie Markham. I can't believe I finally have you."

I tried to squirm from that touch, but I had nowhere to go, not with a blade at my throat. My minions waited, tense, willing to do whatever I asked. Yet, I feared unleashing them might put Jasmine at risk—and my own throat.

"You have her," said a shaking voice from the hall. "I did what I said. Now give me Jasmine."

Moving my eyes, I stared in astonishment. Wil floated in the doorway. He must have followed us after all. He looked at Aeson expectantly. An uneasy feeling built up within me, and everything clicked into place.

"You traitorous son of a bitch!"

Ignoring my outrage, Wil turned pleading eyes to Aeson. "Please. I brought you Eugenie. I kept my part of the deal."

"Yes," said Aeson without even looking at the other man. "You did. And I will keep my word—momentarily."

He kept studying me like I was some kind of treasure or artifact. Like I was the eighth wonder of the world. I appreciated the boost to my ego, but the look in his eyes was actually kind of creeping me out.

"Aeson—" tried Wil again.

"Shut up," snapped the king, still staring at me. The hand on my cheek slipped down and cupped my chin. He smiled, but it was a cold smile, one that didn't meet his eyes. In the corner, I heard Jasmine make a distraught sound. "After all this time, after so much waiting, I can finally beget the heir."

The statement was so ludicrous as to simply bounce off of me without comprehension. "Either kill me or let me go. I hate these idiotic soliloquies."

The entranced look on his face suddenly sharpened, and he blinked. "You . . . you have no idea, do you?" When I didn't answer, he started laughing so hard, I thought tears would form in his eyes. "I've tried so hard to get you, and you never even knew. You really don't know."

"Know what?" I asked impatiently.

"Who your father is."

I didn't really appreciate the *Star Wars*–esque routine. "Roland Markham is my father. And the next time I see him, we're going to come back and kick your ass together. If I don't do it now."

"The next time you see him, you should ask him for the truth about you and Storm King."

"I don't have anything to do with Storm King."

"He's your father, girl. Roland Markham is a murderer and a thief. How could you not have known?"

He might as well have been speaking a foreign language. "Maybe because you're insane. And because I'm human."

"Are you? Funny. You function in this world as easily as one of the shining ones. I've never met a human who could."

"Maybe I'm gifted."

I had on my bitch-bravado face, but his words were sneaking into me. I've heard that the soul often recognizes truth when it hears it, even if the mind does not. Maybe that was what was happening. My logical self was still being stubborn, but something . . . something in his words tickled the back of my mind. It was like some image lay there, covered in a black veil, waiting for me to lift it.

"You are gifted. More than you know." He brushed my

hair out of my face. "Soon I will give you the greatest gift of your life. I'll redeem you for being a blood traitor."

"Shut up." The keres had called me a blood traitor too. "You don't know what you're talking about."

"Then why do you look so pale? Admit it. You've always known. You've always been alone."

"Everyone feels alone."

"Not like you do. Rest easy, though. You won't be lonely much longer. I would have taken you to my bed even if you were ugly, but now that I've seen you—"

There were a lot of ways to have your maniacal tirade cut short, but being attacked by a fox was a new one. I didn't even know where it came from. One minute, Aeson was babbling on about having his way with me, and the next, a red fox was leaping out at him, claws and teeth bared. I'd never thought of a fox as a really dangerous animal, but this one looked lethal. It was the size of a German shepherd, and it hit Aeson like a tank. Its claws left scratches on his face.

The guard holding me released me to help his master, and I retrieved my gun. I fired on him just as he was about to pry the fox from Aeson. It wasn't a killing shot, but it distracted him, halting his progress. I grabbed the wounded guard and threw him as far as the difference in our body weights would allow. He collapsed into a pile, and I shot him again. I turned toward Aeson to check the fox's progress, but the fox was no longer holding the king down.

Kiyo was.

My mouth dropped open. Kiyo. The black hair curled behind his ears, and I could see his muscles straining as he struggled with Aeson, his hands wrapped around the king's throat. Fire flared up from Aeson's fingertips, and I heard Kiyo grunt in response. I started to go to him without conscious thought, but he yelled at me to get Jasmine.

Jasmine. Of course. The reason I was here.

I dragged my eyes from the face I'd been obsessing on

for the past week and approached the girl in the corner. I didn't think she could move any farther against the wall, yet she seemed to do so with each step I took.

"Jasmine," I said, leaning over and trying to sound gentle despite the panic coursing through me. "I'm a friend. I'm here to help you—"

With those pathetic eyes and worn features, I'd expected some difficulty in getting her on her feet. What I did not expect was for her to suddenly leap out and flail at me with both hands.

"Noooo!" she screamed, her shrill voice grating against my ears. I recoiled, not because of the threat she represented but because of the damage I could potentially cause her. "Aeson!" She ran to the struggling men and started beating fists on Kiyo's back. I suspected they had about the same effect as a fly landing on him. He transformed into a fox, and her blows fell on Aeson instead. I reached for her in that moment of surprise, but she was too small and too fast. She slipped away from me and everyone else in the room, and ran out the door before any of us could stop her.

"Jasmine!" I yelled, my cries echoed by Wil as I ran to the door. Kiyo and Aeson still fought, and some distant part of me noted how Kiyo slipped in and out of fox and human forms as Aeson used fire magic against him.

"Eugenie," gasped Kiyo, "get out of here. Now."

"Jasmine—" I began.

"The girl is gone, mistress," said Volusian. "The kitsune is right. We need to get out of here. Cut your losses."

"No." I stuck my head out the door. Jasmine was not in sight. Over a dozen or so guards running down the hall were, however.

"Eugenie!" It was Kiyo again. "Run!"

"Yes, Storm Daughter," laughed Aeson, blood running out of his nose. "Run home. Ask Roland Markham who your father is."

"You bastard—" I wanted to lunge at him, to help Kiyo, but Finn grabbed me.

"Jump now. Back to your world."

The pounding boots in the hall were almost upon us.

"I can't. Not from here. I don't have an anchor."

"Yes, you do."

He glanced over at Wil, who hung there, translucent and utterly useless. If it had been up to me, I would have left Wil and his betraying ass here to be destroyed, but suddenly he had a purpose.

Seeing my uncertain look, Kiyo said, "I'll go as soon as you do. They're here!"

And they were. Men pouring into the room. I probably shouldn't have cared what happened to Kiyo, but I did. I wanted him to get out of this alive. I wanted to find Jasmine and bring her away. But the best I could do now was save my own skin.

Invoking Hecate, I shifted my senses away from this world, reaching out to my own. While doing so, my will grabbed ahold of a startled Wil, dragging his spirit with me. A hard transition like that, without a crossroads or thin spot, theoretically could have dumped me anywhere in the human world. But I had Wil's spirit in tow. It had no choice but to snap back to his physical body, out in the Sonora Desert. If I was strong enough.

"Follow!" I yelled to the minions. Or maybe it was to Kiyo. I didn't really know.

The world shifted, my senses blurring. Crossing worlds in a convenient spot was like crossing through a wall made out of plastic sheeting. It was thin, and it took some struggling and clawing, but you could eventually get through. Jumping without a normal crossover spot, however?

Well, that was like breaking through a brick wall.

Chapter Eleven

Someone was screaming in the desert, and I didn't realize it was me until Tim raced over and grabbed my shoulders.

"Jesus! Eugenie, what's wrong?"

I broke from him, dropped to my knees, and threw up into a convenient shrub. That soon gave way to endless dry heaves, my body's distress too strong to stop. When I finally finished—it seemed like hours but was probably only a few minutes—I ran my hands over my face. It felt like I had shoved my head through a window, cutting my skin to shreds. Yet, when I pulled my hands back, there was no blood.

Apparently convinced I was done bringing up everything in my stomach, Tim carefully handed me a bottle of water. I wiped my mouth with the back of my hand and then drank greedily. When I started to hand the bottle back, he shook his head. "Keep it. What happened?"

"Transition shock," came Volusian's flat voice. "You came through the worlds too hard and too fast, mistress."

"You should be dead," added Nandi. "Or at least segmented."

"Segmented?" asked Tim.

I nodded and drank again. "If you're not strong

enough to make it work, only your spirit will get back here. The body stays in the Otherworld."

He stared. "Will that kill you?"

"Worse."

"What's worse than death?" asked a new voice. Or not so new.

Wil. I'd forgotten about Wil.

I leapt to my feet and spun toward him, gun drawn. Some part of me wondered if I even had bullets left. I'd changed the cartridge once in the Otherworld but couldn't recall how many times I'd fired at Aeson's men.

Tim's mouth dropped open. "Eugenie, put that away!"

"You don't know what he's done. He's a fucking back-stabber."

Wil, sitting on the blanket he'd gone into trance on, froze, too afraid to move. But not too afraid to speak. "I had to. It was the only way to get Jasmine."

"Yeah, it worked pretty well, huh?"

He sounded near tears. "I'd gone a year without any chance of getting her. Then that sprite cut me the deal. Said if I got you to go over, they'd give me Jasmine back. I'm sorry."

I didn't move the gun. "*I* was your only chance to get her back. If you hadn't led us into that trap, we'd be back here with her now."

He groaned, burying his face in his hands. "I didn't know. I didn't know. I just wanted her so badly." He looked back up at me. "What happened? Why did she run away? Was she scared?"

"Maybe. Or it could be that . . . what's that called? Where people help their kidnappers? Stockholm syndrome?"

"What, like Patty Hearst? No. Jasmine wouldn't do that."

I wasn't so sure. She was young and impressionable, and Aeson struck me as a very forceful figure.

"He's too pathetic to kill," observed Finn after studying Wil for a moment.

"No harm in doing it anyway," said Volusian. "Kill him and enslave his soul."

Wil's eyes widened farther.

"Eugenie!" Tim stared at me like I was insane. "You aren't seriously considering that."

Probably not. Sighing, I lowered the gun. "Get out of here, Wil. I don't ever want to see you again."

He scrambled to his feet, face falling. "But Jasmine—"

"You lost your chance. You blew it. Get in your car before I do something stupid."

Wil hesitated, his face pleading and upset. Then wordlessly he headed toward the trail that led out to a makeshift parking area. I watched him leave, bitter anger boiling up within me. In the distance, thunder rumbled.

"Eugenie . . ." began Tim hesitantly. A slight wind ruffled his hair.

"I don't want to talk about it. Take me home."

We gathered up his things and walked in the direction Wil had gone.

"Meet me back at my house," I told the minions. They vanished.

Tim had enough sense to leave me alone on the car ride back. I leaned my head against the window, liking the feel of the cool glass against my fevered cheek. So many things had happened tonight, I had no idea what to fixate on first. Jasmine? Wil's betrayal? Aeson's stupid accusation? Kiyo?

Yes. Kiyo was probably the safest, which was saying something. My heart had leapt at seeing him again. It was stupid, considering the way he'd used me, but my emotions didn't appear to realize that yet. Why? Why did he have this pull on me when I barely knew him? I didn't believe in love at first sight.

And what about the fox thing? I knew of no gentry who could do that, but I did know shape-shifters filled the Otherworld. I'd fought some before but never a fox. Seemed like a weird choice. Perhaps that explained why he hadn't felt gentry. He was something else, not gentry but still Otherworldly. Not much of an improvement.

I left Tim as soon as we got home, seeking out the solitude of my room. Well, as much solitude as I could get with the three spirits waiting for me. I threw myself onto the bed, leaning into the corner where the bed sat against the wall. Exhaustion ran through me, and I did and said nothing, staring into the darkness. Thunder rumbled again but seemed fainter now, like the storm had changed its mind. The spirits simply waited and watched me.

"Tell me what just happened."

"Um, which part?" asked Finn after a minute.

"Any of it. Tell me what Kiyo is. The fox."

"Oh." Finn seemed relieved to have a question he could answer. "He's a kitsune. Japanese fox spirit."

"Roland taught me hundreds of magical creatures. Never heard of a kitsune."

"You don't find them around here much," explained Finn. "And they're not really dangerous."

"He looked dangerous enough to me."

"They carry animal traits into human form," said Volusian. "Strength. Speed. A certain sense of aggression."

I thought about sex with Kiyo. Yeah. That had been pretty aggressive. I closed my eyes.

"Why would he mark me and then follow me?"

"I do not know."

It figured.

"Anything else I should know about him? About them?"

"They're usually female. Men are rare. Perhaps his human blood affected that," said Nandi in her emotionless voice.

"Half-human? Oh. His mother was the kitsune," I mused, recalling him talking about his parents.

"Yeah," agreed Finn. "The women are supposed to be pretty hot. Like sirens. Real seductive. Men can't stay away from them."

"Like a drug," added Volusian.

I opened my eyes. "Could he do that too?"

"Possibly."

Suddenly my obsession seemed less weird than twisted. Had he used some sort of sexual power to lure me in? Was that why I couldn't stop thinking about him?

"I guess half-human isn't so bad," I muttered, speaking out loud without meaning to. I hadn't bedded a full-fledged Otherworldly creature.

"Not bad at all," agreed Finn happily. "He's just like you."

"Stop it," I snapped. "That whole thing . . . what Aeson said . . . it's stupid. I don't want to talk about it."

"And like so much, you ignore what you don't want to hear. Being Storm King's daughter is no small thing." Volusian's red eyes held my gaze.

"Your bluntness is so endearing." My stomach turned, but it was now or never. "All right. I'll bite. Why does Aeson think that?"

None of them had an answer right away. The impression I got from them was surprise more than ignorance.

"Because you are, mistress," said Nandi at last.

"No, I'm not. I'm human."

Volusian crossed his arms over his chest. "You are half-human, mistress. And as I said, your prejudice blinds you from the truth."

"One gentry's accusation isn't the truth. Where are the facts?"

"Facts? Very well. Here are facts. Who is your father?"

"Roland."

"You know what I mean, mistress. Who is your blood father?"

"I don't know. It doesn't matter. My mom always said he was a bastard not worth knowing."

Volusian stared at me expectantly.

"That doesn't prove anything."

"What about your powers? You are rapidly surpassing every other human shaman. You are equal in strength in both worlds. Do you think it's coincidence that the most powerful shaman in remembered history grew up in Roland Markham's household? He brought you there, taking you from Storm King."

"From where? Are you saying I was born in the Other-world?"

Volusian inclined his head. "Storm King abducted your mother and made her his mistress. She bore his child. You."

"You seemly awfully sure about this."

"I saw your mother when she lived in the Otherworld. I have seen her in this world. She's the same woman."

"You're lying."

"By the power that binds us, you know I am not."

He was right. He couldn't lie to me—not so openly, at least. I knew that, and acknowledging that forced me to put my own world into a new perspective. It *might* explain why my mother hated the Otherworld so much. Why she and Roland had been adamant about instilling that hate in me, making sure I could never have any empathy with the gentry or anything else from that world.

I swallowed and realized I was on the verge of tears. God. That would probably blow the show of strength I always tried to hold around these guys. We needed to get through this interview. "So, are you saying that's why Roland eventually killed him? To protect me?"

"Among other things. Storm King's invasion was imminent. He had come to claim you. Roland Markham killed him, both saving you and halting Storm King's plans."

"So Dorian was telling the—wait a minute. He knew! That bastard. He sat there and fed me that stuff about Storm King, knowing who I was!"

"Everyone knows who you are, mistress," said Nandi.

"It's pretty recent, though," added Finn, seeing the look on my face. "Came out only a couple of weeks ago. The same time everyone learned your real name."

"How?" I glared at Volusian. He had known who I was this whole time. "Did you tell them?"

"No."

"Then why didn't you tell me before this? Why didn't any of you tell me when this came out?"

They stared.

"Because you did not ask us," replied Nandi.

"Yes," agreed Volusian. "Had you asked us, 'Am I Storm King's daughter?' we would have gladly—"

"Oh, shut up." I rubbed my eyes. I wanted to sleep. I wanted to sleep forever and forget all this. But I had miles to go before I slept, just like in the Robert Frost poem. "If everyone thought Storm King was so great, then why are they all coming after me? Shouldn't I be some kind of hero? Instead they want to kill me."

"Most aren't trying to kill you, unfortunately. They're trying to bed you, mistress."

"Why?"

"Probably because of the prophecy," said Nandi.

"Prophecy," I said dryly. "Wonderful. Now there's a prophecy."

"Mistress," she said hastily, "had you asked us if there was a prophecy—"

"Yeah, yeah. I know. What's this one say? That I'm a good lay?"

Finn hesitated. "Well . . . it says Storm King's vision will be carried out through his daughter's first son. That the human world will be reconquered."

"You're kidding." Oh, God, I wanted to sleep.

"When they found out you didn't have kids yet, everyone—well, every guy—wanted to get in on the action. Being the one to father Storm King's heir would be a pretty big deal."

"Likewise," added Volusian, "the prophecy says Storm King's daughter will clear the way for her son. Being your consort would carry great prestige."

"Hey, I'm not clearing the way for any invasion. Not that I believe in prophecies. Not that I believe in any of this! In fact, that prophecy proves how stupid this all is. I wouldn't turn against my own kind."

I swear Volusian smiled. "Yes, but which people truly are your own kind? Your loyalties are now divided."

My anger flared. "No. Even if this is true and I am the daughter of the biggest gentry badass ever, I know where my loyalties are. I'm human. I act human. I have no gentry powers."

"As you say, mistress."

"Get out of here. All of you. None of this is true. I'll talk to my parents and clear this up."

Volusian bowed. "A wise idea, mistress."

I said the words to send them away and then lay on my bed. The storm had quieted outside, but one of my own raged inside me. I wanted to shut down my feelings. I wanted to forget all of this, because it wasn't true. It couldn't be. I wanted to take one of the prescription sleeping pills, but I didn't need Roland's warnings to know how stupid that would be. If every gentry was suddenly hot to get me pregnant, I couldn't let my guard down.

I shouldn't have been able to sleep. Not after fighting gentry and seeing a girl run back to them. Not after learning my one-night stand was a kitsune. Not after discovering that I could very well be something I hated. Something that made me question everything I'd ever believed in.

No, I shouldn't have been able to sleep at all, but my body knew better as tiredness flowed over me. My body knew I'd been up all night, that I'd fought and been injured. And most important, it knew my fight wasn't over. Not by a long shot.

Chapter Twelve

I finally worked up the courage to see my mom and Roland a few days later. Tim had left for the day, but he'd apparently baked this morning. A plate of almond poppy seed muffins sat on the kitchen table, and I grabbed two for the road.

My ability to think clearly had improved with some rest, but my anger and pain hadn't really faded. I still felt betrayed and not just by Wil. If anything, I could forgive him more easily than anyone else. He had not fostered a years-long secret. His actions had been open and desperate. They had not been so insidious as Kiyo's, my mom's, and Roland's.

When I arrived at the house, I didn't bother knocking. The front door was open, and I pushed inside, slamming it loudly behind me.

"Genie?" I heard my mom call. "Is that you?"

I walked across the wood floor, my shoes echoing in the foyer. Mom and Roland sat at the kitchen table, eating lunch. Bread and cold cuts were laid out, along with assorted condiments. It looked so normal. So peaceful and innocent. My mom half-rose when she saw me.

"Thank God you're back safe. I've been so—what's the matter?"

I loved these people so much, but seeing them increased my fury, maybe because I did love them so much. For a moment, I couldn't get the words out. I just stared at them, looking from face to face.

"Eugenie?" she asked tentatively.

"Who's my father?" I demanded of her. "Was I born in the Otherworld?"

I saw her go pale, her dark eyes widening in fear. In an instant, Roland was up beside her.

"Eugenie, listen—" The look on his face spoke legions.

"Jesus. It really is true."

I saw him open his mouth to protest, but then he thought better of it. "How did you find out?"

Honesty, at least. "It's all over the Otherworld. Everyone knows. I'm apparently next in line for world domination."

"That's not true," he said. "Forget about it. You aren't like them."

"But I am one of them, right? At least half?"

"By blood only. Everything else . . . well, for all intents and purposes, you're human. You have nothing to do with them."

"Except killing and banishing them. How could you set me up for that . . . if I'm . . . ?" *One of them,* I wanted to finish. But I couldn't get the words out.

"Because you have a talent for it. One we need. You know what they can do."

"Yes. And you've made sure I do, telling me all the horror stories growing up. But there's a hell of a lot more than that. They're weird, yes, but not all evil."

My mother suddenly joined the conversation, eyes wild and frantic. "Yes! They are! You don't know what you're talking about. When did you have this revelation? A day ago? A week ago? I lived with them for three years, Eugenie. *Three years.*" Her voice dropped to a whisper. "Three years, and I never once encountered a decent one. No one who would help me. No one who would keep me from Tirigan."

"Who?"

"Storm King," said Roland. "That's his name. *Was* his name."

"They say you saved her from him."

He nodded. "I was there chasing down a kelpie when I heard rumors of a captured human woman. I went to investigate and found her and you. You were a baby. I slipped you both out of there and hid you."

"But Dorian . . . someone I met . . . said Storm King came looking for us."

"He did. And he found you."

I frowned. From what Dorian had said, I should have been a young teenager then. "I don't remember that."

Roland nodded again. "Once close enough, he could reach out and call to you. He summoned you to him. By the time I tracked you down, you were out in the desert, very near a crossroads. You'd walked miles to get to him."

"I don't remember that," I repeated. In some ways, what Roland told me now was crazier than what I'd learned at Aeson's.

"His magic spoke to yours. He wanted to take you back with him, and you fought against him. You were struck by lightning in the process."

"Wait, I *know* I'd remember that."

"No. I hypnotized you and repressed it. I killed him, but your magic had still been awakened. After seeing what I'd seen, I was afraid you couldn't control it—that it would control you instead."

"I don't have any magic. Not gentry magic anyway."

"Not that you know of. It's hidden away. I made you forget. After that, I started teaching you the craft in the hope of protecting you. I didn't know if others would follow him or if someone else could reawaken you or summon you. I needed to give you the tools you'd need for defense." He suddenly looked tired. "I never realized how well you'd take to them."

I felt as tired as he looked, despite all the sleep. I pulled up one of the chairs and sat; they continued to stand. So I had met Storm King. I had answered his summons. And I had been struck by lightning? That was interesting, because in a lot of cultures, shamans are called to their art through some traumatic event. Lightning strikes are actually common ones. Many of the local Indian shamans—already skeptical of the plethora of New Age white shamans—did not consider me authentic since I'd had no such profound initiation. Turns out I had. Score one for me.

"You made me forget. You got inside my head, and you made me forget. All this time . . . both of you have known and never told me."

"We wanted to protect you," he said.

"And what then? Did you think I'd never find out?" The heat rose in my voice again. "I had to hear it from gentry. I would have rather heard it from you."

My mother closed her eyes, and one tear trailed down her cheek. Roland regarded me calmly.

"In hindsight, yes, that would have been better. But we never thought it would actually come out."

"It's out," I said bitterly. "Everyone knows it. And now everyone wants a piece of this prophecy—and of me."

"What prophecy?"

I told them. When I finished, my mother sat down and buried her face in her hands, crying softly. I could hear her murmuring, "It'll happen to her. It'll happen to her too."

Roland rested a hand on her shoulder. "Don't put much stock in gentry prophecies. They come out with a new one every day."

"Doesn't matter, if they believe it. They're still going to come after me."

"You should stay with us. I'll help protect you."

I stood up, glancing at my mother. No way would I

expose her to more gentry. "No. This is my problem. Besides, don't take this too badly"—I felt myself start to choke up—"but I don't really want to see you guys for a while. I guess you meant well, but . . . I need to . . . I don't know. I need to think."

"Eugenie—" I saw raw pain on his face. My mom's sobs grew louder.

I stood up, averting my eyes from both of them. Suddenly, I couldn't stay here anymore. "I've got to go."

Roland was still calling after me when I practically ran out of the house. But I needed to get away, or I'd say something stupid. I didn't want to hurt them, even though I probably had. But they'd hurt me too, and we all needed to deal with that.

While opening my car door, I looked up and saw a red fox watching me from the same spot as last time.

I strode toward him, close but not too close.

"Go away!" I shouted.

He stared at me, unmoving.

"I mean it. I'm not speaking to you. You're as bad as the rest of them."

He lay down, resting his chin on crossed paws while he continued to regard me solemnly.

"I don't care how cute you are, okay? I'm through with you."

A woman working in her yard next door gave me an uneasy look. I turned my back on the fox, got in the car, and drove home. Yet, as I did, I couldn't help but feel relieved Kiyo had survived. I honestly hadn't known if he would. Strong and vicious he might be, but Aeson had been slinging fire at him. The question was, had Kiyo merely escaped? Or had he managed to kill the king? What had happened to Jasmine?

Tim still wasn't back when I got home. I decided then I didn't want to leave my house that day or make any pretense of productivity. I wanted to hit the sauna, put on pajamas, and then watch bad TV while eating Milky

Ways. It seemed like a pretty solid plan, and I set out to make it happen.

Twenty minutes later, I sat immersed in hot steam, draped in humidity. Heat was great for loosening muscles, although that only made me realize how much I'd hurt them. At least I'd made it out alive. That was the real miracle, considering what a disaster last night had turned into.

I didn't want to think much about it or about Mom and Roland, but it was hard not to. Part of me still believed—still hoped—that all of this was a mistake. After all, wasn't it just everyone's say-so? Of course, somehow I doubted my parents would make all that up. But really. Where was the DNA test? The photographic evidence? I had nothing tangible. Nothing I could see and believe.

Except my own memories. The memories Roland had covered up for me. Hypnotism wasn't uncommon in our line of work. It was just another state of unconsciousness. Shamans who served as religious leaders and healers used similar techniques on their followers and patients to heal the body and mind. Roland and I, as "freelance shamans," didn't really have much need for it. Our contact with the spirit world often became more physical and direct. But I had done some healings and soul retrievals, so I knew the basics.

Leaning my head against the wall, I closed my eyes and thought about the tattoo of Selene on my back. She was my earthly connection, the grounding of my body and soul and mind in this world. I focused on her image and what she represented and then slowly altered my state of mind. Rather than slipping out to another plane, I crossed inward, back into the far reaches of myself and the parts of me buried in my unconscious.

It probably didn't take long, but in that state, it was painstakingly slow. I browsed through pieces of me, both memories and hidden truths alike. All the things that made me Eugenie Markham. I concentrated on lightning, hoping it would snag my attention. Surely a lightning strike couldn't be buried forever.

There. A faint tug. I dove in after it, trying to grasp it and the memory it linked to. It was difficult. The image was slippery, like trying to hold on to a fish. Each time I thought I had it, it wriggled away. Roland had done a good job. Steeling myself, I fought against the layers, clawing and fighting until—

I woke up in bed.

But it wasn't the bed in my house. It was a different bed, a smaller bed covered in a pink comforter. The bed of my childhood. I lay in it, staring up at a ceiling covered in plastic stars just like the one I had as an adult. It was the middle of the night, and I couldn't sleep. I'd been an insomniac then, just as now. This time, however, it was different. Something other than my churning mind was keeping me awake. Somewhere, outside, I could hear a voice calling me. No, not a voice exactly, but it was a pull. A pull I couldn't shut out.

Climbing out of bed, I slipped my feet into dirty sneakers and put a light jacket on over my pajamas. In the hallway, the door to Mom and Roland's room was closed. I moved past as quietly as possible, down the stairs and then out the door.

Outside, the air was still warm. It was high summer. Earlier temperatures had been in the 100s; even now, they had dropped only to the 80s. I walked down the quiet street of our neighborhood, past all the familiar cars and houses. With each step, the call grew louder. I followed, my feet moving on their own. The call led me away from our street, our subdivision, and even the small suburb we lived in. I traveled off of main roads, moving onto trails I'd never known existed.

Then, after almost two hours, I stopped. I didn't know where I was. The desert, obviously, because that and the mountains were all that surrounded Tucson. The foothills were larger than at home, so I must have gone north.

Otherwise, there were no distinguishing features. Prickly pears and saguaros spread out around me in quiet watchfulness.

Suddenly, I felt the air around me charge. There was a presence with me. A person. I turned and saw a man standing and watching me, far taller than my twelve-year-old self. His features were indistinct; I could not make them out no matter how hard I tried. He was only a dark shape, crackling with power.

"Eugenie . . ."

I took three steps back, but he held his hand out to me.

"Eugenie . . ."

I shook off the thrall that had brought me out here. Desperately, I realized I had to get away as quickly as I could. But I no longer knew the way back. The trails I'd followed were a blur. So, I backed up farther, but he kept coming, beckoning to me. My feet stumbled, and I fell. Still facing him, I tried to get up, but he stood over me now. In his indistinct features, I could make out a crown on his head, glittering silver and purple.

"Come," he said, extending his arm to help me up. "It's time to go."

I was trapped. Helpless and trapped and out of options. I had never felt so desperate in my young life. It terrified me. I decided then and there that if I survived this, I would make sure I could never be helpless again. His hand touched my shoulder, and I screamed. As I did, some part of me reached out beyond my body and grasped the power lying around us—

I blinked.

Steam swirled around me in the sauna, and I felt light-headed. I'd been in there too long; it was a wonder I hadn't passed out. Standing up, I had to grip the wall for support and close my eyes. My heart raced from the vision, the vision that finally convinced me all of this was true. I knew—knew with absolute certainty—that the dark man had been Storm King, my father. I could feel it within me. In my soul.

Overcome, I sat back down, needing a few more moments to consider all this and get my bearings.

Yet, the longer I sat there, the more I began to despair. Storm King really was my father. And as for the rest of my life . . . well, things were bad. And they were only going to get worse. Every horny gentry wanted to knock me up; the rest probably still wanted to kill me. I'd never have a moment of peace again.

Minutes passed as I ruminated on all this, falling deeper and deeper into depression—as well as exhaustion. I felt fatigued, too apathetic to care about any of it now. What was the point? I had snubbed my parents today. I'd let Jasmine Delaney down. I had nothing to look forward to ever again except a life of fighting and running. And really, why should I even bother fighting anymore? Nothing mattered. It was hopeless. I should just cross over to the Otherworld and give myself up. At least it'd stop the agony of—

I opened my eyes and sat bolt upright. What was wrong with me? Things were grim, but this . . . this wasn't natural.

I blinked rapidly, trying to gain focus as I took deep breaths. There it was. I could feel it. A thick, unseen darkness wrapping itself around me. It touched me, crawling along my skin. It was trying to drag me down, to suck away all of my energy. All of my hope.

Standing up, no longer dizzy, I pulled my robe off its hook and put it on. Slowly, I opened the door of the sauna and stuck my head out. I saw nothing too disconcerting, but that bleak feeling continued to swirl around me. The light almost seemed dimmer, darker than it should be for late afternoon. I squinted, trying to break the illusion, for that's what it was.

Stepping completely out of the sauna, I tried to assess the source. The sauna was in the center of my house.

Turn left to go to the kitchen and living room, right toward the bathroom and bedrooms. My weapons were in my bedroom; that was where I wanted to be. But if the thing was in the front of the house, I didn't want to turn my back on it. At last, I compromised by putting my back up to the hall's wall and sliding down it toward my bedroom. The distance wasn't far, but when you had to inch your way there, it felt like miles. Creeping, I passed Tim's closed bedroom door, grateful he wasn't here. He knew about my shamanic adventures, but that didn't mean I wanted him exposed to them.

Next came the bathroom. Yeah, the only bathroom. The thing about cute little houses was the "little" part. I loved everything else about this place, but next time, I'd make sure my house had at least as many bathrooms as occupants. Tim and I had gotten into some nasty rumbles when—

A hand reached out for me from within the dark bathroom, but I saw it coming out of my periphery. I ducked and slid across the hall as he lumbered out. A Gray Man. That had been one of my top three culprits for the negativity zone my house had become. Gray Men cast an aura of despair around them, feeding off physical energy and positive feelings.

This one was, well, gray, of course. Other than that, he looked more or less human-shaped, with dark eyes and scraggly white hair. He was even dressed, which I took as a plus since other monsters and sometimes elemental gentry often came over in loincloths or nothing at all, depending on their strength. Considering what everyone wanted to do to me, I was pretty happy about keeping genitalia covered up.

I tried to scramble toward my bedroom, but his long arm reached out and grabbed me by the hair. I yelled out as he dragged me toward him, pressing me to his body. At least he didn't say anything suggestive; Gray Men were apparently strong, silent types. But the way he grappled with my robe left little to the imagination about what he wanted to do. Struggling in his strong grasp, I tried to break free but mostly managed to loosen my robe more. Swearing, I decided if I couldn't get away, then I'd at least delay his amorous actions. My knee jutted up in one hard motion, hitting him in the groin.

His hold on me loosened, and he groaned as one hand instinctively reached down between his legs. I broke away from him, still trying to make for my bedroom. Deciding he could ignore the pain, he lunged toward me, just stopping me from getting to my bedroom doorway. Gripping me by both shoulders, he shoved me up against the wall so that I faced it. Using that hard surface as a constraint, he held me with one arm against it while his other finished pulling off the robe.

I felt his tongue lick my neck, but the truly disgusting nature of that couldn't really permeate me. I was in survival mode now. I struggled against him, hoping to make it difficult for him to get his own pants off. Being pinned liked this gave me fewer options for escape. Moving my hands against the wall, I groped around for something— anything—I could use as a weapon.

Then my fingers brushed over a small decorative mirror that had been my grandmother's. It wasn't very big, but its frame was shaped like a sun—with sharp, pointed metal rays. Not only that, they were silver rays. Grabbing it from the wall, I held it in my left hand, not my dominant hand, but the hand I wore my amethyst ring on. The amethyst could cut through magic and glamour and also focus my own intentions. It wasn't as good as a wand, but it had to do. Concentrating on the stone, I let my will pour into it. The stone amplified my energy and then sent it into the silver frame. In as fluid a motion as I could manage in my confined state, I swung the mirror back, driving it into any flesh I could find.

The Gray Man screamed, and I smelled something burning. He released me, and I turned around, not wasting any time, though I uneasily realized I'd dumped more energy into that silver than I should have been capable of. The mirror had stuck in his side and was smoking. It wouldn't kill him, but having it lodged in there was pretty serious. He reached out toward it with hesitant fingers, knowing he had to touch it to pull it out. I sprinted to my bedroom.

He was only seconds behind me, but it was all I needed to arm myself in my bedroom. He came running in after me, but this time I was on the offensive. I used the silver athame to draw the death symbol on his chest, eliciting a tortured scream from him. Iron was the bane of gentry, but for whatever other reasons, silver hurt anything else Otherworldly. I didn't know why, but I didn't question it either. Especially when it had just proven so handy.

Hurt or no, he pushed me backward. I landed on my bed, head hitting with a crack against the wall. It slowed me, but I had already started connecting beyond this world. I reached out, touched the world of death, and sent that connection through the wand. It leapt out at the Gray Man, sucking him in. He fought it, thrashing as though physical action might fight the pull. It couldn't. A moment later, he vanished.

Almost immediately, the spell of despair in my house disappeared. It was like emerging from underwater. I could breathe again. I let my body slump and relax. I wanted to lean my head against the wall but knew that wouldn't feel too good after the hard blow I'd just sustained.

A loud sound cracked out from the front of my house, like the door being kicked open. I jerked up, adrenaline going a second round as I heard footsteps pounding down the hall. I was reaching for the gun when a familiar voice yelled, "Eugenie?"

Relaxing—only slightly—I watched as Kiyo burst into my room.

Chapter Thirteen

"You're late," I told him, trying to act like my robe wasn't lying out on the hallway floor.

He glanced around, and I couldn't help a small breath of pleasure. Every ounce of him was charged and ready, that muscled body in a fighter's stance. His dark eyes held a hard, savage expression as he assessed for threats. He was magnificent. He looked as though he could have single-handedly torn apart an army then and there. I wrapped my arms around myself, from neither coldness nor modesty.

"I was walking up your driveway and felt something . . . something dark." His body relaxed, the animal fierceness in his eyes replaced by that smoky sensuality as he seemed to notice for the first time that I was naked.

"A Gray Man. He had to go keep an appointment with Persephone."

Kiyo's lips twitched into a smile. "Were you in the shower?"

"Sauna. I impaled him with a mirror."

"Nice."

We stared at each other, a thick tension building up in the air between us.

"Well," I said finally. "Thanks for checking in. You can leave now."

"Eugenie—"

My confusion and lust took their rightful backseat to my indignation. "I have nothing to say to you. I don't want to say anything to you. Get out."

"Not until I've explained everything."

"Like what? How you wanted to get me pregnant, just like everyone else?"

He blinked, clearly surprised. "I—what? No. Of course not. For Christ's sake, I used a condom."

"Yeah, I know. I was there." I could hear the irrational sulkiness in my voice. "Why else would you have done it, then?"

His eyes traveled from my face down my entire body, and then back to my face. "Why do you think?"

I swallowed, attempting to ignore the warmth left from where his gaze had touched me. "Okay. I get the mechanics of it. But you can't sit there and tell me you being in that bar was a coincidence."

"No. It wasn't," he said simply.

I waited for more. "That's it?"

He sighed and leaned against the wall. "I was asked by a friend to find you and mark you so we could keep track of you. I didn't know why; I had no idea who you were at the time."

"What? Someone told you to sleep with me?"

"Er, no. That was my own, um, improvisation. I could have marked you other ways." He smiled meaningfully. "But you were too charming and pretty."

"Hey! Don't use that fox sex magic on me. It's already caused enough trouble. Who told you to do that? To mark me?"

The flirtatious smile disappeared. Silence.

"Look, you're supposed to be the big honesty advocate. If you aren't going to play that way anymore, then I'm going to kick your ass out of here."

A glint of amusement flickered in his eyes. "I think I'd like that." He paused. Finally: "No one you know. Her name is Maiwenn."

"The Willow Queen." I took satisfaction in seeing his surprise. "I know more about the gentry than you think."

"Apparently. When she found out who you were, she wanted to watch you and find out where you stood on your fath—on the Storm King prophecy."

I met his questioning look with incredulity. "Are you seriously asking me? You think I want to see gentry take over the world?"

"No, not really. But Maiwenn wanted to be sure on your position. She opposed Storm King before and has no desire to see an invasion. She'd rather put resources into the Otherworld, into staying there and making that home."

"Smart lady," I said bitterly. "I wish they'd all stay there."

"Don't knock the Otherworld. It has its appeal."

"Yeah? So, what, you consider yourself one of them?"

"I consider myself part of both worlds. It's who I am. It's who you are too."

"No. I'm not part of that world." I stared past him without really seeing, suddenly feeling tired. "Sometimes I don't even feel a part of this world."

He crossed the distance between us and sat down on the bed. Those dark eyes brimmed with concern. "Don't say that."

I looked away so he wouldn't see my eyes getting wet. "I don't know what's going on anymore. Everything . . . everything's changed. I can't turn around without someone trying to rape me. I can't trust the people I love." I turned back to him. "I can't trust you."

His hand reached out and touched my cheek. "Yes, you can. Eugenie, I didn't sleep with you to get you pregnant. I didn't even sleep with you just because you're hot—though that was a definite perk. I liked you. I still like you. I want us to have something."

He'd moved his hand down my neck, to my shoulder, and then to my upper arm. His fingers lazily traced the outline of Hecate's snake. Goosebumps rose on my flesh.

"Don't look at me like that. I don't want to get pregnant."

"Contraceptive technology is a wonderful thing."

"I can't be involved with you."

"Why not?"

The words hurt coming out. "Because . . . because of what you are . . ."

The hand dropped. "I'm the same—"

"I know, I know. The same as me. Kiyo, you've got to understand. . . . I've got a lot to deal with right now. I just . . . well, I just can't. Not yet. Maybe . . ." I looked at him, at the kind and intelligent face, at the smoldering body so close to mine. "Maybe some day, we can . . ."

Something on my face must have given away my feelings, that no matter how terrified of getting close to him I was, I still liked him and wanted him. The old mischievous smile appeared on his face, and his hand cupped my chin. He pressed his lips against my cheek. "Then let me be your friend," he whispered.

I closed my eyes and let his heat envelop me. "Friends don't breathe in my ear like that."

"We'll be special friends."

"Kiyo—"

He drew back a little, still smiling. "Seriously, Eugenie. If we can't be lovers, I still want to be in your life. I want to help you through this. I want to protect you."

I stiffened, and my old snarkiness reared its head through the emotional miasma. "I don't need protection."

"Do you have any idea how bad it's going to get for you?"

"I've handled it so far. I'll handle it again."

"God, you're amazing." His spoke with admiration.

"But you're also annoyingly difficult. Let someone help you. Let me help you."

I stared stonily ahead. His expression darkened.

"They're going to come after you! Do you think I can just sit around when people are trying to hurt and rape you?"

The heat in his voice seared me. He wasn't angry at me; he was angry *for* me. He regarded me in a way no one had ever looked at me before, an expression that said I meant so much to him that he would take on hell itself to protect me. That intensity wrapped around me. It thrilled me. It scared me. I didn't know what to do with it.

Again, he read my face. This time, he pulled me over, crushing my body against his. I didn't fight it. "Let me help you," he repeated.

"How? You live an hour and a half away."

He pressed his face against my hair. "I'll commute."

"Oh for God's—"

"I mean it. I know I can't be with you all the time, but I'll do what I can."

"You're going to trail me like a bodyguard or something?"

"I'll do it as a fox if it makes you feel better."

I laughed in spite of myself, tightening my hold on him. I knew we shouldn't be locked in this kind of embrace, but honestly . . . after everything that had happened, it was comforting. And a turn-on too. But mostly comforting.

"What's that like anyway?"

"What's what like?"

"Being a fox. Is it weird?"

"I don't know. I've always been that way. It's the only thing I know."

"Yeah, but . . . why not just stay human all the time?"

"I'm stronger as a fox. Comes in handy in a fight."

"You're not too shabby as a human."

"Women think foxes are cute."

"Not that cute," I grumbled. I could sense his smile.

"It's a good way to let your instincts take over."

"Which instincts?"

In one movement, he had me flipped onto my back. His hands held mine down while his body pressed against the rest of me. Those lips hovered a few breaths from mine.

"All of them," he growled.

My breath was coming out in rapid bursts, and a voice in the back of my head was yelling, *Hey! Remember how you don't want to be involved with Otherworldly people?* I knew that voice was right, but it was kind of hard to pay attention when my body was melting against his and one of his hands had slid down to the side of a breast.

"I don't think friends are supposed to lay like this."

"I know," he said.

"Or bodyguards."

"I know."

"Or veterinarians."

"That I disagree with."

He crushed his mouth to mine, and it was powerful and ravenous and furious and wonderful. I couldn't think or do anything coherent in that moment, only let him keep kissing me and kissing me.

At last he broke away. He sat up, and I could see his body tremble. The look in his eyes was still hungry and yearning, and there was a visible struggle within him, a warring of two halves. One must have won, because he took a deep breath, and that animal need faded—slightly—from him.

"I need to go," he said at last. "I've got to work in two hours."

"Okay."

We stared at each other for a long time. I pulled a sheet up, letting it cover part of me. A grin lit his features.

"Thanks. That helps." He stood up and moved toward

the door. "Hey, would you mind meeting Maiwenn? She wants to talk to you in person, see what you're like."

"You seem pretty chummy with her," I said. The words came out sharper than I'd intended, but he looked unfazed.

"She's a good friend. And I believe in her philosophies. She wants both our worlds left intact. So do I. She can be a good friend to you too."

"Is she strong enough to come over here?" He nodded. "If she'll do it, I'll meet her. I'm not really keen on going over there anytime soon."

"I'll tell her."

He took a few steps out the door, and this time I called to him. "Hey . . . Kiyo."

"Yeah?"

"All these people and . . . things are coming after me because they think I'm going to be Damien's mother or something . . . but seriously, do you actually think any of it's true? Do you really believe this prophecy could happen? Roland—my stepdad—says prophecies are a dime a dozen in the Otherworld."

"They are," Kiyo said slowly, a slight wrinkle between his eyes as he thought. "And most don't come true. But a lot do, a lot more than you'd think growing up here. The thing about prophecies is . . . well, people sometimes read the wrong things into them. Or, in trying to avert them, they only make the prophecy come true."

I shivered, half-wishing he would have just said prophecies were a bunch of crap. "You mean like Oedipus? How his father got rid of him to beat that prophecy?"

"Exactly. Doing that only ended up making it happen." Seeing my dark look, he smiled. "Hey, don't worry about it. I told you most don't come true. And besides, you're not trying to have kids, so there's nothing to worry about. Concentrate on the now."

I gave him a faltering smile back, hoping he was right. "Thanks."

He held my eyes for a few seconds before stepping out of the room, only to return a moment later with my burnt mirror. He set it on the dresser, regarding it with displeasure. "Sorry I wasn't here sooner."

"Hey," I said, mustering some bravado, "I told you I can take care of myself."

Those dark eyes flashed. "I know. You're a dangerous woman."

I wasn't entirely sure if he referred to my fighting abilities or something else.

When he was gone, I lay back in bed with a sigh, thinking I might not move for a week. Things just got weirder and weirder around here.

Suddenly I felt a faint pressure build in the room. I sat up straight. Red eyes peered at me from a dim corner.

"Volusian? I didn't summon you."

"You gave us permission to come if we acquired information."

"Yeah. I suppose I did. I didn't really think any of you would actually listen to me. What's up?"

"I've come to tell you Otherworldly interest in you has increased."

I stared at him stupidly a moment, then pointed to the bloody athame I'd used on the Gray Man. "Gee, you think?"

He shook his head. "More than these scattered attacks. Before, others were interested in you simply because of your heritage. Now, after seeing you . . . some are more excited still. They find you . . . attractive." I could tell the concept baffled him.

"Great. Now I'm fertile *and* hot. So what's this mean? Should I be expecting daily attacks?"

"More like . . . organized attacks."

"Groups?"

"Worse."

"Worse than a group of guys trying to have sex with me? How?"

"For now, only creatures and gentry who can cross over in physical or elemental form will try. But we are weeks from Beltane, mistress. When the doors open . . ."

"Jesus," I breathed. "Everything with a dick is going to come looking for me."

He didn't bother with a response. But when I said nothing more, he asked, "What will you do?"

"What do you think? The same as I've been doing. I'll fight them off."

He stayed quiet, but I could feel his disapproval.

"What else do you expect me to do? Submit?"

"I expect you to not sit around and wait for the inevitable. You might as well be from one of the bride-by-capture societies. Always being on the defensive will get you nowhere; eventually someone will overpower you."

I laughed without really finding anything funny. "So, what, I go on the offensive? Head over and just start taking on random gentry and spirits?"

"No. You start claiming your heritage. They attack you because you let them, because you kick at one and then wait for the next. You make yourself a victim, yet you are Storm King's daughter. In his day, his rule stretched farther than any of the current monarchs'. His kingdom may be gone now, but his legacy makes you royalty. If you acted like it, they wouldn't attack you so brazenly."

"I doubt they'd give up wanting to father Storm King's heir just because I started calling myself a queen or a princess."

"Oh, they'd still want you, but they would go about it differently. They'd approach you with respect. They would try to woo you. Now they only treat you with disdain. They treat you like the victim—the piece of flesh—that you have let yourself become."

I didn't really like the thought of a bunch of gentry bringing me flowers and chocolate, but I liked it better than rape.

"Yeah, but joking aside, I can't just go in there and say, 'Hey, I'm Storm King's daughter, treat me with respect.'"

"Well," he said dryly, "it would be a start. However, you will drive home your connection to him most when you stop relying on those." He pointed at my weapons. "They make you human."

"I am human."

"You are half-human. If you want them to respect you as one of the gentry, you need to remind them of who you are. You need to draw on the power within you, on your father's legacy."

I thought about what Roland had said, about how he had purposely buried my power. Faint flickers of the vision came back to me, how I'd reached for power just before it ended. "No. I won't use gentry magic."

Volusian sighed. He pointed to the burnt mirror. "Mistress, why did you use that as a weapon?"

"Because a Gray Man caught me unarmed."

"Had you been in full control of your magic, you would have needed no weapons. You could have destroyed him as soon as he crossed your threshold."

I tugged the sheet up and wrapped my arms around myself. The thought of power like that terrified me . . . and yet deep down, I saw its appeal. I didn't like being defenseless at twenty-six any more than I had at twelve. Volusian sensed this.

"Your true nature knows I am right. It longs to be realized."

"If I give in to this nature, I'll become gentry."

"You'll never be fully gentry or human. That you must accept. You must simply take the best of each."

"Even if I wanted to do this"—I swallowed, still uncertain if I wanted the kind of power he was talking about— "I wouldn't know the first thing about tapping it. Roland can't teach me about gentry magic."

"Then you'll have to find a gentry teacher."

"Where will I find one who won't try to rape me first? I don't really have any friends over there."

"Don't you?" He looked at me expectantly.

"You mean Dorian."

"Of all the rulers in the Otherworld right now, only he has ordered his people to leave you alone."

"Seriously? But why? He told me himself he wants to see Storm King's invasion happen."

"Most believe he gave the order simply because he wants you for himself. I, however, suspect he also probably acts out of some ridiculous sense of altruism—and his own pride. Of course, some of his people won't heed the warning, but you will find less of them attacking you than others. Like Aeson and his followers, for example." Apparently Aeson was alive after all. I'd forgotten to ask Kiyo about that in the wake of all the other drama.

"Still . . . Dorian made the attempt, huh?" I thought back to my encounter with him. Of all the gentry, he had been the one I almost felt comfortable with, which was startling, considering how odd he was. And he had helped me. "But I know he wants to have sex with me too. He didn't really make that a secret."

"Of course he does. Which is why he'll help you. He'll help you because he thinks it'll bring you to his bed. And because being close to you will impress his rivals and allies alike. They'll think you're lovers, even if you aren't. He'll like that."

You'll return to me. You won't be able to help yourself.

I shivered, and Volusian continued: "You'll benefit as well. Go to him as an equal, and he will treat you as one. His attitude will go a long way to influence others."

"If I do this, I'll have come a long way from being feared by the gentry to cozying up with one for political reasons. That's quite a leap."

"Not really. Not if you consider how far you've come since your trip to Aeson's."

"That's an understatement." I rubbed my eyes. "I

don't know, Volusian. I still don't know if I'm ready to approach Dorian. I need to think about it."

"As my mistress wishes. But I would advise you to think fast. Decide before Beltane. Siding with Dorian will offer both magical and political benefits."

"Noted. Thanks for the update. And the advice."

He bowed, and I stood up to send him back. Before I did, I couldn't help messing with him. I was still naked, after all.

"Hey, Volusian, you haven't been checking me out, have you?"

He gave me his trademark bland stare. "I assure you, mistress, the only allure your bare flesh has for me is to remind me how easy it will be to slice open."

I laughed. If not for the fact he was actually serious, he'd be so much fun.

Chapter Fourteen

I saw Kiyo a few times in the next week. One of those times I was out on a job, doing an exorcism that turned out to be a setup. The house I'd gone into had no spirit but rather an asag: a demonic creature that literally had a rocklike body. Kiyo had shown up in the midst of the fight, and while I'd thought I had things well in hand, his help sure expedited matters. He didn't use any weapons like I did; he was all body and physical force. Watching him move was almost hypnotic, like admiring a dancer.

His other appearances were similar, showing up when needed and then retreating if I wanted. Once, I reluctantly agreed to lunch after a fight. He watched me with those hungry eyes the entire time, but everything else was friendly and easy between us. It was like when we'd met in the bar, all breezy banter and connection— underscored with simmering sexual tension.

All the other times I saw him, he trailed me around as a fox. And, as much as I hated to admit it . . . he was right. He was pretty cute.

Life was busy now. Whereas before I'd had maybe only one or two jobs a week, I now had at least one every day. Apparently the gentry and other creatures hoping to get a piece of me realized they no longer had to seek me out;

I would come to them if they bothered the right human. It was annoying, to say the least—and exhausting. Of course, since these fights occurred through clients and contracted jobs, I got paid for them. It became a very rich few weeks, though I felt a little bad since my clients never would have needed to pay in the first place if not for me.

I woke up a couple weeks before Beltane, aching and exhausted. I'd had two jobs and an "unscheduled" fight last night. Staring at my ceiling, at the way the late morning sun filtered into funny shapes through my blinds, I drowsily wondered if I was going to be able to keep this up. I'd lose to the Otherworld not through any one encounter, but simply via my own fatigue.

I trudged to the kitchen and found no morning offering from Tim. He must have stayed the night with one of his groupies. Forced to make my own breakfast, I put two chocolate Pop-Tarts in the toaster and fixed coffee while they cooked. Glancing at the table, I saw that my cell phone displayed four missed calls. I'd taken to turning it off, because the calls were always from Lara, and I didn't feel like hearing them anymore. She'd either want to offer me a new job or tell me that Wil Delaney had left yet another message.

I was halfway through my second Pop-Tart when my mom showed up. I hadn't seen her since the confrontation. For a moment, I considered not letting her in, but I promptly dismissed the thought.

She was my mom, after all. She loved me. No matter what had happened, I couldn't let go of that intrinsic truth. She was the one who'd doused my scratches with antiseptic when I was little—and not so little—and tried unsuccessfully to interest me in shopping and makeup as a teenager. She'd tried to protect me from the ugly truths that everyone has to discover growing up. She'd tried to protect me from the path Roland had set me on. And now it seemed she'd tried to protect me from my own past.

Looking back, I tried to piece together things she'd said on the rare occasions I could get her to acknowledge my biological father. *You're better off without him. He wasn't the kind of man anyone could count on. We didn't have a healthy relationship when we were together. There was a lot of emotion, a lot of intensity . . . but it ending was for the best. He's gone—just accept he'll never be a part of your life.*

She'd never exactly lied, I realized, but I'd interpreted the story in a completely different way. I'd read it as a whirlwind affair, one in which her emotions blinded her. With all the bad things she'd implied about his character, I'd just figured he'd up and left one day, unable to handle the responsibilities involved with taking care of me. Little did I know he'd desperately wanted me back.

I offered her a seat at the table, handing her a cup of coffee at the same time. She held it with both hands, lacing her fingers in a nervous gesture. Her hair was braided down her back today, and she wore a red blouse.

"You look tired," she said after a long stretch of silence.

I smiled. It was such a mom thing to say. "Yeah. It's been a busy week."

"Are you sleeping enough?"

"I'm sleeping. Sort of. I'm just too busy when I'm awake, that's the problem."

She looked up, nervously meeting my eyes as though afraid of what she might find. "Busy . . . because of . . . ?"

"Yeah," I said, knowing what she meant.

She looked back down. "I'm sorry. I'm sorry about all of this."

I dunked a piece of Pop-Tart into my coffee. "It's not your fault. You didn't decide to go to the Otherworld."

"No . . . but you were right the other day. I was wrong to keep it from you."

"I was too harsh then."

"No." Her eyes met mine, wide and sad. "I think I thought . . . that if I kept it from you, maybe I could make it go away. Like pretending enough would make it so that it had never happened. I could forget too."

I didn't like to see my mom sad. I don't think anyone does unless they're trying to take revenge for some traumatic childhood wrong. Maybe I had been wronged to a certain extent, but in reflection, it probably couldn't compare to what had happened to her. I knew she had been older when abducted, but in my mind's eye, I could see my mother looking like Jasmine, young and scared. Based on the stories I'd heard before the Storm King paternity news, I'd always envisioned my conception as the result of a torrid affair my scumbag father later walked out on. But that wasn't it at all. The truth was worse. I was a child of rape, born from violence and domination.

"Every time you see me . . . do I remind you of him? Of what happened?"

Compassion washed over her face. "Oh, baby, no. You're the best thing in my life. Don't think like that."

"Do I look like him at all? Everyone says I take after you."

She studied me as though seeking out the answer, but I knew she already had to know. "Your hair, a little. But mostly . . . in the eyes. You got those from him. His eyes were like . . ." She had to clear her throat to go on. "They always changed. They ran every shade of blue and gray you can imagine, depending on his mood. Sky blue when he was happy. Midnight blue when troubled. Deep gray when he was angry and about to fight."

"And what about violet?" I asked.

"Violet when he was feeling . . . amorous."

I'd never heard my mom use that word before. It might have been funny, but mostly it made me consider adding a shot of whiskey to my coffee. Jesus. I'd gotten the eye color my dad had when he was in the mood. So many people complimented me on my eyes, yet to her, they had to bring back memories that were anything but amorous, as far as she was concerned.

"I'm sorry, Mom." I reached out and held her hand,

our first contact since I'd stormed from her house. "It must have been so awful . . . but were there—were there any moments, even a few, when you were happy at all? Or at least not so unhappy?"

Surely . . . surely there had been one moment when it had not all been hatred and sorrow between my parents. Surely I could not have been conceived and born out of so much darkness. There had to have been something. Maybe he'd made her smile just once. Or maybe he'd brought her a gift . . . like a necklace recovered after some looting and pillaging. I didn't know. Just something. Anything.

"No." Her voice was hoarse. "I hated it all. Every second."

I swallowed back a thickness in my throat, and suddenly all I could think about was Jasmine. Jasmine. More than five years younger than my mom had been. Jasmine had been subjected to the same things. She had to have those moments of agony too. Maybe her misplaced affection for Aeson was the only way to cope. Maybe it was better than hurting all the time. I didn't know. I closed my eyes briefly. All I could see was my mom as Jasmine and Jasmine as my mom.

I opened my eyes. "We didn't get Jasmine." I realized I'd never told her that when I'd come over to talk to her. Briefly, I recounted the essential details. Her face blanched as I spoke, and her raw hurt clawed at something inside of me. Jasmine as my mom. My mom as Jasmine.

"Oh God," she whispered when I finished.

"Yeah, I—"

Cold flowed over me. The faintest electric tingle tugged at my flesh.

"What's wrong?" my mom asked, seeing me stiffen.

"Can't you feel that? The cold?"

She looked puzzled. "No. Are you okay?"

I stood up. She couldn't feel it because it wasn't actually a physical thing. It was something beyond normal human senses. On the counter sat my athames, gun, and wand. I didn't go anywhere in the house without them now, not even to the bathroom. I also didn't sleep in anything too delicate anymore. The tank top I wore was still lacy and flimsy, but my pajama pants were cotton with a sturdy elastic waistband. I draped my robe over a chair and considered my armament.

I could tell it wasn't gentry. It was a spirit or demon. Silver, then, not iron. The Glock already had a silver cartridge in it but would have questionable effectiveness if the spirit had little substance. I carefully placed it under my waistband and then picked up the silver athame and wand.

"Stay in here, Mom."

"Eugenie, what's—"

"Just stay," I commanded. "Get under the table."

She looked at my face and complied. I guess you couldn't be an Otherworld abductee and married to a shaman without knowing when to take these things seriously.

I moved slowly and stealthily toward the living room because that was where the feeling centered. I heard no noise, but the silence screamed louder than any sound. I put my back to the wall, sliding along it to peer around the corner. Nothing.

Whatever it was, it couldn't hurt me and stay invisible. It would have to turn substantial to do any real damage. The weird thing was, a spirit also couldn't get me pregnant, not like gentry or some of the monsters could. Spirits were dead, and that was that. One seeking me out seemed odd.

I waited, back up against the edge of the doorway as I peered around the living room. Whatever was going to happen would happen here. It was like a vortex. Power flowed both in and out of this spot.

Something cold brushed against my arm, and then a hand materialized, grabbing hold of me. My reflexes snapped to life, and I cut at the spirit's wrist with the athame in my other hand. The spirit had enough substance to feel the effects of the metal. Plus, the athame's power extended beyond tactile discomfort.

The spirit—a gray, haglike thing—recoiled, but then I felt more cold hands behind me and gave a quick glance back. Five more spirits—more than I'd ever taken on at once. I spun around, but my initial attacker's position was better, giving it a solid hold on me. I didn't break free of its grip entirely, but I struggled like hell, accidentally hitting a small table with a ceramic pitcher on it. The pitcher hit the floor and splintered into sharp, aqua-colored fragments.

The spirit pushed me up against the wall, its skeletal hands clutching at my throat while it stared at me with empty black eyes. It floated such that while it kept me pinned, it stayed out of reach of the athame. It wasn't out of the reach of the wand, however.

Its ghostly companions drifted over, ringing us, as my oxygen began to dry up. Black stars sparkled in my vision, and I tried hard to focus on what I needed to do.

"Be careful," warned one of the observers, "or you will kill her."

Hecate, I prayed in my head, *open the gates.* On the edge of passing out, I felt the snake on my arm tingle. I used that power, letting the farthest limits of my mind brush the Otherworld. I became the gate, a conduit of passage running from my soul to the snake to the wand. The hands on my throat wouldn't let me speak, but the banishing words burned in my mind. It was good enough.

The wand's power flared out at the spirit holding me. It realized too late what had happened and vanished with a piteous scream. One of its counterparts started to move toward me and got sucked away with the other. The other four kept their distance. Meanwhile, I had backed up as much as possible. I needed to open the gates again, but my body informed me I had to allow a moment's recovery time before going a second round.

My throat hurt inside and out from where the spirit had choked me, and the room spun around as I staggered. I took deep, shaking breaths in an attempt to recover what I'd lost.

Two more spirits bore down on me but hesitated a little this time, still keeping some space between us. They circled me, like dancers or boxers, each of us determining what the other would do. Just then, my mom came out of the kitchen holding my iron athame. Screaming, she drove it against one of the other spirit's backs, hacking away. Iron hurt gentry—not spirits. All her actions did was annoy it. It turned slightly, and with one oh-so-casual gesture, it backhanded her with enough force to throw her against the far wall. She hit the wall and slid down into an unmoving pile.

I yelled my fury, charging the spirits around me. Strong emotion is better for physical attacks but not mental ones, and I lost whatever grip I'd momentarily had on the Otherworld. The athame caused some damage to one of the spirits, but the other dodged. It hit me hard, shoving me into my entertainment center. The sharp corners dug into my back, but the adrenaline pumping through me wouldn't let me feel it. Not yet.

I muttered another incantation to Hecate and felt the power shoot up again. The spirit who had thrown me drifted forward. The gates swung open, and I banished it away. Moments later, its injured counterpart followed. That left two.

One of them swooped in, reaching out for me. I ducked past it, hitting the floor, where I half-crawled and half-rolled out of its grasp. My connection to the Otherworld had slipped again; I needed it back. I kept ordering myself to focus, but then I saw my mom lying in the corner. I couldn't get past that. I went after the spirit again, and it hissed angrily as the athame dug into its upper body. I was sloppy, however, and gave one of its hands the opening to grab my wand hand and shove me against the wall. The wand fell to the floor. A moment later, the spirit's other hand twisted my other wrist until I dropped the athame as well. The last spirit floated up and added to the wall around me. Walls were really starting to piss me off lately.

They had me now, trapped and defenseless and injured. I didn't know what exactly they could do, however. Earlier they'd worried about killing me, yet they could have no romantic interest in me. What could they—

My patio door opened, and an elemental walked in. An elemental made of mud, of all things. Its body was very solid, very human, and very male. Oozing, brown-gray sludge dripped off it and onto my carpet.

I renewed my futile efforts to break from the spirits. Volusian's words came back to haunt me. *More organized attacks.* The spirits couldn't have sex with me, but the elemental gentry could. It had sent its minions to subdue me first. Clever.

"Where are the others?" asked the elemental, an almost comic look of astonishment on his face as he glanced around the room.

"She banished them, master," whispered one of the spirits.

"You really are lethal, aren't you?" The elemental approached. "I hadn't believed the stories. I thought sending these six was overkill. Still. I guess even you have your limits."

I sneered at him. "Don't talk to me about limits. You can't even cross to this world in full form."

A look of displeasure crossed that dripping, muddy face. Power was a matter of pride among the gentry. His inability to cross over fully was probably a sore point. Raping me was undoubtedly a way of compensating for all sorts of deficiencies.

"It won't matter," he said. "Once I beget Storm King's

heir, all gentry will pass into this world, smiting the race of humans."

"Okay, Mr. Old Testament. I can't honestly believe you just used 'beget' and 'smiting' in the same sentence."

"So brave and brash. Yet it won't—ow!"

I couldn't free my upper body, but the elemental was close enough that I flipped my lower body upward and kicked him. I'd been aiming for the groin, just like with the Gray Man, but caught his thigh instead. The guarding spirit restrained my legs.

The elemental narrowed his eyes. "You make things difficult. This would be far easier on you if you would submit."

"Don't hold your breath."

"She will submit, master," intoned a spirit. "Her mother lies there on the floor."

I stiffened in the spirit's grip. "Don't touch her."

The elemental turned and walked toward where my mother had fallen. Almost gently, he leaned down and picked her up in his arms. "She's still alive."

"Leave her alone, you bastard!" I screamed. I strained so hard, it felt like my arms would tear from my shoulders.

"Let her go," ordered the elemental.

"Master—"

"Let her go. She will not do anything, because she knows if she so much as steps in this direction"—the muddy hand slid up to my mom's throat, leaving a dirty trail wherever he moved—"then I will snap her neck."

The spirits released me. I did not move.

"I'm going to kill you," I said. My voice was hoarse from the choking and screaming. "I'll tear you to pieces before I send you to hell."

"Unlikely. Not if you want this one to live. Come," he said to one of his servants. "Take her." There was a trade-off, and now a spirit held my mother. "If Odile Dark Swan so much as looks threatening, kill this woman."

"Odile Dark Swan always looks threatening." The

spirit spoke in a deadpan, nonsarcastic voice. Apparently this elemental's minions had as good a sense of humor as my own.

"You know what I mean," snapped the elemental. He came closer to me, so only a few inches separated us. "Now. I will let you live. I will let your mother live. All you have to do is not fight me while I do what I've come here to do. When I am finished, we will depart in peace. Do you understand?"

Anger and fury were raging in me, and I could feel tears burning at the edges of my vision. I wanted to reach out and claw his eyes. I wanted to kick between his legs until no one could tell if he was male anymore. I wanted to deliver him to Persephone in a pile of body parts.

But I was scared. So scared that if I even blinked wrong, they'd break my mother. She already hung uselessly in the spirit's arms like a rag doll. For all I knew, she could have been dead, but something told me she wasn't. I couldn't gamble if she might be alive.

So I nodded in acknowledgment to the elemental and felt one of the tears leak out of my eye as I did.

"Good." He exhaled, and I realized he was as scared of me as I was of him. "Now. Undress."

Bile rose in my throat. I couldn't get enough oxygen again; it was like the air was thick and heavy around me. Another tear stole from my eye, and I slowly pulled down the pajama pants, removing the gun I hadn't been able to use. It occurred to me briefly that I could probably manage to shoot the elemental right now, but I wouldn't be fast enough to save my mother.

What did it matter? If he was telling the truth, I would still live if I could only endure this. I was on the pill. I probably wouldn't actually get pregnant. I'd only have to lay there passively while this big anthropomorphic pile of dirt had his way with me. Things could be worse. Probably.

I looked at him, imagining those hands on me. The air grew thicker to me, making it still harder to breathe. The lighting seemed darker, as it had when the spirit choked me, and I wondered if I was going to faint. Maybe it'd be easier that way. Less to remember.

"The rest," he said impatiently. He too was breathing heavily.

I moved my fingers to the edges of my underwear. I had dressed for comfort in plain, gray cotton bikini-cuts. They were nice but not sexy. They didn't match the pink top. Of course, it didn't matter to the elemental what I wore. Naked desire glowed on his face. I stared at the lumpy, misshapen body and worked hard not to whimper. I knew what I had to do, but I didn't want to. Oh, God. Oh, Selene. I didn't want him to touch me. I didn't want him pressed up against me. Nausea rolled up in my stomach, and I wondered desperately where Kiyo was. I knew he couldn't follow me 24/7, and I suddenly regretted my snide comments about his protection. I wished he were here now. I needed him. I'd never felt so defenseless in my life, not even in that long-lost memory. It was not a state of mind I liked.

As I was about to pull the panties down, a slap of wood on glass made all of us jump. The elemental jerked his head around, and I followed his gaze. The patio door was open, and the wind had blown in, knocking over a picture frame on my coffee table. It was a strong wind, one that kept blowing, scattering papers and other objects around. Yet, outside, the sunshine and azure skies of late spring reflected no such disturbance.

"What . . . ?" began the elemental.

That sharp sound had sort of snapped me out of my anger and fear, and I was suddenly able to notice details more sharply. I could see everything with a new clarity. The air really was thick, the lighting truly darker. I hadn't imagined those things. The angry wind rose and fell with my breathing. Brilliant light slashed the dimness, and we all cried out as it danced around from object to object. At the same time, a deafening roar of thunder filled the room, too big and too loud for the small space. I covered my ears and dropped to the floor.

The elemental turned on me. "Make it stop."

"What . . . ?"

"It's yours! Stop, or you'll kill us all."

I looked around and realized he was right. I couldn't explain it, but I was connected to everything going on in there. The building moisture and humidity. The wind whipping around, scattering things. The electricity charging the air.

I could feel it, but I didn't know what to do with it. *You're mine,* I tried telling it, but nothing happened. This was not like trying to control power with a wand or an athame. This was both within me and outside of me. I could no more stop it than I could stop myself from feeling joy or sorrow or hate.

The wind increased, its fury building. A jagged piece of glass flew into my cheek. "I can't control it," I whispered. "I can't."

The elemental looked panicked. So did the spirits. Whereas a moment ago I had felt weak and defenseless, their fear made mine go away. Their fear fed my anger, and I fed the building tempest. I couldn't actually control the storm, but it was expanding out from me. Something else hit me in the shoulder, and moments later, I barely dodged a book flying toward my head.

I couldn't control this. I didn't know how. I didn't know anything except that I wanted to live and I wanted my mother to live too.

Darkness swirled around us all as great billowing clouds filled the room. More lightning danced around, oblivious to where it traveled. The elemental was right. I would kill one of—

Lightning shot out at the spirit holding my mother, forcing her to fall to the ground. He screamed and screamed. It was the most horrible sound I'd ever heard. It was more than a death knell, more than a tortured cry. I covered my ears again, watching as he glowed blindingly bright, then went black, then was nothing.

The elemental backed away from me, fear palpably rolling off of him. A tingle along my skin told me what he was going to do. He was so scared, he was going to try to cross back to the Otherworld. Right here, right now, with no crossroads. Doing so had nearly ripped me apart. There was no way he could do it, not when he couldn't even transition to this world in his natural form.

He didn't seem to care, however, and suddenly I panicked. What if he could? What if by some miracle he escaped? I couldn't let him get away, not after what he'd done here, not after what he'd tried to do. My need, my anxiety . . . both grew, but I had no way to focus them. I had no idea what had happened to my weapons in this madness. A bolt of lighting blew apart a speaker beside me, and the sound made that ear go deaf.

More lightning flared, so strongly and rapidly that I couldn't tell what was real and what was an afterimage. Somewhere, over the thunder, I heard the elemental screaming, although I could no longer see him. It wasn't as horrible as the spirit's cries had been, but it still made my skin crawl. Lightning hit something else beside me, and sharp pieces of whatever it was flew into my arm.

I was going to die, I realized. With the spirit. With the elemental. With my mother. Who would have thought the spirits I'd just banished to the Otherworld would be the lucky ones?

I buried my face in my hands, trying to block out what I'd created. It didn't help. It was almost like the lightning and clouds existed in my mind as much as in the room. I squeezed my eyes tighter, so much so that they hurt. But nothing changed. The wind roared against me, the thunder shook my house. Dominating it all was the darkness—and the light—as the thunder and lightning came and went.

Darkness, light.
Darkness, light.
Darkness.

Chapter Fifteen

I don't care how old you get or how tough you are. Nothing, nothing at all, can ever replace your mother taking care of you when you're sick.

The feel of a cool, wet cloth touched my head, and the sound of familiar humming just barely penetrated my weary brain. I opened my eyes and saw the same funny-shaped pieces of sunlight cast through my blinds onto the bedroom ceiling. Only this time, their positions had changed, their colors dimmer and darker orange.

The humming abruptly stopped.

"Eugenie?"

"Mom," I croaked. My throat felt torn and raw.

She moved into my field of vision, face drawn with worry. I couldn't believe it. She looked almost entirely normal. Her hair had a bit of a wind-swept look, and I could see a few bruises. Other than that, she seemed fine, not like she'd just endured a paranormal attack and subsequent magically induced maelstrom. For just a moment, I questioned my own memories. Had I imagined what happened? Had it been a trick or a vision? No. I felt like shit. No delusion could have caused this pain.

"You're okay?" I asked doubtfully.

She nodded. "Fine. What about you?"

I tentatively attempted to make contact with the muscles in my body. They told me to leave them the fuck alone.

"I hurt."

She adjusted the cloth on my head, making it fractionally more perfect. As she leaned over, a lock of her hair slipped forward, and I made out muddy fingerprints on her neck. No. Definitely not my imagination.

"I called Roland. He was up in Flagstaff with Bill. He's on his way back now—should be here in a couple of hours."

"Mom . . . how'd you recover?"

"What do you mean?"

"You were really messed up from those spirits. Don't you remember?"

"I got a little shaken up but nothing worse. Nothing like you." She frowned, giving a little sigh. "God, how I wish you were a lawyer instead. Or maybe a pharmacist."

"What do you remember happening?"

"Not much," she admitted. "I remember going after one of those . . . creatures. After that, it's a blur. I must have panicked. Your living room is, uh, going to need some help."

I closed my eyes, feeling tired. My living room would probably need to be bulldozed and rebuilt from scratch. No telling how the rest of the house had fared. It could probably collapse at any moment. My room actually looked kind of normal. A few things were knocked over, probably casualties of stray gusts of wind.

"You've got people here who want to see you."

I opened my eyes. "Who?"

"No one I know. A man and a woman."

"Is the man a fox?"

She stared at me, confused. "A fox? He's very handsome, yes, but, sweetie . . . maybe I should send them away. You don't sound like you're better yet."

"No, no, let me talk to them." I had a feeling the missing

pieces of what had happened during and after the storm
lay with Kiyo. "And I need to talk to them . . . alone."

My mother looked hurt.

"It's not personal. It's business."

She started to argue, then shook her head and stood
up. "I'll go get them."

While she was gone, I dared a hasty assessment of my
appearance. I was still in my underwear and camisole.
The top in particular was ripped and dirty. I pulled the
covers up almost to my neck and ran a hand over my
hair and face. I could feel more dirt on my skin plus a
scab on my cheek, distantly reminding me of a shard of
something flying out and cutting me. My hair stuck out
everywhere. I attempted to smooth it down, but then my
mom returned with Kiyo and a strange woman.

"I'll be in the kitchen if you need me," Mom said pro-
tectively. She pulled the door closed behind her, all but
a crack.

Kiyo's face told me all I needed to know about the way
I looked.

"You should see the other guy," I said.

A small smile broke over his face. "I did. He's in pieces
in the other room."

"Oh."

He beckoned to the woman. "Eugenie, this is Maiwenn, queen of the Willow Land."

I started in surprise. She didn't look like a Willow
Queen. Of course, I'm not sure what exactly I expected—
maybe something akin to Glinda the Good Witch. But
this woman looked like Surfer Girl Barbie. Her skin
glowed with a deep bronze tan. Platinum blond hair fell
in supermodel waves to her waist. Her eyes were the color
of the sea in the sun, blue-green with long lashes. She
wore a simple blue dress, a bit old-fashioned but nothing
that screamed, "I'm a fairy queen." It was looser than the
form-fitting gowns other gentry women seemed to favor

but was still quite pretty. My feelings of inadequacy about my appearance increased tenfold.

"Nice to meet you," I said. I could hear the tentativeness in my voice. Kiyo might swear to her character, but I still carried a lot of apprehension around the gentry, monarch or no.

"And you," she said. Her voice was rich and sweet, her face serene. "I'm sorry I could not heal you too."

"'Too'? Oh . . . was it you? Did you heal my mother? She doesn't remember anything. . . ."

She nodded. "I didn't have the power to heal you both. She was more severely injured, and with your age and stamina—and your blood—well, I thought you'd have an easier time recovering."

I thought about the aches and pains shooting through my body. Easier? That might be a subjective term.

"You made the right choice. Thanks. I'll be fine."

Kiyo stuffed his hands in his pockets and leaned against the wall. "Eugenie doesn't like to admit weakness. It's one of her more charming traits."

I shot him a glare, and Maiwenn offered a small, polite smile. "Nothing wrong with that." She approached me and extended a hand toward my face. "I think I have enough strength for a small healing. May I?"

I nodded, not entirely sure what I was agreeing to.

Her fingertips grazed my cheek, icy cold but gentle. A tingle ran through me, and she drew back, suddenly looking pale and tired. Kiyo started to help her when she stumbled, but she waved him off. "There. No scarring this way." My fingers examined the place she had touched. No more scab.

"Thank you." Silence fell, and I looked from face to face. With me in bed and them hanging around so casually, I didn't really feel like I was having a meeting with a bona fide queen. It was all so informal. "What happened?"

They exchanged uncertain glances. "We're not really sure," he said. "You and your mother were both unconscious.

The elemental was dead, and your living room . . . it looks kind of bad."

"But . . . that was it?"

His eyebrows rose. "What more could there be?"

"There was no storm when you showed up?"

They exchanged conspiratorial looks again, and something about their solidarity rankled me.

"Tell us what you remember," Maiwenn said.

I did, starting with the spirit attack and ending with the vicious storm.

Neither spoke when I finished. Kiyo sighed.

"What?" I demanded. "What happened? You obviously know."

"It's complicated."

"Everything's complicated lately. Let me guess. It was the magic, wasn't it? Storm King's inherited power?"

He didn't answer. She did.

"Yes. It seems it has been passed down after all."

"Can I stop it? Keep it locked up so it doesn't come out again?"

"Not likely. You might be able to bury it so it isn't consciously used, but . . . if it's there, it's likely to burst out again when your emotions let loose. You'll get the same kind of disastrous results if you don't learn to manage it."

"I don't want it." I shuddered, recalling that horrible blackness and deadly lightning. Uneasily, I remembered what Volusian had told me, that embracing my magic could protect me and those I loved. I looked at Maiwenn nervously, hating what I was about to ask. "But I don't want to hurt anyone either. Can you teach me to use it? Or at least control it?"

Kiyo's eyes widened. "Eugenie, no—"

"What do you expect me to do?" I demanded. The expression on his face mirrored what I felt inside. "It's not like I want to do this. But you saw what happened. I destroyed my house, and worse, I nearly killed my mother. And myself."

He sighed but didn't argue. Maiwenn regarded him calmly.

"She's right."

"I know. But I don't have to like it."

"I don't know if I can teach you or not," she murmured, turning back to me. "Your magic—storm magic—is a very physical, outward sort of power. Healing is more internal. Less aggressive. Some of the basics will be the same, but we'll probably have to find you a teacher with similar powers."

Like someone who can call up pieces of the earth and rip castles apart, I thought. I didn't give voice to that. Kiyo and I might be "friends," but I immediately knew he wouldn't like me getting close to Dorian.

"Kiyo says you're against the invasion thing, that you weren't a supporter of Storm King."

"Yes. That was part of the reason I wanted to meet you. I'm happy you survived today, Eugenie Markham, but . . . this possibility of the prophecy coming true alarms me. I've spent years believing Storm King had no children. Your existence causes all sorts of complications."

It occurred to me then that Maiwenn might have slept easier if I'd been killed today.

"So is it true?" she asked. "You have no intention of fulfilling the prophecy?"

"Of course not."

"Turning one's back on such power can't be easy. Even now, you're considering his magic."

"That's a necessity. I don't want it. Besides, none of this is about power. It's about keeping my world safe. You forget that until a few weeks ago, I had no clue about any of this. In most ways—me whipping up a storm aside— I still consider myself human. I'm not going to let some army subjugate or destroy my race."

"You see?" Kiyo said to her. "I told you."

I could still see the doubt on her face.

"I'm serious. I don't want to usher in some terrible era

of gentry domination. I sure as hell don't want to be a plaything for every gentry guy. And even if the worst happens"—I shuddered, remembering the elemental's proximity—"well, there are ways of making sure I don't actually get or stay pregnant." I didn't feel like getting into logistics with her. "Hopefully, I can just keep up the avoidance, though. I'm not jumping into anyone's bed soon."

Sympathy replaced Maiwenn's doubt. "Yes. I'm truly sorry for what you've endured. It sickens me. I honestly can't imagine it. You've surpassed your fearless reputation. I couldn't have coped so bravely."

I thought again about the terror that had filled me when the elemental had me trapped. The tears. The desperation. I didn't know how brave I'd really been.

Kiyo's eyes met mine then, and while Maiwenn looked distracted with thought, I think he might have glimpsed a little of my emotion. Affection for me burned on his face, and I fell into it. The moment shattered when a loud voice sounded outside my room.

"What the fuck happened in here? No way am I cleaning this up!"

Kiyo straightened up, alarmed, but I waved away his concern. "Don't worry. It's just my housemate."

Sure enough, Tim burst in, outrage written all over him. He wore buckskin pants and a matching vest over his bare chest. Feathers decorated his black hair. Beads ringed his neck. His face fell as soon as he saw me.

"Oh God, Eug. Are you all right?"

I started to give him the "other guy" line, then opted for simplicity. "Fine."

He jerked his thumb behind him. "That room's in pieces."

"I know. Don't worry. I'll clean it up."

"What happened?"

"You're better off not knowing. Tim, this is Kiyo and Maiwenn."

Remembering himself, Tim raised his right hand in a sort of "How, white man" kind of way. "I am Timothy Red Horse. May the Great Spirit smile down upon you." This latter part seemed to be for Maiwenn in particular. She smiled formally. Kiyo appeared to oscillate between hilarity and disgust.

Greetings done, Tim walked over to me, shaking his head ruefully. "You're into some crazy shit."

"You might want to find another place to stay," I said seriously. "I don't think it'll be safe around here."

"Are you kidding? I'm never going to find this good a deal. What's a little death and destruction?"

"Tim—"

His face sobered. "Don't worry, Eug. I know what you do. If things heat up, I'll get out."

"Did you see the living room? That's pretty hot."

"Yeah, but so long as the house is standing . . ."

"You're more difficult than I am." I remembered I was supposed to find a witch to boost the wards around my house. I'd forgotten. Instead, I had created some wards of my own, but they weren't very strong, as evidenced by the recent invasion. A witch couldn't keep everything out but would do a better job than me.

Tim grinned. "Well, let's not get carried away. Anyway. You look like you're in the middle of something. You want anything? Chicken soup? Foot massage?"

"You can get me a Milky Way. And see if my Def Leppard CD survived the war zone."

"Don't get your hopes up on that last one." He said goodbye to the others and left.

"An odd man," mused Maiwenn.

"You have no idea."

Yet, while Tim and I had bantered, I'd noticed Maiwenn and Kiyo speaking quietly to each other in the corner. She had rested a hand on his arm as they talked, and there had been something almost . . . intimate in the way they stood together. Like they were comfortable being in each other's personal space. Very comfortable. I remembered Kiyo's resolute support of her, his claim that he worked with her because he believed in her cause. But was that truly it? Or was there more? She was a "good friend." They stood apart now, but a jealous, ugly feeling kindled in my chest.

She finally turned away from him and gave me a small, tight smile. "I don't mean to be rude, but . . . I'm not feeling well and must return home."

"It's no problem. Thanks for coming, and . . . thank you for healing my mother."

Maiwenn nodded, and I could tell she really was sick. Weariness ringed those lovely eyes. "I'm happy to. And I'm glad we were able to talk. You have no idea how relieved I am to see where you stand. I'll do what I can to keep others from trying to . . . take liberties with you."

Kiyo's fingertips brushed her arm to stop her, and I watched that contact with a critical eye. "Wait for me outside."

She nodded and then swept out of the room in all her golden beauty. Kiyo walked over to my bed and sat down, running a hand along my cheek.

"I'm glad you're okay. When I walked in . . . I thought you were dead."

"I'm hard to kill," I said lightly.

He smiled, shaking his head with exasperation. "I can believe that."

Reaching down, he picked up my hand and brought it to his lips, eyes on mine. He lingered a moment, and my skin burned where he kissed me. Then carefully, gently, he laid my hand back down, lacing his fingers with mine.

"I'm going to make sure she crosses over okay, and then I'll be back to stay with you."

"You gonna take care of me? Massage my feet and feed me chicken soup?"

"Anything you want," he promised. "That's what

friends do." He kissed my hand again and then stood up. "Be back in a few minutes."

I could still feel where he'd kissed me, but for once, my infatuation with him went on hold. I was thinking about the conversation I'd just had. It still bothered me, but I'd meant what I said. Learning gentry magic was about the scariest thing—other than rape by a mud elemental—that I could imagine right now. Yet, I wanted no more storms in my living room, no storms anywhere that I was incapable of controlling.

And for what it was worth, that meant getting a grip on my power. I knew whom I had to go to for that control, and it held its own set of terrors. Necessary evils, though. I had no choice.

So while I waited for Kiyo's return, I began a mental to-do list. Summon Volusian. Plot strategy. Buy high-heeled shoes . . .

Chapter Sixteen

I slept the rest of the day and most of the following one as well. Only the essentials got me out of bed—food, the bathroom, one phone call, and a meeting with Volusian after Kiyo had to leave for Phoenix.

I was dozing around dinnertime that second day when Tim's angry voice in the living room woke me up.

"No! I don't care. She needs to sleep, okay? I'll give her the message, but stop calling."

I'd heard Tim use that tone only on a few people, so I had a good idea whom he spoke to. For whatever reason, despite having never met, he and Lara hated each other. Throwing on my robe, I shuffled out to the living room and saw him talking on my cell phone. The only progress we'd made in cleanup thus far was to sort of clear a walking path through the debris. He pulled the receiver from his face.

"It's that bitch secretary of yours. I wouldn't have answered except that she keeps calling and calling. I told her you can't take—"

I reached for the phone. "It's fine. I need to talk to her."

Glaring, he handed it over.

"Did your asshole roommate just call me a bitch?" demanded Lara. "He has no right—"

"Let it go," I ordered. "Tell me what's up."

"Well, I got your message. Did the shoes show up?"

"Yeah, they're great. What about the witch?"

"I set it up. He's going to come ward the place tonight. He'll need you to let him in."

"No prob. I won't be here, but Tim will."

"Okay, and about the other thing . . ."

"Yeah?"

A long pause. "Well, I don't think I heard that part of the message right. It sounded like you said you needed a dress too."

"I do need a dress."

Silence.

"What's the matter? Didn't I leave you my size?"

"Yeah, you did, it's just that . . . a dress? I mean, you've asked me to get you some pretty crazy stuff before—and I'm still kind of uneasy about that one time with the nitroglycerin—but this is really out there, even for you."

"Oh, stop it. Just take care of this."

I wasn't keen on the dress either, but Volusian had insisted during our earlier bedside strategy session. If things fell into place with Dorian, I'd attending an Otherworldly party on Beltane rather than waiting for an attack back here. Volusian had insisted I start making arrangements. What an age we lived in when spirit minions advised on fashion.

"Any special requirements?"

I considered. "Nothing bridesmaid or prom-ish. Think cocktail party. Simple. But elegant."

"Sexy?"

"Moderately."

"Color?"

"As long as it looks good."

"All right. Got it. I'll have it by next week. Oh, yeah, Wil Delaney called again."

"You don't have to let me know anymore. I sort of take it as a given by now."

"So you don't want to return it?"

"No."

We disconnected, and I hit the shower. Beltane eve, the big night, was fast approaching. Tonight was the warm-up. The night I made my deal with the devil.

After digging out my dusty blow-dryer, I dried and brushed my hair until it gleamed. I didn't usually go for makeup—not having the patience—but a little foundation went a long way to hide the small bruises on my face from yesterday's blowout. I considered mascara superfluous with already dark eyelashes, but when combined with some smoky eye shadow, it did make my eyes look bigger. More lipstick, and I barely recognized myself. I didn't look slutty or anything, but it had certainly been a long time since I'd looked so polished.

I considered a skirt but couldn't go that far. Instead, I opted for tight jeans and the new half-heeled sandals. The tank top I selected was olive green, the same color as my moleskin coat, with thin straps meant to rest slightly off the shoulder. Each strap had a tiny ruffle along its edge, as did the low, cleavage-showing scoop neckline.

Examining my reflection, I couldn't help a wistful sigh. I looked better tonight than I had when I met Kiyo. If only he could see me now.

I spritzed on some Violetta di Parma, grabbed my coat and weapons, and headed for the door. Tim nearly fell out of his chair when he saw me.

"What are you doing? Are you going out? You can't do that! Not after what happened yesterday."

"I'm feeling better," I lied. Actually, it was only partially a lie. Did I feel good? No. Did I feel better than yesterday? Yes.

"You're crazy."

"Sorry. Got business that can't wait."

"Dressed like that?" he asked skeptically.

Ignoring him, I drove out to the gateway in the desert. The transition to the Otherworld was a little rough in light of my weakened physical state, but I managed. Volusian and Nandi waited for me at the crossroads when I arrived. Finn hadn't felt like showing. It was one of the downsides of not having him bound to me. We set out along the road.

Shortly into the walk, I realized wearing heels was the Worst Idea Ever. I took them off and carried them the rest of the way. If I was going to keep seeing Dorian, I would need to leave an anchor at his place to facilitate crossings.

"Don't cross his threshold without asking hospitality first," warned Volusian. "They'll disarm you before you can enter. You don't want to do that without protection."

I agreed, though I didn't like the idea of disarming in the first place.

No one ambushed us this time, and I practically walked up to the gates without incident. The guards recognized me and locked into a defensive stance, weapons drawn.

"Our mistress comes in peace," said Nandi mournfully. "She would speak with the Oak King and ask his hospitality."

"Do you think we're stupid?" asked one of the guards, eyeing me watchfully.

"Not exactly," I said. "But I do think you were here last time and saw that I didn't cause any trouble. Maybe you also noticed I spent a lot of time in your king's bedroom. Trust me, he'll want to see me."

They conferred briefly and finally sent one of their number away. He returned minutes later, granting me admittance and hospitality—once they had indeed disarmed me. They walked me through the same hallway as before but not up to the throne room door. Instead, we wound deeper into the keep until we stood at a set of glass doors leading out to some sort of garden or atrium.

"Our lord is outside," explained one of the guards, about to open the doors.

Volusian blocked his way. "Get a herald to announce her. She's not a prisoner anymore. And use her titles."

The man hesitated, glanced at me, and then called for a herald. Moments later, a stout man dressed head to foot in teal velvet hurried in. He looked at me and swallowed nervously before opening the doors. A handful of elegantly dressed gentry stood out in the gardens, glancing up at our entrance.

"Your majesty, I present Eugenie Markham, called Odile Dark Swan, daughter of Tirigan the Storm King."

I winced. Yikes. I'd had no idea I'd had that much appended to my name now.

The soft conversation dropped. Apparently I should get used to having this effect while attending social events in the Otherworld.

From inside, I had expected a small courtyard type of garden, but this looked like it stretched out indefinitely. The grass was still green, but many of the trees had leaves in orange, yellow, and red. None were the dying brown of late autumn. These showed the perfect, beautiful hues one saw at autumn's finest. Heavy apple trees laden with fruit clustered in corners, and in the air, I could just faintly smell a bonfire and mulling spices. It was earlier in the day here than when I'd left Tucson. The end of the afternoon was giving way to twilight, the sky painted in shades of gold and pink that rivaled the leaves' splendor. Torches on long poles were set up to offer light.

The group parted, and Dorian strode forward. His red hair streamed behind him, and over a simple shirt and pants, he wore a robe-type garment made of wine-colored satin and gold brocade. I approached him, and we met in the middle. My spirits waited near the doorway.

"My, my. What a lovely surprise. I didn't think I'd see you again so soon."

Dorian reached for my hand, and this time I let him take it. A flicker of mischievous amusement glinted in his eyes at this small concession, and I knew I had already piqued his curiosity.

"I hope you don't mind me dropping in like this."

He kissed my hand, just as Kiyo had yesterday. Only Dorian's kiss was less of a *hope you get better* kiss and more of an *imagine my lips in other places* kind of kiss.

"Not at all." He drew his lips back and laced his fingers with mine. "Come. Join us."

I recognized a couple of the gentry standing there from dinner. The other two people hanging around looked like servants, waiting anxiously with long mallet-type things in their hands. I peered at them, then at the wickets spread out in the grass.

"Croquet? You're playing croquet?"

Dorian's face broke into a grin. "Yes. Do you play?"

"Not in years." The gentry played croquet? Who knew? I supposed it was technologically simple as far as games went. It made more sense for them to play that than video games.

"Would you like to now?"

I shook my head. "You're already in the middle of something. I'll just watch."

"As you like."

He took a proffered stick from one of the servants. Watching him line up a shot, I could see he intended to hit his ball and knock out an opponent's near a wicket. A faint breeze ruffled his hair and the folds of his robe, and he had to take a moment to brush the fabric out of his way. When he finally hit his ball, it went wide, considerably away from his opponent's ball.

"Ah, well. It was close. I nearly had it, don't you think so, Muran?"

Muran, a lanky guy dressed in lavender, jumped at being addressed. "Er, uh, y-y-yes, your majesty. Very close. You were almost there."

Dorian rolled his eyes. "No, I wasn't. It was an

abominable shot, you wretched man. Let Lady Markham have your turn. Give her your mallet."

Now I jumped. *Lady* Markham?

But the aforementioned Muran practically shoved the thing at me. Hesitantly, I approached his ball. I was pretty sure I'd been ten the last time I'd played, off visiting one of my mom's aunts in Virginia.

Remembering Dorian's hang-ups on his robe, I paused to slip off my coat. A servant immediately raced over to take it from me, folding it neatly over his arms. I turned back to the ball and mallet, sizing up the shot. I tossed my hair back over one shoulder and hit. The ball half-skittered, half-rolled through the grass and went through one of the wickets.

"Exquisite," I heard Dorian say.

I glanced back at him but saw he wasn't watching the ball at all. His eyes were all over me. I tried to return the mallet to poor Muran, but Dorian wouldn't hear of it. He made me finish the game in Muran's stead. As we played, I immediately picked up on something peculiar.

Dorian was a terrible player—too terrible to be real. He was obviously faking it, but his subjects could not bring themselves to do better than their king. So they too faked their own sort of appalling game play. Watching it was comical. I felt like I was in a scene from *Alice in Wonderland*. Having no such qualms about winning, I played normally, and even with aching muscles and no practice, I won pretty handily.

Dorian couldn't have been happier. He clasped his hands together, laughing. "Oh, outstanding. This is the best game I've played in years. These sheep won't know what to do now." He glanced at his fellow players and beckoned them toward the building. "Go, go, your shepherd is tired of you all."

I watched them go. "You don't really treat them . . . respectfully."

"Because they deserve none. Did you see the preposterous way they acted in that game? Now imagine that happening every second, every day of your life. That's what it's like to be royalty, to live at court among courtiers. Be happy you have no true throne yet. It's all simpering and groupthink."

I almost heard a touch of bitterness in his light voice. Almost.

A servant handed my coat back, and Dorian addressed her and a couple of guards. "Lady Markham and I are going to take a walk now through the eastern orchard. Seeing as she's dressed for business, I imagine she wants to speak alone. Follow, but keep your distance."

Turning, he offered me his arm again and led me off into one of the garden's winding turns, into a dense apple orchard. Like the other trees I'd seen, these were filled with fruit. Still more apples lay on the ground, round and red and waiting to be eaten.

When we were sufficiently alone, I said, "I'm not dressed for business, not in these shoes. I was dressed for business the last time I was here."

He gave me a sidelong look. "Women who show up looking as lovely as you do after barely stomaching my presence last time do not come on pleasure. They come for business."

"You're a cynic."

"A pragmatist. But, business or pleasure, it becomes you." He sighed happily. "I do so wish more of our women would wear pants like those. The warriors often do but not nearly so tight."

"Thanks . . . I think."

We walked on at a leisurely pace while the sky turned orange and scarlet.

"So I imagine you've changed in other ways since our last encounter. The very fact that you've come here so congenially indicates as much."

"Yes." I narrowed my eyes. "You know, I don't appreciate you telling me that Storm King bedtime story when all the time you knew I didn't know what was going on."

"Mean, perhaps. But also amusing—were you in my place. Besides, I did you a service of sorts. I provided necessary background information, Lady Markham."

"Don't say 'Lady Markham.' It sounds weird."

"I've got to call you something. Our normal rules of etiquette don't exactly outline anything for your situation. You are the daughter of a king without a kingdom. You are royalty but not quite royal. So you are addressed like a noble."

"Well, then, only use it in public. Or stick to 'Odile.'"

"What about 'Eugenie'?"

"Fine."

Silence fell between us. The orchard seemed to go on forever.

"Do you want to tell me why you're here yet? Or should I think up some other pleasantries to discuss?"

I repressed a laugh. Dorian played flamboyant and scattered, but he wasn't a fool.

"I need a favor."

"Ah, so it is business after all."

I stopped walking, and he stopped with me. Looking down at me, he waited patiently, his face pleasantly neutral. I shivered as another breeze stole through, and he took my coat from me, helping me slip it on.

I wrapped my arms around myself, grateful for the coat's warmth. Sexy was cold.

"I conjured a storm yesterday."

"Did you now?" His voice held less levity and more calculation. "What happened?"

I told him the story, just as I had for Maiwenn and Kiyo.

"What were you thinking when it happened?"

At first, I thought he was chastising me. Sort of like when you do something stupid and your mom asks, *Are you insane? What were you thinking?*

"Like how I felt? What was going through my head?"
He nodded.

"I don't know. I guess I went through a lot of moods. When it all started . . . I mean, I felt the same as for any other attack. Planned out what I would do, focused for a banishing. But once my mom got involved . . . I started to lose it."

"And when Corwyn had you trapped?"

"Who?"

"The elemental. He was one of Aeson's men. The spirits you banished came back telling tales, though admittedly, no one's heard this part, seeing as you didn't leave any witnesses."

"I felt . . . scared. Weak. Defenseless."

"You don't strike me as someone who's scared a lot."

"No, actually. I'm scared all the time. Stupid not to be. What's that saying? Only the dead are without fear? Or is that hope? Dunno. At that point, I sure as hell didn't have any hope either. I felt like I was out of options."

"And so you chose the only option left to you."

"I didn't choose it exactly. Not consciously."

"No. But sometimes our souls and the secret parts of our minds know what we need."

He walked over to a large, sheltering maple tree. Presumably it too had those wonderful colors, but the near-darkness made such things impossible to see. Taking off his robe, he spread it on the ground and sat down, leaving space beside him. A moment later, I sat down as well.

"So what have you come to ask me, Eugenie Markham?"

"You already know. I can hear it in your voice."

"Hmm. So much for crafty subterfuge."

"I need you to teach me how to use the magic. So it doesn't take over again. I don't want to kill someone the next time I freak out."

"Or," he added, "you just might want to kill someone with it. On purpose, that is."

"Maybe." I shivered. "I don't know."

He didn't speak right away. The darkness around us grew deeper.

"What you did to Corwyn was akin to using a brick to swat a fly when much finer, much simpler methods would suffice. The storms you can conjure are great and powerful things, absolutely. The gods know your father made effective use of them. But I think you'll find your real power is in controlling the storm's finer elements. A child can throw paint on a canvas; a master works with fine brushstrokes. You learn the small things, and then the storms will be second nature."

I took a deep breath. "So can you teach me? *Will* you teach me?"

Even in the dark, I knew he had that laconic smile on his face. "If someone had told me during our last meeting that we'd have this conversation, I would have flogged him for insolence."

"I don't have anyone else to go to. Maiwenn offered, but she doesn't have—"

"Maiwenn?" he interrupted. His tone startled me. "When did you talk to her?"

"After the attack." I explained the circumstances of our meeting. When he didn't respond, I grew defensive. "There's nothing wrong with that. If anything, it's kind of nice to have someone on my side who doesn't want to see me get pregnant and take over the world."

"And for that very reason, you shouldn't trust her. I want to see Storm King's heir born. Therefore, I have good reason to make sure you stay alive. She does not."

I remembered thinking how Maiwenn would have had a lot less to worry about had I died in the attack.

"She didn't seem so sinister," I replied haltingly, suddenly struck by a thought. If Maiwenn's noble philosophy involved killing me, then would Kiyo follow her in that?

"The sinister ones never do."

"You're just trying to sway me to your side."

"Well, of course. I'd be trying to do that regardless of her involvement."

I sighed. It was all plots and posturing after all. Above all else, Dorian was still one of the gentry. "Maybe coming here was a mistake."

"Coming here was the smartest thing you've done so far. So tell me, what will you give me for teaching you to control your power?"

"You can't get something for nothing, huh?"

"Oh, please. Don't sound so superior. I helped you last time without asking anything in return, and now here you are again asking more of me. You demand a lot of the gentry you consider so greedy."

"Fair enough." I leaned against the tree a little. "If you'll help me . . . I'll let . . . I'll let people think we're, you know . . ."

There was a pause, and then his warm laughter filled the orchard. "Sleeping together? Oh, you really have made my night. That's not fair. Not fair at all."

I blushed furiously in the dark. "You'll one-up Aeson. He'll think I'm willingly giving you what he tried to take by force."

"And all the while, I'll actually be getting nothing except tantalizing glimpses of you in outfits like this."

"I'll cover up more if it makes a difference."

"What would make a difference is if you were sleeping with me for real."

"That's not fair either. Not for a few magic lessons."

"'A few'?" He laughed again, his voice carrying the kind of incredulity that seemed to amuse rather than upset him. Jesus. Did nothing bother this guy? "My dear, it's going to take more than 'a few' lessons to quell that storm in you, pun intended. Especially with your temper. It's going to make focus hard."

I felt indignant. "Hey, I've been focusing since I was a

kid. I can clear my mind in the middle of a fight to banish spirits. I go to trance in seconds."

"Perhaps," he conceded grudgingly. "But I'm still not sure this is fair. You'll be getting more than lessons. Assuming you are my 'lover,' people will be hesitant to assault you. You'll find your status soaring."

"Christ. Nothing gets past you, does it? Apparently Volusian and I have a lot more to learn about subterfuge too."

"Who?"

"My servant."

"Ah. The sullen one with red eyes?"

"Yes."

He made a disapproving click with his tongue. "He's both dangerous and powerful. You're brave to keep him."

"I know. I couldn't send him to the Underworld, so I bound him to me."

"If I helped you, we could probably send him on."

The thought astonished me. With Volusian securely in the world of death, I'd probably be a lot safer.

As though reading my mind, Dorian added, "Things will get nasty if he ever breaks loose on you."

"I know. He tells me on a regular basis—in graphic detail. Still . . . he's been useful. I think I'll keep him around for a while."

We sat quietly in the darkness again. I realized it must be getting past the castle's dinner hour. Part of the reason for showing up at this time had been to get invited to dinner. With gentry pride in hospitality, Volusian had thought it would please Dorian to show off his resources, especially since being half-gentry meant I could safely eat in this world now. Finally, a legitimate perk to all this insanity. I half-smiled imagining a hall full of hungry gentry, pounding their silverware on the table. With the way everyone danced around Dorian's moods, however, I had no doubt they'd wait hours if need be.

"If you're going to pretend to be my lover, it will involve more than just say-so. You've seen how free we are with our affections in public. If you keep ten feet away from me, no one's going to believe it."

I froze, suddenly remembering that other dinner. I hadn't entirely considered the implications.

He chuckled softly, a low and dangerous sound beside me. "Oh, yes, you didn't think about that, did you?"

He was right. I'd figured Dorian and me disappearing into his bedroom for lessons would be convincing enough. But now I had to picture sitting on his lap, letting him touch me and kiss me. I had trouble with the image. He was one of the gentry, the beings I'd hitherto kept a wary eye on and tracked down my whole life. Discovering Kiyo's true nature had been a shock to my system, one I was slowly starting to reconcile. How could I handle someone who was completely of the Otherworld?

Yet . . . the more I hung around Dorian, the easier it became to think of him as just a person. Weird or not, there was something comfortable about being with him. So, yeah. I could handle this. Maybe. It was just a little making out, right? It wasn't sex. And wasn't it a small thing to ensure I didn't tear anyone else apart inadvertently?

"I'm not going down on you or anything," I warned, using flippancy to cover my discomfort.

He laughed again. "As saddening as that is, it might actually be too much. You're human enough that they'll expect some modesty."

Small blessings. "All right. I'll hold up my half if you hold up your half."

"Well, in distribution, I think I'm actually doing three-quarters of the work here. But yes, I'll do the same. Shall we shake on it? Isn't that how you humans seal a deal?"

I extended my hand in the darkness, and he took it. Suddenly, he pulled me to him and kissed me. I immediately pulled back, aghast.

"Hey!"

"What? You don't expect to have our first kiss in public, do you? We want to be convincing, remember?"

"You're a sleazy bastard, you know that?"

"If you truly believe that, then maybe you'll feel better finding another teacher."

I thought about that. Then I leaned forward and tried to find his lips in the darkness. I didn't realize I was shaking until his hands gripped my arms.

"Relax, Eugenie. This won't hurt."

I took a deep breath and calmed myself. Our lips found each other. His reminded me of flower petals, soft and velvety. Whereas Kiyo was all about animal passion and aggression, Dorian seemed more about . . . precision. I suddenly remembered his metaphor about the difference between slapping paint on a canvas and fine brushstrokes.

Don't get me wrong, Dorian wasn't exactly sweet and chaste. There was heat in those soft lips. He seemed to want to draw out the experience, almost in a taunting way, so much so that I found myself impatient and eager when his tongue finally darted in between my lips. He pushed it farther into my mouth, the rest of the kiss intensifying. He smelled like cinnamon and cider, like all the good things in an autumn night. Finally, he pulled away.

"You're still afraid of me," he noted, amused by that fact just like everything else. "Your body still won't relax."

"Yes." I swallowed. It had felt good, the kind of good that sends heat down your body and makes your toes—and other parts—curl. But my fear had underscored it all, that fear of gentry and otherness that I still couldn't quite shake. It was a weird combination, physical pleasure mingling with fear. Very different from the way it was with Kiyo—physical pleasure mixed with a larger, all-encompassing sense of chemistry and mutual affection, despite my unease over his half-kitsune heritage. "I can't help it. This is all still strange for me. Part of me says it's wrong. It's hard to change what I've always believed overnight, you know."

"Do you want to go back on the deal?"

I shook my head. "I don't go back on my deals."

I could feel him smiling in the darkness. He leaned over and kissed me again.

Chapter Seventeen

To his credit, he didn't really manhandle me too badly that night. At dinner, he kept a hand on mine or an arm around my shoulder but little more than that. As he pointed out to me in a quiet moment, anyone could make a brazen display of fleshiness. What really indicated intimacy was how two people interacted with each other, what their body language said. So I worked on looking comfortable and happy in his presence, and from the shocked expressions on people's faces, we must have done a pretty convincing job.

He took me to his bedroom after that, looking smug and presumptuous to those watching. But when we got there, he actually gave me my first lesson. Honestly, it was a bit disappointing. I'd been ready for fireworks. What I got was a lot of practice on quiet meditation and focus. He claimed if I couldn't control my own mind, I couldn't control the power.

So I spent the next couple hours with him working on this and found my most difficult challenge was in not slipping into trance or astral travel. Those behaviors came so automatically to me in still moments that I kept lapsing. The kind of meditation he wanted me to do involved turning my senses outward rather than inward, which seemed strange to me since I had thought magic came from within.

We finally ended the lesson with him giving me a heavy gold ring that he'd put part of his essence into. It was an anchor. Now if he left the Otherworld through a thin spot, he could transition to mine without appearing in a corresponding thin spot. He would simply travel to wherever the ring was. It would save both of us extraneous travel time.

What it also meant was that he planned on coming to my world for some of the lessons. I had mixed feelings on this. Certainly it would be more convenient for me. But the fact that he could even jump with an anchor like that indicated how powerful he was. That realization was just a teensy bit unsettling, as was the thought of him in the human world at all. And yet, by being there, his powers would diminish. He would be safer—or rather, humanity would be safer.

Back home, the following couple of days were more of the same: fights, fights, and more fights. Yet, as Dorian had predicted, some of the traffic dried up. I liked to think this was because my reputation was scaring would-be suitors away. More likely, my new connection to the Oak King made my assailants think twice about incurring political fallout.

As it turned out, I had to deal with my own share of fallout over this alliance—from Kiyo.

"Are you sleeping with Dorian?"

He stood in my doorway, his dark hair backlit by the late afternoon sun. He wore a white lab coat with KIYOTAKA MARQUEZ, DVM on the pocket. He must have driven here straight from work.

"Good news travels fast," I said. "Come on in."

I offered him a drink and a seat at my kitchen table, but he just kept pacing around restlessly. He reminded me of a wolf or a guard dog. I didn't really know anything about fox behavior.

"Well?" he asked.

I poured myself a cup of coffee and gave him a sharp look. "Don't take that tone with me. You have no claims to what I do."

He stopped pacing, and his expression softened. "You're right. I don't."

It wasn't exactly an apology, but it was close. I sat down in a chair, folding my legs up underneath me. "All right, then. No. I'm not sleeping with him."

His face stayed the same, but I saw visible relief flash in his eyes. It was petty, I realized, but knowing he'd been jealous made something warm flutter up inside of me.

Grabbing a chair, he turned it around and sat down so that his chin rested on its back. "Then what's up with the stories?"

I told him. When I'd finished, he closed his eyes and exhaled. A moment later, he opened them.

"I don't know what bothers me more. You turning to magic or you turning to Dorian."

I beckoned behind me. "Have you seen my living room? I am not going to be responsible for inflicting Hurricane Eugenie on Tucson."

That made him smile. "Tucson already deals with Hurricane Eugenie on a regular basis. But yeah, I get your point. What worries me . . . I don't know. I don't really use magic, but I've spent half my life around people who do. I've seen how it affects them. How it can control them."

"Are you questioning my self-control? Or my strength?"

"No," he replied in all seriousness. "You're one of the strongest people I know. But Storm King . . . I saw him once when I was little. He was . . . well, let's put it this way. Dorian and Aeson and Maiwenn are strong. Compared to other gentry, they're like torches beside candles. But your father . . . he was more like a bonfire. You can't use that kind of power and walk away unscathed."

"I appreciate the warning, Gandalf, but I don't know that I have a choice."

"I guess not. I just don't want to see you changed, that's all. I like you the way you are." A smile flickered across his lips and then faded. "And as for working with Dorian . . . well, that just makes the situation worse."

"You sound jealous."

"Of course." He answered without hesitation, not really ashamed to fess up to his feelings. "But he's power-hungry too. *And* he wants to see the Storm King conquest happen. Somehow I doubt he'll be content to have you be his pretend-lover for long."

"Well, hey, remember I've got a choice in there too. Besides, contraceptive technology is a wonderful thing, right?"

"Absolutely. But Maiwenn says—"

"I know, I know. All sorts of wise and compelling things."

Kiyo eyed me warily. "What's that supposed to mean?"

"Nothing. Just that I think it's funny for you to talk to me about Dorian when—"

"When what?"

I set down my cup of coffee and looked him in the eye. "Honesty again?"

He returned my stare unblinkingly. "Always."

"You two seemed . . . more than chummy. Is there anything going on between you? Romantically, I mean?"

"No." The answer came swift and certain.

I reconsidered. "*Was* there anything going on?"

This got a hesitation. "Not anymore," he said after a moment.

"I see." I looked away and felt my own wave of jealousy run through me as my cruel mind pictured him and that beautiful woman together.

"It's over, Eugenie. Has been for a while. We're just friends now, that's it."

I glanced up. "Like you and I are friends?"

His lips turned up wickedly, and I saw the temperature in his eyes dial up a few degrees. "You can call it whatever you want, but I think we both know we aren't 'just friends.'"

No, I supposed not. And suddenly, after so much time with him and the fact that I'd made out with a full-fledged gentry, Kiyo being a kitsune wasn't really a problem anymore. The lines that organized my life had all blurred. That scared me because I wanted Kiyo, and suddenly I had no excuses standing in my way. And honestly, I realized, it was a lot easier having excuses. Excuses meant you didn't have to work or open yourself to someone else and be vulnerable. If I really wanted to be near and with Kiyo now, I was going to have to look beyond sex. Sex was easy—especially with him. What was going to be hard was remembering how to get close to someone and trust him.

I looked away, not wanting him to see the fear on my face, but he already had. I don't know what it was about him, but sometimes he seemed to know me better than I knew myself.

He stood up and moved behind me, his hands kneading the kinks in my neck and shoulders. "Eugenie," was all he said, voice warm.

I relaxed into him and closed my eyes. "I don't know how to do this." I referred to him and me, but considering the rest of my life, that statement could have applied to any number of things.

"Well, we stop fighting, for one. Let's drop this other stuff and go out."

"Now? Like on a date?"

"Sure."

"Just like that? Is it that easy?"

"For now. And really, it's only as easy or hard as we choose to make it."

We took Kiyo's car, a pretty sweet 1969 Spider, to one of my favorite restaurants: Indian Cuisine of India. The name sounded redundant, but the latter part of it had been a necessary addition. Considering all the local restaurants that served Southwest and American Indian cuisine, a lot of tourists had come in expecting to find Navajo fry bread, not curry and naan.

The tension melted between us—the hostile kind, at least—though he did have one pensive moment in which he asked, "All right, I have to know. Is it true you kissed him?"

I smiled enigmatically. "This is as easy or hard as we choose to make it."

He sighed.

After dinner, he drove us out of town but wouldn't say where we were going. Almost forty minutes later, we were driving up and around a large hill. Kiyo found an area with other cars but saw there were no spots left, forcing him to drive back down and park a considerable distance away. Twilight was giving way to full night, and it was hard to find the path up the hill with no lighting. He slipped his hand in mine, guiding me. His fingers were warm, his grip tight and secure.

It took us almost a half hour, walking until the path finally crested to a small clearing. I hid my astonishment. It was filled with people, most of whom were setting up telescopes and peering up at the clear, star-thickened sky.

"I saw this advertised in the paper," Kiyo explained. "It's the amateur astronomy group. They let the public come out and hang with them."

Sure enough, everyone there was more than happy to let us come and look through their telescopes. They pointed out sights of particular interest and told stories about constellations. I'd heard a lot of them before but enjoyed hearing them again.

The weather was perfect for this kind of thing. Warm enough to not need jackets (though I still wore one to hide weapons) and so perfectly clear that you could forget pollution existed. The Flandrau Observatory, over at the university, had fantastic shows, but I loved the casual nature of this one.

While listening to an older man talk about the Andromeda galaxy, I thought about just how vast our existence really was. There was so much of it we didn't know about. The outer world, the universe, spread on forever. For all I knew, the inner world of spirits continued on just as far. I only knew about three worlds: the world we lived in, the world the dead lived in, and the Otherworld, which caught everything in between. A lot of shamans believed the divine world was beyond all of this, a world of God or gods we couldn't even imagine. Looking up at that snowstorm of stars, I suddenly felt very small in the greater scheme of things, prophecy or no.

Kiyo shifted beside me, and I felt his arm brush mine. My body kept an exact record of where we touched, like some sort of military tracking system. He caught my eye, and we smiled at each other. I felt at peace, almost deliriously happy. For this moment, all was right in the world between us. Maybe I'd never fully understand what pulled two people together. Maybe it was like trying to comprehend the universe. You couldn't measure any of it. It just was, and you made your way through it as best you could.

"Thank you," I told him later, as we walked back down the hill toward the car. "That was really great."

"I saw the telescope at your house—er, what was left of it anyway."

"Oh. Yeah." Being up here had sort of taken me away from reality. I'd forgotten that my home was in a state of disaster. "Mine couldn't really compare to any of these. Maybe I'll have to upgrade now."

We passed the other cars and finally finished the long trek back out to his car. The temperature had cooled down a little, but it was still nice out. Kiyo wrinkled his nose as we walked.

"Smells like . . . dead fish out here."

I inhaled deeply. "I don't smell anything."

"Consider yourself lucky. You probably couldn't smell how many people hadn't showered back there either."

I laughed. "I remember how you smelled my perfume back in the bar that night. I thought it was crazy. So super-smell is another kitsune perk?"

He shook his head. "Depends on what you're smelling."

We got into the car. He started to put the keys in the ignition, then decided he wanted his coat.

"Can you reach it? It's behind my seat."

I unfastened my belt and shifted around, practically hanging through the seats to reach his coat. It was crumpled and lying on the floor.

"Jesus," I heard him say.

"Are you staring at my ass?"

"It's practically in my face."

I snagged the troublesome coat and leaned back, but his arm caught me and pulled me onto his lap. It twisted me in an awkward position, and I squirmed to straighten out my legs. I finally ended up sort of straddling him.

"I can't believe you lectured me earlier about the dangers of losing control," I chastised. His hands had slid down to the ass he so admired.

"What was I supposed to do?"

"Hey, I'm not complaining. Just surprised, that's all."

"I think it's the fox in me."

"Never heard that excuse before."

"No, it's true. You'd be amazed how simple the instincts are—and how strong. Sometimes I have to fight to not jump every woman I see. And then I always want to eat. Like I have this paranoid fear if I don't stock up now, I could be starving later when winter comes. It's really weird."

It was compelling too, but wrapped up against him, I realized this conversation was wasting perfectly good make-out time. I unfastened his seat belt and then put my hands palm down on his chest. Leaning forward, I kissed him, pushing myself harder into his lap. His grip on me tightened.

"I thought you didn't want to get involved with a kit-sune."

"Well . . . I happen to think foxes are cute."

I wriggled out of my coat and then pulled off the tank top underneath, neither of which was easy to do with the steering wheel behind me. I rose up on my knees a little, putting my breasts near his face. His mouth showered my cleavage with kisses while his hands tried to undo the bra.

Meanwhile, my own hands unfastened the button on his pants. I reached down and slid my hand into his boxers.

"Eugenie . . ." he breathed. He managed to combine a cautionary tone with an utterly turned-on one. "We don't have condoms."

I moved my hand farther, suddenly very turned on myself by the thought of having nothing between us. "The pill, remember? Besides, contraceptive technology is a—"

The car suddenly lurched dangerously onto the side we weren't sitting on. My back jammed into the steering wheel, and we half-tumbled onto the other side. Kiyo's arms went around me, pulling me toward him in an effort to shelter me with his body and keep me from falling. Guess I shouldn't have undone his seat belt earlier. Fortunately, the car didn't flip all the way over, and a moment later, it slammed back down on the side we were sitting on with a jaw-rattling crash.

"What the—" I began.

In the dark, I could just barely discern Kiyo's wide eyes staring beyond me, through the windshield. "I think we should get out of the car," he said quietly, just as something heavy and solid slammed down on the hood behind me. I heard headlights smash. The entire car shook.

I didn't need to be told twice. We kicked open the driver's side door, and I scrambled out. A smell like rotting fish slammed into me. Kiyo started to follow me out, and then the car was lifted up from its front end and slammed back down to the ground. Glass and metal crunched as the motion tossed Kiyo back in the car. The windshield cracked like a spider's web.

Fear for him shot through me, but then I finally saw the culprit, and fear for me shot through me.

It looked like one of the fuaths, I thought. A fachan, possibly. If so, he was far from home since they were native to Ireland and Scotland. Still, the Otherworld had become as global as the human world, and you never really knew what could pop up where.

He looked like something you might get if Bigfoot had sex with a cyclops and then their offspring moved to the Deep South and interbred for another century or so. He was almost eight feet tall and every part of his grossly muscled body was covered with hair—matted and smelly hair that needed a thorough washing. One giant eye, its color indeterminable in the starlight, peered out at me. One extra hand extended weirdly from the right side of its chest, and an extra leg hung off of its hip. The leg didn't seem to help him walk; I wondered if it and the extra arm did anything at all or were just used for effect.

Seeing me, he left the car alone and started lumbering forward. Hopefully Kiyo would be able to get out now. I reached for my gun and discovered it was gone. Son of a bitch. It had slipped its holster either from grappling with Kiyo or when the car had tipped.

"Get my gun out!" I yelled back toward the car.

Meanwhile, I took a few cautious steps back, assessing how to handle the fachan. Fachans, despite inhabiting the earth, originated in the Otherworld. They could therefore be banished back there. They also crossed to this world in a physical form, which meant they could be killed. I had both athames in my belt. Silver would be more effective, but iron would probably do some damage too. Okay. I just had to manage one of those while keeping it from getting too fresh with me. No problem.

He swung one of his long, almost awkward-looking arms at me, and I intercepted it, stabbing him in the hand with the silver athame. I pushed as hard as I could, shoving through tendons and bones. The creature shrieked and jerked his hand back. My hand was on the hilt, but he moved too quickly, too strongly. He took the athame with him. Shit.

"Kiyo!" I yelled.

I took out the iron athame and darted over to his right side, opposite the car. The fachan was bigger, but I was smaller and therefore faster . . . right? My blade snaked out, digging deep into the soft flesh of his stomach. This time I made sure to bring the athame back with me before he moved and took this one too. Blood, looking black in the dim lighting, gleamed where I'd cut. I put some distance between us. I just needed to slow him so I could snag a few moments for the banishing.

But he wasn't slowing. He hadn't seemed happy about the injuries, but he still kept coming for me. I kept the distance between us, wanting to injure him without getting within his range. It was kind of hard when it felt like his arms were as long as my body.

He swung out his uninjured fist, and I ducked it, using the opportunity to draw blood again. As I did, something occurred to me. His blow, had it landed, would have done some serious damage. Very serious. It had had no purpose, save to inflict as much brute pain as possible. I could understand the tactical advantage of rendering me unconscious before sex, but being in a coma—or dead—might complicate the prophecy a bit.

My blade bit into him again, and I followed with a sharp kick to his side, dodging at the last minute. We soon developed a little dance. His large, muscled arms would swing out at me, and I would sidestep and get in my slash or kick. Considering my fight with the mud el-

emental had been two days ago and I wasn't entirely in
peak condition yet, I felt my performance here wasn't
too shabby.

At least until I moved too slowly, and he caught me
with the edge of his hand—his extra hand. Apparently it
wasn't useless after all.

It was a glancing blow, but I flew backward, into the car,
up onto the roof, and into the windshield. The glass—
already cracked and fractured—shattered upon impact,
and sharp, excruciating pain burned through the side of
my stomach as I hit. The skin there was still bare and uncovered from where I'd stripped in the car. My head felt
like a cartoon character had just dropped an anvil on it,
and for a few seconds, I couldn't get my body to do the
things I wanted it to do.

The fachan lurched toward me, his limbs and their
bulging muscles swinging, and I didn't have anywhere to
go. He grabbed me by my shoulders and lifted me up
high. I knew in those slow-motion seconds that he was
going to slam me down and that I would be dead. As it
was, the jerking, lifting motion alone made my addled
brain scream.

Suddenly, the fachan's head tipped back, and a look
of agony crossed his face. His hold on me released, and
I dropped back to the hood. It was much less painful
than what he'd been about to do, but it still hurt. I frantically tried to sit up and see what had happened, but
everything spun.

Some wolf was attacking the fachan. No, no wolf. The
colors and shape weren't quite right. The ears were
more defined, the tail haughty and white-tipped. It was
a fox. It was Kiyo. But he was bigger than I'd ever seen
him, which was why I'd mistaken him for a wolf. He was
huge, muscled and powerful, and his teeth were tearing into the fachan's back.

The fachan turned and swatted him away. Kiyo took it

with grace: hitting, rolling, and then getting right back up. I wished I could do that.

I still felt like crap, but my vision had righted itself. Peering into the car, I could see where my gun had rolled across the passenger seat and lodged between it and the door. Beyond me, I heard blows and yips as Kiyo and the fachan continued their fight.

Gingerly, I started crawling back into the car on all fours, careful to avoid the shards of glass ringing the gaping remains of the windshield. I didn't do a very good job and brushed sharp points in a few places. They stung my skin. Worse, I could do little to protect my hands when forced to creep over the broken shards covering the dashboard.

At last I made it inside and retrieved the gun. Grabbing it, I worked my way back to the driver's side seat and took aim at the fachan still grappling with Kiyo. Only, my hand could barely hold the gun up. That was no good. I shifted and held the Glock two-handed. My arms still shook, but I was steadier now.

I watched them pace and attack each other, moving fast. Too fast, I worried. I was likely to shoot Kiyo in the process. But I had to try. Nothing was hurting this thing. It was unstoppable. I didn't want to try to banish it at full strength, particularly since I'd never get close enough to put the death symbol on him and speed his passage. I therefore needed him wounded and easy to send over.

Taking aim, I waited for a window of opportunity, for a broad target on the fachan. There. The bullet bit into his back, and he jerked in surprise. It slowed him just enough. I fired again. I kept firing until I'd unloaded the entire clip into him. He made horrible noises and staggered slightly. I half-expected him to keep coming, but then Kiyo the Giant Fox leaped at his chest and knocked him to the ground, teeth tearing into what appeared to be the fachan's throat. Ew.

My wand was in the car. I swapped it with the gun, and

called upon Hecate, focusing on the snake wound around my arm. My mind slipped this world, opening the gates, and I aimed for the fachan's spirit. My will, pouring through the wand, seized him and ripped a hole between the Otherworld and my world. It was harder than usual. "Mind over matter" might be the adage, but the mind was reluctant to obey when the body was so weakened and had had its head slammed into a windshield.

My path to the Otherworld was clear. But then, seeing him start to get up, despite Kiyo's mauling, I decided I didn't want him potentially coming back. So I pushed my mind past the Otherworld, brushing the gates of the world of death instead. I felt Persephone's butterfly flare on my arm as I connected with her domain. The fachan roared as it recognized the tug. He resisted me, his body and spirit presenting a formidable match for my own.

I focused harder, pushing every ounce of me into forcing him through the black gates. I called on—no, I begged—Persephone to take him.

At last he went through, his physical body disintegrating as the Underworld sucked his spirit through.

Only it was pulling more than him through.

I'd pushed so hard that my spirit had touched more of the world of death than I normally allowed. In my weakened state, my focus wasn't as sharp about keeping me out. My mind felt like it was being sucked in by a whirlwind, and I had the impression of ghostly, skeletal hands pulling at me.

"No, no, no, no!" Whether the words were in my head or on my lips, I didn't know.

I struggled against the hands, trying to gain a grip on the human world. I would have even settled for the Otherworld. There I could survive, but from the world of death, there was no return. Half of me prayed to Hecate to pull me back through the gates while the other half of me prayed to Persephone to block me out.

At last I fell back with a snap, my spirit returning firmly to my physical body. My physical and mental senses burned. Almost immediately, I slumped forward, unable to support myself. Only my hand on the edge of the steering wheel caught me from falling out of the car.

I felt nauseated and dizzy, with too many parts of me hurting to count. Kiyo, still as that giant fox, stood by me, gleaming eyes watching me with all seriousness.

"Hey," I said, reaching out a tentative hand. His fur was as soft as silk. I stroked it carefully, my motor control still not all it could be. Those fine hairs touched my skin like the lightest of kisses. "That was some trick. How'd you do it?"

He neither answered nor changed shape, merely nuzzling my hand with his nose. I smiled but then felt too tired to keep holding my arm up. I dropped the hand to my side, feeling something wet and sticky. Pulling my arm up, I saw blood covering my fingers, dark and glistening.

"Oh, man," I muttered. The world had started spinning again; black spots danced in front of me. "We need to . . . go . . . somewhere. Do something. Change back; I can't drive."

He kept watching me, eyes solemn and intent.

"I mean it. Why aren't you changing? Are you hurt?"

He rested his chin on my knees, and I petted him again, even though I got blood on that gleaming fur. I didn't get why he wasn't changing. Could he not hear me in this form? No, he'd always understood before.

Well, if he wasn't going to help, I needed someone who could. I had a cell phone in the car somewhere. I could call Roland or Tim. But where was the phone? I couldn't climb in the backseat, not in this shape. Could foxes fetch?

Maybe I could summon a spirit for help. Not Volusian, not like this. But maybe Finn? What were the words? How did I call him? It was suddenly too hard to think.

"Help me . . ." I whispered to Kiyo. "Why won't you help me?"

White spots now danced with the black ones. I closed my eyes, and it felt better.

"I'm going to lie down," I told him, stretching back. "Just for a minute, okay?" I rested my head on the passenger seat, lying perpendicular to the seats.

I heard a soft, almost doglike whine. He must have stood on his hind legs, because I next felt paws and a head resting near my knee.

"Why won't you help me?" I asked again, feeling tears spill out of my eyes. "I need you."

I heard the whine again, mournful and contrite. My hand reached out, grasping for soft fur. I clutched the strands as though they alone could keep me alive. Then, my fingers lost their grip and slipped away as my hand dropped.

Chapter Eighteen

It was like déjà vu. Two fights, two blackouts, and two "mornings after" back in my own bed. Talk about tedious.

Only this time, I wasn't alone in bed. I knew Kiyo was with me even before I opened my eyes. I recognized his smell, the way his arms wrapped around me. They held me with delicacy now, not with the fierceness that usually seized him.

"You don't quit," I murmured, blinking the sleep out of my eyes. "Even wounded, you're still trying to get me back in bed."

"I've already got you here." He lay on his side, his eyes staring into mine. Smiling, he ran a hand over my hair, smoothing it back. "I was so worried about you."

I snuggled against him, slowly dredging up memories from last night. "I was worried about you too. What happened? Why wouldn't you change back?"

"I did . . . eventually."

Well, that was obvious. I waited expectantly, needing more.

"Being a kitsune isn't just about the novelty of turning into a fox. It's more than that. It's like . . . I also can turn into—I don't know—a fox god. No. That's not right. I don't know how to describe it."

"A superfox?"

His soft laughter vibrated against my forehead, and he kissed the skin there. "That's not quite right either. The foxes of the Otherworld are like the progenitors of mortal foxes in this world. They're stronger, more powerful, wilder. I can change into one of those, but to do so . . . I almost have to give up my humanity. They're too animal, too . . . I don't know, primordial. When I'm a normal red fox, I'm still pretty much the same as I am now unless I've been in that form for a really long time. Then the human part starts to go. But for your 'superfox,' I'm already gone in one transformation. I can hang on to only a few human instincts—like that I had to fight that thing and that I had to protect you."

I took all this in, frowning. "But that doesn't explain why you didn't change back."

"It takes time to go in and out of that form. The change is more than physical. I have to give up my human nature to go in, my fox nature to come out. Both are hard. That's why it took me awhile to even help in the first place. I had to make a quick call, even though it left you undefended. I thought I'd do more damage in the other form."

"Yeah, you did do a pretty good job. But you sure scared me there." I fell silent, recalling those terrible moments of uncertainty while I bled all over myself. "When did you finally change back?"

"Not long after you passed out, I think."

"That would explain why I'm still alive."

He nodded. "You lost a lot of blood. You needed ten stitches."

I blinked. "Did you take me to a doctor?"

He grinned. "You bet I did."

It took me a moment to catch on. I pulled back the covers and lifted the skirt of one of my racier and rarely used nightgowns—how'd I get dressed in that anyway?—

and saw black stitches standing out starkly against my skin, off to the side of my stomach.

"You did this?" I exclaimed. "You stitched me up? Without a doctor?"

"I *am* a doctor. I do this all the time."

"Yeah . . . to cats and dogs. Not to people."

"It's exactly the same. We're animals too."

I eyed the stitches uneasily. The skin around them was red. "Was everything sanitized?"

He made a disparaging sound in his throat. "Of course it was. The standards are the same. Come on, stop worrying. It was either that or let you bleed to death in the car. I had a kit in the back and used it."

"How'd you have enough light out there?"

"The overhead lamp still worked."

I couldn't believe he'd stitched me up in a smashed car with a vet's kit. Improvisation at its best. "Did the car actually start?"

"Sort of . . . I got us back to the freeway before it died. I found your cell phone and called Tim."

"Poor Tim. When I first told him I was a shaman, I think he thought it was as fake as his own Indian charade."

"Wait—he's not actually Indian? I've been trying forever to figure out what tribe he's from."

"He's from the tribe of Tim Warkoski. It's ridiculous, but—"

The air in the room rippled, pressure building. I had to blink a few times to ensure the shimmering around us wasn't in my head.

Kiyo propped himself up, alert and wary.

The pressure abruptly faded. A rift from the Otherworld opened up in front of us, and suddenly Dorian stood on a small table in the corner. Not unexpectedly, it promptly broke under his weight, making a horrible crashing sound as its pieces and contents fell to the floor. To his credit, he sidestepped the disaster rather gracefully, easily landing both feet on the floor. I winced, seeing the anchor ring lying among the debris. I'd set it on the table, not considering the consequences of Dorian arriving exactly where it lay.

"What the hell—" Kiyo started to climb out of bed, but I was in his way. I laid a restraining hand on his chest.

"No, it's all right. He's here for our next lesson. Jesus . . . I can't believe it's that time already." I'd lost a lot of time since the car.

Dorian wore his usual simple but fine clothes, covered by another elaborate robe. This one was black satin, edged in silver and small seed pearls. If the present circumstances surprised him, he didn't show it. He kept his face typically unimpressed and sardonic. His smile twisted as he regarded us.

"I can come back later if it's more convenient. I do so hate to interrupt."

"No, no," I said hastily, sitting up and swinging my legs over the bed's edge. The movement uncomfortably tugged the skin around my stitches. "We were just, um . . . resting."

Dorian arched an eyebrow. "You rest in that?"

I glanced down, flushing. I'd worn this exactly once when Dean and I had gone to Mexico for a weekend. The nightgown was pale green, its top and bottom hems ornamented with elaborate green leaves and tiny pink flowers. The mid-thigh-length skirt was sheer chiffon. Note to self: Never let Kiyo dress me again, unconsciousness notwithstanding.

Tim chose that moment to walk in, summoned by the noise. "Eug, what . . ."

His mouth dropped—and not just because of me. I looked around at us all: me in my nightgown, Kiyo bare-chested, Dorian in his extravagant robes, and Tim in his Native getup.

"God," I muttered, standing up, "we look like the Village People."

I pulled the terry cloth robe over me, wondering how I always seemed to be half-naked lately. Tim continued to stare, wearing the shocked look of one who has just walked in on his parents having sex.

"Everything's fine," I told him. He still didn't move, and I waved a hand in front of his face. "Hey, wake up. Think you can make some breakfast?"

He blinked. "It's three in the afternoon."

I gave him a pathetic look. The familiarity of it seemed to snap him back to normal. He could never resist it. That, or he felt he owed me food for the free rent.

"What do you want?"

"Eggs and toast."

"Healthy or unhealthy toast?"

I considered. "Healthy."

"Are your, uh, friends eating too?"

I glanced at the other two men.

"I'd love to," replied Dorian with a cordial half-bow. "Thank you."

"Famished," said Kiyo, eyes still narrowed on Dorian.

"Thanks, Tim, you're the best." I practically pushed him out the door.

"Charming man," remarked Dorian politely. He glanced around. "And a charming room." The broken table aside, the room's other contents included: a pile of laundry, the wicker chair, a case of ammunition, a dresser, and a small desk with my laptop and a half-finished puzzle of the Eiffel Tower. The room didn't have a lot of space, so everything had been jammed in. It all seemed so chintzy compared to the opulence of his bedroom.

Kiyo also got out of bed, wearing just a pair of jeans. "You want to tell me again what's going on?"

"I already did." I opened my dresser and pulled out a pair of jeans and a shirt that said I'LL GIVE YOU SOMETHING TO CRY ABOUT on it. "We're doing my next lesson."

"She can't do it today," Kiyo told Dorian. "She was in a fight last night."

"Unless I'm mistaken, she gets in a fight every night."

"This one was bad. She was injured. Didn't you see the stitches?"

"My humble eyes had better things to occupy themselves with than her stitches."

"Hey, guys?" I snapped. "I'm still here, you know. Stop talking about me in the third person."

Kiyo walked over and touched my arm. "Eugenie, this is crazy. You need to go back to bed."

"Today's lesson will not require physical exertion," said Dorian primly.

"There, you see?" I said. "I've got to keep going with our deal."

Kiyo looked darkly from me to Dorian. "Your 'deal' doesn't seem to be doing a lot of good. I thought it was going to keep your would-be rapists away."

I had turned my back to them, opened the robe, and started pulling my jeans on. I froze, considering.

"The fachan wasn't trying to rape me," I said slowly. "He wanted to kill me."

"Are you sure?"

"He tried to throw me through a windshield. That's not very romantic."

"A fachan?" asked Dorian.

I shed the robe and nightgown and pulled the shirt over my head before turning back around to face them. I gave Dorian the short version of what had happened.

He stood up from where he'd been leaning against my desk and strolled over to the window, hands clasped behind his back.

"A fachan," he mused. "Here. Curious."

"Not really. Not compared to anything else that's happened to me," I reminded him.

He pointed out the window. "You live in a desert. Fachans like bodies of water. You have a lot of enemies, my dear, but I doubt any fachan would hate you enough to show up here of his own volition."

"What are you saying?" asked Kiyo.

"That someone went to considerable trouble to summon him here. Someone with either a lot of raw power or simply an affinity for water creatures."

"Who could do that?" I asked.

"Any number of people. Maiwenn could."

Kiyo took a few dangerous steps toward him. "Maiwenn didn't do that."

Dorian smiled, unfazed by Kiyo's intimidating presence. They were the same height, but Dorian's frame was lean and slim, Kiyo's broader and more muscled.

"You're probably right," Dorian said after several tense moments of silence. "Particularly since she's been so under the weather lately." Kiyo's face grew darker.

I glanced back and forth uneasily, uncertain as to what I was in the middle of. "Do you guys know each other?"

Dorian extended a hand to Kiyo, cool and collected. "I know *of* you, but I don't believe we've been properly introduced. I am Dorian, king of the Oak Land."

Kiyo grudgingly took his hand. "I know who you are."

"This is Kiyo," I said.

"Delightful to meet you. You're a . . . kitsune."

Dorian said the word in an odd tone. It wasn't exactly disrespectful, but it clearly implied they were not equals.

I grabbed both their arms and steered them out. "No pissing contests. Come on. It'll only take Tim about five minutes to whip up the food."

Whatever antagonism existed between Kiyo and Dorian, it took a break as the gentry king entertained himself with the rest of my house. He was like a kid, unable to keep his hands off of everything. Well, everything that wasn't made of plastic or an iron affiliate. My living room was a veritable wonderland, with everything conveniently piled up in junk heaps for him to explore.

"What's the purpose of this?"

He held a fluorescent pink Slinky, tossing it from side to side so he didn't have to touch the plastic extensively.

My impression was gentry could touch the taboo substances in small doses with minor discomfort; prolonged exposure grew much more uncomfortable. Charge it up with power, and it could kill them.

"It doesn't really have a purpose," I decided. "You just sort of . . . play with it when you're bored."

He tossed it back and forth, watching it spring up in arches.

"Let me see it," I said.

I held it, closing my eyes. My focus was back now with the excruciating pain vanquished. I concentrated on the Slinky, putting a small piece of my essence into it. I handed it back.

"Wrap it up and take it with you. It'll be my anchor."

He grinned. With so many other distractions, we eventually had to drag him to the kitchen table when the food was ready.

"Haven't you ever been in the human world before?" I asked, once we all sat down.

"There you go again, assuming we all just traipse over here for no good reason."

"So you haven't."

"Well, actually, I've vacationed here a number of times. Not in this desolate place, of course, but several other nice spots."

I rolled my eyes and slapped butter on my toast. It was made of good, hearty bread, chock-full of whole wheat and about a billion other grains. You could use this stuff as sandpaper.

I doused my coffee with sugar and cream, gulping it to chase down some ibuprofen. I might not be dying anymore, but myriad aches and stiffness filled my body. I didn't think I could handle regularly getting into high-magnitude fights every other night.

When the whole prophecy thing had surfaced, I had joked that I preferred attempts on my life to sexual advances. I didn't really believe that anymore. At least when the bad guys wanted my clothes off, it bought me some time. That fachan, however, had had no intentions short of crushing me. And he'd done a pretty good job of doing that. I had never fought something so massive before. Most of my fights, before this all started, had been with spirits and elementals. I could take them out with barely any effort. The fachan had been in a different league. The spirit army from the other day had also been new.

Dorian's words rang back to me. The fachan had been deliberately sent. But by whom? One of the many who had a grudge against Odile? Someone like Maiwenn who wanted the prophecy to fail? Maiwenn herself? This latter thought bothered me. She'd seemed more or less trustworthy, despite her bland personality. If she turned into an enemy, it was going to create some serious friction between Kiyo and me.

We finished breakfast, and Dorian declared we had to go outside for our lesson. I took one look at him and the scalding sunshine and saw imminent disaster for that perfect, alabaster skin. Figuring he wouldn't want my prissy, vanilla sunscreen, I dug him out a wide-brimmed cotton hat of Tim's that looked only mildly ridiculous.

"Are you going to be able to do this?" I asked, leading Dorian out to my back patio. Tim had left for drumming practice, but Kiyo followed us, still watchful. "Your magic's weaker on this side."

Dorian draped his elegant robes over a lawn chair. "Not me who needs to do the magic. And really, I doubt you will either. Not in the way you're thinking of. Hmm . . . yes, this area may work better than I'd hoped."

He surveyed the patio area and the small grassless yard surrounded by a stucco wall. Dragging up another chair, he set it near the center of the patio, facing the house, and beckoned me to it. I sat down.

"Now what? More meditation?"

He shook his head. "Now we need a bowl of water."

"Kiyo? Can you grab us one? There's a big ceramic bowl in the back of one of my cupboards."

Kiyo silently complied, looking as though leaving us alone for even one minute would result in Dorian trying something. I found that protectiveness endearing, albeit a bit over the top.

And then Dorian did try something.

"What are those?" I exclaimed.

"Think of them as . . . learning aids."

He had produced a handful of silken cords from the deep pockets of his robe, all in different colors.

"What are you—no. You are not serious."

He had moved behind my chair and grasped my hands. I jerked away.

"You're trying to tie me up?"

"Not for sinister purposes, I assure you, although if you'd like to experiment with them later, I'd be happy to show you their various and sundry uses. For now, simply trust me that they'll be useful."

I continued to regard the cords warily. He shook his head, smiling. Moving behind me, he gently ran his hands down my arms. "You still don't trust me. And yet you do. An interesting mix. You fear me but want to connect with me. Do you remember what I said the night we met?" He knelt down, speaking softly in my ear. "This is exactly the way it will be when you come to my bed. You'll surrender yourself, and though it'll scare you, you'll exult in it too."

"I think you're imagining more to our charade than there is. And I don't really see myself feeling exultant over being tied up."

"Have you ever tried it?" His fingers slowly slid back up to the sleeves of my shirt, like butterflies on my skin. It was . . . nice. I shrugged him off.

"No. And I don't need to. Besides, whatever your kinky intentions are, it doesn't matter. I've got something going with Kiyo."

"Ah. Of course you do. From what I hear, he's always 'got something going.'"

I stiffened. "Don't try to cause trouble."

"I'm attempting nothing of the sort. Just stating a fact. A man with human blood is just as appealing to our women as you are to our men."

"I already know about Maiwenn."

"I see. What do you know?"

"The truth. They used to be involved. Now they're not."

"Ah. And that doesn't bother you? Especially considering it's likely she'll try to kill you someday?"

I turned around as much as I could and glared at him. "I meant it: Don't try to pick a fight. I trust Kiyo, and I like Maiwenn. End of story. Now if you're going to tie me up, just get it over with."

He rose from his crouch, the sensuality gone from his voice as he began the business of binding me. "I'd never dream of picking a fight. Your pet fox in there will break my neck if I so much as look at you the wrong way."

"Don't act like you're actually afraid of him. You can supposedly bring down buildings." I relaxed back in the chair and let him tie my hands together behind me. He took a long time in doing it, like he was weaving or braiding.

"Why, Eugenie, are you saying you'd wager on me in a fight? I'm touched. Very touched. Although, I do hear foxes have very sharp claws. How are those scratches on your back, by the way?"

Kiyo walked out just then, carrying the bowl of water. He froze when he saw Dorian tying a cord above my breasts and around my upper arms.

"What's this?"

"An awakening," said Dorian.

"It's fine," I said. "Set the water over there."

Kiyo did so and then stood next to me, arms crossed and eyes on the gentry king.

Again, Dorian took his time in tying my upper body. He used multiple cords, and able to see better this time,

I realized he had indeed woven them into an intricate pattern. Aesthetic and functional.

"There." With a last tight knot, he straightened up and regarded his work. "Not bad. It seems I haven't forgotten how to tie a decent knot after all. One more thing, and we're set."

"One more thing" turned out to be a blindfold.

"No way," I said.

"Eugenie, my sweet, your outraged protests are adorable, but they only continue to slow us down. If you want me to help you, then let me. If you don't, then take me to one of those places where human women wear revealing clothing and quickly lose their virtue through alcohol."

I let him blindfold me, feeling uneasy. I trusted Kiyo and sort of trusted Dorian, but the other bindings had already unsettled me. I didn't like being trapped or in someone else's control. The bright world went dark as fabric covered my eyes.

"This is all giving me a bad feeling," Kiyo said nearby.

"On the contrary," said Dorian, "it's giving me a very warm, very pleasant feeling. But I suppose we should return to the lesson at hand, hmm?"

"Is this the part where you explain the bondage getup?" I asked. "Or where I find out you just did it for fun."

"No, no. As hilarious as that would be, I do have my reasons. Now. I'm going to pick up this bowl of water that Kato so kindly fetched—"

"It's Kiyo," came the irritated response.

"So sorry. Anyway, I'm going to set it somewhere out here in this miniature wasteland, and you will tell me where it is."

"Oh. I get it. I'm supposed to, like, work on my non-visual senses? Listen to where you set it?"

"You won't use any of your physical senses at all."

I heard him walk away, presumably with the water, but I couldn't tell where he set it. He paced and paced in circles, kicking rocks and scuffing his shoes so I was clueless by the time he returned to me. When he spoke next, his words were right by my ear again.

"Now, given freedom, even with just a blindfold, you'd be inclined to move and want to use something—*anything*—to find the water. You'd turn around, sniff the air, whatever. Now you have to accept that all of that is gone. You cannot rely on what you usually can. You are trapped and powerless—more or less. Give in to that. Open yourself up to whatever comes. Find the water."

"How?"

"By reaching out to it. Tap into a sense other than the usual five. Remember the exercises we did last time, about reaching beyond yourself—in this world, not the spirit one."

"I thought magic was inborn. Isn't that what separates humans and gentry?"

"It is inborn. And your inner magic summons and controls storms. To do that, you must summon and control the appropriate elements. And to do *that,* you must be able to find them. Hence, you focus outward."

"How do I do that?"

"Just concentrate. But relax too. Think about the water. How it feels, what it's like. Spread your consciousness out around you, but don't go into a trance and let your spirit slip out. That'd be cheating."

"How long does it take?"

"As long as you need."

He retreated, and I sat there and waited for some revelation. Okay. Somewhere around me was a bowl of water. And something inside of me was supposed to be able to sense it. I wouldn't have believed any of it if the living room on the other side of the patio door didn't stand as proof of my supernatural powers. But I hadn't had to think to cause the storm. This was different.

All I mostly felt at first was my own body. Dorian's binds didn't hurt me, but they were snug. The stitched-up cut stung a little. The back of my head ached. My leg muscles felt stretched and inflamed. I slowly took inventory of every part of me, assessing how each one felt. I could feel the beat of my own heart, the steadiness of my breathing.

After that, I started concentrating on the stuff around me. I heard someone, Dorian maybe, slide up a chair and sit down. A plane droned overhead. One of my neighbors kept a bird feeder, and sparrows regularly chirped and squabbled around it. The harsher cries of less melodic birds sounded in the distance. My street had few houses and was removed from real traffic, but a block or so away, a car started and then drove off.

I thought about water, its appeal growing as the sun beat down. I had put on my own sunscreen and was grateful for it. Still, I could feel sweat pouring off of me. Water would be cool, refreshing. My mom's house had a pool, and suddenly I wanted nothing more than to dive into that crystal-blue surface.

I thought about the bowl of water, thinking of its cool temperature, the wetness on my skin. I tried to feel it, to call to it.

"There," I said at last. I don't know how much time had passed. Awhile.

"Where?" asked Dorian.

"Four o'clock."

"What?"

"She means over there," I heard Kiyo say. Presumably he pointed.

"No," said Dorian.

"What?"

"Sorry."

"Was I close?"

"No."

"Not even a little?"

"No."

"Damn it! Get me out of this." I wriggled against my constraints.

"Hardly." Dorian's voice held mild surprise. "We must try again."

"Oh, dear lord. This might be even more boring than the meditation," I grumbled. "Can I at least get something to drink?"

He hesitated. "Actually, I think your odds will increase if you're thirsty."

"Oh, come on—"

"Here we go," said Dorian. I heard him get up and walk around again, and once more, I couldn't tell where the bowl ended up.

When he returned to his chair, I tried again. More time passed as I concentrated my little heart out. At one point, I heard someone get up and move toward the door.

"Who is that?"

"Me," said Dorian. "I'm bored."

"What? You're my teacher."

"The kitsune will call if you need me."

"I don't believe this," I said when he was gone.

"Hey, this was your idea," said Kiyo.

I heard him shift in a chair, getting comfortable.

I was on the verge of my next guess when Dorian came outside again.

"There. Nine o'clock."

Kiyo must have pointed again.

"No," said Dorian.

He made me do it again, and by then, I was furious. My poor muscles, already put through enough, were locking up from lack of movement. The heat was unbearable. To make matters worse, Kiyo asked if Dorian wanted something to drink and then went inside. He returned, and I heard the sound of a two-liter of pop opening, followed by the filling of two glasses.

After that, they started carrying on casual conversation.

"Eugenie will be at my Beltane ball," Dorian explained, "as my special guest."

"Sounds great."

"Your enthusiasm is palpable."

"Just not my thing, that's all."

"Ah, pity. Because if you wanted to come, I'd be happy to extend the invitation."

"I wouldn't want you to go to any trouble."

"It's no trouble at all. You could come with Eugenie. I always make special arrangements for dignitaries' entourages and servants."

"Will you two shut up?" I asked. "I'm working here."

They fell silent.

Water, water. I needed that goddamned water so that Dorian would untie me and I could return to air conditioning. I'd also drink a gallon of water while I was at it. Maybe two or three. In fact, when I found that stupid bowl, I'd dump it over my head.

Sweat pooled along the hem of my shirt and where the cords and blindfold pressed against my skin. I'd probably sweated away the sunscreen and would burn. As if my body hadn't been through enough. Where the hell was that water? Why couldn't I find it?

I thought again about my mom's pool, vowing I'd pay her a visit tomorrow. God, it was so hot. I just wanted to be cooler. Water, water, water. I felt like Helen Keller. Or maybe one of those people in the Lakota sun dances where excessive heat exposure induced hallucinations. Maybe I could imagine the water.

I sighed, and then, somehow, I felt coolness touch me. It was a reprieve from the heat. I straightened up as much as I could. Had I done it? Was this what it felt like to touch the water? The third time was the charm. Yes. There it was again. Like cool, moist air blowing at me from the east. I could taste its dampness, hanging around me like humidity in the sauna.

I inclined my head in the direction I'd sensed the cool air. "I've got it. Three o'clock."

"No."

"The hell it isn't!"

I heard Dorian get up. He sighed. "I think we'd better quit for the day."

"But I swear I had it! I could feel it! I was thinking about water so hard."

"I know you were."

He undid the blindfold, and I looked up. Billowing clouds, colored like lead, inked out the sky. Wind blew at me from the east—not imagined after all—picking up in strength. Great, heavy drops fell around us, landing with loud splashes.

Water at last.

Chapter Nineteen

Dorian wasn't nearly as impressed as he should have been by the storm.

"You couldn't control it," he told me. "It did you no good. Until you master the small things, you'll never control the large ones. They'll control you."

He didn't seem upset; he simply showed that infinite patience and good-natured attitude he always had. Still enchanted by human stuff, he wanted us to take him into the city and show him entertaining things—particularly the aforementioned women with low inhibitions. Considering the car ride would have literally killed him, we ordered pizza instead.

You could tell it was sort of a letdown for him, but he still enjoyed it. He found delight in everything, I realized. Well—except for those extreme moments of boredom that seemed to plague him, although even in those he still managed to find some sort of joke. I didn't know many people like that.

I saw him once more that week, this time at his place. He made me repeat the boring water experiment five times, but it only yielded the exact same results. At least this time I didn't conjure any storms. When I asked if we could do something else next time, he laughed and sent me home.

The day before Dorian's ball, I mustered up the courage to do something I'd been thinking about for a long time now: visit Wil Delaney.

He still left messages with Lara almost every other day, but that wasn't what finally made me go see him again. Ever since my mom's visit, I hadn't been able to shake the idea of her locked away, miserable and alone, in Storm King's castle. The pain of that image transferred to my impressions of Jasmine, and no matter how reluctant the girl had been to leave, I knew she was still a victim. I wanted to do something—anything—to help her but had no idea where to start or even how to do it, considering last time's disaster. Talking to Wil again seemed like a semireasonable beginning.

Kiyo went with me, driving us in his rental car since his poor Spider was out of commission. This car was a brand-new Toyota Camry that seemed pretty nice to me, though it obviously caused him considerable distress.

When we knocked on the door, Wil didn't answer right away.

"You sure he's here?" Kiyo asked.

"Yeah. I don't think he ever leaves. We're probably being thermal-scanned or something."

Kiyo gave me a puzzled look.

"Just wait," I warned.

A minute later, I heard the legion of locks and bolts being undone, and Wil's face appeared.

"Oh, my God," he gasped, face lighting up. "You're back. Wait. Who's that?"

"A friend. Now let us in."

Wil gave Kiyo a hesitant look and finally opened the door wider. As we walked in, I could tell from Kiyo's expression that he was having exactly the same reaction I'd had to the weirdness of Wil's lair. In particular he paused in front of a magazine lying open on a coffee table. An article's large headline read: THEY'RE USING YOUR DNA TO TRACK YOU! WEAR A HAIRNET WHEN LEAVING THE HOUSE!

"I knew you'd come around," Wil burbled out, leading us into the kitchen. "When are we going back?"

"I don't know that we are, Wil."

"Then why—"

I held up a hand to silence him. "I just want to talk right now, that's all."

His face fell, but he nodded and walked to the refrigerator. "You want something to drink?"

"Sure. What do you have?"

He opened the refrigerator. Inside were about ten jugs of water whose labels guaranteed ultra-ultra-ultra purification and refinement against impurities.

"Water," he said. "Most soft drinks are laden with—"

"Water's fine."

He poured three glasses and sat down with us, watching me expectantly.

"I want to know more about Jasmine," I explained. "If we're ever able to go back . . ." Again, that pale face loomed in my mind. I swallowed. "It might not do us any good if she doesn't want to go. Is there anything about her . . . anything you can tell us that might sort of explain that?"

The fanatical gleam left his eyes, replaced by something sober and sad. "I don't know. I mean, I guess half of it's being fourteen, you know? Not that she ever seemed all that impressionable. I guess she could have been brainwashed. There's lots of documentation on that; the government does it all the time. I imagine even fairies have conditioning techniques . . ."

He started going off on that, and I felt Kiyo's hand rest on my thigh under the table and give a slight squeeze. It was less of a sexual thing and more of a *What the hell have you gotten us into?*

Keeping my expression blank, I finally interrupted Wil's lecture. "Can you give us any information about her? Like . . . what she was into? Likes? Dislikes? If we could just get some idea about that, it might help us understand her better."

"Well," he said doubtfully, "I could show you her room."

He took us farther into the house, which was just as dark as the kitchen, and into a small room that smelled of dust and disuse. Probably making a great sacrifice to his values, he flipped on the lights. For half a second, I was relieved that Jasmine's room did not mirror the rest of Wil's crazed existence. It looked like a normal teenage girl's room.

At first.

Then I saw the fairy posters.

They were interspersed with other airbrushed fantasy pictures—unicorns and dreamscapes—but fairies definitely made up the dominant theme splashed against the room's rose-pink walls. These images weren't accurate representations of the very humanlike gentry but depicted more of what pop culture perceived fairies to be like: small and winged, playing with flowers and fireflies. Those sorts of beings did exist in the Otherworld, though technically they were pixies.

"You didn't think this was relevant?" I breathed, gazing around.

"This is fluff," said Wil dismissively. "Stuff girls are into. She's liked this stuff since she was little."

I walked farther into the room and knelt in front of a small bookcase. J. R. R. Tolkien. C. S. Lewis. J. K. Rowling. More and more fantasy titles. A shrine to escapism.

Glancing around, Kiyo seemed to be thinking along the same lines I was. "Are there any photos? Any friends of hers?"

Wil shook his head. "She didn't have a lot of friends." He sat down on the ruffled pink bed and found a small album on the floor. "Here are a few pictures."

Kiyo and I sat next to him. The album was sort of a record of Jasmine's childhood. There were some baby pictures and some shots of her as a little girl. Wil figured into a lot of the pictures, but we saw little of their parents. I recalled his bitter comments about their chronic absence. We did find a few pictures of her with other children, but as she grew older, those became more rare. Mostly these seemed to be candid shots that someone— Wil, most likely—had snapped while she was busy with something. One showed her curled up with a book, another found her lying in a backyard hammock while bright sunshine lit up her strawberry-blond hair. She had noticed the photographer in that latter one and regarded the camera with a sad, sweet smile.

"What did she do for fun?" I asked when Wil closed the album. "Hobbies? Sports?"

He gestured to the shelves. "She liked to read, obviously. And she liked being outside. She went for walks, sometimes planted flowers. Wasn't really into sports or anything like that."

"She must have hung out with some people," I pointed out. "Didn't you say she was at a party when she was taken?"

"Yeah . . . kind of surprising, actually. But she went to things like that once in awhile. Not often. But sometimes. I mean, she did things with me sometimes too. We went to Disneyland once. Saw movies. But mostly she was alone."

"Do you know why?"

"No. I think . . . I think she just had trouble relating to kids her age. She was smart, always sort of ahead of her time."

His voice was wistful, and I realized no matter how unstable he might be in some ways, he did truly love and miss his sister.

"Was she this reclusive before your parents died?" asked Kiyo gently.

"Yeah. She was always kind of this way."

After a bit more investigating around the room, we

finally left. Wil pushed me hard on what I was going to do about Jasmine, but I had no answers to give him.

"Well," Kiyo said after a few quiet minutes on the road, "that was depressing."

I didn't answer right away as I stared off at the road ahead of us.

"Eugenie? You all right?"

"No. Not really." I sighed. "That poor girl."

"Starts to make more sense, though, doesn't it?"

"Yeah. Isolated from the real world, she starts living in a fantasy one. Then suddenly Aeson gives her the chance to actually live in that one."

He nodded his agreement. "Of course, abduction and rape probably weren't the ways she envisioned escaping off to fairyland."

I stared off again for a while. "She reminds me of me."

The glance he gave me was wry. "You dissociated into a make-believe world that you hoped would become real?"

"No. But I was kind of a loner too. I think I had more friends than her, admittedly, but I always had trouble relating to others. It got worse once Roland made me his apprentice. Hard to get excited about boy bands when you're learning to exorcise ghosts."

"I don't think you missed anything there."

I rewarded him with a smile as I continued thinking. "Even though I didn't have many friends, I always wanted them, wanted to be noticed. If Jasmine's the same, then she probably likes being Aeson's mistress, as sickening as it is. He probably showers her with attention."

"You're right . . . though I wonder if there's more to it."

"How so?"

"I think a lot of teens feel disconnected sometimes, like no one understands them. I mean, I felt that way lots of times. Not sure I would have welcomed what happened to her as some sort of salvation."

"Me either. But I suppose everyone copes in different ways. I took up solitary things. Running. Swimming."

"Puzzles?"

"Hey," I said. "How'd you know about that?"

"Because you have about a hundred of them in your closet."

I laughed, then reconsidered something he'd just said. "What was it like for you, growing up? You knew from the beginning what you were, right?"

"Yeah. My parents never made that a secret. They accepted that they were from different worlds—literally—and didn't fight that. Growing up with that duality sort of became second nature. Like I said before, I like both worlds, which is why I certainly don't want to see some conquest of this one. Of course, I had plenty of times in my life, particularly when I was young and moody, when I'd get mad at one of my parents. Then I'd swear I'd be all kitsune or all human, depending on who'd pissed me off."

"Your teenage angst must have been a terrible thing," I teased.

"You have no idea."

"Are your parents still together?"

"No. Still amicable. My mom finally stayed in the Otherworld for good once I got older. I see her from time to time. It broke my dad's heart—he was crazy about her—but he remarried and seems to be better off."

I leaned back against the seat. "Now that I know what I am . . . I kind of wish I'd known sooner. I would have liked to get a head start on my magic and go blow Aeson's castle apart and get Jasmine back."

"You don't know that you can actually do that," he warned. "You're half-human. You may not have gotten all his power."

"Did you get everything your mom has?"

He hesitated. "Yes."

"I can't leave Jasmine there. Not knowing what I know. But I don't know how to get her back."

Kiyo reached over and squeezed my hand. "We'll think of something. Don't worry."

It was a little comforting, but I think we both knew it was the sort of empty, kind statement you say to make someone feel better. I doubted he had any better ideas than I had on how to get Jasmine back.

Kiyo didn't have to work until the next morning, so we decided to go hiking at Sabino Canyon. Physical exertion seemed like a good way to forget about abducted girls, and it was. The temperature pushed into triple digits, and we were exhausted and sweaty as we finally made the return trip down, both of us greedily drinking from water bottles.

I saw him watching me at one point while we stopped to take a break. There was a content and admiring expression on his face, not purely sexual, for a change.

"What?" I asked.

"Your hair. I never realized how red it is. The sun lights it up like a flame."

"Is that a good thing?"

"Very good."

The comfortable look on his face shifted, and I saw the familiar glint of need surface. We didn't say much after that. The rest of our hike and subsequent ride home proceeded in silence, but the air burned between us, hotter than anything we'd felt outside.

Tim was nowhere to be found when we arrived home. Just as well. I turned on the shower, eager to remove the sweat and grime, and Kiyo hopped in with me.

"We're here to get clean," I warned.

"Sure," he said, pushing me up against the wall.

Water poured down on us as we kissed and touched and attempted some semblance of washing ourselves. I don't know how good a job we did. I think some parts got significantly soaped down more than others.

I wouldn't have minded sex in the shower, but we had no condoms in there. Sometimes I thought the double birth control was overkill; in eight years, I'd never had problems with the pill. But we both knew how high the stakes were. A condom was a small thing to ask.

We fell onto my bed, still kind of slick and soapy. He slipped the condom on in like two seconds, and I moved on top of him. Foreplay apparently wasn't going to play a big role in our relationship. His hands grasped my hips, halting me for a moment.

"You took your pill today?"

"Yes, yes," I assured him.

He relaxed and released me, letting me move down and take him into me. A soft sound, half-groan and half-sigh, escaped his lips. He opened his eyes and smiled at me.

"You are . . . the most right thing in my world."

I smiled back, knowing exactly what he meant. We felt good and right together, like the last month's tension hadn't existed. We were where we should be, picking right up after our first night together.

His hands clenched my sides, his nails touching my back as my body shifted up and down. A tingle of apprehension ran through me whenever those fingers came near my back, but he continued to show restraint. The scratches were finally healing, albeit slowly.

He let me stay on top only about a minute or so before he flipped me onto my stomach and took me from that position, all aggression and furious passion. I slyly tried shifting us once, and he playfully returned me back. Maybe it was the fox thing, or maybe it was just his own human nature, but something in him liked being the dominant one. I decided not to fight it, far too busy swimming in the bliss and fire of him moving inside of me.

When he finished, he rolled off and pulled me to him. Happy, I buried my face against his body, drinking in his scent and feel like an intoxicant. Clinging to each other, we listened to our ragged breathing calm down. For the first time in awhile, I felt safe and at peace. Things were exactly as they were supposed to be.

He stayed with me that night, and our bodies wrapped around each other in the darkness. My body fell into its old bad habits, and I found myself lying awake long after he'd fallen asleep. I twisted and turned, counting stars on my ceiling and attempting to force my mind into calmness.

I tried too hard, apparently, because my mind slipped into trance, one off from wakeful consciousness but not really asleep either. Recognizing this, I started to shift out of it until an image appeared in my mind, a familiar one of a barren area I didn't recognize and a dark, crowned figure standing over me.

The memory I'd half-started in the sauna returned, flooding my mind's eye. I suddenly found myself looking up at Storm King. The fear was there, the fear that I couldn't escape him and that he would take me away.

Then, just as before, I reached for something both within and without. Power surged through me, and the air grew thick. Dark clouds formed out of nothing, covering the sky. Soft thunder echoed around us. I still couldn't see his face in this memory, but I could sense his amusement.

"Are you going to try to fight me, little one?" A different power built up around us as he gathered his own magic. "I like your attitude—though you're fighting a losing battle. For now, at least. Come with me, and I'll show you how to really use your gifts."

He gently nudged his power toward me, attempting to quell mine. I sucked in more of my magic, letting it course through me. It burned, but it was wonderful. Amazing. Like nothing I had ever felt before or could have conceived of. I was more than a human in that moment, more than Eugenie Markham, more than a god. It filled me, but even then, I could not control it. Not yet. Lightning flared above us, followed immediately by thunder.

Storm King was still pushing against me. I don't think

I was really more than a match for him, but he hadn't quite expected this much of a fight. I tried to focus my power, to get ahold of it and use it against him. It was slippery, though; I couldn't keep a hold. Lightning blazed again, and I reached out with my mind to seize it, willing it to strike him down.

Only my aim was off. It hit me instead.

I screamed, pain ripping through me as I became the lightning's conduit, its means of grounding itself. It couldn't kill me, however; it couldn't even really hurt me—that much. I was one with the storm, and the magic I'd summoned was my own. It shot into my body, terrible and magnificent, a burning pain laced with pleasure, an ecstasy I didn't ever want to let go of. . . .

I jerked upright in bed, gasping for air. Immediately, Kiyo was beside me, asking what was wrong. I couldn't answer right away. That fiery, exultant power was emblazoned in my memory. Yet, even as I sat there, I could feel the memory fading, the remembered sensation going with it. Some part of me cried out for it, willing it to stay. But it was going.

"Eugenie?" I think it was the hundredth time he'd spoken my name. "What's wrong?"

"A dream," I murmured, closing my eyes. Even with that magic gone—gone for years, really—my body shivered with delight. I felt alive, my flesh tingling with an awareness of both itself and the world around me. I opened my eyes and turned to Kiyo, resting my hands on his arms, curling my fingers into his skin.

"What's the—mmm."

His words were swallowed by my kiss. My mouth fed so ferociously at his that I tasted blood from where I'd bitten his lip. In an instant, I felt his animal lust answer my own as his hands gripped my hips and tried to pull me down. But I was already pushing him down, moving myself on top of him.

"Don't fight me on this," I growled, digging my nails against him.

He smiled. I think he thought I was joking, little knowing the power and aggression suddenly churning through me. His hands slid over to my wrists. Gripping them tightly, he rolled me over, pressing his full weight down on my body. "A little fighting's not bad," he teased.

"No." My words were fierce. Unchallengeable. Still wrapped up in the dream's fleeting power, I surprised both of us and flipped *him* over. It was a lot like when we'd had sex earlier today, only now the roles were reversed. My own strength astonished me.

"Don't fight me," I repeated, voice low and dangerous.

His eyes widened in the near-darkness. There was only a heartbeat's pause. "Anything you want." Ostensibly, he sounded excited and amused, but there was an undercurrent of nervousness there too.

Burning and exultant, I moved my mouth and hips down. We both gasped as I took him inside me. No condom, nothing between us. I shuddered at the contact, growing aroused at the thought of him directly feeling me and all my wetness. Skin to skin. Maybe I should have moved slowly, letting him savor the new sensations, but my body was too impatient. I rode him as fiercely as he had me earlier, something within me needing to assert my dominance and claim him as mine. My nails drew blood, and he cried out each time our hips slammed together.

I felt powerful, in control. Like I could do anything and conquer anyone. The warmth and bliss of orgasm started building up inside of me, and some very small part of me wondered if I was getting off on thrusting him inside of me or simply on the thrill of domination. And if it was the latter, whom was I exerting my control over? Kiyo? Storm King?

The ecstasy in my lower body grew more intense, more urgent. I pushed aside the nagging speculation and gave myself up to my own selfish wants. I stared

down at Kiyo; he looked back as though he scarcely recognized me.

"Mine," I gasped, holding back my release. "Right
now, right in this moment, you're mine."

Kiyo made a strangled noise of pleasure, head tipped
back.

I was on the edge; I couldn't hold my body back much
longer. I didn't *want* to hold back much longer. I was the
powerful one here. I was taking what I wanted. But first,
I needed to make sure he knew that.

"Say it," I told him between heavy breaths. "Tell me
you're mine. Tell me, and I'll let you come. I'll let you
come in me. I'll let you explode in me."

"Eugenie . . ." he moaned when I started to slow my
pace.

"You're mine," I told him again. The lovely agony between my thighs was almost too much to bear. I was
going to lose it.

But Kiyo lost control first. "Yes . . . yes. Oh, God, Eugenie. I'm yours."

The power of that admission set me off, both physically
and mentally. Crying out, I threw back my own head as I
came. I didn't need to see his face to know he was coming
too. I could feel it, feel it in the way his body spasmed
inside of mine. Squeezing him tighter, I earned another
moan of pleasure from him and another orgasm for me.
It was glorious. We both shook from the force of our own
reactions.

When we finally collapsed apart, sweating and panting,
neither of us could say a word. Finally Kiyo rested his head
on my chest as though seeking comfort or protection.

"Yours," he murmured at last, just before falling
asleep.

Chapter Twenty

I became merely mortal the next morning, the last lingering memories of magic recalled only in theory, not in feeling. I wanted to try to explain the dream-memory to Kiyo, how I'd at last recalled what happened between Storm King and me before Roland killed him. But I didn't know how to explain it. I barely understood magic at all and found recapturing that terrifying yet glorious feeling nearly impossible.

Besides, I had other things to worry about today. It was Beltane Eve.

I found myself busy almost from the crack of dawn. Beltane—or May Day—ushers in the return of life to the year; many western European cultures consider it a peak day for fertility and conception. Apparently many Otherworldly creatures do too. Like Halloween—or Samhain—the gates between the worlds open, facilitating passage between humans and the Otherworldly alike. Midnight on May 1 was the ultimate opening, but the passages steadily increased throughout the day on April 30.

Since my presence at Dorian's party tonight was common knowledge, many must have decided to get in their chance before I left the human world. Fortunately, most of these same gentry and assorted creatures were those who could not have passed through under normal circumstances. This meant they were considerably weaker and hence easier to banish or destroy. Unfortunately, when they came in a steady stream, they also became a huge and exhausting annoyance.

I got home around dinnertime, not long before I was supposed to show up in the Otherworld. Hastily, I shed my sweaty clothes and took the world's fastest shower. Afterward, I managed a makeup job rivaling the last one, but it cost me time. With minutes ticking away, I threw on the dress Lara had procured and ran a quick brush through my damp hair. There was nothing else to be done with it. I threw a little mousse into it to avoid frizz, and then I was off to the desert.

Dorian had wisely put my Slinky anchor in a more secure place than a flimsy table. I appeared in a small chamber where a servant had awaited my arrival. He gave me a polite bow and then took me straight to Dorian's room. Inside it, I found pandemonium.

Male and female servants ran in and out, doing God only knew what. Dorian stood in front of a giant mirror, checking himself out in an azure blue robe. A stout man hovered nearby with about a dozen other robes weighing down his arm. It was the same man, I realized, whose place I'd taken in croquet.

"Eugenie Markham," announced my escort.

Dorian gave me half a glance. "Lady Markham, so nice to—sweet gods. She's wearing beige."

I looked down. Lara had found me a clingy silk dress in a shade she termed "champagne": a warm ivory tinged with gold. I wouldn't have thought the color worked for me, but she apparently knew me better than I did. The strapless bodice was gathered and decorated with a bit of iridescent beading meant to imitate buttons down the middle. From the waist down, the skirt cascaded in smooth, shining folds. It fit snugly against my silhouette, flaring slightly only when it hit my ankles.

"It's 'champagne,'" I corrected. "And what's wrong with it?"

"Nothing. It's lovely." He turned back frantically to his valet. "It's not going to match any of these, Muran. What else do we have?"

Muran bit his lip. "There's the green velvet, your majesty. Its trim has that shade in it. Paired with an ivory shirt, it would look quite stunning."

Dorian made a face. "Silk or satin would be better. Grab it anyway, and see if there's anything else we're missing. Oh, and send someone to do Lady Markham's hair."

"What's wrong with my hair?"

"Nothing, were you sprawled in my bed after a night of passion." A young woman hurried forward, and he jerked his head in my direction. "See to her, Nia."

Nia, a tiny thing with olive skin, curtsied to me and led me to the parlor where Dorian and I had first chatted. I couldn't see what she did, but her fingers worked as deftly and intricately in my hair as Dorian did when tying the cords around me. I'd only once had my hair done by a stylist, and it had been for a wedding in which a cruel friend had required me to wear orange taffeta. The event still woke me with nightmares.

A slight tingle occasionally brushed my skin as Nia worked, and I realized she used magic in the styling. I supposed it was handier than a curling iron, but geez. What a disappointment to discover you had the magical equivalent of cosmetology when other gentry got healing and the ability to tear buildings apart.

"There you are, my lady."

She took me to a mirror, nervously assessing my reaction. Scattered braids ran toward the back of my head where the rest of my hair had been gathered up into a high ponytail. She'd smoothed and curled most of that hanging hair, but a few tiny braids hung in it here and there. Long, smooth locks framed my face, curled slightly at their ends. Violets and dark ivory sweetheart roses adorned some of the braids.

"Wow," I said.

Nia wrung her hands. "My lady likes?"

"Very much."

She beamed. With her petite frame and smooth face, she looked about sixteen but could probably actually boast a century. "I didn't know how humans wore it."

I smiled and gave her arm a small pat. "It's wonderful."

She looked ready to swoon with joy, and I recalled how eagerly Dorian's staff always jumped to obey his commands. Was I inspiring that kind of loyalty? Or fear?

Dorian swept into the room then, resplendent in a forest green robe made of silk. The edging contained an intricate pattern of ivory, russet, and gold, set off by the black slacks and ivory shirt underneath.

"Much better," he said, taking my hand. "Come, we're late."

Muran and a few others followed as we headed for the throne room. Dorian didn't actually run, but an urgency underscored his movement.

"Why the rush?" I asked. "Don't they wait on your every pleasure?"

"Certainly. But I have to be in there before the other monarchs arrive, or we'll create a complication of etiquette. Everyone will bow when we enter, but the other monarchs don't have to. If they're in there before me, it'll be awkward."

"What do you mean by 'bow'? Does that mean—"

A herald hurled open the double doors and announced in a booming voice: "His royal majesty, King Dorian of the House of Arkady, caller of Earth, protector of the Oak Land, blessed of the gods."

"Whoa," I breathed. Dorian squeezed my hand.

"—with Eugenie Markham, called Odile Dark Swan, daughter of Tirigan the Storm King."

I didn't think I'd ever get used to being titled, but my astonishment over that faded compared to what happened next. Everyone in the room turned toward us and fell to their knees, heads bowed. Dead silence followed. Slowly, almost in a glide step, we walked down the center aisle, and I tried to look straight ahead and not at the sea of obeisance.

Civilizations rose and fell in the time it took us to reach the throne. When we did, Dorian turned us around to face the assembly and made a small, nondescript gesture. I don't know how the others saw it with their heads so low, but they all rose and the drone of life and music promptly returned. People moved again, mingling and laughing. Servants scurried to and fro with drinks and trays. It could have been any human party, save for the occasional troll and wraith sipping wine. The men dressed in variations of the Renaissance look Dorian seemed to favor, but the women's gowns ran the gamut of bell sleeves and velvet to Grecian wraps and gauze.

"And now, my dear, we must part ways."

I jerked my gaze away from the assembled throng. "What are you talking about?"

He waved his hand. "These are the greatest nobles in my kingdom, not to mention the other kingdoms. I must mingle, listen to their simpering, act like I care. You know how it is."

Panic seized me as I looked back at all those gentry faces. "Why can't I go with you? I mean, we coordinate and everything."

"Because if I keep you on my arm all night, I'll look possessive and insecure. Leaving you on your own shows I have absolute confidence that you'll leave with me tonight, regardless of other solicitations."

"Oh, my God . . . I'm going to be hit on all night."

He laughed. "Don't worry, that's all they'll do—unless

you wish otherwise. Anyone who touches you against your will would incur the wrath of my entire guard, not to mention most of the guests. It would be a shocking insult."

"And yet I could apparently go off with anyone if I wanted to."

"Of course. You're free to choose as you like."

"Wouldn't that be an insult to your manhood or something?"

"A bit. But then I'd just take five or so women to my bed and redeem myself fairly quickly."

"Whoa. I feel like I'll be holding you back."

"Don't worry. I'll recover once you're gone tomorrow."

I swallowed and looked around, the jokes unable to allay my anxiety. "I don't even know anybody."

He turned me to him and gave me a soft kiss on the lips. I had to consciously work to keep my body relaxed. It was still a shock each time he did that.

"You'll just have to meet them, then," he said.

He strolled off toward the first group of people he saw, and I heard a flurry of exuberant greetings at his approach. Feeling stupid and awkward, I wondered where I should go and whom I should talk to. I didn't really do big parties. Too much of my time was spent in solitude to really know how to interact in a group like this. That wasn't even taking into account that these were all Otherworldly residents. Two of my deepest phobias combined into one long evening.

"Wine?" asked a servant who had suddenly appeared at my side.

"Yes, please."

I seized one of the goblets from her proffered tray and took a hasty gulp of a sweet, fruity red. Picking a direction at random, I took five steps and was immediately intercepted by a tall gentry in scarlet velvet. He had black hair and a neatly trimmed beard.

"Lady Markham," he oozed, taking my free hand and kissing it. "It's a pleasure to meet you at last. I am Marcus, lord of Danzia in the Rowan Land."

"Hi," I said, knowing I would never again remember his name once he left.

He kept holding my hand and let his eyes run over me from head to toe. I suddenly wished the dress wasn't so tight or the neckline so low.

"I must say," he murmured, "I'd heard reports of your beauty, but they are paltry things compared to the reality."

"Thanks."

I tried to take back my hand, but he held on to it.

"My family's nobility extends all the way back to the migration to this world. We are renowned for our fierce warriors. Magic runs strong in our blood, usually calling to one of the elements. My own inclinations run toward control of the air."

As if to emphasize the point, I suddenly felt the slightest of breezes blow against my arms.

"My heirs will inherit a vast estate. My house has always served in an advisory capacity to royalty. Even now, I am a close personal friend of Katrice, the Rowan Queen. She is a powerful ally."

I realized then he was laying out his pedigree for me, quickly and efficiently, much as a breeder might show off a prize dog's papers. I opened my mouth, ready to tell him I wasn't interested, but he just kept going.

"Some men would fear having a warrior consort. They would seek to control you and seize the power for their own uses." He inclined his head ever so suggestively toward where Dorian conversed with a tall, dark-skinned woman. "Not me. I would not use you to further my own ends. You would rule by my side as an equal, sharing in the guidance of our children."

Yikes. This wasn't even our first date. I managed to break my hand free of his. "Thank you, but this is all kind of sudden. It's been really great talking to you, though."

Anxiousness flooded his face. "But I haven't even told you about my famed reputation as a lover—"

"I've got to be somewhere right now. Sorry."

I took two steps back, turned, and practically ran into another man. Beyond him, a few others attempted to linger inconspicuously. In fact this one, I realized, had simply been waiting for me to reject Marcus. He gave me a dazzling smile.

"Lady Markham, it's a pleasure to meet you at last. . . ."

I sort of lost track of time after that. I never got much farther than that spot and my wine remained forgotten and undrunk. Listening politely to each guy's sales pitch, I amused myself by considering just how much I could push the limits of the hospitality rule before getting in trouble with Dorian. Yet, no matter how annoying each guy got, I squashed my rebellious instincts and kept to good behavior.

After a couple hours, I caught sight of Shaya, the black-haired woman who had captured me that first night. She walked alone through the room. Brushing off my current suitor, I broke free of the next contender and hurried over to her.

"Hey, Shaya, how's it going?"

She looked at me in astonishment, not surprising considering I hadn't spoken to her since my capture. Her gown was midnight blue velvet with a full skirt, tight sleeves, and a high collar. I didn't entirely understand her whole background, but apparently she was the younger daughter of some noble and had ended up in a military career as part of Dorian's guard.

"Lady Markham," she returned. Mild curiosity showed on her face. "What can I do for you?"

"Oh, nothing. Just thought we'd . . . you know, talk."

One delicate eyebrow rose. She glanced over at the eager throng of men and turned back to me with a half-smile. "It seems like you have plenty of guests to talk to."

"Please," I whispered. "I know we aren't friends, but

just talk to me like we are. Just for a minute. I can't stand it. I need a break. I'm so tired of hearing about how big each guy's estate is . . . not to mention other things."

She laughed, the sound rich and sweet. Linking her arm through mine, she led me idly around, like we were indeed friends.

"I've heard stories about the things you've faced down. And yet, in the end, it's a group of desperate nobles who undo you."

She allowed me a few minutes' solitude, and we talked about trivial things. As we did, I realized something: She was really funny. And intelligent. And . . . nice. I'd dismissed her upon our first meeting as a prissy gentry bitch, my attitude fueled partially by my capture and partially by the antagonism at dinner. But here she was, hanging out with me like any other person would, her comments both witty and astute.

"I have to go. Rurik's looking for me," she said at last, letting go of me. She smiled again, amused and compassionate. "Put up with them a little longer. They're nothing more than a nuisance."

I shook my head. "They're so blunt and straightforward. It's strange." Kiyo and I had once mocked the pretenses in dating, but right now, a little less honesty had its appeal.

"Then be blunt back. If you're too nice, they'll think they have a chance and will try another time. Most now consider you a high-ranking noble; arrogance is expected. They won't think you're rude."

I thanked her and watched her leave, just as a hand tapped my shoulder. I sighed. Time to face the wolves again.

Or fox, as it turned out.

"Hey," I said. "Nice threads."

Kiyo stood before me in a beautifully tailored tux, its clean black and white lines standing out in sharp contrast beside the flowing colors of the other men.

"I wore it for you. Figured you might like a change from velvet and silk. And as for you . . ." His smoky eyes did a quick assessment of me. "I've been hearing a lot of guys drool over your dress tonight."

"You've been here for a while? And didn't come talk to me?"

He grinned. "You looked pretty busy."

"Well, stay with me now. Maybe they'll leave me alone if they think I'm occupied with someone."

We found a two-seated bench against a wall, padded with brocade-covered cushions. I sighed and leaned my head against his shoulder. He put an arm around me.

"I wish I was out patrolling like I usually do tonight. Fighting spirits and whatnot isn't half as exhausting as this."

"And so Tucson goes undefended, eh?"

"Roland's on it, much to my mother's dismay. I just hope I've drawn a lot of the action here instead of back there."

We sat quietly for a while, watching the party. It reminded me of the bar. Alone but not alone. Like any other party, people were getting more drunk as the night progressed. That unabashed sexual contact popped up more and more frequently, and a number of people danced wherever they found room. They moved in graceful strides, reminiscent of ballroom styles I knew.

"I've been thinking . . . about last night."

I looked up at him. "Yeah. I've thought about that a few times myself."

"You were . . . I don't know. I've never seen you like that. Not that we've done it all that much, but . . . wow. You marked me up pretty good."

"Is that a bad thing?"

He smiled. "No. I don't think so." His fingers brushed my chin and tipped my face up. "But what was going on? How'd a nightmare bring that on?"

I turned my face away. "It wasn't exactly a nightmare."

"What, then?"

"Just a dream . . . or a memory. It was about my father. And magic."

"What happened?"

"I . . . well, it's hard to explain."

"Eugenie—"

I kept my demeanor light and playful. "Forget about it. For tonight at least, okay? It isn't the right time. We can talk later."

He hesitated, then nodded. I moved my face closer, and he brushed his lips against my forehead, down to my cheek. I closed my eyes and sighed, luxuriating as his lips moved delicately down the side of my neck. We turned toward each other, our mouths drawn by some unseen force. And as we kissed, I forgot all about the crazy propositions tonight. There was only this. Me and Kiyo.

"No groping," I warned, seeing his hand slyly move toward forbidden areas. "I don't care how many other people are doing it. Or how much attention we don't draw to it."

"Then let's go somewhere private," he murmured, trailing kisses along my shoulder.

"I can't. You know I have to leave with Dorian. Nothing's going to happen," I added, seeing him open his mouth. "It's just for appearances. We can get together tomorrow."

He considered and nodded. "All right. But I'm giving you a good sendoff tonight."

He moved back, and we continued our kissing for a bit until a voice said, "The gods know I've seen some strange things in my life, but never did I expect to find a kitsune trying to make himself ruler over all of us."

We looked up in surprise. I hadn't expected another suitor while clearly busy with Kiyo.

Aeson stood there.

Chapter Twenty-One

I shot up, anger coursing through my body as I stared at that smug face. A heavy, bejeweled crown sat atop his brown hair, and he wore a close-fitting black satin dinner jacket.

"Don't look at me like that, Lady Markham," he told me in a voice both pleasant and hostile. "Dorian will not protect you if you start trouble in his home, no matter how advantageous you are as a lover."

"Fine. I'll just have to kill you somewhere else."

"Your plan didn't work so well last time."

"Neither did yours."

He leered. "That dress is exquisite, you know. It outlines every part of your body beautifully."

I crossed my arms instinctually. "Don't waste my time with compliments."

"Just tossing in my own bid for your body, just like everyone else here."

"Yeah? Haven't you paid attention? None of their compliments have worked either."

"Bah. They're petty lordlings and leeches scraping for power," he said with a sneer. "The general consensus is that you've refused everyone simply because you've yet to be approached by anyone worthy." He cut a glance at Kiyo as he spoke.

"Or maybe because I'm with Dorian. Not that it makes any difference. I'd fuck that trowe over there before I'd go anywhere near you."

"I think I'd like to see that, especially considering he comes to your knees."

"If this is the part where you tell me how well-endowed you are, save it. There's nothing you can say that would get me near your bed, so just give it up and leave."

His features hardened, a cold and sardonic smirk turning up his lips. "I suppose I can't argue with that. Not that it matters. I won't be alone tonight."

He stepped aside, just barely, and inclined his head. I followed the motion across the room. Jasmine Delaney stood among a group of gentry nobles. She was watching us, an unreadable look on her face. A long dress, heavy with brocade and jewels, draped her slight form, and her gray eyes looked even more enormous than last time.

I clenched my fists, remembering the look on my mom's face when she described her captivity. Wil's picture of a lonely girl, lost in her fantasy world, circled around my mind. "I *will* kill you, you bastard. But first I'll make sure you beg me for it." I sounded like Volusian.

"Eugenie," murmured Kiyo, laying a hand on my wrist. His voice was firm and cautionary. He apparently feared I'd do something stupid. It was a good fear.

Aeson seemed unconcerned. "Those are kind of extreme measures, don't you think? Especially when there are much simpler ones."

"Such as?"

He shrugged. "I'll turn her over to you tonight."

"Let me guess. If I go live with you instead?"

"No such commitments. Come with me just for Beltane. One night, and both you and she walk free. Not a bad offer, especially since there are still a number of men out there plotting to carry you off for an extended period.

Considering the other drivel that's approached you, you could do a lot worse. I'm powerful. Rich. Influential. A worthy consort."

I looked Aeson up from head to toe, glanced at the still-watching Jasmine, and then turned back to him. "I think I'd rather just kill you."

He gave me a mocking bow, face still hard. "I look forward to the attempt." He started to walk away, then gave Kiyo a considering look. "I suppose you could pick worse men to father your child. This one's already proven he can do it."

Aeson swept away from us and headed back to his group. Sliding a possessive arm around Jasmine, he leaned over and kissed her hard, pressing her body up against his. With the difference in their heights, he looked like he was molesting a small child—which, I supposed, he actually was. Puberty be damned.

The anger that sight inspired in me solidified into ice as I turned back around to face Kiyo. The look on his face made something inside of me curl up into a ball.

"What's he talking about?"

He started to open his mouth and then paused, apparently reconsidering what he wanted to say. My incredulity exploded.

"Kiyo! This is where you tell me he's full of shit and you have no idea what he's talking about."

"Eugenie . . ." he began slowly.

"Oh, my God." I turned around. The ice inside of me melted and made me queasy. "You have a kid you never told me about. You have a kid somewhere."

"No. Not yet."

I spun around. "What the hell is that supposed to—" I stopped. "Maiwenn. Maiwenn is pregnant."

Poor Maiwenn. Poor sick and weak Maiwenn. I'd heard a number of comments made about her condition and never questioned it. It was a sign of my distraction in the last month. Gentry didn't really get sick. They could get killed in battle, die from an infected wound, or die of old age. That was about it.

Even now, looking across the room, I saw her sitting and talking with a few others. She was smiling but looked pale under her tan. The dress she wore was loose and voluminous. The one she'd worn at my house had been similar, albeit not made of silk. She wasn't currently showing off her body.

"You should've told me," I whispered.

"Yes," he said simply. "I should have."

"You should have told me!" I repeated, my voice loud and strained. Most of the room's noise muffled my cry, but a few people nearby gave us curious looks.

"Shh." Kiyo took my arm and steered us back toward the wall. "I was waiting. Things were so uncertain between us. I wanted to have a steady foundation before I told you."

"Did you ever consider that telling me now might help that 'steady foundation'? What happened to all the honesty rhetoric?"

"And how would you have taken it?" he asked quietly. "You've had a hard enough time knowing she and I were together at all."

"No, I haven't."

"Eugenie, I see it in your face whenever her name's mentioned."

"It doesn't matter. This is big."

He shook his head. "It happened in the past. She and I aren't together. We're friends now. You and I are together."

"So what? You're not going to do anything with this baby because you guys aren't together anymore?"

"No! Of course not. I'll be there for the baby, and I'll support Maiwenn as much as that requires."

"Then that's not the past," I snapped. "That's your future. *My* future too if you were planning on being with me."

His face turned even more sober than it had been. "You're right," he said after several drawn-out moments. "It was wrong of me. I'm sorry. I thought I was protecting you."

I gave a harsh laugh that bordered dangerously on being a sob. "Yeah. Everyone wants to protect me lately. My parents did too. You guys think if I don't hear bad things, then they won't exist anymore. But you know what? They *do* still exist, and I *do* end up hearing them. And I wish to God that I could have heard them from the people I love first."

I turned and started walking away. Kiyo grabbed my shoulder. I tried to tug out of his grasp.

"Don't touch me," I warned. "We're done here."

"What are you saying?"

"What do you think? You think I'm going to smile and forgive all this? I can barely forgive my parents, and I've known them my whole life. I've barely known you for a month. That doesn't really count for much."

He flinched. The hand on my shoulder dropped.

"I see," he said stiffly, face darkening. "Then I guess we are done here."

"Yeah."

We stood staring at each other, and where heat once had smoldered between us, only a lonely chasm remained. I turned on my heels and stormed across the room without even knowing where I went. Eager men approached me, but I brushed past them all, apparently showing the arrogance Shaya had said was expected of me. I just couldn't face them right now.

It was too much. All of it. The crazy propositions. My so-called legacy. Aeson and Jasmine. Maiwenn and Kiyo.

Oh, God, Kiyo. Why had he done this to me? I'd tried to write him off after our first night together, and he'd made me care about him again. Now it only hurt twice as much. The words from last night came back to me.

You're mine.

Apparently not.

I stopped in the middle of the crowded ballroom floor with no clue where I was going. I'd gotten disoriented somehow and forgotten where the exit was. The throne was over there, so that meant—

"Yo, Odile. Some party, huh?"

My navigation attempts were interrupted by Finn's approach. I still hadn't adjusted to seeing him in his more humanlike Otherworldly form.

"Finn! I need you to get me out of here."

He frowned. "You can't leave yet. Etiquette says—"

"Fuck etiquette," I snarled. "Get me out. I want to be alone."

His standard cheery expression faded. "Sure thing. Come on."

He led me not toward the main doors but rather to a small doorway tucked near a corner. Delicious smells wafted out from inside. This was some sort of back way to the kitchen. A number of scurrying servants gave us startled looks as we passed through twisting corridors and banks of ovens, but Finn moved with purpose, never breaking stride. People tend not to question if they think you know where you're going.

With a flourish, he gestured me to a small alcove far from the bustle of the cooks. Hooks with cloaks and coats covered the walls, and I realized this must be where the staff had stashed their personal things. A small bench sat below the hooks.

"Good enough?" Finn asked.

"Yes. Thank you. Now go away." I sat down and wrapped my arms around myself.

"But shouldn't I—"

"Just go, Finn." I could hear the tears in my voice. "Please."

He gave me a mournful, almost hurt look and then walked away.

The tears took a long time to come, and even then,

they did so reluctantly. Only a couple streaked down my cheeks. I had felt helpless with the mud elemental, but this was a different kind of helplessness, one with mental, not physical, consequences.

My heart ached inside for Kiyo, and my stomach burned with fury against Aeson. Neither ailment looked to have a remedy anytime soon.

I don't know how long I sat there before Dorian came. I could only make out his shape in my periphery, but the scent of cinnamon gave him away. He sat down beside me for a long time, saying nothing. Finally, I felt his fingertip gently run along my cheek and wipe away one of the tears.

"What can I do?" he asked.

"Nothing. Not unless you'll let me break hospitality and go do some damage."

"Ah, sweet one, if that were possible, I would have long since strangled several of my nobles, lest I be forced to listen to more of their idiotic blather."

"What's the point of being a king, then?"

"Not sure that there is one. The food maybe."

"You make a joke out of everything."

"Life's too painful not to."

"Yeah. I guess."

We lapsed into silence until Dorian called someone's name. A moment later, a small, harried servant appeared. "Bring us some of that chocolate cake Bertha made. Two slices." The man hurried off.

"I'm not hungry," I mumbled.

"You will be."

The cake arrived. It was one of those flourless kinds, so it was more like cake chocolate than chocolate cake. Raspberry sauce pooled around it. I found myself eating every bite.

"Better?" Dorian asked.

"Yeah."

"You see? I told you it was the food."

I set the plate on the floor and tried to give voice to an idea that had slowly been percolating in the back of my head. An idea that probably would never have dared surface had I not been so furious at Aeson and Kiyo tonight. Indeed, it was Aeson's preposterous proposal that had reminded me of it.

"Dorian?"

"Yes?"

"When we first met . . . you told me that if I slept with you, you'd go with me to get Jasmine. Does that offer still stand?"

The first surprised look I'd ever seen on him crossed his face. I took a certain amount of pride in realizing I'd finally caught him off-guard.

"My, my," he said softly. "This is unexpected. So. Desperation and fury achieve what all my charms could not, hmm?"

A flush spilled over my cheeks. "Well, no . . . it's not like—"

"No," he said abruptly. "The offer does not still stand."

"But I thought—"

"I saw you fight with Aeson and the kitsune. I won't have you come to my bed out of some misguided sense of revenge on the two of them."

He was right in a way, I realized. This was my means of getting back at both them. Aeson for flaunting Jasmine. Kiyo for breaking my heart.

"Please," I said. "I'll do it. I-I don't mind. And anyway . . . I have to get Jasmine back. I can't handle her being with him anymore."

Dorian was quiet for a long time. Finally he said, "All right."

I snapped my head toward him. "You mean it?"

"Certainly. We'll go back to my room and see how you do."

"See how—? What's that supposed to mean?" Was the deal contingent on how good I was in bed?

He smiled. "I'll get Nia to take you back. I have to mingle a bit more and will join you soon."

Nia arrived as if by magic and did exactly as he'd said. Once alone in his massive chamber, I paced restlessly, reconciling myself to sex with a full gentry. It would be easy. Nothing to it. I just had to lay there. Gentry didn't carry diseases like humans. I couldn't get pregnant. One night, and I could finally get revenge on that bastard Aeson and the smug look on his face. And yes, Dorian had been right: I'd be getting revenge on Kiyo too. Who knew? Maybe sleeping with Dorian would fill the terrible, aching hole Kiyo's betrayal had left in me.

"Admiring the view?" asked Dorian when he finally entered. I stood by the huge picture window, staring at my own reflection in the dark glass.

"I'm never here in daylight. I've never seen what it looks like."

"It's lovely. You'll see it in the morning."

I supposed I would. He took off the heavy robe, poured a glass of wine, and sprawled back on the pile of pillows on his bed. The move seemed less an initiation into sex and more of an expression of fatigue. He looked very ordinary. Very human.

"You look tired." I leaned against the bedpost, watching him.

He exhaled heavily. "It's hard work amusing one's admirers—as you can no doubt attest to. How'd you like your first royal party? Tell me who you spoke to. Your night must have been more tedious than mine."

Gingerly, I sat on the bed's edge and recounted the night for him. I gave my opinions and offered up as many details as I could on my many solicitations. Names eluded me, but Dorian could identify the culprits pretty easily based on other identifying information. He laughed so hard at my accounts and opinions, I thought he'd start crying.

Swinging himself up gracefully, he slid over on the

satin coverlet to sit beside me. "You poor, poor thing. No wonder you like hunting us down. Although, I confess after my own equally inane experiences tonight, I might have a few names to give you."

"You shouldn't say things like that."

He shook his head and laughed. "Stay here long enough, and you'll say them too."

Those gold and green eyes watched me, glimmering with both affection and desire. For a moment, I could almost believe Dorian wanted me for *me* and not for my human fertility or connection to a prophecy.

Resting his hand on the back of my neck, he kissed me, and I had no more time for questions. We'd kissed a lot by now, and his lips still held that same silky softness, that careful precision and control. I was used to this, and it warmed up every part of me, but tonight's inevitable conclusion loomed before me. My lips almost faltered but still managed to kiss him back. I could do this. It was easy . . . right?

He gently lay me back on the bed, still kissing me as he rested his body partially across my own. The heat and weight of him triggered something pleasurable within me, even as some part of my brain suddenly started pining for Kiyo and recalling every bad thing I'd ever been taught about gentry. My breath quickened but not from passion. *No, no,* I chastised myself, forcing my body to not go rigid. *This is Dorian. There's nothing to be afraid of.* But I was afraid. This didn't feel right. I couldn't let myself do it, even though I knew there was no reason not to. I hung out with gentry now. I had titles. I wanted to learn their magic. I wanted to kill Aeson. And yet, somehow, some part of me refused to give into this final—

Dorian broke away from me and sat up. "It's as I thought. You don't want to really do this. You're afraid of me."

I half sat up, propping on my elbow. Swallowing, I

tried to breathe more steadily. "Didn't you say once that you wanted me to be afraid?"

"Not *this* afraid. Besides, your heart is a bit muddled tonight."

He rose from the bed and casually poured another goblet of wine. Sipping from it, he walked over to the window and stared at the nothingness, just as I had earlier.

"W-what are you doing?"

"I told you before. I don't take women who don't want me." He kept his back to me, but his voice held that usual carefree tone. Like everything was still just one big joke. I wondered if he was upset. I couldn't read him at all.

"Er, wait . . ." I scrambled off the bed and grabbed his arm, nearly spilling the wine. "What are you saying? We have to do this. I swear, it doesn't matter. I want to do this. Really."

"Maybe. You don't look at me like you do the kitsune, but I've felt your desire before. It's a fleeting thing, though, and it can't quite win against that part of you that says not to submit to one of the shining ones."

"Maybe we can ignore that part."

He laughed and touched my cheek. "I adore you, you know that? I'm so happy I met you."

I swallowed, anxious and desperate. "Please, Dorian. I want to get Jasmine. We have to do this."

"We aren't doing anything like that. Not tonight, I'm afraid." He walked away and sat back on the bed near the headboard, just as he had earlier. "I will, however, make you a deal. We will postpone our arrangement until you're ready. In exchange for this grace period, I add the further caveat that we won't go to Aeson until you've made some suitable progress with your magic."

I thought about our last couple of dismal lessons. "That might take awhile. . . ."

"Then it takes awhile. Really, if you want every edge you can get to defeat him, you'll be better off knowing something about your power, even if it's small. Your weapons are strong, but if they're gone . . . then they're gone."

I wanted to fight him on this, to tell him I couldn't wait that long. Fuck the magic. Fuck my prudish resistance. We should get the sex over with and just grab Jasmine.

But I knew he was right. On all levels. He didn't deserve my body without my mind being into it, and I did need every advantage I could get.

"Well, then . . . can we practice tonight? Seeing as how nothing else is going on?" If I distracted myself, maybe I'd stop hurting for Kiyo.

"No point in bothering with tact, eh? Very well, then, let's see what we can accomplish."

I dragged a chair into the middle of the room while Dorian produced some more cords from his neverending supply.

"Beige and violet," he said, holding them up. "To match your dress."

"It's 'champagne.'"

He didn't tie my hands this time, but he did completely bind my torso. Again, he used intricate patterns as he worked, integrating unique braids and weaves. The purple silk crisscrossed around my breasts, and each time his hand brushed some sensitive part, a secret thrill would run through my body. What was the matter with me? If I could have these physical reactions, then why couldn't I have sex with him?

The binding took forever, just like always. It made me so impatient, but Dorian clearly enjoyed it. He worked with infinite patience, careful of every weave and knot. When he finally finished, he stood back and surveyed me, just as he had the last two times.

"Very nice," he observed, eyes taking me in.

A strange thought occurred to me as I sat there. I willingly let him do this to me, but really, it was a leap of faith. My arms might be free, but as he stood over me, I realized how helpless I was. How totally in his power I was if he wanted to abuse it.

But he didn't. He never did. After blindfolding me, I heard him fetch the water pitcher from the other room. Once it was apparently hidden, he returned to the bed. I heard the bed shift under his weight, the sound of more wine pouring out.

"Have at it," he said.

I focused just like I'd done in our last two lessons. My mind expanded, reaching out into the room, trying to find the water I supposedly had an affinity for. I repeated the same exercises, visualizing moisture and wetness. The way it felt and tasted.

Yet, when I pointed to where I thought the water jug sat, he told me I was wrong.

So I tried again. Three more times, to be precise. Failures each time.

I heard him yawn. "Would you like to call it a night? I dare say this bed is big enough for us to sleep chastely in. Or, if you wish, I have no qualms about sleeping on the sofa in the other room."

"No," I said stubbornly. "I want to try again."

"As you like."

Again, I went through the motions, hating them yet burning with need. I wanted to do this. I wanted to control the power. I might have failed at sex tonight, but I would not fail at—

"It's there," I said suddenly.

"Where?"

I pointed, and in my outstretched hand, I could almost feel something wet. It was so easy. How had I not noticed this before?

"It's right beside you. Really close. If you're still lying on the bed, I'd say . . . elbow level. Maybe on the table."

He stayed quiet.

"Well? I'm right, aren't I?"

"Check the rest of the room."

My hopes crumbled. "I was wrong again."

"Just check. See if the water is somewhere else."

I didn't get his game. Why the vagueness? Had I found it or not?

But I tried again, reaching out into the room. That spot near him pulsed to my senses. The water was there, I knew it. So what was this all about?

Another spot suddenly called out to me. I reached for it without using my hands this time, and that same strong pulsing reached back. And with that sensation came a slight tingle, only a spark, but it whispered of the power I'd felt in the dream-memory.

"Okay. Right by the door. On the floor, I think."

"Yes." The response was surprisingly simple and clear. No jokes or games.

"Right? I'm right? Really? You're not just messing with me so we can go to bed?"

I heard his soft laugher as he walked to the door and then approached me. Taking my hand, he dipped it down into a ceramic pitcher, and I felt cool water slide over my hand. I laughed, ecstatic and empowered. I felt like splashing it on both of us.

"So what'd I find the first time then? By the bed? It must have been something, judging from your reaction."

"Indeed it was."

He took the pitcher away, walked toward the bed, and returned to me. I felt his arm move toward me, and then the scent of something strong and fruity touched my nose.

"The wine," I realized. "I found the wine."

"Yes. Quite remarkable too, considering I'd almost drank it all." He set the decanter down and untied my blindfold. "Now, my dear, it's time to go to sleep."

He knelt before me and started the tedious process of undoing all those ties and knots. I waved my free hands.

"You want help?"

He shook his head. I could smell the wine on him. "No. Leave me my simple pastimes, please."

"Are you drunk?"

"Probably."

He worked steadily on freeing me from the cords, his fingers a little less precise than they'd been earlier. I again felt that strange chill over being so ensnared.

Released at last, I stood up and stretched. "Can I have some of that?"

I wanted to celebrate, and after weeks of good behavior, I realized I could safely drink here. Funny that the safest place for me now would be in a gentry's keep.

He held up the decanter. There was probably only one glass left. He eyed it askance for a moment and then took off his shirt. Perplexed, I watched him walk over to the door and stick his head out.

"Yes, sire?" I heard a voice say.

"We need more wine!" declared Dorian in a booming voice. "Lady Markham and I have a lot more to do tonight."

"Right away, your majesty!"

"Hurry, man. You have no idea how demanding she is. I can barely keep her satisfied as it is."

I heard boots running on the stone floor. Dorian shut the door and turned to me.

"Your wine will be here shortly, and my prowess will no doubt be proclaimed throughout the castle."

I rolled my eyes at his show. "So did I pass the test?"

"Hmm?"

"You said I had to make progress in magic before we could go get Jasmine."

"Oh. That. Well, this wasn't exactly progress."

"The hell it wasn't."

He sat next to me on the bed. "You found the water. Now you have to do something with it. Your enemies won't be impressed when you inform them there's a lake just over the next hill."

I sighed. Great. "So what's the next step?"

"Next you make the water come to you."

"Huh. Well. That at least sounds more exciting."

"Not really. Mostly we do exactly the same thing except you just sit around and try to make it move."

"You're the most boring teacher ever."

He grinned and gave me a quick kiss on the cheek, just as a knock sounded at the door. "It all depends on what you want me to teach you."

Chapter Twenty-Two

I didn't give Lara all the details the next day, only that I'd just broken up with a guy.

"Ice cream," she advised me through the phone. "Lots of ice cream. And tequila. That's the key."

"I can't do a lot of drinking right now."

"Hmm. Well, maybe get one of those liqueur-flavored ice creams. Like with Kahlúa or Irish cream."

"Any other hot tips?"

"Chick flicks."

"Good God. I'm disconnecting right now."

"Well, then, try this." She sounded huffy. "I just got a call from a guy who thinks there's a troll in his basement. Seems like beating one of those up would be therapeutic."

"Lara's full of shit," Tim told me later when I recounted the phone call. "Why do women turn to ice cream? It makes them fat, then they hate themselves and start going on and on about how they'll never find anybody, blah, blah. It's stupid. Now, if you've got some peyote squirreled away, that'd be a different matter. . . ."

"No," I said. "No peyote. Not after what happened last time."

He made a face. "All right, then. My best advice? Don't

call him. He's probably going through all sorts of regret and guilt. You call him, he'll feel smothered and put up his defenses. Let him stew for a while, and he'll call you."

"I don't want him to call."

"Sure, Eug."

I ended up taking down the troll later that day, but it didn't really do much for me. Neither did the Kiss puzzle I put together that night. With my doldrums growing, I was only too happy when my next lesson with Dorian came the following day.

Considering his fascination with human things and novelty in general, I thought he'd like eating out somewhere. I didn't know why I bothered; we probably should have gone straight to the lesson. Maybe I felt guilty about the sex thing. Maybe I was lonely.

After a quick drive, I arrived at the Catalina Lodge, a prissy hotel about a mile or so from Catalina State Park. I parked in a remote spot, hopefully away from watchful eyes, and sat down on the ground with crossed legs. The ring sat beside me on the asphalt. Slipping on my sunglasses, I leaned against the car and waited.

My timing couldn't have been more perfect. A few minutes later, I felt the pressure and tingling, and then Dorian materialized beside me. He'd left the robes and cloaks at home, wearing dark pants and a blousy, sage-colored shirt that looked only moderately out of place. He squinted up at the bright sunlight and then noticed me on the ground.

"Isn't it ever cloudy in this infernal place?"

I straightened up, and he offered a hand to help me rise. "I could arrange that if you wanted."

"And risk you wiping out half of your fair city? No thank you."

"Figured you'd appreciate that. It'll make your world domination easier. One less place to conquer."

"No. I need this place intact. I plan on keeping prisoners and exiled enemies here. Where exactly are we today?"

"Mere steps away from the best food of your life, if rumors are true."

He flashed me one of his trademark grins. "Pleasure before business? My, my, you never fail to astound me."

"Hell, wait'll you hear me identify every water source in the restaurant." That, at least, had been a good thing to come from Beltane. I could now feel cactuses, wells, and any other water source within a certain distance. I could even sense people now since the human body was supposed to be, what, 65 percent water? That meant no one could sneak up on me.

Inside and seated, Dorian found watching his surroundings far more fascinating than anything on the menu.

"Pick something for me," he said distractedly, watching a family leave with four small children in tow. He cocked his head curiously. "By the gods, do all those little ones belong to them?"

I glanced up. "Likely."

"And their mother looks pregnant again. Incredible. Back home, those people would be worshipped as fertility deities. A family with two children is remarkable enough."

The waitress returned. I ordered spinach-stuffed ravioli for me and some sort of spicy chicken for him.

"A lot of middle- and upper-class families actually go out of their way to only have two kids. And a lot of them don't even start until they're older than me."

"Baffling." He propped his elbow on the table, resting his chin in his hand. "A woman your age could have had that many children by now."

"Hey, I'm like twenty-six. I'm not that old. I don't even look my age."

"That's your father's blood. And I wasn't insulting your age—merely making an observation." He sighed. "I'd give up half my kingdom for just one child."

I smiled slyly. "And the chance to be the father of Storm King's grandson?"

"I'd be just as happy to father his granddaughter too. I'd be happy to father anyone's child."

"Then why don't you find some nice girl and do it?"

"Believe me, it hasn't been for lack of trying." His face held a rare seriousness, but the expression vanished as quickly as it came. "Ah, now there's a fetching young woman."

Following his gaze across the restaurant, I saw a tall blond woman exit the restroom. She was stuffed into a tiny spandex dress, her chest practically spilling out. I didn't have the heart to tell Dorian there was probably a lot of silicone in there. His eyes lingered on her, then his charm-alarm must have gone off for fear of neglecting me. He turned back around.

"Not that you don't look lovely today too."

"You don't have to pacify me." I laughed. "You're welcome to ogle other women."

Our late-afternoon meal proceeded nicely, and everything about it continued to enchant Dorian. The credit card I used to pay with at the end especially captivated him.

"It has information about me stored in it," I tried to explain. "That information lets the restaurant get money from me."

He picked up the returned card gingerly, turning it over and over in his fingers. "Intriguing. I imagine this has to do something with electricity? The blood of your culture?"

His wry tone made me smile. "Something like that."

It wasn't until we were on the mile and a half walk to Catalina State Park that things got a little tense.

"Heard from the kitsune lately?"

"He has a name," I snapped.

"Heard from Kiyo lately?"

"No."

"Really? He hasn't tried to contact you and beg for forgiveness?"

"No," I repeated between gritted teeth. Something about the way he said it made it sound like I'd been dealt a great insult.

"Odd. I think that's what I'd do if I'd offended my lady-love. Of course, I suppose when a man spends half his existence as an animal, you can't really expect him not to act like one."

I halted and turned on Dorian. "Stop it. Just stop it, okay? Stop trying to poison me against him."

"You don't need me to do what he's already done."

"Damn it, Dorian. I'm serious."

We started walking again, but it was me who brought up the subject again after several minutes of silence. "You knew. You knew Maiwenn was pregnant and didn't tell me."

"It wasn't my secret to tell. Besides, I got in trouble the last time I spoke badly of her. You accused me of trying to turn you against her."

"I'm not sure this is really the same thing. We're talking about Kiyo now. Last time it was about Maiwenn wanting to kill me."

"And you don't think they're the same thing?"

I stopped walking. "What do you mean?"

"Kiyo is her friend, formerly her lover, and now the father of her child. He stands firmly with her against Storm King's invasion. Yet, where would he stand if it came to a choice between you or her? What if Maiwenn decided you were too great a threat? What would he do? What would he do if you accidentally got pregnant?"

A chill ran through me at his words. I abruptly turned away and barely recognized my own voice when I spoke.

"I don't want to talk about this anymore."

He held up his hands in a pacifying gesture, face calm and affable. "I honestly intended no harm. Pick another topic. We'll discuss anything you like."

But I didn't really feel like talking anymore, so the rest of the walk proceeded in silence. When we finally entered the park, the sun was well into its descent. We still had plenty of light and set out to pick a good place to work. We ended up following one of the less traveled trails and then deviated from it into a semi-treed area. We had nothing even close to dense forest coverage, but rock outcroppings, some scraggly pines, and distance from the path promised relative privacy.

The routine proved to be the same. Dorian had me sit on the ground, leaning against a rock. He had another stash of those silk cords and again wrapped them around me. The rock didn't make a suitable attachment, so he simply let my hands rest in my lap and bound them together at the wrist. Naturally, he did his usual artistic weave on them, intricately wrapping red and blue cords together.

When he moved on to wrapping the cords around my chest and arms, his eyes flicked to mine and then back to his handiwork. "You aren't really going to stay mad at me for the rest of the day, are you?"

"I'm not mad."

He laughed. "Of course you are. You're also a terrible liar. Lean forward, please." I did, letting him tie the knots behind me.

"I just don't like you playing games, that's all. I don't trust them."

"And pray, what games am I playing?"

"I don't even know half the time. Gentry games, I guess. You speak the truth, but it always has an ulterior motive behind it."

He leaned me gently back against the rock and crouched on his knees to look me in the face. "Ah, but I *do* speak the truth."

"I just can't tell what you want sometimes, Dorian. What your plans are. You're hard to read."

That delighted smile of his spread over his face. "I'm

hard to read? This from the woman who alternately hates and fucks Otherworldly denizens? The same woman who claims not to trust me even while I tie her up, putting her completely at my mercy?"

I wiggled in my bonds. "Well, I trust you with this."

"Are you sure?"

He pressed a hard kiss against my lips. It startled me, but I couldn't do anything about it. This man, this gentry—the one who could be either helping me or using me—had me trapped. I couldn't do anything except let him keep kissing me. The realization triggered a response in me that was quite startling, considering my issues with control and helplessness. It made me feel vulnerable . . . and excited.

I turned my head away as much as I could, attempting to break off the kiss. "Stop that."

He leaned back on his heels. "Just making a point."

"No, you weren't. You were just trying to kiss me."

"Well, yes, you've got me there. But the fact remains: Tied up or free, you can trust me. I do nothing that I don't firmly believe is in the interest of your well-being. The same holds true for casual comments about your love life. Now then." He stood up. "Shall we commence this lesson?"

"No blindfold?" I asked, still a little shaken.

"Not needed. You know where the water is. Or you will in just a moment."

He produced the canteen I'd brought along and took off its lid. Searching the area, he found a large boulder, reaching almost to his shoulders. He set the open canteen on top of it and then selected a spot for himself near some scrubby bushes where he had a clear vantage of me and the canteen.

"You feel the water?"

"Yes."

"Make sure of it. If you accidentally reach one of

the trees and end up calling its water, you'll kill the poor thing."

I extended my senses, considering what he said. After a few moments, I felt certain I had the water sources all differentiated. "No, I've got it."

"All right, then. Call it to you."

"Am I supposed to make the canteen rise or something?"

"No. You have no connection to it. But you do connect with the water. You feel it. You touch it with your mind. Now coax it to come to you, to come out of its container. You've already done it with storm systems. The trick now is doing it on a small, specific level. Forget about your body—it's useless to you now. This is all in your mind."

"That's all the instruction I get, coach?"

"Afraid so."

He stretched out, rolling onto his side to get comfortable. For someone who took such care with his clothes, he seemed nonchalant about getting them dirty. I supposed laundry was a small concern when you had a full staff to take care of it.

Sighing, I turned back to the canteen. What I attempted seemed ludicrous—but, then, so had feeling the water in the first place. So, I followed what he said as best I could. My grip on the water was so tight, I might as well have held it in my hand already. But no matter how hard my concentration focused, I couldn't make the water move. It reminded me of the wind. I could feel it but not control it. Well, actually, if my training progressed, I might actually be able to control it some day. But the analogy stood, nonetheless.

Time dragged. Extensively. I tried and tried to order the water around, but it refused to obey.

More time passed. It crawled.

I finally decided it was a good thing the cords covered my watch because I'd be pissed off if I discovered how much time had elapsed. Hours had slipped by; I felt certain of it. The light had grown dimmer and dimmer. Looking over at Dorian, I swore he was asleep.

"Hey," I said. No response. "Hey!"

He opened one eye.

"I'm not getting anywhere with this. We should call it a night."

He sat up. "Giving up already?"

"Already? It's been like two hours. Probably three."

"Miracles don't happen overnight. These things take time."

"How much time? I'm starting to wonder if you made this magic rule just to procrastinate on getting Jasmine."

"Well. You can believe that if it makes it easier for you. The truth—if you trust me enough to hear it—is that this is for your own protection. In a perfect world, we would go in and extract the girl quietly. In the real world, we will likely fight Aeson's guards and Aeson himself. I would prefer we both walk out of this alive. You didn't fare so well last time."

"This is going to take forever. This training."

I knew I was being whiny and petulant, but my back hurt, and mosquitoes had come out. At least in identifying the water source, I'd been able to take guesses. Here I could do nothing more than just wait and stare. If nothing happened, nothing happened.

"I'm sorry," I told him. "I'm just tired, that's all. Didn't mean to bitch you out."

He seemed untroubled by my reaction, just like always. Indeed, I could see his face regarding me kindly in the twilight. "No problem at all. Let's go, then."

He walked over to the canteen and recapped it. Closing my eyes, I leaned my head back against the rock to wait for him to release me. As I did, I felt something cool and wet, like mist, spread out behind my back and neck. To my new water senses, it didn't feel . . . right. Moments later, before I could ponder the difference, the mist coalesced into slimy skin.

"Dori—"

My scream was cut off by cold, clawed hands. One covered my mouth, and the other gripped my throat. Dorian had spun around before my cry, making me think he'd sensed something before I had. He leaped toward me, but four wet, human forms materialized in the air before him, blocking his way. Nixies. Water spirits.

Two were male; two were female. Legends whispered they could shape-shift into more beautiful forms, but here they appeared drab. Clammy skin, mottled and gray. Clothes sodden and dripping. Seaweedlike hair hanging down. The one holding me pushed me down flat to the ground, all the better to cut off my oxygen that much faster. Water dripped onto me from her hair, and her eyes gleamed a sickly green in the waning light. She hissed with pleasure and pressed harder while I frantically assessed my options.

I finished the assessment pretty quickly because I had no options. I was fully armed but unable to reach anything because of Dorian's fucking bondage fetish. Covering my mouth stopped me from summoning a minion. The world flickered with starbursts as my air disappeared. My lungs and throat heaved, trying desperately to latch onto something. Her claws dug into the tender flesh of my neck, and I half-wondered if she'd rip it out rather than wait for suffocation.

My only hope was Dorian, but he wouldn't get to me anytime soon, not with his own army of—

Every stone and pebble in the area suddenly lifted off the ground. Shortly thereafter, the really large stones and boulders followed suit. Those big ones exploded, fracturing into thousands of tiny shards. All those little pieces of rock rose higher, joining each other, slowing rotating in a clockwise manner.

My captor's grip had lessened slightly, probably from

surprise. It didn't return my air, but I twisted my head enough to see Dorian standing with his arms raised up like some sort of symphony conductor. Above him, that cyclone of sharp rocks spun faster and faster, a blur to the eye. Then, as though giving the song's grand finale, he brought his arms down sharply.

And down came the rocks.

A portion of that maelstrom swooped and soared, the primitive predecessors of bullets. At first their movements seemed chaotic, and I feared falling into their path. But it turned out every rock had its own plan, its own target. Those sharp pieces honed down on the nixie holding me, piercing and slicing with a fierce precision. She opened her mouth in a silent scream as blood splashed onto me, and her torn body collapsed in a bloody, wet pile. I twisted out from under her, taking in big gulping breaths of air.

Beyond her, Dorian gave another downward motion, urging his orchestra to its next climactic moment. The rocks swooped into another nixie, cutting it to pieces. Then another . . . and another . . . until the nixies were nothing but ribbons of blood and gore. Their task complete, the rocks gently fell to the earth, as soft and placid as drops of rain.

The entire counterattack had taken less than a minute.

Immediately, Dorian knelt by my side, helping me sit up as I gasped my way back to life. "Easy, easy," he warned. Blood covered both of us. "Small breaths."

"Untie me! Get me out of this!"

He pulled the silver athame from my belt. In moments, he sliced open the cords, freeing my arms and hands. I jerked away, my adrenaline still surging. He reached for me, but I flailed against him.

"Damn you! You almost got me killed!" I yelled, hearing the hysteria in my voice. "You almost got me killed!"

He grabbed my upper arms with a solid strength,

pulling me to him and forcing me to stillness. "Eugenie, calm down. *Eugenie!*"

He shook me—hard—where I still struggled, and I halted abruptly, quelled by the harsh sound of his voice and ferocity of his grasp. I could no longer find the silly, languid gentry king. There was a stranger holding me, his face hard and commanding.

"Do you think I'd let anything happen to you?" he demanded, almost shouting. "Do you think I'd let anything harm you?"

I swallowed, still in pain from the nixie's claws on my throat, and found my body shaking. His grip was so tight, I might as well have been tied up again. He scared me, having turned into someone else. Someone powerful and awe-inspiring. Looking into his eyes and seeing the sweat on his face, I realized fear had touched more than just me. He was scared too, not for himself, but for what had almost happened to me. Something inside me eased up, and I nearly slumped into him.

"I can't believe what you did," I whispered. I killed all the time without much thought or effort, but this . . . this had been something else entirely. And he wasn't even at full strength in this world. "You slaughtered them."

"I did what I had to do." The heat in his voice had faded, replaced with a deadly calm. "And you'll be able to do the same someday." One of his hands released me and moved to my head, smoothing my hair back. He pressed our bodies together and rested his cheek against mine so his soft words could spill into my ear. "You will surpass me, Eugenie. Your power will be so great, none will stand against you. Armies and kingdoms will fall, and they will bow down before you."

I found myself trembling again, feeling the same fear and excitement that had filled me during our last kiss. Only this time, I didn't know if my feelings came from his body's proximity . . . or the promise of power he offered.

Chapter Twenty-Three

The similarities between the fachan and nixie attacks weren't lost on me. Both types were water creatures, and all had seemed much more interested in killing Storm King's daughter than fathering her child. Recalling how Dorian had said someone powerful would have had to force them to come out to the desert, I decided that figuring out who that could be needed to move to the top of my list of priorities. Rape was horrible. Death was . . . well, final.

Unfortunately, I wasn't really sure I trusted my new gentry contacts to give me unbiased advice. So I turned to my next-most relatively neutral sources.

Like always, my spirit minions took a long time in answering my question. Nandi and Volusian were compelled to answer eventually, but I think they always sort of tried to wait each other out. This time, it was Nandi who finally gave in.

"Mistress, there are many among the shining ones who could summon such creatures. Far too many for you to hunt down or investigate. To do so would be akin to counting grains of sand on a beach. The task is impossible. Were you to try, you would fall into a despair so dark and deep that it would undoubtedly shatter your mind and force you into insanity."

Volusian sighed loudly and shuffled so that he stood farther into the shadows of my bedroom. "Metaphors aside, mistress, she is correct. Perhaps there are not *quite* so many suspects but still enough to make a search difficult."

Finn, moving around my room in lazy circles, stopped his flight and scoffed. "Why are you wasting your time with all these other people? It's obvious who's doing it. Maiwenn is."

I sat cross-legged on the bed and swallowed a piece of my Milky Way. "Maiwenn can't control water. Besides," I added bitterly, "everyone keeps going on about how weak and sickly she is lately anyway." I honestly didn't get what the big deal was with her being so debilitated by pregnancy. I'd worked at a restaurant in high school, and there'd been a waitress there who'd stayed on her feet until the day she delivered.

"Maiwenn doesn't have to do it herself," argued Finn. "She's the mastermind. Other people hated Storm King. She's probably collaborating with them and directing them to attack you."

"That seems kind of elaborate."

I swear, Volusian almost smiled. "Spend more time around the gentry courts, mistress, and you'll find a plan like that would be childishly simplistic. Nonetheless, I find it unlikely the Willow Queen is involved. It is not in her nature. She would not kill without provocation. She is more likely to wait and observe than act on her emotions."

"Unless there was something more personal involved," said Finn slyly. "You know, maybe a little jealousy . . ."

Apparently my romantic difficulties were no secret. Honestly, I didn't get how gossip spread so fast in the Otherworld, particularly considering how they had no telephones, TV, or Internet.

I glared at him. "She has nothing to be jealous about. Not anymore."

"Agreed," said Volusian. "Besides, the Willow Queen is not an adolescent girl who would risk her rule to take petty revenge. She—and her peers—are far too clever. And ruthless."

Finn crossed his arms and glared at Volusian. It was kind of a bold move, considering Finn looked like a cartoon character and Volusian looked like he ate the souls of small children. For all I knew, he probably did.

"Of course you'd say that. You're trying to throw Odile off Maiwenn's trail. Makes it easy, doesn't it? Then Maiwenn's assassins can do your dirty work for you. We all know you're just waiting to kill her off." Finn jerked his thumb in my direction.

Volusian went rigid, his eyes narrowing to red slits. "Make no mistake. When I kill our mistress—and I will— I will not depend on some gentry to do it. I will rip her flesh and tear her soul apart myself."

Silence fell.

"Truly, mistress," Nandi said at last, "it is a wonder you even have the will to carry on."

"Enough," I groaned, rubbing my eyes. "Being around you guys is like being on the *Jerry Springer Show* sometimes. As much as I hate to admit it, I agree with Volusian." Finn started to speak, and I cut him off with a gesture. "But I still want to talk to Maiwenn. If she is guilty, maybe I can find out. If she isn't, maybe she'll help me figure out who is."

"You're crazy," exclaimed Finn. "You're playing right into her hands."

"And your opinion has been duly noted for the record. I don't need to hear it anymore."

He disappeared with a huff. I shook my head and turned to the others.

"Show me where the closest crossover to her home is."

It turned out to be an hour and a half drive from

Tucson, but considering how much Otherworldly travel I probably would have had to do by crossing somewhere else, I didn't mind. This proved doubly true when the crossroads in the Willow Land deposited me within eye-sight of her castle.

It was only a small consolation, considering it was still freezing in her land. Back home, the weather had been hot and perfect. Worst of all, today was Cinco de Mayo. I should have spent the rest of the day drinking copious amounts of tequila, followed by a blissful blackout under a table somewhere.

At least there was no wind now, but the air held a sharp, biting chill. It was dry too; I could sense its lack of moisture. Ice and snow drifts glittered with crystalline beauty in the stark winter sunlight, but it was a dangerous beauty. If you stared at the blankets of white too long, you could almost get afterimages from the brightness.

I trudged down the cold road, admiring the castle in spite of myself.

Unlike Aeson's and Dorian's, it lacked the blocky, fortress look. It was . . . well, pretty. Graceful, fluid spires rose up, their silvery white surface gleaming and sparkling. The entire structure had a curved, almost sinuous look, like a calla lily. I wondered if this simply resulted from the difference between male and female monarchs. Maybe Maiwenn just had better taste.

The guards turned rightfully alarmed when I informed them who I was. They tried to coax me inside to wait for Maiwenn's admittance, but I refused to take one step until they'd requested hospitality for me. It took awhile—during which time the number of guards circling me doubled—but Maiwenn finally sent back word that I could see her and would be under the protection of her home.

A lady-in-waiting led me to Maiwenn, and she made it clear in both body language and words that I had no business disturbing her queen. She led me through twisting halls, at last leaving me in a cozy, brightly lit sitting room. Maiwenn rested in a comfy plush chair, propped up by pillows. A heavy satin dressing gown wrapped around her, and someone had tucked a blanket over her lap. Even pale-skinned and messy-haired, she looked gorgeous.

She smiled at me and gestured for the servant to leave. "Lady Markham, what a pleasant surprise. Please, sit down."

Uneasily, I eased onto a delicate plush pink chair. "Call me Eugenie."

She nodded, and we both sat there awkwardly. Watching her, all I could think about was how she was carrying Kiyo's baby. It would create a lifelong bond between them that I could never share. Not that I wanted anything like that, of course. Kiyo was out of my life.

Maiwenn's sense of propriety, being better than mine, soon kicked in. "I'm happy to receive you, but I suspect this isn't a social call."

"No . . . I'm sorry. I wanted to talk to you about . . ." I hesitated, suddenly feeling foolish. What had I been thinking to come here and ask her outright if she wanted to kill me? Well, it was too late to back out. Might as well go for it. "I've had a couple of nasty attacks lately. Attacks meant to kill me. And I was wondering if . . . if maybe you knew anything about them. . . ."

Her turquoise eyes regarded me knowingly. "Or more to the point, you want to know if I had anything to do with them."

I averted my eyes. "Yes."

"It's no wonder Dorian likes you so much. Your bluntness must amuse him to no end." She sighed and leaned her head back in the chair. "You may believe me or not, but the answer is no. I neither ordered nor know anything about any attempts on your life. What happened?"

Figuring it couldn't hurt regardless of her involvement, I told her everything about the fachan and the nixies. Her face stayed mostly blank, though I did see surprise flash in her eyes a few times. When I finished, her response was not what I expected.

"Why do you live in a desert anyway? Willingly even?"

I felt surprise cross my own face. "It's my home. It's not that bad."

She shrugged. "If you say so. But Dorian is right in his assessment of getting those creatures to you in the first place. Someone powerful and motivated would have had to do it."

"Do you know who?"

"No. Like I said, you have no reason to believe me, but I had nothing to do with this."

She was right. I had no reason to believe her. And yet . . . some part of me noted that Kiyo trusted her. Whatever anger I felt over his withholding of information, I had to believe he wasn't an entirely unreliable judge of character.

"Could you give me names of people who could do it?"

"I could give you dozens. Wouldn't do you much good."

I scowled and slouched into my chair. The same response as the spirits.

"I'm sorry I can't be more help." She sounded sincere. "I won't lie: The thought of you having Tirigan's grandson terrifies me. But I don't believe in punishing you for something that has not yet happened—especially when you are trying to *not* make it happen. However . . ." That placid expression turned hesitant. "May I ask you a question?"

"Sure."

"I know what you told me, and yet . . . well, I hear more and more stories about your involvement with Dorian. Kiyo said . . ." She tripped over the name. "Kiyo said I had nothing to worry about."

"You don't. It's an act. Dorian's teaching me to use my

magic, and in exchange, I play his girlfriend." No point in mentioning our recent bargain.

She considered. "So you've decided to embrace your heritage after all."

"Only enough to not do something stupid."

"You're right to do that . . . though I'd feel better if you had another teacher. Your bargain may seem safe enough for now . . . yet I doubt he'll let it stay that simple for long. Don't let his charm blind you to his agenda. He'll use you to get what he wants—and he wants the prophecy fulfilled."

"Hey, I can handle Dorian. And his charm."

"There's more to it than just that, however. Your very life may be at risk."

"From Dorian? I doubt it."

"From his enemies."

That was a new one. "I didn't really know he had any unless . . . well, you and he differ in opinion . . . and I guess he and Aeson don't get along either." I sat up straighter. "Do you think his enemies are the ones trying to kill me? To get back at him?"

"Any number of people could be trying to kill you. The list of his enemies is no shorter than the ones I referred to before. Most of his have nothing to do with where he stands on the prophecy. He's powerful, and many fear that—with good reason. When this part of the Otherworld rearranged itself, he fought to seize much more of it than he did. Only at the last minute did Katrice, queen of the Rowan Land, emerge as a contender and slice up more. The land recognized her and allowed her a portion, cutting Dorian out of larger territory."

I shivered. I had heard Roland speak of the Otherworld's sentience, how it continually changed form and boundaries. Still. The thought of it "allowing" someone to do something creeped me out.

"Many know he has never accepted that outcome," she

continued. "He would like to expand, and they see you as the means of doing it. Your human powers have been feared for years. If you manifest Storm King's as well, they believe you and Dorian will conquer the other kingdoms. And possibly beyond."

"Everyone's so obsessed with conquest," I grumbled. "Why can't they just leave things the way they are?"

"Your king has grander plans than that, I'm afraid."

I wondered not for the first time who was getting the better end of this deal Dorian and I had contrived. What was it he really wanted from me? "So even people who agree with the prophecy don't necessarily like him."

She nodded. "They would rather see your son fathered by someone less ambitious—someone they could control. Those same people could very well attempt to remove Dorian. Or, others who wanted Storm King to succeed in theory secretly believe it will never happen, so now they simply worry about the immediate threat you present to the kingdoms here."

This new development, that I was a threat because I wanted to conquer the Otherworld, was almost more ludicrous than the prophecy. "Why the hell would I want to rule in this world? Haven't they noticed I'm human? Or at least half? I don't have any claim on gentry real estate. And I don't want any."

"The shining ones view things differently than humans. Humans always feel the need to point out any drop of foreign blood in a person. As far as we care, you have our blood, and that suffices. You may have a human mother, but for all other intents and purposes, most of us now regard you as one of our own."

I thought about how common "outsider" labels were back in my own world: African American, Asian American, etc. She was right. People usually called attention to "foreign" blood.

"Yeah, but all that aside, I've made a career out of

hunting them down. Doesn't that bother anybody or seem weird for a potential queen?"

"Some, yes," she conceded. The slightly distasteful look on her face informed me she was among them. "And they won't get over that anytime soon. But really— for everyone else—well, as I said, most consider you one of us now, and killing wantonly isn't that out of line for a powerful leader. Nothing that Tirigan or Aeson or Dorian hasn't done."

I exhaled loudly. "This doesn't make me feel better. I suddenly feel like I have more enemies than before."

"I'm sorry. If it's any consolation, Dorian's enemies may seek you out because of your connection to him, but that very connection will compel him to protect you by whatever means he can. Conniving or not, he's a powerful ally."

I remembered the nixies. "Yeah. He is."

Another uncomfortable silence descended, and we sat there watching each other. Regardless of how wussy I thought her condition was, she did look pretty exhausted. I hadn't really decided if she was an enemy or not. Honestly, I'd received more things to worry about than any sort of answers from this visit.

"Well," I said stupidly, "thanks for the . . . help. I guess I should go."

She nodded and gave me a faint, tired smile. "You're welcome here anytime."

"Thanks."

I stood up and moved to the door. My hand was on the knob when she called my name.

"Eugenie . . ."

I turned. A pained look crossed her face, one that had nothing to do with her physical discomfort.

"He loves you," she said haltingly. "You should . . . you should forgive him. He didn't mean to hurt you."

I held her gaze for several painful moments and then

walked out without another word. I didn't want to think about Kiyo.

And then, as irony would have it, I ran into him when I was about halfway out of the keep. The universe was harsh sometimes. Whatever feelings her words had kindled in me dried up at the thought of him coming to visit her. The look on his face implied I was the last person he'd expected to see there.

I forcibly kept my expression cold, trying hard not to show how much I was drinking in his appearance and presence. He was as stunning as ever with that tanned skin and silky black hair curling slightly behind his ears. I wanted to run my hands through it. The heavy coat he wore couldn't hide that graceful, athletic body.

"Eugenie," he said softly, "what are you doing here?"

"I had to chat with Maiwenn. You know, girl talk." I hoped my tone conveyed that I did not want to elaborate on our conversation. He picked up on the hint.

"Well. It's good to see you. You look . . . good. How have things . . . I mean, have you been okay?"

I shrugged. "The usual. Propositions. Attempts on my life. You know how it goes."

"I worry about you."

"I'm fine. I can take care of myself. Besides, I do have some help."

Those dark, caring eyes narrowed slightly. "I suppose you mean Dorian."

"He saved me from a pretty nasty attack the other day and," I added, feeling mean, "he's going to help me go get Jasmine."

"That's a bad idea."

"Which part? Getting her or relying on Dorian?"

"Both."

"Well, you knew I was going to go for her one of these days. Better sooner than later." I started to walk past him, and he caught my arm. Even through the coat, his touch sent shock waves through my body.

He leaned close to me. "I want to come with you."

"I don't need your help."

"You need all the help you can get."

"No." I broke his hold.

He moved and blocked my way again. I could feel some of that animal intensity radiating off of him. "Last time you didn't want gentry help because it hurt your pride. You're doing the same thing with me for the same reasons, and there's no point. Forget how much you hate me, and worry about what's best for the girl. I'm going with you."

He had a point about what was in Jasmine's best interests, but his attitude bothered me. "What, you think you can make something happen by just telling me it will? You're not going, so get over it."

"There's nothing to get over. If you're in danger, I protect you. I'll be there."

"Well, I guess you're going to have to go stake out Aeson's 24/7, because I'm sure as hell not letting you in on the secret planning meetings."

Some of his feral demeanor dropped, and suddenly he was relaxed, collected Kiyo again. "There are secret meetings? What are you guys now, the Superfriends?"

I rolled my eyes and walked past him, back to the crossroads and the warmer weather of Arizona. That ache in my chest, the one I'd had since Beltane, burned steadily the entire time. I hated what had happened to us, but I didn't know how to fix it. I didn't know how to forgive Kiyo.

I tried to get my mind on something else as I drove home, like planning the logistics of the next Jasmine rescue. Or, considering her resistance, maybe it would be more like a smash 'n' grab. Regardless, I was eager to get it over with. Damn Dorian's clause about my magic. And his stupid nobility about sex.

I was almost home when I drove past a Barnes &

Noble. An idea leapt into my brain, a strange one admittedly, but one that couldn't hurt.

I hadn't stopped thinking about how much potential I allegedly had with magic. For years, I'd relied on human magic—or rather the human ability to extract magic from the world. I could banish spirits and monsters. I could walk worlds. But this so-called power within me offered so much more, according to both Dorian and Maiwenn—not to mention my own barely remembered longings. I had resisted it at first, but now . . . now I wanted so badly to advance to higher levels. Dorian and I would meet tomorrow night for another session, and I hated the thought of more inactivity. He'd told me I had a lifetime to catch up on magic, but I didn't want to wait that long. I wanted to close the gap.

Naturally, the store had no books on real magic. They only carried the silly and trumped-up commercial type stuff. But they did have a science section, and within that, I found a couple shelves on weather and meteorology.

I doubted these books would make me a magical dominatrix overnight, but actually knowing the science behind what I worked with had to help. It was something tangible, something I had more experience with than the weird, esoteric nature of magic itself. Volusian had once commented that as a child of both worlds, I could take the best of each lineage. I was both gentry and human. Magic and technology.

I spent over an hour skimming through books on storms, the atmosphere, and assorted weather phenomena. When the store made its closing announcement, I could hardly believe it. Time had flown by. Scooping up the ones I deemed most useful, I paid and went home.

"Reading is hot," Tim told me when I walked in the door with my heavy bag.

I ignored him and retreated to my room. Dumping the books on the bed, I picked the most remedial-looking one and sat down at my desk, where the Eiffel Tower still lay unfinished. I hadn't had time for puzzles lately. With a wistful last look, I swept the pieces up into the box and put it away. The tower would have to wait.

Shifting my legs into a comfortable position, I spread out the glossy, full-colored textbook. Flipping through the title pages and introduction, I finally found the meat of the book.

Chapter One: Moisture and the Atmosphere

Chapter Twenty-Four

Whatever snide comments Dorian and Maiwenn might make, Tucson is the best place in the world to live.

Standing at the desert crossroads the following evening, I paused a moment to take in my surroundings before crossing over. Dorian's kingdom was certainly beautiful, but it just wasn't the same. It wasn't home. A soft wind cut through the dry air, ruffling my hair and whispering that spring would yield to summer soon. The breeze carried all the delicious smells of the desert, and I caught the sweet scent of mesquite—not the barbecue kind but the delicate perfume emitted by its fuzzy yellow blooms. Above me, the sun beat down without remorse, warning the weak to get the hell out. The tourist season tended to drop off with the sharp increase in temperatures, but I loved this time of year.

And all around me, in this dry and unforgiving heat, I could feel the unseen water. It was in the saguaros and the cactus wrens and the mesquite trees' tap roots. There were even tiny bits in the air, despite the ostensible aridness. Everywhere there was life, there was water. Sensing it was second nature to me now. Calling it still remained a challenge.

Closing my eyes, I let my mind reach through the boundaries and send me into the Otherworld. Practice really did make perfect with these transitions; they were effortless now, just like sensing water. My body slipped through, pulled toward the corresponding thin spot near Dorian's home. Before I could arrive there, however, I reached out toward the Slinky, using my stored essence as a magnet to pull me there instead of the road. Moments later, I appeared on Dorian's bed.

"Presumptuous," I muttered, swinging off of it and standing up. I picked up the Slinky and tossed it around, watching its rings arch and fall.

"Is that you, my lady?" I heard a tentative voice call. Seconds later, Nia's young face peeked in from the other room. "His majesty is in the conservatory. If you'll follow me?"

Wow. I'd never heard of anyone actually having a conservatory, outside of the game Clue. When Nia led me inside, I found Dorian standing in front of a canvas with a painter's palette and brush in his hands. *Dorian, in the conservatory, with the candlestick,* I thought. *Er, paintbrush.*

He smiled when he saw me. "Lady Markham, you're just in time. Perhaps you can amuse Rurik. He's become terribly unreasonable."

I glanced over to the side of the room where Rurik, the massive warrior with platinum blond hair, sat on a delicate chaise lounge upholstered in lavender velvet. He wore full leather and copper armor, and the entire juxtaposition made me wince.

"I don't mean to be unreasonable, your majesty." He spoke through gritted teeth. "But sitting here and not moving—while in armor—isn't all that easy."

"Bah, you're whining. Most unseemly for a man of your station. Why, Lady Markham can stay still for hours—and in far more uncomfortable circumstances too, I might add."

Rurik glanced at me, both startled and pleasantly intrigued.

"Don't move! Look back here."

Rurik's leer faded as he turned back toward his king. Dorian's canvas faced away from me, so I had no idea what his masterpiece looked like. I started to walk around and check it out, but he waved me off with the brush.

"No, no. Not until I'm finished."

Shrugging, I pulled up another lavender chair—the entire room was that color, actually—and slouched into it. Dorian spoke without looking up from his work.

"So what have you done today, my dear? Anything entertaining?"

"Not really. Slept in. Banished a shade. I actually read for most of the day. Kind of lame."

"What are you reading? I really enjoy that one human's works . . . oh, I forget his name. He was very popular for a while. Shakemore?"

"Shakespeare?"

"Yes, that's the one. Has he written anything new?"

"Um, not in, like, four or five centuries."

"Ah, pity. So what did you read about instead?"

"The weather."

He paused midstroke. "And what did you learn?"

"Storm-formation stuff. How water molecules build up and condense, how charged particles discharge to form lightning. Oh, and there was something else about high and low pressure, but I've got to go back and reread that. Kind of confusing."

Both men treated me to brief, blank looks, and then Dorian returned to his work. "I see. And do you think this will facilitate your learning?"

"Not sure. But I kind of like knowing what the end result is supposed to be."

Silence fell as Dorian continued painting. Rurik persisted in looking miserable, occasionally sighing loudly to express his discontent. I'd never entirely forgiven him for the ice elemental thing, so seeing him suffer had its perks. Unfortunately, it grew boring after a while. I crossed my arms and slumped farther into the chair, catching his notice.

"Sire, your lady's restless. I'm sure you have more interesting things to do with her. We can work on this another time. I don't mind."

"Nonsense. I'm almost done."

The first happy expression I'd seen since arriving showed on Rurik's face. It vanished when Dorian turned the canvas around to display his work.

We stared.

"Sire, am I . . . wearing a bow?"

I cocked my head. "It does kind of look that way. But the rest . . . man, that's actually pretty good. I didn't know you could do faces so well."

Dorian glowed. "Why, thank you. I can paint you too someday if you'd like."

"It's a *bow*," protested Rurik.

Dorian glanced at the canvas, then back to the warrior. "It matches the chaise. I had to add it; otherwise you would have clashed."

Back in his bedroom, Dorian went through his usual motions, flinging off his silver-gray cloak and pouring a glass of wine. He drank some type of blush tonight.

"Ready to start?"

I nodded, sitting down in the chair in the middle of the room. As I'd said, I didn't really think the meteorology books would give me that much of an edge yet, but I felt more empowered after reading them. Like I was starting to take my training into my own hands.

He took another drink of his wine, procured more cords, and approached me. Putting one hand on his hip, he surveyed me carefully, not unlike how he'd scrutinized his canvas.

"That's a very pretty shirt." I glanced down. It was a black tank top with a chain of red daisies embroidered near the top. "Hmm. Let's try this."

He abandoned the pastel-colored ties he held and

replaced them with red and black ones. Placing my arms flat against the chair's arms, he wrapped each of mine down with black first, making X patterns. The style reminded me of the way a ballerina's slippers laced up. When that was finished, he went back over each arm with red.

"These are more like ribbons than your usual ones," I observed. "Or maybe sashes. Do you own, like, every possible form of constraint known to man?"

"Nearly," he said. "All right. Let's get started. The water's over there."

He indicated a table near the window where my old friend the pitcher sat, but I'd already known it was there. Settling as comfortably as I could in the chair, I stared at the pitcher and immediately let my mind reach out to the water. It flared like a beacon to me. Beyond it, I could sense all the other water in the room too. Me and Dorian, the wine, water vapor. I directed my attention to the pitcher's water.

I can feel you, now come to me.

But, as many practices had already demonstrated, wanting didn't make things happen. God, that pissed me off. I honestly didn't know how Dorian could stand waiting around through all of these sessions. It had to be boring as hell. I was bored, and I actually got to do something. Sort of.

No, no. That was a bad attitude. Forget the boredom. Focus on the task at hand.

Hours passed again. If Dorian was still awake—which I doubted—I knew he'd close off the session soon. The knowledge irritated me, but I understood. I was already feeling tired, my eyes bleary. I kept blinking a lot to regain focus and keep them from drying. I think that made me notice what happened next.

"Dorian, look at the pitcher."

He sat up right away and followed my gaze. A moment later, he walked over and touched the pitcher, brushing his fingers along its side. Water quietly ran down the ceramic surface, pooling on the table's glass surface. A slow, delighted smile spread over his face.

"You've seized it. It's listening to you. Now make it come farther—all the way out of the jug."

With tangible progress before me, my excitement grew. I thought hard about what I'd been doing, trying to repeat it. About a minute later, I could see water spilling down the sides of the jug, much faster and in greater amounts. The puddle on the table grew too full, dripping onto the floor.

"I'm ruining your carpet."

"Never mind the carpet. Bring it farther." I could hear the anticipation in his voice.

Some logical part of me saw carpet as tough terrain to navigate, and the water's progress slowed. Soon, I decided, that was only in my head. The carpet had nothing to do with anything. Only my control of the water mattered.

As soon as I made that leap, the water shot over the carpet in a curving rivulet, almost like a snake. It reached my feet, and I could feel it waiting for some further instruction. Only, I didn't know what to tell it. I simply wanted it to come to me.

I'd barely given form to that thought when the water sprang up before me and hovered in the air. My mouth dropping, I watched it splinter into hundreds of drops. They hung there, suspended like strings of crystal beads. I gaped, fascinated, but had no idea what to do next. My grasp on them slipped away, and the drops disintegrated further into a fine fog. Seconds later, the cloud dispersed altogether, evaporating into the rest of the air. As they faded, so did the tingly, euphoric feeling racing through my blood.

Neither Dorian nor I did anything right away. Then, I started laughing. And I couldn't stop. It was too wonderful. I wanted to do it again and again but had no more water. The wine would be too messy.

An idea occurred to me. Sensing the moisture in the air, I sent my power out to the air right in front of me. Suddenly, tiny flecks of water condensed on my skin, like I'd been sprayed by a light mist. I laughed again.

Dorian, grinning as broadly as me, walked over and ran his fingers over each of my cheeks. Touching his fingers together, he rubbed the water into his skin, almost as if testing it was real.

"I did it."

"You did do it."

His eyes shone with unadulterated pleasure. You might have thought he'd been the one to do this. Funny that he should take such joy in this, I thought, when it was a paltry thing compared to his magic. He untied me and clasped my hands to help me rise.

"I think a celebration is in order." He poured another glass of wine and handed it over. We clinked our glasses together. "To clever pupils."

"With good teachers."

He took a sip. "Hardly. I actually slept most of tonight."

I laughed as I drank. "Do you . . . when you use your magic, do you feel something . . . I don't know, something *good* burning in you? Like pleasure or exhilaration . . . and not just from, like, mental satisfaction either . . ."

I couldn't put it into words, but his face told me I didn't have to. "Yes. I know exactly what you mean. Wonderful, isn't it?"

I drank more of the wine. "Yes. Yes, it is."

"Just wait. You've just had a sip of it. Once you come into your full power, you won't know how you did without."

I grinned at him. I felt so thoroughly pleased with myself and life, I could hardly stand it. When had I been this happy? Aside from being with Kiyo? And if I had this kind of reaction now, what would happen when I really moved into the big leagues? Dorian spoke of it like an addiction, but it sure sounded like a good one.

Looking up, I saw his eyes all over me. He set his glass

down and spoke in a soft voice, almost wonderingly. "You shine . . . did you know that? Power suits you."

He made me as happy as everything else in the world just then. Warmth built in my chest and radiated out through the rest of my body. I don't know how that feeling expressed itself on my face, but it must have conveyed something because he leaned over and kissed me.

I could taste wine in that soft kiss, wine and heat. One of his hands pulled me against him while the other carefully removed my glass. Still pressing us together, he eased me onto the bed. I answered his sweet, taunting kisses with hard, demanding ones. It didn't take him long to adjust to this shift in style. He rolled me to my back and lay down on top of me, twining one hand in my hair to hold my head in place as an eager need suddenly filled his kisses. He consumed my mouth with them while his other hand slid unabashedly between my thighs, rubbing me through my jeans.

My body arched up against his, and I felt an aching cry rise up in my throat, only to be lost in the pressure of his mouth on mine. I knew then it would finally happen. The dangerous allure of this . . . the exoticness of sleeping with someone who was still such an unknown quantity . . . it all enflamed me that much more. We would do this. We would come together, and I would give myself to him.

Give myself to him.

A tightness seized my chest, conflicting sharply with the burning pleasure in the rest of my body. His touch made me crave more, almost made me beg for it, and yet that angry part in the back of my mind was screaming again. It told me if I made this choice, if I deliberately chose to do this with him, then I was giving in to the enemy. I didn't really know who that enemy was exactly, but it didn't matter. The instinct pulsed through me, defensive and afraid. It warred against the rest of me, against my body's needs and even against my own conscious wishes. I knew and liked Dorian. Why couldn't I overcome that base fear? In some ways, the fear was tit-illating. I had a feeling if I could just get over that first crest of difficulty, the problems would go away.

But damn it, that was a high peak to get over.

And like last time, Dorian could feel my reluctance. He broke our embrace, almost jerking away from me. Before he turned his face from mine, I saw emotions I'd never seen before. Frustration. Unhappiness.

"Dorian . . ." I said. "Dorian . . . I'm so sorry . . ."

He rubbed his face with both hands and exhaled. His voice was flat when he spoke. "It's late, Eugenie. Too late for you to leave." He stood up and stretched, and when he finally turned around, he'd once more cleared his face of its dark expression. His cheerful countenance was also missing; he simply looked tired. "I'll take the sofa in the parlor; you stay on the bed."

"No, I—"

He gestured me off as he walked into the other room without a backward glance, saying only, "Take it. It'll be the best night of sleep you've ever had."

Elaborate French doors connected the two rooms. He closed them, leaving me to my own misery.

I sat on his massive bed, attempting to sort out a tangle of warring emotions. What was wrong with me? Why couldn't I make this work? I'd slept with guys I liked a lot less than Dorian. Why couldn't I cross this last line? Why keep fighting it?

I blew out all the candles and torches in the room before taking off my jeans and sliding under the covers. Dorian was right. This had to be the most comfortable bed I'd ever been in. Unfortunately, there was no way I could sleep. I kept thinking about my magical elation, alleged desire, and subsequent breakdown. My body wanted him. My mind did too. Only my instincts still fought it.

The world's most comfortable bed must have felt in-sulted over all the tossing and turning that followed. At least its size gave me all the fidgeting room I could want.

My eyes grew accustomed to the darkness very quickly, and I could discern the shapes of furniture and corners in the partial moonlight. Outside the giant window, stars glittered—thousands more than I'd seen the night with the astronomers. We'd lost the stars in the human world, despite our success in reaching them. Humans and gentry were almost like two sides of a coin, each supplying what the other lacked.

The answer to my problems with Dorian was a long time in coming, but come it did. It was still pitch black when I finally got up and padded into the adjoining room. The doors opened silently, and I paused upon reaching him. He couldn't quite fit on the sofa, so his legs dangled off the end. He still wore the same clothes and had pulled a flimsy throw blanket over his body. He faced the direction I stood, eyes closed. One hand draped above him, and his hair spilled onto his cheek, its fiery color indiscernible in the poor lighting.

He was a king, with thousands of people who answered to him, yet he lay crammed onto this couch because of me. I had hurt someone I didn't think could be hurt. I stood there thinking about this in the still, dark room before finally kneeling down beside him.

I tentatively reached out a hand, but his eyes opened before I made contact. "What's the matter?" he asked. He sounded alert, concerned.

I couldn't talk right away. Silence pooled as thick as the blackness around us. He neither spoke nor moved as I deliberated; he simply watched and waited.

"I want you to tie me up."

That was the great thing about Dorian. Most people would have hesitated or asked questions. Not him. He followed me out to the other room and promptly retrieved the same sashes he'd used earlier in the chair.

I settled on the bed, unsure where to position my body, but he gently adjusted me. He started to extend my arms up over my head but then stopped. Moving his hands down to my stomach, he caught the edges of my shirt and gave me a questioning look. I nodded, and he carefully pulled it off and over my head. Returning to my arms, he raised them above me toward the headboard and tied my wrists together, still incapable of rushing his careful bindings. With the next sash, he bound my wrists to the intricate scalloping of the headboard and then used another to reinforce the binding. When he finished, my arms lay somewhat relaxed on the pillows above me, but my hands and wrists were tightly secured. Weirdly, something inside of me eased upon realizing I was trapped.

The length of the tying process surprised me. I would have thought he would want to expedite things, but his patience seemed undaunted. He settled back on his knees and studied me, just as he always did after completing one of his tie-ups. Near darkness or no, I felt exposed in just my underwear and wondered if it was my naked skin or the silk sashes that so captivated him. Probably the combination of both.

He slid off the bed and stood up so he could take his own clothes off. As they fell to the ground, more and more of his body was revealed. The moonlight caught his white skin, and it practically gleamed. He reminded me of some ancient Grecian or Roman statue, all marble and smooth lines.

He crawled back onto the bed, looking down on me, and my heart started racing again. Shadows bathed him now that he was away from the window's full light, and he seemed larger and more powerful compared to me. I had no means of getting out of this unless I wanted to attempt some crazy kicking maneuvers.

The time and tension stretched out between us. It made me anxious yet stimulated as well. Why the delay? Why wouldn't he touch me? Why did he just keep looking at me like that?

Finally, he knelt by my feet and kissed my toes. Such a small touch, but it made my body shudder after all that waiting. He alternated between both feet, his lips caressing toes and ankles before steadily moving up my legs. Kiyo had done a similar physical examination during our first night together. I wondered if there was some sort of psychological or personality analysis you could make based on whether a guy started at the top or the bottom.

Up, up. Dorian's mouth moved on. My pelvic muscles tightened in anticipation, and I felt wetness growing between my thighs. But then, he simply skipped past my underwear, continuing with my stomach. He ran his hands along the smooth skin, still taking his time, cautious around the healing fachan cut. When he finished there, he moved to my neck, bypassing my breasts. My neck was pretty sensitive too, and his mouth's intensity had increased. The sensation forced my breathing into anxious, ragged gasps, but a frustrated complaint slipped out nonetheless.

"Why are you skipping all the good parts?"

He paused, just barely lifting his lips from my skin. "Do you want me to go back?"

I bit my lip. He was trying to make me dictate the terms here, but that wasn't what I wanted. For once, I didn't want the power here. That was why I'd asked to be tied up. I wanted the choice taken away from me. I stayed quiet.

He returned to my neck, moving his mouth along my collarbone and shoulder, then up to my cheek and ears. Our lips soon came together again, and I tried to channel my eagerness and passion into that kiss, as I had done earlier. But now he kept himself just out of reach, just enough to tease but not fulfill. I shifted my body upward, touching as much of his as I could. That, too, he held slightly away. It was frustrating, and in my need, I forgot about who was supposed to be in control.

"Okay—go back."

He complied as efficiently and quickly as he had to my initial bondage request. His hands and their delicate fingers cradled my breasts, holding them in place for his mouth. I closed my eyes and tilted my neck back, lost in those burning twirls of his tongue as he woke the nerves in my flesh and delicately sucked the nipples. When he finally broke away, I made a soft sound of protest until I realized where he went next.

Looping his fingers through the sides of my panties, he pulled them down, stopping abruptly when they reached midthigh. For a moment, I thought it was more of his teasing until I suddenly grasped the situation.

"It's, um, called a Brazilian wax," I explained, voice still breathy.

"Oh." His own voice held wonder. "Oh my."

His fingers ran over that delicate area, both for sensuality and his own curious exploration. With a happy sigh, he removed the underwear altogether and carefully spread my thighs apart. Then, his mouth was upon me, his tongue running along that most sensitive of spots in one smooth motion.

It was like a spark to a powder keg. My whole body bucked up as heat exploded throughout me, and I made some sound vaguely like a whimper. Both of his hands slid up and held me firmly in place, reminding me again that I'd given up the power here. That same conflicting mix of fear and need flared up inside of me, scared that he could do anything he wanted to me and half-hoping he would.

When he grew convinced I wouldn't thrash anymore, he let one hand slide back to my thighs. His mouth had never stopped in its fervent feeding, and now his fingers moved in, pushing into me with smooth motions timed to work with his mouth. I moaned against his touch, my head thrown back and upper body arched. He had an uncanny knack for pulling back each time orgasm was about to occur. So, when he finally allowed me that release, it almost caught me by surprise.

My flesh ignited, electric and glorious. I shivered as my muscles contracted, as that scorching ecstasy poured through my body. Even when that tide broke, he kept his mouth down there licking and probing until I begged him to stop, too overcome by the flood of sensation. He took his time in obeying the request, finally moving away and laying his body on top of mine.

Every part of him pressed against me, hard and wonderful, and I writhed under him, yearning for more. He moved his hands back up to my arms, again firmly pinning me in place. His mouth crushed mine, forcing me to taste myself on his lips. Struggling did no good.

When he released me from the kiss at last, his face moved only a fraction of an inch away from mine.

"I know why you're doing this," he said. "Why you wanted to be bound. It's because you want the decision taken out of your hands. You knew once you were here, there'd be no turning back. You wouldn't have to be burdened with the decision of willfully coming together with me. You would have no choice in the matter and hence relieve yourself of any guilt or anticipation."

He kissed my cheek and then lingered on my ear a little. "In a moment, I swear I can ravage and take you as much as you want, if that's what makes it easier. But your choices aren't gone yet. We can stop if you want. Or I can untie you. You can tell me you want this and join with me not in submission, but as an equal."

The words were on my lips. *Yes, untie me. Make love to me. Fuck me. I want to be with you.* I could have said any number of things to change the balance of power. I could have gained both control and freedom again. Yet, I said or did nothing. Maybe it was because it was the only way I could go through with this. Or maybe I just wanted it this way. Maybe I even enjoyed it. Regardless, I stayed quiet, and he read the answer in that.

He rose up, looming over me. He was a conqueror, coming to collect, and I was a prize, open flesh waiting to be seized. That fear lurched up in me, and I thrived on it. It was delicious. Thrilling. I gave up my power. I gave myself to him.

Almost on his knees, he spread my legs apart and pushed in. I screamed, almost more from mental than physical sensation, my arms straining uselessly against the ties. He filled me, punctuating each powerful movement into me with a soft grunt in his throat I thought even he wasn't aware of.

I wanted to reach up and wrap my arms around him, pull him against me. But all I could do was lay there, lay there and let him push into me over and over, the enemy I'd somehow come to crave.

He shifted his body so that he was completely on top of me, still moving urgently and possessively, save that now I had even less mobility than before. He held me down, grip tight. And me? I was all aching and burning flesh, letting him take whatever he wanted from me. I floated in a warm, liquid place. It was like being wrapped in golden silk, molten bliss spreading over my body.

"I told you," he said through his labored breathing. "I told you you'd come to me. And now . . . now I realize I could have simply taken you the instant I'd tied you up. You didn't need any of the rest. You've had this desire and never even known it . . . this desire to simply be had in any way your lover wanted." He paused a moment, swallowing and catching his breath. "I'm right, aren't I? I could move you into any position I wanted, make love to you in any place I wanted, and you'd love every moment of it. . . ."

I couldn't really manage any coherent answers, and most of my noises had lapsed into primal, unintelligible cries. All I wanted to focus on was us being together, the way it felt to have him pushing and rubbing, the way it must feel for him to be inside of me. I'd slid up on the bed; my head was practically in danger of hitting the headboard soon.

Suddenly, he pulled out abruptly and hovered back over me. His eyes, dark in this light, watched me, and I sensed that laconic, playful expression on his face. Both of us panted. I waited for him to return, feeling irate at this interruption. I'd been on the verge of coming again. Somehow I suspected he'd known that.

"What are you doing?"

"Waiting. Waiting for you to tell me to keep going."

He wasn't being cruel or mean. He was teasing me, toying with me the way he so enjoyed among the people around here.

"You fucking bastard," I said. Somehow the profanity carried mild affection.

He laughed. "Should I take that to mean you want me to continue?"

"You know I do."

"Then say it outright. Unless you're going to get up and take me yourself."

"Did I mention you're a bastard?"

"Tell me you don't want me to stop. Beg me. Beg me, and we'll do this for the rest of the night."

It was merely a game, another dimension of this power play and his dominance over me. And, much to my chagrin, it was a turn-on.

"Please," I whispered.

"Please what?"

"Please . . . don't stop. I want . . . I want you to keep . . ."

"Keep what?"

I sighed. "I want you to keep fucking me."

He was back in me almost before the words had left my lips. I yelled out again as moments later, the delayed orgasm exploded in me. I shook and burned as that glittering sensation crackled through me. All the while, our bodies kept moving together. His face was near mine, watching with pleasure as I panted and struggled against a joy that was almost too intense.

"I hate you," I gasped out.

He laughed and rained kisses down on my face. "No, you don't."

He was right.

Chapter Twenty-Five

"I know what you're thinking."

I stretched my arms above me, tucking my hands between my head and the pillow. Sunlight poured over me from the giant window but did little to help my troubled mood. I'd been sullen and quiet all morning. "Not likely."

Dorian reached over to a tray of assorted pastries and sweets that had been sitting by the bed when we awoke. That and the newly built-up fire were only a couple of signs that tidying servants had been up and around in here. Their presence shouldn't have bothered me; everyone had already believed Dorian and I were sleeping together. Yet, knowing others had moved around us while we slept still felt odd.

He popped a marzipan-stuffed tartlet into my mouth. I made a surprised sound but ate it anyway. He had excellent cooks. "Well, then, let me guess anyway. I do so love trying to reason out your thoughts."

He grinned at me, every inch the lighthearted and frivolous man I usually knew. He bore almost no trace of the impassioned lover from last night, the one who'd repeatedly told me in explicit detail exactly what he could do to me if he wanted—and then proved that he could.

I rolled to my side, putting my back to him. "Knock yourself out."

"All right. You're now realizing you did the unthinkable. You made love to me—one of the shining ones. You crossed over that invisible line, and now the horror and regret of that is eating you up."

"No."

"No?"

"No, that's not what I'm thinking."

"Oh."

I heard him shift again and then felt a cookie balanced delicately on my arm. I snagged it and munched on it, getting crumbs on the sheets while he reconsidered. Lemon sugar.

"Very well. How about this: You're thinking about the kitsune. About Kiyo. You miss him and lament what happened. Being with me makes you feel guilty."

I hadn't been thinking about Kiyo, but mentioning him suddenly brought him to mind. I did miss Kiyo. I missed the easy way we interacted, his solid and steady presence. I missed the way he held me and made me feel safe.

"No."

"Hmm. Well, then. My perception appears to be off this morning. It has been known to happen once or twice before."

I stared out the window, unsettled emotions turning over and over in me. Finally, I said, "I'm bothered by . . . how it was last night. How rough it was."

"Truly? I really don't know you so well. I thought you enjoyed it."

"I did."

He waited a beat. "Forgive me, then, but I don't quite grasp your concern."

I rolled back over toward him, and it all spilled out. "Don't you get it? All this time I've been trying to avoid hordes of gentry and monsters from raping me. And yet . . . that's essentially what happened last night. I let you . . . I let you be aggressive and possessive. And then I liked it. What's that say about me? What's wrong with me?"

Dorian's face shifted to that rare and serious concern that sometimes seized it. He reached out and cupped my face with both of his hands. "Oh, gods, no. Is that what's upset you? Eugenie, Eugenie. That's not rape. Rape is brutal. Rape is done against your will, usually with someone you hate—or at least like a little less than me. What we did last night . . . that was a game. I believe it initially helped you get over a mental stumbling block, but after that . . . there was nothing violent or bad. It was a . . . novel way of approaching sex. You consented. There's nothing wrong with you for liking it."

Maybe he was right, but it still made me feel strange. "I've just never done anything like that. I've had rough sex before but never anything so . . . kinky."

"Kinky. Fantastic word. It always takes us awhile to catch up with your world's slang."

"It makes things weird between us. I mean, weirder than usual."

He ran his hand over my cheek and through my hair. "Then tell me how to make things right."

"I don't know."

"Perhaps this will cheer you up: We're ready to go to Aeson's now."

"What?" That didn't cheer me up so much as surprise me. Where had this come from?

"We can go whenever you wish."

"You're giving in because I have morning-after regrets?"

"I'm 'giving in' because you crossed the point I wanted you to with your magic."

I scoffed and rolled away. "Bullshit. I can make water drops appear in the air. Somehow I doubt that's the life-or-death difference needed on this mission."

"The life-or-death factor here is that you can control a

fine portion of your magic now. I needed that to happen before I felt comfortable on this venture. I couldn't risk your emotions flaring and creating a storm that might kill us. Now, you may very well still have some sort of magical breakdown, but I believe your current skills will go far to at least minimize the impact."

"Then what you said before—about it being protection in case I was defenseless . . ."

"Yes. I'm afraid that was a ruse. I'd hoped the thought might spur you on to try harder."

Typical Dorian. His absurdity made me half-smile.

"You're happier now?" he asked.

"I don't know if happy is the right word, but I will be when the Jasmine thing is over."

"Excellent. Come here."

He motioned me into his outstretched arm, and for a moment, I expected an advance. Like a *Hey, baby, I'll make you happier* type thing. I moved over tentatively, and he only put his arms around me. Just that simple. No jokes. No kinkiness. Just a simple embrace between two people, two people close enough to have rattled the headboard last night. I took comfort in it, relaxing into his warmth and security. He wasn't Kiyo, but he felt nice.

At last he moved his face away so he could look at me. "Very well, then. Tell me how you would like this to unfold."

Staging another heist turned out to take a fair bit of planning and didn't actually unfold until later the next day. We assembled all three of my minions in one of Dorian's lounges. They waited patiently for orders, each watching me as their minds undoubtedly stirred with their assorted neuroses. As Volusian had once pointed out, they had little to lose. They couldn't die. When Dorian called in Shaya to join us, I couldn't help an exclamation of surprise.

"Remember the distraction we discussed?" he asked me.

I did. Before getting out of bed, we had come up with

the tentative outline of a plan. Part of it had included a major distraction near Aeson's home, enough to draw the attention of his guard so we could enter undetected. My spirits had long since verified that the siege tunnel had been blocked off.

Shaya, he explained, would be our distraction. She had the power to command small ranges of vegetation. In particular, she could summon and order around trees—something she'd apparently done before to great effect. Dorian's thought was that Shaya would have a small regiment of said trees attack the western side of Aeson's hold. On the eastern side, we knew there was a servants' entrance we could slip into. Normally, that would be too exposed but not if the castle's security was preoccupied elsewhere.

I nodded, thinking it was a good plan. Shaya crossed her arms and looked thoroughly displeased.

"You got a problem with it?"

"I don't think it's our place to interfere with Aeson's affairs, nor do I feel this is worth risking my king's life over."

I glanced between her and Dorian uneasily. "So you won't do it?"

"Of course I will. My king gives a command, and I obey. I am merely expressing my honest opinion first. I would be doing a disservice otherwise."

Dorian touched her cheek, smiling at her stern expression. "And that is why you are so valued."

"It's a bad idea," said Finn suddenly.

We all turned to him.

"What do you mean?" I asked.

"What's a few trees? It screams, 'Hey, look at our obvious distraction.' It'll make them suspicious. You want to really get their attention, send him in." He inclined his head toward Dorian. "A little bit of that rock mojo, and they'll think there's an all-out assault going on."

"We can't. I need him as my backup," I argued, "and

protection for Jasmine. Shaya can do her thing and get out of there quickly. If I go in without him, then we're in exactly the same situation as before."

"Except without the army waiting for you," said Finn.

Shaya shook her head, glossy black braids swinging. "I don't like the idea of my king left alone."

"He'll be in and out, no problem. And if he has to face off, he can take anything Aeson's people throw at him."

"Unless it's Aeson himself," mused Dorian.

"Is he stronger than you?" I asked.

"We're very evenly matched."

"Huh. That surprises me. I mean, Kiyo walked away alive from a fight with him."

"King Aeson wasn't using his full power then," said Nandi. "Most likely he feared burning down his home." Seeing my startled look, she continued. "It would have created a terrible inferno from whence you would not have escaped. Your skin would have melted, only your bones left behind."

"So you're saying he wouldn't have to worry about that outdoors. He could unleash as much as he liked." Something struck me, and I turned back to Dorian. "What about you? Are you limited indoors?"

"Hypothetically, no. Realistically? Well . . . I still have to operate in a way that won't bury us alive." He smiled, seeing my consternation. "Don't worry, my dear. I'll still be of use to you."

"More use outside," said Finn. "We won't even need extra backup, not if nobody's inside to find us."

I sighed and rubbed my eyes. I'd walked into Aeson's with a lot less planning last time, and foolish or not, it had been a hell of a lot simpler than this. I turned to the room's darkest corner, which had been silent thus far.

"Volusian?"

He straightened up from where he'd slouched in the shadows. "I will be very surprised if we emerge from this without any sort of confrontation, regardless of who creates the initial distraction. If I must honestly answer what will keep you alive"—he sighed, obviously unhappy about that outcome. I suspected Nandi's horrific description of my death by fire had kindled warm and fuzzy feelings in him—"then yes, bringing the Oak King affords more protection for you and the girl, mistress."

"Then it's settled."

Finn pouted and turned his back on us, pacing around sulkily.

After that, it simply became a matter of waiting. We wanted to go under cover of darkness. Dorian and Shaya left to pursue household duties, and the spirits flitted off to do whatever it was they did. This left me with a lot of downtime. I paced the castle's grounds, ruminating over the same old things: Kiyo, the upcoming raid, and the prophecy.

The appointed time came, and our strike team reassembled for a few last-minute details. Most of it was simply a repetition of what we already knew. The spirits drifted along, but the rest of us set out on horseback. Shaya rode with the physical grace that permeated her normal movements, but I was surprised to see how agilely Dorian rode as well. He seemed so languid and comfort-oriented in his day-to-day affairs that I never thought of him as having athletic abilities, his feats in bed notwithstanding.

We crisscrossed the assorted kingdoms. It seemed to take longer than last time, and Volusian affirmed as much for me.

"The land has shifted its layout," he explained.

"It does that," said Dorian, seeing the panic on my face. "It's normal. We're on the right path."

"Yeah, but will we make it there before sunrise?"

"Certainly."

He smiled too broadly, and I could tell he didn't know for sure. I looked up. Right now we had perfect blackness, lit only by stars. The moon was dark tonight. Persephone's moon. I could feel the tingle of the butterfly on my arm and felt reassured. Before, I'd needed Hecate to escape back to my own world. Here, that wasn't an issue. Staying alive and sending my enemies on to death was the issue now, so I didn't mind the boost to my connection with the Underworld.

"How much farther?" I asked a little while later. I felt like a kid on a road trip but couldn't help the anxiety tickling my brain. I might have imagined it, but I swore the eastern sky now looked deep purple rather than black.

"Not far," said Shaya, voice calm.

Sure enough, we pulled off and secured the horses, going the rest of the way on foot, traveling through trees and undergrowth. I couldn't see anything, but we soon reached some significant point. Shaya split off from us to do her thing. Dorian squeezed her arm before she left, and she made a solemn bow of acknowledgment. I watched her disappear before I turned and joined the others to continue straight ahead.

Aeson's fortress finally loomed up before us as we reached the edge of the tree line. It could really be perceived only through its blockage of the stars. Otherwise, it appeared almost as black as the sky beyond. We stopped just before the terrain cleared, staying under cover. Studying the building further, I could make out small black figures moving back and forth in front of the wall. Guards. Presumably there were lookouts on the towers too.

"Now we wait," I muttered. I was tired of waiting. I wanted action.

Almost opposite us, on the other side of the forest, Shaya should have been preparing to summon her tree warriors. She and Dorian swore it would be a noisy affair, so there'd been no need for a secret countdown or anything like that. The castle was too far away for me to make out any identifiable features, but the spirits indicated the spot containing the side door.

Minutes dragged by, and I imagined all sorts of horrible fates for Shaya. Oh, God. What if they caught and killed her? She'd come here out of loyalty to Dorian, and no matter what else had happened, I'd come to respect her immensely. I didn't want her to die because of this.

Dorian approached my right side and put an arm around me. "Don't worry. This will be finished before you know it. Ah—there we are."

In the distance, we heard it. Wood crackling and splitting. A low roar. Faint shouts of alarm carried over the air, and the guards in our view took off running toward the noise. We waited until they'd cleared the area.

"Now is our time," murmured Volusian. "Go."

We streaked across the open area, toward the doorway. I could hear the noise on the other side. The sound of something breaking. More shouts. Shaya's plan had been to send about a dozen massive trees to beat on the walls over there. What a wake-up call that had to have been.

"W-wait! Hold it!" I suddenly cried.

The spirits stopped instantly. Dorian took a moment longer to slow down and gave me an odd glance. "What's wrong?"

I peered around. My senses tingled. I could feel water, lots of it. The way I felt in crowds or at Dorian's. Water in numerous condensed clusters. The water sources were people. Lots of them.

We'd been set up. Again.

"Fuck!"

They seemed to come out from everywhere, though I knew they all had to have been hiding in the castle's vicinity or else I would have felt them sooner. They came down from the roofs, out the door we'd been staking out, from around the corner. And somehow I knew the ones who ostensibly had run off would return.

I heard Dorian yell, "They won't kill you—not if they don't have to!" Then, the side of the castle exploded in a downpour of huge black rocks, causing those above and still scaling to fall down to death or at least serious injury. Others standing nearby were buried by the fallout.

My spirits had standing orders to attack anyone attacking us, and I saw them flare up for battle. As for me, I'd come packing two guns tonight, again courtesy of Lara. Both had steel cartridges, and my pockets held more clips still, plus a few silver ones. I kept what distance I could from the thick of the fray and fired, aiming for heads and faces if I could, but mostly happy if I could bring anyone down at all.

Regular range practice paid off, and I hit almost everyone I fixed on. No one ever managed to get too close to me. The spirits I ignored. They couldn't die, and only another shaman or Dorian-caliber magic user could banish them.

After his spectacular wall demolition, Dorian had resorted to a more conventional method: a copper sword he'd worn sheathed under his cloak. It glowed red in the darkness, and I realized he could enhance its power since copper came from inside the earth. He didn't fight with brute force, but he moved with speed and skill, surprising me as much as the horse-riding had. I wouldn't have minded another show of that earth power, but all magic took its toll. It would do no good for him to burn himself out yet.

Suddenly, I saw one of the guards moving up on him, just out of Dorian's line of sight. I started to cry out a warning, and then a large, four-legged form ran forward, snarling as he threw his weight into the guard. Dorian gave a quick glance of surprise but quickly returned to fighting. I couldn't recover so quickly and could only stare as Kiyo, in what I had jokingly dubbed the "superfox" form, clawed and ripped at his victim. The man did manage to slice Kiyo's side, making me wince, but the fox seemed unaffected. Shaking my head, knowing I could neither wonder how he'd shown up nor worry about his safety, I returned to my own battles.

A few victims later, I had my aim on someone when I sensed another form sneaking up behind me. I turned but wasn't quite fast enough. He grabbed my arm and bent the gun away from him, forcing me to the ground. With my left hand, I managed to drag out the other gun. It was more or less smothered as his body tried to pin mine down, and I had no real target. It didn't matter. I just sort of aimed in an upward direction and fired. He screamed and recoiled enough for me to push off and fire again with more precision.

Someone else took advantage of my distraction and grabbed me from behind. I'd stuffed the extra gun back in my pants and now struggled against him with the first gun when suddenly it grew hot in my hands. Burning hot. I yelped and dropped it, staring as it lay sizzling on the ground, glowing faintly orange.

I didn't have to hear his voice in my ear to know who held me.

"Eugenie Markham, lovely of you to pay me a visit."

"I'm going to kill you," I hissed.

"Yes, yes, you told me that before, and yet, I see it's not really working out. You should have taken me up on my earlier offer." He barked out a command to a nearby guard who ran up to us. "Disarm her before she kills anyone else."

With all the confusion, none of my other allies noticed what was happening. I opened my mouth and began chanting the ritual words to bring the spirits. They were currently too far out of range to simply hear me shout. Realizing what I attempted, Aeson threw me onto the ground, using his body weight to hold me while one hand covered my mouth.

"Hurry!"

The guard removed my athames and wand. For the

extra gun, he wrapped his hand in the folds of his cloak to retrieve the weapon and then hastily tossed it away.

"You're a damned nuisance—and a deadly one," muttered Aeson. "Keeping you alive for nine months may be more trouble than it's—ow!"

I didn't see what happened to him but heard a *thunk* above me.

"You used your power to toss one rock at me?" he exclaimed, an almost comic note of incredulity in his voice.

"On the contrary," I heard Dorian say pleasantly. "I didn't use magic for that. I just threw it."

Aeson tossed me toward his guard, just as flames rose up from the ground. In the darkness, the bright light hurt my eyes, forcing me to glance away. Heat rolled off that scorching orange wall, instantly heating up my skin. The guard attempted to scramble back and hold me at the same time, doing a half-assed job at both, though he still managed—just barely—to keep me restrained.

My gaze stayed on the fire's flickering colors until I suddenly felt the ground shake. Jerking my head up as much as my restraint allowed, I saw a cloud of darkness rise above the flames. It crashed down, like the palm of one's hand, and the fire abruptly went out, extinguished as pounds of dirt slammed it to the ground.

Without missing a beat, Dorian gestured to the spot Aeson stood on. I felt shaking again and saw the earth ripple, like a wave of water moved under the surface. It knocked Aeson off-balance, and then a storm of rock shards—much as I'd seen with the nixies—swirled around, taking aim. Still on the ground, Aeson lifted his own hands. Waves of heat blasted away the rocks, scattering them in different directions. Some of them melted, dripping back to the earth in a molten shower.

Ashes filled the air, and I could hear Aeson coughing as he stumbled to his feet. The ground trembled again, pushing him back to his knees. He supported himself with one hand and gave a shaking, raspy laugh.

"It didn't have to come to this," he said. "If you would have just shared her, she might already be with child."

A shower of rocks spattered Aeson as Dorian strode forward. They weren't razor sharp, but they looked like they hurt. The Alder King winced and shielded his face.

"I don't share," Dorian said flatly. The earth near Aeson coalesced into ropes of dirt, winding their way around his limbs. Score one for bondage fetishes.

"Too bad. You might have lived had you felt differently."

Aeson suddenly burst up, breaking through the bonds of earth. As he did, fire blasted from all around him, outlining him and then shooting forward. My scream was smothered in my captor's hand as I saw Dorian fly backward. Aeson charged forward, his hands controlling and shaping the flames into a ring around Dorian's crouching form. The walls flared up high and thick, so hot they gleamed blue and white. I wouldn't have thought Dorian could survive that inferno, but Aeson kept talking to him as though he were still alive.

"Too many theatrics, Dorian, and not enough strength left now to free yourself."

I looked around desperately. There weren't many guards left. In the distance, I saw Kiyo nail some guy pretty handily—the man's pain-filled scream affirmed as much—but he was too far to help, just like the spirits. I realized then my guard's hold had slackened; he was apparently transfixed by his master's showdown. Others, just as captivated, stopped and stared.

Taking advantage of the guard's lack of attention, I shoved my elbow back into his stomach and attempted to spring free. I didn't really expect to achieve that goal, but it did uncover my mouth. I spoke the summoning words, and Nandi and Volusian appeared.

"Get Aes—" I began, just before the hand slammed on my mouth again. Another guard joined mine to help with the confinement.

The spirits shifted from humanoid form to something else, still vaguely anthropomorphic but more like a cloud of energy. They swooped toward Aeson, one shining and blue, the other black and silver.

He deflected them with flames while still holding the walls on Dorian. An instant later, I saw a wand in one of his hands. No. He couldn't—

He spoke banishing words, and I felt the surge of power in the air as he tore open a hole to the Underworld. The form that was Nandi trembled and then exploded, disappearing in sparkles. She'd found her peace at last—and without another two years of service to me.

"Call the other one off," snapped Aeson, "unless you want to lose him too."

The hand on my mouth lifted. I hesitated. I had nothing to lose if Volusian won or lost. In fact, Aeson's request likely indicated he couldn't banish the spirit to the land of death. Gentry rarely had that kind of power anyway, so Aeson probably couldn't do what I had been unable to do. But if he fought Volusian, it was possible he could have enough strength to break my control and enslave him as a minion. That was not an option. Better for the spirit to be destroyed than turned against me.

"Hold, Volusian."

He retreated immediately, coalescing back into his normal shape.

Aeson returned to Dorian. The Alder King held up his hand and brought his fingers together in a fist. The burning walls contracted, resembling more of a cocoon than a cylinder now. Through the crackling of flames, I heard Dorian scream.

Helplessness choked my heart. Just like with the mud elemental. Just like with the nixies. I had no weapons and no freedom. This was exactly the kind of situation Dorian kept speaking of. The time magic would be handy. I couldn't use it, however. My abilities included only miniscule water manipulation and out-of-control storms and their consequences.

Yet, suddenly, I didn't care about the consequences. I wanted to summon a major storm, a storm to devastate this whole area. Maybe it'd kill my friends and me, but things didn't really look good for us anyway. Focusing my mind on that, I tried to recall the angry tempests I'd created before.

Only . . . it didn't work. Maybe it was because I'd never consciously done such a thing before. Or maybe it was because I could no longer see storms as a whole. They were pressure and charged particles and—most importantly— water. Dorian had taught me to compartmentalize the elements, and that's all I could do now. I thought about storms, but all my mind did was reach out and touch all the water sources nearby. Damn it. Finding water did no good, not unless I could move a whole lake and douse the fire. I doubted I could command that much water, even if I had a source like that nearby.

But I didn't need one that big.

I only needed to summon a smaller water source, one my powers could manage. I refocused. My magic reached out, grasping and connecting with the water molecules I wanted. They recognized me, and I called them forward. They resisted a little. There were more of them here than had been in the pitcher.

Obey me! I shouted to them. *Come to me! I am your mistress.*

Only a few seconds passed while I struggled for control of the water. Meanwhile, Aeson was still holding his arms up, collapsing the walls slowly in what was probably a sadistic effort to prolong Dorian's pain. Still, I needed the delay as I pushed and pulled the water more fiercely.

A funny look crossed Aeson's face just then, and he glanced around, as though trying to find something. Yet, he didn't know what that was.

Come to me!

I could feel the water breaking free, unable to resist

my command. A look of horror twisted Aeson's face. His hands dropped and clutched his head, almost as if he would claw it off. Behind him the flames around Dorian abruptly faded and disappeared, almost as if a lake had dropped onto them after all.

But as I'd noted, I hadn't needed a lake. I'd only needed a smaller source. I'd needed Aeson. The water in him was a size I could manage, the source I'd called out to and commanded. After all, the human—or gentry—body is 65 percent water.

And a moment later, all of it came to me. The other 35 percent didn't.

Chapter Twenty-Six

A fairy king's explosion will sort of get everyone's attention.

I don't know how they all knew I was responsible, but suddenly, the eyes of my allies and foes alike were on me as all fighting ceased. The guy holding me released his grip, backing up and away. Fear glittered in his wide eyes. It occurred to me then I'd nearly forgotten about my captivity while working the magic. The experience had actually been remarkably like when Dorian kept me tied up. Maybe there'd been more to that method than his own kinky tendencies.

None of Aeson's guards—the few who were left— moved from where they stood. I wondered if it was like in those films where killing the head zombie stops all the rest. Kiyo trotted up to me. Blood and dirt spattered his fur, but his eyes shone with eagerness and anticipation, like he could have fought all night. Volusian stood nearby, watching all with an unreadable expression on his face.

Looking around myself, I received the full impact of what I'd just done. Whatever else wasn't water in the body lay scattered out in a wide radius from where Aeson had stood. I recognized blood and bits of bone, but most of the debris consisted of slimy, nondescript blobs. Bile rose up in the back of my throat, and I worked to swallow it down. God, what a mess. No wonder the guards looked at me like some kind of monster. I had craved the strength Storm King's inherited power could give me, but this . . . well, I didn't know if I could handle this on a regular basis.

"Sire!"

Shaya came tearing through the trees, breaking into the clearing. She looked remarkably fresh compared to the rest of us, but then, she'd probably spent most of our battle time running back to us, once she'd set the trees in motion. She knelt beside Dorian, cradling his head. I'd almost forgotten him in the aftermath.

Running over, I dropped beside her. To my surprise, he looked more dirty than burnt. His skin appeared to have the nastiest sunburn of his life, and his clothes had singed and melted in some places. He looked exhausted, like he could keel over at any minute, but he still had the strength to push Shaya away when he saw me.

"I'm fine, I'm fine." He struggled to sit up. "Eugenie—"

"How the hell did you survive that?" I exclaimed.

"Earth shield. It's not important. Listen to me, you have to—"

"Your majesty, we have to get you to a healer. We can't stay here."

I nodded my agreement. "She's right—"

"Damn it! You're both welcome to fuss over my body as much as you like later. Right now, you have to act." Reaching out, he grasped my arm, fingers digging in painfully to make his point. "You have to act now if you want to put Aeson to rest."

I glanced around at the gore. "He's pretty rested. And I don't feel his shade. He's gone."

Dorian shook his head. "Listen to me. Find his blood, er, what sort of passes for it." He scanned and caught sight of a small puddle of water that looked to have some dark blobs in it in the poor lighting. "There. Touch it, and then stick your hand in the ground."

Shaya made a small sound of surprise.

"Why . . . ?" Bad enough I'd caused this mess. Now I had to touch it?

"Just do it, Eugenie!" His voice was ragged but forceful, and he reminded me of the time he'd fought the nixies, hard and fierce.

"He's right," came Volusian's more subdued tones. "You must finish what you started."

Still not understanding, I did as they asked. The liquid was still warm, and I felt my stomach turn again as I dipped my hand in it. I sensed a tension in Aeson's guards as they watched, but none of them intervened.

"Now put your hand in the earth," said Dorian.

Frowning, I tried. "I can't really go in. The ground's too hard."

And then it wasn't. My fingers sank in. It was easy. The previously hardened dirt turned soft, like quicksand, pulling my hand in until I was wrist-deep. I wondered if Dorian had done something magical.

He shifted over to me. "Tell me what you feel."

"It . . . it's soft. And, well, it's dirt."

"Nothing else?" His voice surprised me. Anxious. Desperate.

"No, it's just—wait. It feels . . . warmer. Hot almost. Like it's moving . . . or alive." I looked up at him, frightened. "What's happening?"

"Listen to me, Eugenie. I need you to think about . . . life. Vitality. Picture it in your mind. Whatever setting makes you feel alive when you're outdoors, makes you feel connected to the rest of the world. Cold. Rain. Flowers. Whatever it is, visualize it as sharply as you can. For me, that life is autumn on my father's estate when the oaks are orange and the apples are ripe. For you, it will be something different. Reach out to that. What it looks like, smells like, feels like. Hold that image in your mind."

Still scared, I attempted to focus my befuddled mind into a coherent image. For a moment, his vision stuck in my head, the cool breezes and blazing colors of his land. But no, that wasn't what made me feel alive. Tucson did. Dry heat. The desert's perfume. The sun pouring down on the Santa Catalina mountains. The dull-colored stretches of sandy dirt adorned with splotches of green from low shrubs and plants. The colors and hues of blossoms on cacti after the rain.

That was life. The world I'd grown up with and longed for whenever I was away from it. Those images burned into my mind, so real I could almost reach out and touch them.

The ground below me shook. Startled, I jerked my hand out of the dirt, but the trembling didn't stop. The land groaned, and before my eyes, it shifted and twisted. The guards' low cries of fear came to my ears, and nearby, Shaya muttered what sounded like a prayer. The trees of the forest behind me melted, sinking into the ground they'd sprouted from. The green carpet of grass we'd fought on faded, replaced by gravelly dirt. A moment later, shrubby patches of grass shot up from that dirt, along with small, scraggly plants. Cholla. Agave. The land beyond the fortress rose, forming into sharp angles and plateaus, like the foothills of a mountain range. Thin pines grew on those slopes, covering it in patches. The moisture in the air dropped, and the temperature increased ever so slightly. Finally the cacti came, popping up everywhere, and they were covered in flowers. Too many flowers to be real. We never had that kind of an outburst, yet there they were, a riot of colors vividly apparent even in the dusky light of dawn. Saguaros sprang up among the flowering cacti, in a matter of seconds reaching the sizes that normally took hundreds of years.

The land started to quiet, except for the spot beside me. It trembled from the force of something trying to get out. I scrambled away lest it impale me. Moments later, a tree burst from the earth, springing up with unreal speed. Reaching almost twenty-five feet in the air, its spiky gray-black branches spread out. Purple blooms sprang all over it like a cloud or a veil.

Then all went still. I gaped. I had a Tucson summer around me. Only it was better. The kind of summer you always wished for but rarely achieved.

We all sat there frozen, peering around for what would come next. Only Dorian and Volusian seemed nonchalant.

"What is this tree?" Dorian asked softly, looking upward.

I swallowed. "It . . . it's a smokethorn." My mother had a couple of them in her yard.

"A smokethorn," he repeated, lips turning up in delight. I stared at him, still in shock.

"What . . . what just happened?" I managed. The sweetness of mesquite came to me on a light breeze, heady and delicious.

"He's given you a kingdom," said a clear, soprano voice. "You stole what I should have gotten."

Jasmine Delaney stood just on the outskirts of our little gathering.

She looked wraithlike in the early morning light. Her strawberry-blond hair hung long and loose, and a form-fitting blue gown covered her slim body. Her wondrous, enormous gray eyes appeared black without full illumination. Finn stood next to her.

I clambered to my feet. Beside me, Dorian did the same, albeit awkwardly. He touched my arm. "Be careful."

Something was wrong here, but I couldn't put my finger on it yet.

"Jasmine . . ." I said stupidly. "We've come to take you home."

Her lips formed a flat line, not exactly a smile and not exactly a grimace either. "I am home. After putting up with humans all that time, I'm finally where I should be."

"You don't know what you're saying. I know you think you want to be here, but it's wrong. You need to come home."

"No, Eugenie. I'm saying what you should have been saying all along. I recognized my birthright, and I came for it. Whereas you . . ." She shook her head, anger kindling in her words. The intensity of that hate seemed absurd with her young, high voice—as did the fact that she'd actually used the word "birthright." Too much time with the gentry. "You became the biggest rock star around here. You could have had it all, but you couldn't handle it. You spent all your time bitching and moaning, acting like it was so hard to be you. It was stupid, but they all ate it up. Even Aeson did."

She sounded near tears, and a lump formed in my throat. Not because I felt sorry for her but because I knew with a deadly certainty what she was going to say.

"He thought because you were the oldest and had your stupid warrior thing going that you'd be the one to have the heir, not me. He was going to toss me aside, even though I've been faithful to him the whole time— even before he brought me over. It didn't even matter. He was ready to get rid of me for you."

I closed my eyes for a moment, trying to block out her eyes. Those enormous gray eyes, gray like the sky on a rainy day. Just as mine were the violet of storm clouds gathering. Wil's words came back to me, lamenting their childhood: *Our dad was always off on some business trip, and our mom was constantly sleeping around on him.* Their mom had indeed slept around—with one of the gentry, on one of Storm King's assorted liaisons in the human world. There had been a reason Jasmine reminded me of myself.

"Jasmine . . . please. We can deal with this. . . ."

"No. I'm tired of you, Eugenie. You're the worst sister ever, and you aren't going to be the one who gets to have the heir and start the conquest. I am."

I glanced over at the lanky form beside her. "Finn . . . ?"

He shrugged, as chipper as ever. "Sorry, Odile. I gave you the chance. I spread your identity around, hoping you'd see reason. You think I wanted to be some shaman's toadie? I picked you because I thought you were going places. You blew it, so I traded up."

My shock over these developments shot into anger. Finn had betrayed us. He'd let Aeson know we were coming. He'd even tried to stack the deck against us by separating Dorian from me earlier.

Before I—or anyone else—realized what I was doing, I strode over to where my captor had tossed my assorted weapons. In a flash, I held the wand. I touched Persephone's gate and said the banishing words. Finn's mouth dropped open in astonishment, but he was such a weak spirit—never meant to be more than a toadie, after all—that his resistance was a nonevent. My will, channeled through the wand, pulled him through the pathway I'd created. A moment later, he vanished, transported into the Underworld.

Banishing him didn't really fix the mess I was in, but it made me feel better.

Jasmine's face darkened, her eyes narrowing with bitter hatred for me. Christ. I still couldn't believe this. She was just a kid.

"Your staff got downsized," I told her.

"I've got more."

I felt a surge of water in the air and a dozen translucent, feline forms appeared beside her. They reminded me of lions, but their bodies moved like water swirled inside them, dynamic and restless, just underneath their translucent skin. Their eyes glowed an almost neon blue, and their teeth and claws looked about ten times longer and sharper than a normal lion's.

"Yeshin," Dorian murmured in my ear. "More water creatures."

I caught the implied message. Maiwenn had had nothing to do with the fachan or nixies. Jasmine had sent them, using the power inherited from our father to attempt to kill me. She'd wanted to get me out of the way so she'd be the only one in line to fulfill that crazy prophecy. Maybe I should have been outraged, but mostly I felt jealous. Jasmine could summon water denizens, and I could not.

The yeshin moved toward me with a sinuous grace, saliva—or was it simply water?—dripping from their fangs. For a moment, I couldn't act. Then Kiyo moved in a golden-orange streak beside me, tackling one of the yeshin to the ground. Their limbs and claws bit into each other as they wrestled, rolling over and over in the dust.

I came to life, grappling on the ground for my gun. Finding it, I ejected the clip and dug through my coat pockets until I found a silver one. Meanwhile, four other yeshin advanced. Dorian waved a hand, and a small dust cloud rose up and swirled in the creatures' eyes. With his other hand, he pointed at me and yelled at the guards.

"All of you! You know your duty. Defend her."

The guards stayed fixed, staring uneasily between the yeshin and me. Then, one stepped forward, sword raised. He let out a battle cry and charged forward to the yeshin nearest him. A moment later, the others followed suit.

"Stay back from this, your majesty," I heard Shaya say. "You're too weak now."

She was right. Dorian was pale beneath his burns, barely able to keep himself upright. Giving me a brief glance first, Shaya closed her eyes in concentration. Seconds later, two saguaros ripped themselves from the earth and lumbered toward a yeshin. Their weight and grappling helped immobilize it. I took aim and fired until the yeshin moved no more. Straightening back up, the saguaros plodded on to their next victim. I followed them, ready to repeat the process.

Nearby, Kiyo looked to be on his third yeshin. I watched as he pinned it down, his sharp teeth tearing into its skin. Liquid leaked out, not blood but water. Still, it made a valiant effort to fight him, one clawed paw snaking out and gouging his side. Blood appeared on him, but it didn't seem to faze him. He kept moving, tearing into the beast until it died. Then, without hesitation, he moved on to the next one.

The guards—my guards?—fought yeshin in small groups while Volusian aided with his magic. Shaya had created another set of moving saguaros but looked tired. She had her sword drawn and hovered near Dorian, watchful and protective through her fatigue.

The saguaros had another yeshin pinned. I fired and heard only a click. I'd run out of bullets. This was my second silver clip; I'd brought no more. Swearing, I stuffed the gun away and pulled out my wand. Fixing on the yeshin the saguaros held, I sent the creature out of this world. It took more energy than firing a gun. Working my earlier magic had apparently tired me out. No wonder Dorian and Shaya were weakening.

Three yeshin were left. Kiyo was moving onto one of them; I swore he'd taken down half the group himself. Blood covered him, but he bared his teeth and lunged at his next foe. One of the saguaros went down to a yeshin's attack, but the cactus' partner distracted the cat enough for a banishing. The guards had encircled the third and were having a rough time of it. One of them was thrown from the fray, landing roughly and painfully. Another fell in the way of the yeshin's claws and screamed.

I still didn't entirely get why they fought for me, but I moved to help them, trying to get a good fix. Suddenly, as I approached, I heard a horrible, strangled cry from where Kiyo fought. I knew it wasn't the yeshin, but I couldn't turn around. I had the guards' yeshin in sight already and had started the words. Forcing myself to stay on task, I drove it from this world. The guards turned to me in surprise.

"Thank you, your majesty," one said gratefully. I didn't dwell on the fact that he wasn't thanking Dorian.

The last yeshin was stalking away from an inert form—

a fox-shaped form. My guards were on the cat in a flash, and it succumbed almost immediately. It had already been severely weakened.

Jasmine, I barely noted, was nowhere in sight.

Without giving her another thought, I fell to Kiyo's side. He wasn't moving. I rolled him over to his back, trying to feel a pulse or breath. Nothing. I screamed his name, wondering what to do. Could you perform CPR on a fox? Desperate and hysterical, I shook him, saying his name over and over. A hand reached out and took my arm, moving it away.

"He's gone, Eugenie," Dorian said quietly. Shaya knelt beside him, face sober.

"No," I whispered. "No."

"Can't you feel it? His spirit left this body. It travels to the next world."

I blinked, suddenly back in control. Traveling. Maybe not there yet. A banishing sent the spirit on instantly. Real death had a slight delay; that was how people had near-death experiences.

"But not quite there," I said, relaxing my body and clearing my mind. The butterfly burned as I reached out to Persephone. I was already in the Otherworld, one step closer than usual to the world beyond it.

Dorian shot me a look of alarm, recognizing what I was doing. He reached for me. "Damn it, don't—"

He stopped abruptly, realizing I was already gone. Disturbing me in that state would be deadly. I vaguely saw his hand drop as he stared helplessly at my entranced body, the body that no longer held my spirit.

I had moved on—on to the land of death.

Chapter Twenty-Seven

Traveling in spirit is a lot different than traveling in the body. The body gives you more strength—and more risk—but the spirit can see things beyond normal physical senses. As I rose up and up from the Otherworld, I saw it in all its beauty and power. People and objects were ringed in light, some brighter than others—like Dorian, who shone like a small sun. All around him and the others, the Alder Land glittered with its own aura, an aura that called out to me in a funny way. Leaving it felt strange, like part of me was being abandoned back there.

As for me, my soul grew wings as I crossed into the Underworld. I was dark, nearly black, and wore a graceful, avian shape. I was the Dark Swan, my totem, the shape my spirit naturally traversed the worlds in. I hadn't had to use this shape in some time. I'd first developed the ability to move my spirit into the Otherworld wearing a shape nearly identical to my physical presence; I'd later learned to go over entirely in my own body. But this was not the Otherworld, and I needed the protection of my swan shape. The land of death did not like to give back its souls, and the closer I got, the more risk I faced. I could only pray Kiyo hadn't fully entered it yet.

Feeling him was easy. My physical body was still close

to his, and he and I had enough of a mental and spiritual bond that I could track him. But, as it turned out, he was far ahead of me. Too far. He had crossed the black gate. If I wanted to follow, I would have to enter the land of death in earnest. My return was doubtful.

And yet . . . I couldn't just let him go. Not yet. Not when he'd died because of me. Not when he'd still followed, despite my rejection of him. Not after what we'd shared together.

Onward I flew, my wings sweeping over currents of power. I saw no gate per se, but I felt when I crossed it. The connection to my physical body trembled, and I knew I had just endangered it. Too much time here, and it would sever altogether. With that knowledge came another sensation as I crossed over, one so sharp and sudden that I might as well have been slapped in the face. It felt like a belly flop into a freezing pool—remarkable considering the soul did not feel physical sensations. Well, at least that was what I'd been taught. I'd never known any shaman who crossed over and survived to tell about it. Once I actually entered the world, I was suddenly awash in tactile feelings. Warmth swirled around, mixed with those streaks of icy cold.

For just an instant, I saw a world so beautiful, it made me ache inside. Color and light and wonder. Glimpsing it, I felt my connection to something much greater than myself, something I had never understood in the worlds of the living. I was drowning in it, in that burning bliss that made the euphoria of magic seem trivial. And just for a second, I nearly grasped all the meaning to life and death.

Then, in a blink, it was all gone, and I was plunged into darkness. I silently cried out, longing for the return of that beauty. Where had it gone? Why wouldn't it come back?

A voice answered me, vaguely female. It spoke in my mind, reverberating through me and my being.

This world becomes what you bring to it. What do you bring?

The blackness shifted and became solid. I saw no light source, yet I could just barely make out the area in front of me. Ground appeared, cold and dead. Black rocks jutted out at odd angles, sharp and ugly. A chill wrapped me up. My field of vision was limited in that weird illumination. Everything beyond it was unfathomable darkness. In front of me, I made out a deeper blackness, surrounded by a faint gray outline. A doorway or a tunnel.

Was this what I was? Had I shaped my surroundings into cold darkness?

The voice spoke again: *This world is what you make it.*

Inside the tunnel, I could feel Kiyo. With no more thought, I took flight again, moving forward.

The darkness swallowed me once more. Then I emerged into an empty clearing. It looked like I was in a cave, surrounded by that same cold stone. An indeterminable source illuminated the room with stark light. There was no way out. I felt Kiyo ahead still but saw no way to get to him. Behind me, the path I'd come from was gone.

And then I wasn't alone anymore. Shapes materialized around me. I recognized almost every one of them. The keres. The fachan. Finn. Some of the yeshin. An assortment of spirits. Countless other monsters. Countless gentry. Every being I had ever banished to this world. They filled almost every inch of space in the enclosure, crowding around me.

Their faces were horrible. Twisted reflections of what I used to know. They opened their mouths, screaming their terror and pain, reliving when I had killed or banished them. The group closed in, hands reaching out. They clawed at me, trying to gouge me and scrape away my skin.

Skin?

The feathers were gone. I stood in my human form, quite ordinary-looking in casual clothes. The hands and faces closed in tighter, and I screamed as the mob tore me apart. Agony shot through every part of me, a terrible and consuming pain. I sank to the floor, trying to ward them off.

What will you give us? they seemed to ask as one. *What will you give us to let you pass?*

"What do you want?"

You sent us here without thought. You ripped our essence out of one world and into another. Do you know what that is like? To have your essence torn asunder?

"Show me," I whispered.

They did.

It started inside of me. Like a small spark, noticeable only by a faint twinge. Like getting shocked with static electricity. Then it grew, spreading out like a mass of wriggling worms, eating me from the inside out. Only it was more than physical. It was like . . . a spiritual cancer. I could feel everything about me disintegrating. First, all the superficial things. My love of pajamas and Def Leppard. This was followed by the removal of things that identified me, that made me unique: my physical abilities, my shamanic powers, even my newfound magic. Next, my emotional connections were stripped away, making me forget everyone I knew or loved. My parents, Kiyo, Dorian, Tim, Lara . . . they all vanished, their memories blown to the wind. Finally, my base essence disappeared. Me as a physical and mental being. Eugenie Gwen Markham. A woman. Half human, half shining one. It was all gone, and I was nothing. I wanted to scream but had no means of doing so.

And then, I was back.

I sat huddled in a ball, alone in the cavern. Unfolding myself, I saw that I was whole. My self-knowledge had returned. Still shaking, I looked up and saw that a doorway had appeared. It was a way out, a way toward Kiyo.

I walked into the next tunnel, again entering the darkness. When I emerged, I found myself in a cavern exactly like the other. Only this time, I wasn't alone. A man stood on the far side, his back to me as he studied the wall. Sensing my presence, he turned around.

He had reddish hair, streaked with silver and just barely touching his shoulders. The features of his face were striking, a square jaw and sharp angles. Handsome in a harsh sort of way. He wore clothes like the gentry, most of him covered by a sweeping cloak as rich as anything Dorian might own. Rich purple velvet. Jewels worked into the edges. A crown sat on his head, made of a gleaming metal too bright to be silver. Platinum, I thought. It was a masterpiece of metalworking, all scalloping and flowing edges, like a circle of entwined clouds. The edges of it met in a small point at the top of his forehead, like a faux widow's peak. Diamonds and amethysts set among the lacy curves glittered in the weird lighting.

But it was his eyes that really seized me. They would not hold one color. They shifted, like clouds on a windy day. Azure blue. Silvery gray. Rich violet.

"Hello, Father," I said.

The eyes held at a steady, deep blue as he looked me over. "You are not what I expected."

"Sorry."

"No matter. You will do. In the end, you're only a vessel anyway. Your magic will grow, and those around you will eventually see that what needs to be done is accomplished, once your child is born."

I shook my head. "I'm not going to have your heir."

"Then you will not pass. You will die here."

I didn't say anything. Anger hardened his already fierce features, and whatever attractiveness I'd noted before vanished. I remembered my mother's reaction, her pure and unwavering hatred for him. His eyes flickered again, turning from blue to a gray so dark it almost looked black.

"You are a stupid, foolish girl who has no idea what you're doing. The fate of the worlds hinges upon you, and you are too ignorant and too weak to do anything about it. No matter. You are not the only one who can carry on the dream."

"What, you mean Jasmine?"

He nodded. "She lacks your power and war instincts, but again, she is only a vessel. More important, she is willing. Aeson made sure of that. He visited her years before finally taking her. She knows her duty. She will see it through."

A cold, heavy lump settled in my stomach. I had gone out of my way to avoid pregnancy, but Jasmine would not. She would be seeking it, purposely trying to have Storm King's heir. All my smug contraceptive practices would mean nothing.

Storm King read my thoughts. "Maybe if you were the one, you could control the situation. Maybe it wouldn't be as bad if you were the heir's mother. If your sister is the one, there will be no reprieve."

"Don't fuck with me just to get your way. It won't work."

The eyes darkened further. "Whatever you want, then. It makes no difference if you die here and stay with me."

I stared at the far, blank wall, willing the stone to open. Beyond it I could feel Kiyo slipping away from me. My heart—if I had one in this form—beat more rapidly.

I closed my eyes. "What do you want me to do?"

Hands reached around from behind me, closing around my waist.

"Submit just once," Aeson said in my ear. "Submit just once to me, and you can pass on."

His hands pulled me against him, and I tried to squelch my rising nausea. Some reasonable part of me said it didn't matter. None of this mattered. I wasn't here in body. I couldn't get pregnant. This wasn't actually happening.

Yet . . . it seemed so real. And for all intents and purposes, it was. His hands upon me. His breath against my neck. It felt exactly as it would in physical form, as I knew it was intended to.

I opened my eyes and saw my father watching me. Beyond him, Kiyo moved farther away.

"All right," I said, barely recognizing my own voice.

Aeson turned me around and kissed me, harsh and bruising, uncaring that my lips stayed inert and did not kiss him back. He pulled me down, putting my back against the sharp planes of the stone. The last thing I saw before all went to blackness was Storm King looking down at me, face cold and uncaring. I closed my eyes, trying to ignore the mental and physical hurt.

When I let myself see again, I sat on the ground, palms down against the hard surface. Just like before, I felt no more pain, and I could tell my clothes were whole once more. Another illusion . . . one my body had no memory of but which would stay etched in my mind for some time, I suspected. Standing up, I moved forward, on toward Kiyo.

Someone else was waiting for me in the next chamber, a man I'd never seen before. He was slim and small, dressed in scarlet velvet bordering on outlandish. He held a small cloth-wrapped bundle in his hands and paced around nervously. When he caught sight of me, his face brightened with relief.

"There you are, your majesty!" he exclaimed. "I've been waiting."

"Waiting for what?"

He proffered the bundle before me. "To give you your crown. You have to put it on."

I eyed the bundle nervously and then looked at the smooth, blank wall between Kiyo and me. "Is that what I need to do to get through? Put on the crown?"

He nodded, shifting from foot to foot. "Hurry. We're running out of time."

I knew what the crown was for. I knew what Dorian had done outside of Aeson's fortress. Somehow, some way, I had gained the Alder Land. I had become its queen. I sure as hell didn't want it, though. If I made it away from here alive, I'd definitely rectify the problem. But if wearing the crown here was what it took to pacify this next sadistic torment, then I would do it. It was a whole lot easier than everything else I'd been through.

"Fine. Give it to me."

He handed me the bundle. I unwrapped and nearly dropped it when I saw what lay inside.

Aeson had worn a gold circlet. Dorian's crown, which he rarely wore, was similarly simple. It resembled a ring of leaves, beaten out in different metals: silver, gold, and copper. Presumably Maiwenn and the rest of the Otherworldly monarchs wore similar items.

But this . . . this was not a simple circlet. It was heavy and platinum, an intricate swirl of metal set with diamonds and amethysts. Storm King's crown. Only it was smaller. A bit more delicate. Designed for a woman.

"What is this?" I exclaimed.

The man gave me a puzzled look. "Your crown."

"This isn't the Alder Land's crown. This is my father's crown."

"What else would you wear, your majesty?"

I tried handing it back to him, but he stepped away from it. "I don't want it. I won't wear it."

"You have to. It's the only way."

He looked at me pleadingly, almost like he wanted me to move on to the next stage of this game as much as I did. I didn't need his entreaty. I wanted to move on too. Badly. Badly enough to finally lift the crown up with shaking fingers and rest it on my head.

Instantly, I no longer stood in the chamber. I was on a high, cragged peak, overlooking vast sweeping plains. The sky was dark and heavy with clouds, and lightning danced among them. Below, on the plains, armies stretched as far as the eye could see. Armies of gentry and spirits and the myriad creatures living in the Otherworld. The crown felt heavy on my head yet did a poor job of holding down my hair as the wind whipped it around. A gown of indigo velvet embraced my body, and a black and silver fur cloak draped my shoulders. In my left hand, I held my wand, and in the crook of my other arm, I held a baby.

It was wrapped up in white blankets, its eyes closed. A fine haze of hair, its color indistinct, swept over its head. I had no idea who its father was—I didn't even know if it was a boy or girl—but some instinctual part of me knew it was mine. Tentatively, I reached out with my fingers and touched that fine hair. It felt like down, like the softest, finest silk imaginable. The baby stirred slightly at the touch, snuggling against me, and something inside of me stirred as well.

I jumped as a hand encircled my waist, and a warm body moved next to mine. Dorian. A sword hung at his side, and a new crown sat on his head, more elaborate than his former circle of leaves. It was made of thick gold, heavy with jewels and dazzling to behold. But it wasn't as big as mine.

"They're waiting for your order," he said.

I followed his gaze out to the fields of people and saw that they were all on their knees before me, heads touching the earth. Above them, thunder rumbled as the storm swirled restlessly.

"I don't know what to do," I told him.

"What you have to do."

As though moving of its own accord, the hand holding my wand rose into the air. The armies rose with it, like I was a puppeteer pulling marionettes to life. A great roar sounded among them, swords banging on shields and magic flaring in salute. One downward motion, and I knew they would march. One motion from me, and I would unleash hell itself. The roar intensified. Dorian's body shifted closer. The baby stirred again.

My hand felt heavy and started to fall. . . .

I stood alone in the stone chamber. No man. No crown. The doorway had appeared, and I lunged for it.

The darkness engulfed me, and I swear the tunnel had grown more narrow than before. Still I moved onward. I could feel Kiyo growing closer and closer. I ran, needing to find him, needing to reach out to him, needing to—

And there he was.

He lay on a small dais in this new chamber, wearing his human shape. He was on his back, whole and perfect, his hands clasped on his chest like a sleeping fairy-tale princess.

I moved toward him, and a woman moved in front of me.

I didn't know how I hadn't seen her before. She had just appeared. I looked at her and squinted, trying to focus, but had trouble. Her appearance kept shifting. One instant she was golden and lovely, honey-blond hair pouring to her ankles. The next she was pale as death, black hair sweeping behind her like a funeral shroud, yet still beautiful in a frightening sort of way.

Persephone herself blocked my path, and I knew there was no way I could go through her.

"Let me have him. Please. I've passed all the tests, just like you wanted."

What I wanted? It was the same voice I'd heard before, only now amusement tinged its edges. *None of that mattered to me. They were not my tests. This world is what you bring to it. Most of the dead bring guilt or regret. You brought your fears.*

I peered beyond her to Kiyo, my soul screaming out to his.

"What do you want? What do I need to do to take him?"

What makes you think I'll give him to you? He's mine. I received him fairly. The dead do not leave my realm.

I racked my brain, turning over every story or myth I'd ever heard.

"What about Orpheus? You let him take Eurydice."

But in the end, she did not leave. He was not strong enough. She stayed.

"You don't need him, especially since I've sent you so many other souls."

Was it truly for me? Or your own ends?

"Does it matter?"

Perhaps not. But now I have two more, and I do not have to give them up.

"Then do it as a favor," I begged.

A favor? Her amusement grew. *Why would I do that?*

"Because I've served you faithfully. And because we're the same. I'm trapped in two worlds too, and I don't think I can get out of that. I'm torn in two forever now."

I touched the butterfly tattoo on my arm, half black and half white. Just like Persephone, who spent half her existence as a goddess of springtime and half as a ruler of death. Just like me, half human and half gentry. Half lover, half killer. In *Swan Lake,* Odile is the dark swan and Odette is the light swan, yet both are played by the same dancer.

She only stared, and I desperately tried to think of something. "You said this world is what we bring. I brought love too. Doesn't that count for anything?"

She considered. *That depends. Will you give up your love? Sacrifice it to me? Promise you will stay away from him forever, that you will forsake your love.*

I stared at Kiyo's inert form, thinking how it would be to never see him again. Something inside of me died at that thought, but I didn't hesitate.

"All right. I agree."

Persephone stared at me a moment, then Kiyo vanished.

It is done.

"You sent his soul back? He'll live?"

If his body is healed soon, then yes, he'll live.

She continued staring at me, and I realized I'd made no such guarantees for my own return. In fact, I could no longer feel that glittering connection to my own body.

You are trapped here, she affirmed.

"I know. It's okay. It's worth it." And I meant it. Kiyo's life meant more than my own.

Her blue-to-black-to-blue eyes held me. Then, as improbable as it seemed, she sighed.

Go back. Go back to your dual existence. I will see you again someday, and then you will stay.

Her fingers touched my forehead, and a searing pain ran through me. My form disappeared in a flurry of feathers and black wings, and I felt myself being pulled out of this world. Just before I left completely, she spoke again. Her voice was tired and maybe just a little sad.

Keep your love. I have no use for it anymore.

An instant later, I woke up in my physical body, gasping and choking for air as I returned to life.

Chapter Twenty-Eight

About two days passed before I had enough of a grip on consciousness to get out of bed. I had dim recollections of a commotion outside Aeson's stronghold after returning to my body that night but little more. Shaya had cradled me in her arms. Dorian had yelled for a healer. But best of all, beside me I'd seen Kiyo stir.

Now I woke up in one of Dorian's many guest rooms. It was smaller than his but as opulently decorated as everything else around there. I'd come to a few times before this but only now found the strength to stay up. Nia, who had hovered by my side the entire time, remained less convinced.

"You shouldn't . . . you need to sleep more. . . ."

I was stripping off the long chemise they'd put me in, trading up for my recently laundered clothes. "If I sleep any more, I'll be dead, and I've already come too close to that. Where's Dorian? I need to talk to him."

"I'm sure he'd come to you, your majesty."

I winced at the title. "No. Just take me to him."

Despite her protests, her sense of duty couldn't disobey the order. She led me through the maze of corridors where I earned a number of curious looks from the various occupants. Since my initial arrival, I'd become sort of a common fixture around here, accepted and ignored. Now people regarded me with the same frightened curiosity I'd first received.

Outdoors, we found Dorian in one of the gardens, standing over a small, fluffy dog. Muran hovered nearby, and between them, they tried unsuccessfully to coax the dog to lie down and roll over. It merely sat looking at them, tail thumping.

Dorian noticed me first, his face breaking into a wide smile. The healers had been at work on him too; no trace of the burns remained. "Queen Eugenie, lovely to see you out and about."

Muran nearly fell all over himself to bow. "Y-your majesty."

"We need to talk," I told Dorian firmly. "Alone."

"I never tire of being alone with you. Nia, take this unreasonable beast away with you. And take the dog too." He waved them off.

Once alone with him, I demanded, "What the hell were you thinking?"

"There are so many incidents to which you could be referring, I don't even know where to start."

"Yes, you do. You made me queen of Aeson's kingdom."

"Your kingdom now, my dear."

I paced around in the grass irritably. It was the middle of the day, crisp and sunny. "I didn't want it. You had no right to do it."

"It's done. Besides, if I hadn't, someone else might have snatched it up. Would you have liked to see your charming little sister on the throne?"

That stopped me. Extensive searching had found no trace of Jasmine. She seemed to have gotten away cleanly during the yeshin fight.

"Give it to someone else. There has to be a better choice than Jasmine or me."

"Give it away?" He laughed his wondrous melodic laugh, the one that declared all the world was a joke.

"The land recognized you. You can't go back on that. It's yours forever . . . well, at least until you die. Or pass it on to an heir."

"Great. Here we go again. I might have known you'd start pushing that."

"I did no such thing, but . . . since you brought it up . . ."

I stopped pacing and glared at him. "Quit it. I don't want to talk about it. I don't even want to think about it."

Some of his humor faded. "Maybe you should. Jasmine certainly will be. If she has a son first, all your good intentions won't matter. You say you don't want it, but you know . . . it could all turn out differently if you beat her to it."

It was so alarmingly close to what Storm King had told me in the Underworld that I didn't even know what to say at first. Was this a coincidence? I felt pretty sure that all I'd seen there had been an illusion, meant to test my resolve and make me face my fears.

"What's wrong?" Dorian asked, seeing my face. There was nothing sly or knowing in his expression, only worry.

"Nothing. Look, forget about the prophecy for a minute. Go back to the Alder Land thing. If you were so worried about it falling into the wrong hands, why didn't you just seize it for yourself?"

"Why, Eugenie, do you think me so power hungry?"

"Yes. I do. I've heard and seen as much. When these kingdoms were formed, you wanted more. And you had your chance when Aeson died." He didn't answer, and I pushed on, knowing I was right. "But that would have upset a lot of people, wouldn't it? Maiwenn and the others might have turned against you. But by making me Alder Queen . . . you got a placeholder. No one can say anything because I defeated Aeson fairly in battle, and now you have easy access to the same power. You plan to use me and this fucking title to extend your control."

"You have a very low opinion of me. No wonder you're so upset."

"Come on. Why else would you have done it?"

He stared in astonishment. "Why, because I love you." He said it as though it was the most reasonable thing in the whole world. Like I should have known this already.

"You barely even know me."

"We've known each other almost as long as you've known the kitsune, and I daresay you think you're in love with him. Your little foray that night demonstrated as much. By the gods, that was one of the most foolish things I've ever witnessed. You stopped breathing. I thought you were dead."

I heard the catch in his voice, and it really struck me that he just might love me after all. It gave me a strange feeling, one I didn't know how to cope with. Dorian loving a person was almost incomprehensible. I thought of him as loving only his own amusements and ambitions.

"I do love Kiyo," I said in a low voice. "And if we can work it out . . . I'm going to—"

He shrugged, carefree and lax again. "It doesn't matter. I don't mind sharing you."

"You told Aeson you don't share."

"As a general rule, no—and certainly not with the likes of him—but I don't think you'll give me exclusivity, so I must compromise."

"There isn't going to be any exclusivity *or* compromise."

"So you say. You also said you'd never come to my bed in the first place. Or that you'd ever use magic. You probably said a dozen other things too. We all saw how those turned out."

"Stop it. I'm serious about this."

"And so am I. You're a queen now. You control part of this world. Ally with me, and we'll be the greatest power since your father."

"I don't want the power or the Alder Land."

"It's the Thorn Land now."

"I—what?"

"The land conformed itself to you. The Alder Land was Aeson's domain. Yours is the Thorn Land. You're the Thorn Queen."

"The smokethorn," I recalled. If someone tried to force a crown of thorns on me, that was going to be seriously fucked up.

"Very fitting actually. A tree covered in beauty yet possessing a sharp and deadly core."

I shook my head. "I don't care about metaphors. I don't want to rule this kingdom."

He moved into my space, something passionate kindling in those gold-green eyes. "So what? You think you can just ignore it? Pretend it'll go away? *The land conformed itself to your will!* You can't turn away from that. Its survival depends on you—particularly since, for reasons only the gods know, you turned it into a wasteland."

I faltered. "Well . . . I'll get one of those people . . . you know, someone who rules in your place . . ."

"A regent? That'll only work for so long. You can't avoid the land. You have to come back and visit it, or it will die. You're connected now."

"I didn't want this, Dorian." I felt tired. Maybe getting up hadn't been such a good idea after all. "You shouldn't have done it."

"We'll have to agree to disagree on that, but I'll do what I can to make amends. Take Shaya. She'd make an excellent regent. And I'll give you Rurik and Nia and any other servants you seem to like reasonably well."

"I don't really like Rurik."

"No, but he'll be as loyal as that dog I just had. More so, actually, considering what an unreasonable little bastard it was. Rurik will sift through what's left of Aeson's guard and keep only those who'll support you."

"You mean who support Storm King."

"It's the best I can do," he said with a shrug. "You may take it or not. And you'll still have to fill other positions yourself. Nia will do nicely for a lady-in-waiting, but she's not quite up to being a seneschal. You'll need one of those. And a herald too."

He spoke like he was reciting things I needed to pick up at the grocery store. "Oh, God. I'm trapped in the fucking *Chronicles of Narnia.*"

"I'm sure that would be an amusing reference, if I understood it. For now, I can do no more. I'm giving up some of my favorites for you. The rest is in your hands." There was a smile on his face, but his eyes were serious. "No matter what you think of me and my motivations, I swear to you I wouldn't have had you seize Aeson's land if I didn't think you were worthy. There's power burning inside of you, Eugenie. I meant it when I said you'd surpass us all."

I shook my head and turned away, unable to hear this. "I'm leaving now. I really don't want to see you again. Nothing personal. Well, yeah, actually it is." I started walking toward the door.

"What about your magic lessons?"

I froze. "What about them?"

"Don't you want to continue them?"

I slowly turned around. "I have some control now. Not great control, but enough to keep me from doing something stupid."

"And that's good enough for you?" He took a few steps toward me. "You killed one of this world's greatest magic users with a novice's control of water. Imagine when you master it—and the other elements."

"No. I'm not going to. I don't need to."

"I thought you liked the way it made you feel."

The ghostly memory of power flared up in my mind, and I swallowed, willing it to go away. I shook my head at him. "Goodbye, Dorian."

I started to turn again, but he caught my shoulder and pulled me into a kiss. He deserved to be slapped, but the kiss was exquisite, just like all his kisses. And feeling him against me reminded me of our night together, how he'd brought me to a wildness I didn't think myself capable of.

"That's the last time you're going to kiss me," I warned when it ended.

He smiled knowingly, and in his eyes, I could see his own memories of that night. "So you say."

I left him and returned to my own world.

Kiyo found me a few days later, as I'd know he would. I'd been out running errands and came home to see him sitting on my doorstep, in human form. He wore a white cotton shirt, tucked neatly into khakis. The black hair was brushed away from his face, and his dark eyes were as smoky and sensual as ever. He looked good— and healthy. Like Dorian, he'd enjoyed the benefits of gentry healing magic. In fact, Kiyo had received the very best: Maiwenn had tended him during his recovery.

"Come on in," I said, unlocking the door.

He entered wordlessly, following and waiting as I put away my keys and purse. I offered him iced tea and then sat down with him on the couch, wanting to say so much and not knowing where to start.

"You look better than the last time I saw you," I finally said.

His teeth flashed in a lovely smile. "Wouldn't take much."

I looked away. "Maiwenn did a good job."

I felt his hand reach out and turn my face toward him. Those fingers held the same warmth I remembered, the same electric tingle.

"The way I hear it, it was more you than her."

"I didn't do so much."

He *tsked* me. "Honesty, Eugenie."

"All right, it was bad. Really bad. But I'd do it again."

"You're a crazy, wonderful woman. I can't repay what you did."

I started. "There's nothing to repay. Why on earth would you think that?"

"Because I didn't deserve it. Not after the way—"

"No. Forget it. I . . . I shouldn't have freaked out over it. Not over something that happened before you even met me." What I didn't add was that I could suddenly empathize with how dangerous certain bits of information could be to a relationship. Like, say, revealing how a gentry king had initiated you into sexual bondage.

"I still should have told you."

"Yeah," I conceded, "you should have. But it's done. I can live with it."

His arm had snaked around me in that subtle way he had. "What are you saying?"

"You know what I'm saying. There's too much between us . . . I'm not ready to give that up yet."

The arm pulled me closer, and there was a slight tremble in his voice when he spoke. "Oh, God, Eugenie. I've missed you so much. You're like a part of me."

"I know."

We held each other for a quiet moment, and then I heard him say in carefully measured tones, "I hear you're a queen now."

"That's what they say."

"How do you feel about that?"

"Use your imagination."

"Dorian had no right to do that." There was a growl in Kiyo's voice.

"You're preaching to the choir here. I already had that argument with him. He doesn't see it as wrong. He thinks I should keep progressing in magic too."

The hand stroking my face stopped moving. He pulled away slightly so he could look me in the eyes. "That's an even worse idea. You aren't going to, are you? I mean, you got what you needed from him, right?"

"Right."

He visibly relaxed, again touching my cheek with a sensual languor. "We'll get you through the queen thing. I won't let anything happen to you."

"There you go again with the macho protectiveness thing. Who brought who back from the dead?"

"Fair point."

I gave voice to something I'd wondered about for a while now. "How . . . how did you know when I was at Aeson's anyway? Did you really stake out his place and wait for me?"

His eyes crinkled with seductive mischief. Moving his hands to my back, he let his fingers trace the still-healing scars from where he'd scratched me. "There's no place you can go that I can't find you."

I groaned. I'd forgotten about that. "Those damned things are going to heal one of these days."

"I'll make more."

We leaned into a kiss, and like that, things were solved between us. We didn't need many words to get across how we felt. Maybe that's how it is with someone you really love, someone you're connected to. That wasn't to say we didn't have reams of communication to hash through in the future, not if we were going to attempt some sort of relationship. But for now, the kiss conveyed enough. It was an exchange of heat, an exchange of love, and it felt like coming home.

"I've still got to make amends," he told me, his lips only a fraction of an inch from mine, "no matter how magnanimous you're feeling. You know, the usual. Chocolate. Flowers."

"Whatever. I don't need the covert signs to know you want to have sex with me. There are plenty of more obvious ones."

"Like what?"

"Like your hand on my breast."

"No. This is still subtle." He pulled my body to his, melding us together. "Now, when my mouth is there, then you'll know—"

"You're such a freak. Sex got us into this mess. I don't know that it's healthy to rely on it to fix everything."

"Only one way to find out."

Queenly authority or no, I didn't do a very good job of protesting. And when he pushed me down on the couch, I didn't do a very good job of protesting that we should go to the bedroom. Fortunately, Tim never came home, so I didn't shock his sensibilities again.

Whatever words he'd withheld in our conversation came out as Kiyo made love to me, telling me he wanted me, would love me forever, and would do anything in the world for me. They were the sort of promises all people make when they're falling in love, but that didn't make them any less powerful. I floated on them long after he left that evening, awash in emotion and contentment and residual lust.

I was getting dressed in my bedroom when a voice behind me said: "He's a mistake, you know. So is the Oak King. You're better off without either of them."

I jumped and spun around angrily on Volusian. "Don't sneak up on me like that! Christ. Were you watching me out there? What is it with you Otherworldly types and your fetishes? Exhibitionists and bondage and voyeurism. Good grief."

His red eyes regarded me levelly as I finished pulling on my shirt. "I was not joking, mistress."

"About Dorian and Kiyo? What's the matter with them? Well, Dorian's kind of obvious, but Kiyo's all right."

He shook his head. "Hardly. He is a fox, and part of him thinks like one. He regards you as his mate, and that is a dangerous thing. He and Dorian are both zealots in their way. They sit at different ends of the spectrum, perhaps, but both are fixed in their beliefs. Each will have his own agenda for you—even the kitsune, whose views you tend to agree with. They will each try to dominate you and make you think it was your idea."

For one uneasy moment, I thought about how sex had been with each man. Aggressive. Controlling. I'd had small pieces of control, but in the end, I had always been pushed to submission, a submission I welcomed. There was only the one night with Kiyo—the night I'd woken up in the afterglow of remembered power—that I had truly been the dominant one.

"You would do better to find someone milder and more malleable. Someone less ambitious."

I considered his words. Maybe he was right. Maybe. "Men without ambition are boring."

"And that attitude, mistress, is why the females of your kind continue to struggle for equality. And why they continue to fail."

I sat on the bed and clasped my hands in front of me. "I didn't summon you. Was that all you came to tell me, Dr. Love?"

"No. I came to tell you that you need to visit your kingdom sooner rather than later. The people are nervous and restless. You are their queen, and that means something, no matter how much you loathe it. Your people need to see a strong monarch right away."

"I was hoping to put that off." My people, huh?

"I wouldn't recommend it. Not unless you want a disaster on your hands."

"So should I appoint you as one of my advisers now?"

"You may do anything you like. As for me, I tend to share Finn's view. If I cannot rip you apart yet and must be enslaved to someone, I would rather it be to someone more important than a human shaman."

I'd been teasing him, but my feelings sobered at the thought of Finn and poor Nandi. "You're the last man standing, Volusian. Who would have seen that coming?"

"I did, mistress." The incredulous look on his face resembled Dorian's when he'd told me he loved me. "There was never any question. They were inferior."

I laughed. "I never thought I'd say this, but after everything that's happened, you're the only normal thing I can rely on."

He didn't reply.

"Go back to the Otherworld and stay with Shaya. Tell her I'll be there soon. Only cross over if there's a message I need to hear."

"As the Thorn Queen wishes."

"Oh, be quiet."

I spoke the banishing words and sent him on. After that, I stretched out on my bed and tried to assess my life thus far. I was still a shaman, one of the most powerful around if the stories were true. I possessed human means of working and controlling magic, using it to fight and banish anything nasty that slipped into this plane. But I was also gentry, the daughter of one of the Otherworld's biggest tyrants, and I could supposedly be the one to bring about a terrible prophecy—provided my woman-child sister didn't do it first. I was dating a guy who could turn into a fox and who might very well turn on me if I ever got pregnant. I had the love of a king who could tie damned good knots and wanted my help to take over his world and my own. Somehow I'd developed the power to call storms and blow up people. I'd been to the land of death and returned. And finally, I was a queen: the Thorn Queen, which didn't exactly sound flattering. Why couldn't I have been the Violet Queen or something? Why trees and not flowers? There was no accounting for Otherworldly tastes.

I needed tequila and Def Leppard right away.

I walked out to the kitchen, hoping to uncover one or the other but found neither. Instead, I settled for water from a large glass pitcher we kept chilled in the refrigerator. I poured a cup for myself and then set to refilling the pitcher while my mind spun.

Why had everything turned so confusing lately? I didn't want any of this. I just wanted Kiyo and the occasional exorcism. Love and a way to pay the mortgage. That was it. I didn't need all this Otherworldly entanglement or the gentry and their games. They offered me nothing. I didn't want anything from any of them.

Angrily, I slammed the faucet off and turned toward the refrigerator. I didn't realize how wet my fingers were until the glass pitcher slipped from my hands. Everything after that happened in the space of a heartbeat. The pitcher fell. It hit. It shattered. Without thinking, my senses reached out and seized the water, ordering it to stay where it was. There was nothing to be done for the glass—

Yet, it didn't move. The shards hung frozen in midair, just like the water, suspended in the pattern created from the impact. I stared, dumbstruck, until a faint breeze brushed my skin and I realized the fragments trembled slightly. Cautiously, I reached out to that air with my mind and felt its answering resonance. Stretching further, I could sense the currents of power running from me to the space around the glass. The air shifted there as its molecules fought to keep the pieces from falling. Somehow, without even knowing how, I'd made the air obey me, just as I had the water.

Only this was a lot more difficult. I gradually became aware of exactly how I affected the air molecules, and the longer I did it, the harder it was. The pieces of glass felt like bricks, their weight heavy on my senses as I kept holding them up. With a casual thought, I sent the water away to my sink. Forcing all of my attention to the glass gave me a little more strength, but I knew my control would give out soon. Still, I held on. I suddenly wanted to dominate the air, understand how it worked and what I needed to do to command it.

Imagine when you master it—and the other elements.

As I connected to the air, I felt that burning, glorious feeling start to run through me. It still had yet to ever come close to the levels in the dream-memory, but the surge I felt now was stronger and sweeter than anything else I'd felt from controlling water alone.

Tim walked in just then, freezing midstep when he saw me. "Eugenie?"

Fatigue beat at my muscles, and sweat broke out along

my brow. The glass would fall any moment now, and when it did, the magical high would disappear. I fought as long as I could, but when the glass started to shake violently, I hastily ordered the air to carry the pieces to a nearby garbage can. My control was clumsy; only some of the glass made it.

I thought you liked the way it made it made you feel.

Gasping, I sat down in a chair, staring at the glass on the floor. Tim was staring at me.

"Eug . . . what just happened?"

The euphoria of power flickered briefly as I desperately tried to summon the air again. No luck. That achingly wonderful glory drained out of me, like embers fading from orange to gray. Some part of my soul screamed for it as it disappeared, begging it to come back, swearing that I would do anything at all for it to return. I closed my eyes and swallowed.

"Eugenie," Tim tried again, "what was that?"

I opened my eyes and followed his gaze to the glass that still lay on the floor. It took me a moment to find my voice, and when I did, it came out soft and husky.

"I don't know. But I think I want it."

Some days, a girl just can't catch a break . . .

. . . especially when the girl in question is Georgina Kincaid, a shape-shifting succubus who gets her energy from seducing men. First there's her relationship with gorgeous best-selling writer Seth Mortensen, which is unsatisfying on a number of levels. It's not just that they can't have sex, in case Georgina inadvertently kills him (generally a turnoff for most guys). Lately, even spending time together is a challenge. Seth's obsessed with finishing his latest novel, and Georgina's under demonic orders to mentor the new (and surprisingly inept) succubus on the block.

Then there are the dreams. Someone, or something, is preying on Georgina at night, draining her energy and supplying eerie visions of her future. Georgina seeks answers from Dante, a dream interpreter with ties to the Underworld, but his flirtatious charm only leaves her more confused—especially as the situation with Seth reaches crisis point. Now Georgina faces a double challenge— rein in her out-of-control love life and go toe-to-toe with an enemy capable of wreaking serious havoc among mankind. Otherwise, Georgina, and the entire mortal world, may never sleep easy again. . . .

Please turn the page for an exciting sneak peek of Richelle Mead's
SUCCUBUS DREAMS,
coming in October 2008!

Chapter One

I wished the guy on top of me would hurry up, because I was getting bored.

Unfortunately, it didn't seem like he was going to finish anytime soon. Brad or Brian or whatever his name was thrust away, eyes squeezed shut with such concentration that you would have thought having sex was on par with brain surgery or lifting steel beams.

"Brett," I panted. It was time to pull out the big guns.

He opened one eye. "Bryce."

"Bryce." I put on my most passionate, orgasmic face. "Please . . . please . . . don't stop."

His other eye opened. Both went wide.

A minute later, it was all over.

"Sorry," he gasped, rolling off me. He looked mortified. "I don't know . . . didn't mean . . ."

"It's all right, baby." I felt only a little bad about using the *don't stop* trick on him. It didn't always work, but for some guys, planting that seed completely undid them. "It was amazing."

And really, that wasn't entirely a lie. The sex itself had been mediocre, but the rush afterward . . . the feel of his life and his soul pouring into me . . . yeah. That was pretty amazing. It was what a succubus like me literally lived for.

He gave me a wary smile. The energy that flowed through me was no longer in him. Its loss had exhausted him, burned him out. He'd sleep soon and would probably continue sleeping a great deal over the next few days. His soul had been a good one, and I'd taken a lot of it—as well as his life itself. He'd now live a few years less, thanks to me.

I tried not to think about that as I hurriedly put on my clothes. He seemed surprised at my abrupt departure but was too worn out to fight it. I promised to call him— having no intention of doing so—and slipped out of the room as he lapsed into unconsciousness.

I'd barely cleared his front door before shape-shifting. I'd come to him as a tall, sable-haired woman but now once again wore my preferred shape, petite with hazel-green eyes and light brown hair that flirted with gold. Like most of my life, my features danced between states, never entirely settling on one.

I put Bryce out of my mind, just like I did with most men I slept with, and drove across town to what was rapidly becoming my second home. It was a tan, stucco condo, set into a community of other condos that tried desperately to be as hip as new construction in Seattle could manage. I parked my Passat out front, fished my key out of my purse, and let myself inside.

The condo was still and quiet, wrapped in darkness. A nearby clock informed me it was three in the morning. Walking toward the bedroom, I shape-shifted again, swapping my clothes for a red nightgown.

I froze in the bedroom doorway, surprised to feel my breath catch in my throat. You'd think after all this time, I would have gotten used to him, that he wouldn't affect me like this. But he did. Every time.

Seth lay sprawled in the bed, one arm tossed over his head. His breathing was deep and fitful, and the sheets lay in a tangle around his long, lean body. Moonlight muted the color of his hair, but in the sun, its light brown would pick up a russet glow. Seeing him, studying him, I felt my heart swell in my chest. I'd never expected to feel this way about anyone again, not after centuries of feeling so . . . empty. Bryce had meant nothing to me, but this man before me meant everything.

I slid into bed beside him, and his arms instantly went around me. I think it was instinctual. The connection between us was so deep that even while unconscious we couldn't stay away from each other.

I pressed my cheek to Seth's chest, and his skin warmed mine as I fell asleep. The guilt from Bryce faded, and soon, there was only Seth and my love for him.

I slipped almost immediately into a dream. Except, well, I wasn't actually *in* it, at least not in the active sense. I was watching myself, seeing the events unfold as though at a movie. Only, unlike a movie, I could *feel* every detail. The sights, the sounds . . . it was almost more vivid than real life.

The other Georgina was in a kitchen, one I didn't recognize. It was bright and modern, far larger than anything I could imagine a noncook like me needing. My dream-self stood at the sink, elbow deep in sudsy water that smelled like oranges. She was hand-washing dishes, which surprised my real self—but was doing a shoddy job, which did not surprise me. On the floor, an actual dishwasher lay in pieces, thus explaining the need for manual labor.

From another room, the sounds of "Sweet Home Alabama" carried to my ears. My dream-self hummed along as she washed, and in that surreal, dreamlike way, I could feel her happiness. She was content, filled with a joy so utterly perfect, I could barely comprehend it. Even with Seth, I'd rarely ever felt so happy—and I was pretty damned happy with him. I couldn't imagine what could make my dream-self feel this way, particularly while doing something as mundane as washing dishes.

I woke up.

To my surprise, it was full morning, bright and sunny. I'd had no sense of time passing. The dream had seemed to last only a minute, yet the nearby alarm clock told me six hours had passed. The loss of the happiness my dream-self had experienced made me ache.

Weirder than that, I felt . . . not right. It took me a moment to peg the problem: I was drained. The life energy a succubus needed to survive, the energy I'd stolen from Bryce, was almost gone. In fact, I had less now than I'd had before going to bed with him. It made no sense. A burst of life like that should have lasted a couple of weeks at least, yet I was nearly as wiped out as he'd been. I wasn't low enough to start losing my shape-shifting, but I'd need a new fix within a couple of days.

"What's wrong?"

Seth's sleepy voice came from beside me. I rolled over and found him propped on one elbow, watching me with a small, sweet smile.

I didn't want to explain what had happened. Doing so would mean elaborating on what I'd done with Bryce, and while Seth theoretically knew what I did to survive, ignorance really was bliss.

"Nothing," I lied. I was a good liar.

He touched my cheek. "I missed you last night."

"No, you didn't. You were busy with Cady and O'Neill."

His smile turned wry, but even as it did, I could see his eyes start to take on the dreamy, inward look he got when he thought about the characters in his novels. I'd made kings and generals beg for my love in my long life, yet some days, even my charms couldn't compete with the people who lived in Seth's head.

Fortunately, today wasn't one of those days, and his attention focused back on me.

"Nah. They don't look as good in a nightgown.

That's very Anne Sexton, by the way. Like 'candy store cinnamon hearts.'"

Only Seth would use bipolar poets as compliments. I glanced down and ran an absentminded hand over the red silk. "This does look pretty good," I admitted. "I might look better in this than I do naked."

He scoffed. "No, Thetis. You do not."

And then, in what was an astonishingly aggressive move for him, he flipped me onto my back and began kissing my neck.

"Hey," I said, putting up a halfhearted struggle. "We don't have time for this. I have stuff to do. And I want breakfast."

"Noted," he mumbled, moving on to my mouth. I stopped my complaining. Seth was a wonderful kisser. He gave the kind of kisses that melted into your mouth and filled you with sweetness. They were like cotton candy.

But there was no real melting to be had, not for us. With a well-practiced sense of timing that you could probably set a watch to, he pulled away from the kiss and sat up, removing his hands as well. Still smiling, he looked down at me and my undignified sprawl.

I smiled back, squelching the small pang of regret that always came at these moments of retreat.

But that was the way it was with us, and honestly, we had a pretty good system going when one considered all the complications in our relationship. My friend Hugh once joked that all women steal men's souls if they're together long enough. In my case, it didn't take years of bickering. A too-long kiss would suffice. Such was the life of a succubus. I didn't make the rules, and I had no way to stop the involuntary energy theft that came from intimate physical contact. I could, however, control whether that physical contact happened in the first place, and I made sure it didn't. I ached for Seth, but I wouldn't steal his life as I had Bryce's.

I sat as well, ready to get up, but Seth must have been feeling bold this morning. He wrapped his arms around my waist and shifted me onto his lap, pressing himself against my back so that his lightly stubbled face was buried in my neck and hair. I felt his body tremble with the intake of a heavy, deep breath. He exhaled it just as slowly, like he sought control of himself, and then strengthened his grip on me.

"Georgina," he breathed against my skin.

I closed my eyes, and the playfulness was gone. A dark intensity wrapped around us, one that burned with both desire and a fear of what might come.

"Georgina," he repeated. His voice was low, husky. I felt like melting again. "Do you know why they say succubi visit men in their sleep?"

"Why?" My own voice was small.

"Because I dream about you every night." In most circumstances, that would have sounded trite, but from him, it was powerful and hungry.

I squeezed my eyes more tightly shut as a swirl of emotions danced within me. I wanted to cry. I wanted to make love to him. I wanted to scream. It was all too much sometimes. Too much emotion. Too much danger. Our increased flirtation and sexual taunting fed a complication that didn't need any more stroking.

Opening my eyes, I shifted so that I could see his face. We held each other's gazes, both of us wanting so much and unable to give or take it. Breaking the look first, I slipped regretfully from his embrace. "Come on. Let's go eat."

Seth lived in easy walking distance to the assorted shops and restaurants adjacent to the University of Washington's campus. We got breakfast at a small café, and omelets and conversation soon replaced the earlier awkwardness. Afterward, we wandered idly up University Way, holding hands. I had errands to run, and he had writing to do, yet we were reluctant to part.

Seth suddenly stopped walking. "Georgina."

"Hmm?"

His eyebrows rose as he stared off at something across the street. "John Cusack is standing over there."

I followed his incredulous gaze to where a man very like Mr. Cusack did indeed stand, smoking a cigarette as he leaned against a building. I sighed.

"That's not John Cusack. That's Jerome."

"Seriously?"

"Yup. I told you he looked like John Cusack."

"Keyword: *looked*. That guy doesn't look like him. That guy is him."

"Believe me, he's not." Seeing Jerome's impatient expression, I let go of Seth's hand. "Be right back."

I crossed the street, and as the distance closed between my boss and me, Jerome's aura washed over my body. All immortals have a unique signature, and a demon like him had an especially strong one. He felt like waves and waves of roiling heat, like when you open an oven and don't stand far enough back.

"Make it fast," I told him. "You're ruining my romantic interlude."

Jerome dropped the cigarette and put it out with his black Kenneth Cole oxford. He glanced disdainfully around. "This place? Come on, Georgie. This isn't romantic. This place isn't even a pit stop on the road to romance."

I put an angry hand on my hip. "What do you want?"

"You."

I blinked. "What?"

"We've got a meeting tonight. An all-staff meeting."

"When you say all-staff, do you mean like *all*-staff?"

The last time Seattle's supervising archdemon had gathered everyone in the area together, it had been to inform us that our local imp wasn't "meeting expectations." Jerome had let us all tell the imp goodbye and then banished the poor guy off to the fiery depths of hell. It was kind of sad, but then my friend Hugh had replaced him, so I'd gotten over it. I hoped this meeting wouldn't have a similar purpose.

Jerome gave me an annoyed look, one that said I was clearly wasting his time.

"When is it?"

"Seven. At Peter and Cody's. Don't be late. Your presence is essential."

Shit. I hoped this wasn't actually *my* going-away party. I'd been on pretty good behavior lately. "What's this about?"

"Find out when you get there. Don't be late," he repeated.

Stepping off the main thoroughfare and into the shadow of a building, the demon vanished.

A feeling of dread spread through me. Demons were never to be trusted, particularly when they looked like quirky movie stars and issued enigmatic invitations.

"Everything okay?" Seth asked me when I rejoined him.

I considered. "As much as it ever is."

He wisely chose not to pursue the subject, and we eventually separated to take care of our respective tasks. I was dying to know what this meeting could be about, but not nearly as much as I wanted to know what had made me lose my energy overnight. And as I ran my errands, I also found the strange dream replaying in my head. How could it have been so vivid? And why couldn't I stop thinking about it?

The puzzle distracted me so much that seven rolled around without me knowing it. Groaning, I headed off for my friend Peter's place, speeding the whole way. Great. I was going to be late. Even if this meeting didn't concern me and my impending "unemployment," I might end up getting a taste of Jerome's wrath after all.

About six feet from the apartment door, I felt the hum of immortal signatures. A lot of them. The greater Puget Sound area had a host of hellish employees I rarely interacted with, and they'd apparently all turned out.

I started to knock, decided an all-staff meeting deserved more than jeans and a T-shirt, and shape-shifted my outfit into a brown dress with a low-cut, surplice top. My hair settled into a neat bun. I raised my hand to the door.

An annoyed vampire I barely remembered let me in. She inclined her chin to me by way of greeting and then continued her conversation with an imp I'd only ever met once. I think they worked out of Tacoma, which as far as I was concerned might as well be annexed to hell itself.

Others walked around—vampires, lesser demons, etc.—and I nodded politely as I made my way through the guests. It could have been an ordinary cocktail party, almost a celebration. I hoped that meant no smiting tonight, since that would really put a damper on the atmosphere. No one had noticed my arrival except for Jerome.

"Ten minutes late," he growled.

"Hey, it's fashionably—"

My words were cut off as a tall, Amazonian blonde nearly barreled into me.

"Oh! You must be Georgina! I've been dying to meet you."

I raised my eyes past spandex-clad double-D breasts and up into big blue eyes with impossibly long lashes. A huge set of beauty pageant teeth smiled down at me.

My moments of speechlessness were few, but they did sometimes occur. This walking Barbie doll was a succubus. A really new one. So shiny and new, in fact, it was a wonder she didn't squeak. I recognized her age both from her signature and her appearance. No succubus with any sense would have shape-shifted into that. She was trying too hard, haphazardly piling together an assortment of male-fantasy body parts. It left her with a Frankensteinian creation that was both jaw-dropping and probably anatomically impossible.

Unaware of my astonishment and disdain, she took my hand and nearly broke it with a mammoth handshake.

"I can't wait to work with you," she continued. "I am *so* ready to make men everywhere suffer."

I finally found my voice. "Who . . . who are you?"

"She's your new best friend," a voice nearby said. "My, my look at you. Tawny's going to have a tough standard to keep up with."

A man elbowed his way toward us, and whatever curiosity I'd felt in the other succubus's presence disappeared like ashes in the wind. I forgot she was even there. My stomach twisted into knots as I ID'd the mystery signature. Cold sweat broke out along the back of my neck and seeped into the delicate fabric of my dress.

The guy approaching was about as tall as me—which wasn't tall—and had a dark, olive-toned complexion. There was more pomade on his head than black hair. His suit was nice, expensive and tailored. A thin-lipped smile spread over his face at my dumbstruck discomfiture.

"Little Letha, all grown up and out to play with the adults, eh?" He spoke low, voice pitched for my ears alone.

Now, in the grand scheme of things, immortals had little to fear in this world. There were, however, three people I feared intently. One of them was Lilith the Succubus Queen, a being of such formidable power and beauty that I would have sold my soul—again—for one kiss. Someone else who scared me was a nephilim named Roman. He was Jerome's half-human son and had good reason to want to hunt me down and destroy me some day. The third person who filled me with fear was this man standing before me.

His name was Niphon, and he was an imp, just like my friend Hugh. And, like all imps, Niphon really only had two jobs. One was to run administrative errands for demons. The other, his primary one, was to make contracts with mortals, brokering and buying souls for hell.

And he was the imp who had bought mine.

Unwrap a Holiday Romance
by
Janet Dailey

Eve's Christmas

    0-8217-8017-4   **$6.99**US/**$9.99**CAN

Let's Be Jolly

    0-8217-7919-2   **$6.99**US/**$9.99**CAN

Happy Holidays

    0-8217-7749-1   **$6.99**US/**$9.99**CAN

Maybe This Christmas

    0-8217-7611-8   **$6.99**US/**$9.99**CAN

Scrooge Wore Spurs

    0-8217-7225-2 $6.99US/$9.99CAN

A Capital Holiday

    0-8217-7224-4   **$6.99**US/**$8.99**CAN

Available Wherever Books Are Sold!

Check out our website at **www.kensingtonbooks.com**